EV... ...KE
...AGAIN ...

T... ...nade of wood. The ... ...t, the scent of stale beer, and cigarettes. The music keening quietly from the neon-stroked box in the corner is nearly a decade behind the mode. The two-legged humans seated on stools at the bar scattered around are dressed in ragged natural fibers and cheap plastiwear.

The music fades into silence. Two-legs turn their heads and look. Tikki stands on the threshold in her human guise, and she is nude.

"Give me your clothes."

The woman objects. A man stands to fight. As he goes down, two more arise, ready to fight.

Before the last have fallen she is like a creature out of their nightmares—half human, half beast—her face an inhuman mask, her arms and upper body massive with muscle, fangs gleaming from among her teeth. The barman brings up a shotgun, but it is too little too late. The two-legged female who started it all frantically wrenches off her clothes, screaming, stinking of terror, and runs naked for the door.

Tikki dresses, then turns to face those who remain. The hunting is begun, and now she needs a car.

SHADOWRUN—
WHO HUNTS THE HUNTER

DARING ADVENTURES

☐ **SHADOWRUN #9: SHADOWPLAY by Nigel Findley.** Sly is a veteran who has run more shadows than she cares to remember. Falcon is a kid who thinks he hears the call of magic and the voice of the Great Spirits. Together, they must face deadly confrontation between the world's most powerful corporations—one that could turn to all-out warfare, spilling out of the shadows and onto the streets themselves.   (452283—$4.99)

☐ **SHADOWRUN #10: NIGHT'S PAWN by Tom Dowd.** Although Jason Chase was once able to shadowrun with the best, time has dulled his cybernetic edge. Now his past has come back to haunt him—to protect a young girl from the terrorists who want her dead, Chase must rely on his experience and whatever his body has left to give. And he needs everything he's got, as he comes face to face with an old enemy left for dead.   (452380—$4.99)

☐ **SHADOWRUN #11: STRIPER ASSASSIN by Nyx Smith.** Death reigns under the full moon on the streets of Philadelphia when the deadly Asian assassin and kick-artist known as Striper descends on the City of Brotherly Love. (452542—$4.99)

☐ **SHADOWRUN #12: LONE WOLF by Nigel Findley.** Rick Larson thinks he knows the score when it comes to Seattle's newest conquerors—the gangs. But when the balance begins to shift unexpectedly, Larson finds himself not only on the wrong side of the fight but on the wrong side of the law as well.   (452720—$4.99)

Prices slightly higher in Canada.

Buy them at your local bookstore or use this convenient coupon for ordering.

PENGUIN USA
P.O. Box 999 — Dept. #17109
Bergenfield, New Jersey 07621

Please send me the books I have checked above.
I am enclosing $_____ (please add $2.00 to cover postage and handling). Send check or money order (no cash or C.O.D.'s) or charge by Mastercard or VISA (with a $15.00 minimum). Prices and numbers are subject to change without notice.

Card #_____ Exp. Date _____
Signature_____
Name_____
Address_____
City _____ State _____ Zip Code _____

For faster service when ordering by credit card call **1-800-253-6476**

Allow a minimum of 4-6 weeks for delivery. This offer is subject to change without notice.

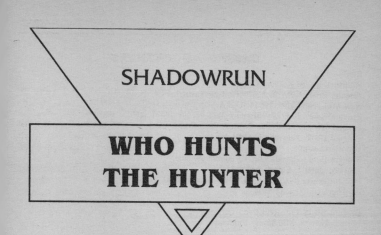

SHADOWRUN

WHO HUNTS
THE HUNTER

Nyx Smith

A ROC BOOK

ROC
Published by the Penguin Group
Penguin Books USA Inc., 375 Hudson Street,
New York, New York 10014, U.S.A.
Penguin Books Ltd, 27 Wrights Lane,
London W8 5TZ, England
Penguin Books Australia Ltd, Ringwood,
Victoria, Australia
Penguin Books Canada Ltd, 10 Alcorn Avenue,
Toronto, Ontario, Canada M4V 3B2
Penguin Books (N.Z.) Ltd, 182–190 Wairau Road,
Auckland 10, New Zealand

Penguin Books Ltd, Registered Offices:
Harmondsworth, Middlesex, England

First published by Roc, an imprint of Dutton Signet,
a division of Penguin Books USA Inc.

First Printing, May, 1995
10 9 8 7 6 5 4 3 2 1

Series Editor: Donna Ippolito
Cover: Romas Croallus

REGISTERED TRADEMARK—MARCA REGISTRADA

SHADOWRUN, FASA, and the distinctive SHADOWRUN and FASA logos are registered trademarks of the FASA Corporation, 1100 W. Cermak, Suite B305, Chicago
IL 60608.

Printed in the United States of America

To Artie Falbush, Jr.

For more things than we can remember,
For things no one else could have done,
For caring, for trying, for doing,
For getting it right every time . . .

Special thanks to readers John S. Francavillo, Fern R. Francavillo, Scott Lusby (Aspiring Author), Paul Sitomer, Ted Swedalla (the Wonder Stud), and Dave Zimmerman for their remarkably insightful critiques of the original manuscript; Shirley Barnes, for letting Dave actually read the manuscript; Robert N. Charrette, for things past and present (need I say more?); Romans, fellow countrypersons, enigmatic humanity, nature, and the universe for no particular reason, and also the Face, LF, wherever you are, for getting it started.

And, of course, Lucy the howler . . .
Welcome to the club.

When the stars threw down their spears,
And water'd heaven with their tears,
Did he smile his work to see?
Did he who made the Lamb make thee?
        —*The Tyger,* William Blake

1

Death stalks silently—

Moving from cover to cover, from tree to brush to gully. In the dying light of the setting sun she is a four-legged phantom in black-striped fur the color of blood. Her eyes and ears, all her senses, her whole being, are focused on the antlered creature standing barely ten meters away.

The creature pauses and turns its head. It grunts discontentedly. Does it know? Does it see, does it smell?

Wait—the phantom freezes—look, smell, listen. Creep forward. Ears flat against skull. Tail down. Almost near enough now . . .

One step more . . .

The forest is draped in winter, snow and ice cover the ground, and for one fleeting instant the cold clear air hangs on the treacherous razor-edge of perfect stillness.

The elk turns and looks away.

The phantom explodes through the underbrush, plowing through snow drifts, springing, leaping, hurling herself over the corpse of a fallen tree. She is not Tikki, not Striper. She is 350 kilos of primitive meat-eating savagery. She is carnivore incarnate.

The elk recognizes the threat—hears smells sees her coming—and fights through the snow to flee, but Tikki closes the distance in instants.

And in the last instant, the elk turns to face her.

Tikki feints, dodges the menacing antlers, then slams bodily into the elk's flank and with one final merciless lunge seizes the animal's neck in her jaws.

That is the death grip, the killing grip. Her jaws are a steel-sprung trap crushing the animal's neck, snapping bone, tearing through flesh, even as she bludgeons and batters the creature with paws like massive mallets. The elk staggers and falls beneath her assault. Its rapid panting breaths become a desperate pounding rhythm punctuating the final moments of its life.

Then it ends. As nature intended it should end.

Blood trickles into the snow. The elk's carcass steams in the frigid air. The aroma of death arises. Tikki lifts her nose, drinking in the scent, relishing it, and growls deep in her throat, fangs bared, instinct satisfied.

This is right. How it should be. The right way for things to end. She is nature's weapon, born to hunt, designed for the kill, just as this elk and all creatures like it were meant to be prey. No one who could see her in this moment, in this her natural form, could possibly doubt it. No one, especially her, could doubt that the creature lying beneath her is hers by natural right. It is a defining moment, a proof of everything she has ever believed about herself, and a repudiation of all things human and metahuman.

Two-legs. She has no need of them now. She is better off without them, in fact. They make things complicated.

Here in the wild, survival is the only concern.

Tikki looks at the fallen elk, lowers her head to sniff it. The elk's big, even bigger than her. Dragging it through these snow-laded woods will not be easy. Too bad she has no choice.

Her cub must have meat. The cub can't come to the kill, so the kill must go to the cub. Tikki had three cubs. One was flawed in some obscure way and died shortly after birth. Another was killed by hellish dogs breathing fire, dogs she systematically hunted down and slaughtered. The third, the smallest of the litter, was hurt by the dogs and seemed slow to recover. Since then, she has kept it in the old cabin where her supplies are stashed, where animals cannot get at it, and where, wrapped in the hides of dead dogs, it will be warm.

The cub is healed now. It grows stronger. Soon it will be strong enough and large enough to follow her on the hunt, to watch, hidden among the trees and brush, to learn the making of a kill, the quiet movements, the sudden charge, the crushing grip . . . all that the kill involves. That will make life less difficult.

Tikki could make the passage back to the cabin less difficult by first eating her fill, but the smell of that much spilled blood would attract every kind of scavenger and that would lengthen her journey. She will drag the carcass back whole to some point near the cabin, near enough for the cub to reach without trouble, but not so near as to attract other predators to her lair.

She grips the elk around the neck and begins dragging.

The journey is long and full of hardships. The carcass is heavy; dragging it proves awkward and tiring. The snow in places is a meter or more deep. The elk's antlers catch on trees and scrub. And always instinct haunts her. Prey worth the trouble of catching is difficult to come by in these northern forests. Rabbits and other small animals are plentiful enough, but unless she can catch them asleep they are not worth her cost in time and effort.

Tikki has spent many days hungry since the first cold winds of Fall came blowing. And now her stomach grumbles. Her limbs twitch with the urge to tear the elk open. Her ears flick with impatience. Instinct tells her to gorge herself on the carcass, fill herself to bursting with life-giving meat—now! at once!—while she has the chance. She would do it without hesitation but for the one thought foremost in her mind, the image of the cub waiting for her in that far-off cabin.

The cub has changed things. That young life has become as important to Tikki as her own. She does not really understand how this can be so. She's pondered the point till her head aches from thinking and still she reaches no conclusions. Carrying the cub in her belly and getting it out through her loins took a great effort, but she has known great efforts before and none has ever affected her in quite the same way. Maybe suckling the cub had something to do with it. Maybe it's some kind of magic.

All she really knows is that she would lay down her life for the cub—this she knows absolutely—and so she has come to accept the one thing that seems most incredible of all. That some things, perhaps this one thing only, mean more to her than her own survival.

Until now, she would not have thought that possible. Until now, she had considered her own life to take precedence over practically everything else in the world. How can this be? She puzzles over the point constantly.

It is, perhaps, beyond understanding.

The smoldering sun sinks behind the tops of the mountains. Twilight fades into the dusky grays of night. From out of the distance comes the menacing howl of a creature Tikki has seen only once, a strange two-legged beast with wings and a single horn. Not an ordinary two-leg. Tikki lets go the elk to lift her head and roar her warning. Only silence answers and that is well. She has staked out a large territory and she guards it jealously. Good prey is scarce. Sharing her domain with other hunters would leave her that much less to eat, and less for the cub.

She continues on. Soon she spies the skull of a creature like a bear, but with short, curving tusks, sitting on the stump of a tree. More skulls: deer, moose, something like a wolverine but larger, something resembling a lion but with spikes at the end of its tail. Many of these skulls, picked clean by scavengers, hang in trees and sit on stakes. They are her warnings to two-legs, to creatures with senses too dull to detect the clear and obvious signs she has left on trees and brush for kilometers around the cabin, signs that mark this part of the forest as her personal possession.

The snow beneath her paws grows hard and crusty with icy crystals. Odd smells touch her nose. Tikki lifts her head again to test the air. The smells are faint but harsh and set her nerves to twitching. They begin speaking to her of humans and human machines. The last time she smelled anything of machines was at the start of winter, when Raman, her cub's sire, rode away on his motorcycle. The cold made him shiver. The promise of snow turned his thoughts constantly to the south. He said he would return here to Maine with the Spring, and Spring is still weeks away.

Tikki abandons the elk and goes loping, running toward the cabin. When she hears the noise of an idling engine, she charges. The sound is wrong. Wrong, wrong, wrong. It is not Raman's cycle. It is like the turbine-inflected whining of a panzer.

More smells come. Weapons and synthleather and the distinctive aromas of intruders.

Elves.

Terror and fury send her crashing through brush, skidding and spinning down icy slopes. Her legs piston frenetically. Breath roars through her throat. The scattered bones of prey, hidden by the snow, crackle and crunch beneath her pounding paws.

The cabin comes into view, sitting in a snowy clearing ringed by soaring white-dusted pines. Before the cabin lurks a boxy air-cushion vehicle, a Mostrans hovertruck, lying belly-down in the snow. In front of the ACV's cab stands a tall lanky figure, a male in gray and white camo, holding a fully outfitted assault rifle. The kevlar mask over his face and the hood covering his head do nothing to hide his elven scent. Nor that of the two elven females just then stepping out of the cabin, carrying a large gray case.

Smells in the air tell Tikki that her cub is outside the cabin. Where? Very near. Near enough for her to see it plainly, and yet all she sees are the elves and that large gray case.

Instinct fills in the blanks. *Her cub is in that case!*

Tikki hurtles toward the elves. The two females hustle the gray case toward the cargo door of the Mostrans. The male retreats a few steps. Their smells are watchful and wary and hint of a rising tension like fear. Tikki is barely ten meters away when the pod atop the Mostrans' cab snaps open, revealing an autocannon, already tracking.

The first stammering burst batters her chest and head. Hide splits, ribs crack. Something unseen tears at her right eye. She staggers and slips on a patch of ice. The Mostrans' turbine begins keening louder. The female elves heft the gray case in through the ACV's cargo door. Tikki seizes the crystalline earth in her paws and hurls herself forward. A second burst batters her flank and snaps her right hind leg. She tumbles down and scrambles up. The male elf points his rifle. The glaring light of a laser-sight flashes across Tikki's face like fire. The rifle clatters, the autocannon stammers. She's struck in the head, shoulder, and body. The impacts pitch her off-balance and send her sprawling. A final assault leaves her blind in both eyes, ears ringing, blood boiling into her mouth.

The cargo door on the Mostrans bangs closed. Tikki drags herself up. Another burst of the autocannon nearly tugs her right foreleg from her shoulder. She sags into the snow, gulping air in huge gurgling breaths. The Mostrans whines, ice and snow swirl through the air like sleet, and the vehicle rushes away.

With it goes the scent of the cub.

Tikki opens her mouth to roar, but the pain is overpowering and she is sliding down through nothingness into the great unending dark of a vast pit.

2

The sign glares in stroboscopic color:

**WELCOME TO NEW BRONX PLAZA
SITE OF THE VILLIERS ARCOLOGY
A NEXUS OF GOLDEN OPPORTUNITY & VALUE**

The plaza extends for blocks in every direction. The walls of the Villiers Arcology rise forty stories into the neon-lit night. The massive project has been plagued by delays like the terrorist bomb that left a blackened wound in one wall. The skeletal framework of supporting steel rises another twenty or thirty stories above the walls, but never seems to attain its zenith.

In the time it's taken for the arc to reach this stage of near-half-completion, a horde of condoplexes and office towers have risen around the plaza and along the banks of the Harlem River. People are calling it a renaissance, the re-vitalization of a part of the South Bronx that's been decaying for decades, ravaged by gangs, infested with vicious devil rats. Bandit wonders if that's so. This is the year 2056 and the masters of the corporate over-world, the likely engineers of this renaissance, have never seemed particularly altruistic.

Most of the people living in the new plexes and working in the new towers look like salarymen and execs from Manhattan. So do the thousands of suits now crossing the gold-hued tiles of the plaza. Promo skimmers drifting by overhead and the laser adverts gleaming in midair proclaim the amazing values inherent in whole body re-fits, custom apparel, executive limousines, and high-rent security condos. If the SINless and the indigent have any place in this so-called "renaissance," Bandit can't see it. But that is the way of the world. Or so it seems.

Bandit sits along the curvilinear base of the fountain ded-icated to some ancient samurai with paired swords and mul-tiple rings. He plays his wooden flute and watches the passing suits. The song he plays flows from within. The magic he makes is subtle but persuasive, enticing, enchanting. The suit who pauses to drop a few bits of corporate scrip into the begging bowl at Bandit's side turns to go, but pauses again to stare at the bowl, then drops a few more notes. Bandit nods his head in a particular way, as if in thanks, and plays a particular strain on his flute. The suit hesitates, adds a silver credstick to the collection in the bowl, then goes on his way. That, too, is the way of the world.

The way of the world is the way of nature, and the ways of Raccoon are as much a part of nature as anything else in nature: people, animals, mountains, and streams. Cities and deserts. Nuyen and New Guinea. Raccoon is of course a sort of thief. He prefers strategy and tricks to any kind of confrontation, because violence between thinking creatures is wasteful of the energies of life and, possibly, an affront to nature itself. Raccoon goes his own way, seeking value and things of interest, such as items of power, useful in his special brand of magic. Petty thefts are usually beneath him. But when the means of the theft are clever and the ends are good, well . . . that changes everything. To persuade a salaryman, perhaps one of the corporate elite, to give up his nuyen for the sake of the poor . . . well, that is a good trick, indeed.

There is only one small problem with it.

A faint glimmer in the air catches Bandit's eye. He shifts to astral perception. The small spirit he finds crouching beside his begging bowl takes the form of a raccoon. This is the watcher he assigned to watch the astral terrain in the vicinity of the fountain.

The spirit points. *"Master, look!"*

Bandit looks.

Through the thousand auras of the suits moving around him burn a few that are particularly bright, hot with anger and resolve and the readiness to do violence. Bandit does not need to see the gray and black uniforms of corporate security forces to know who these people are, or what they intend to do. He has no System Identification Number, no corporate ID. He is on a plaza that Villiers International defends like its own exclusive property. The guards always come. It is part of the way of things, part of nature.

But the guards will be several more moments forcing their

way through the evening crowds. There is time. Bandit lays a folded paper dragon on the base of the fountain. A small thing of great beauty in exchange for all the money he's collected. A fair exchange. More than fair. For Raccoon need not give anything for what he takes, and this time he takes only money. Money may have its uses, but it is essentially valueless scraps of paper or small bits of metal with electronic encoding. Of no use in magic whatever.

"Out of the way!" a voice bellows.

Quickly then, Bandit stuffs money and credsticks into the pockets of his long coat, grabs the begging bowl and runs.

"YOU!" someone shouts. "HALT!"

The guards are close and the crowds are densely packed. Bandit points his flute and whispers a word. Discreetly, a winding path opens before him as people, like currents in a stream, shift just slightly out of his way. And like currents passing around a tree limb or rock, they rejoin into a single waterway to his rear.

"Above you, Master!" a voice whispers in his ear.

From out of the neon-stroked night comes the silent form of a helicopter with flashing red and amber beacons. Bandit knows it comes for him. He has eluded the forces protecting this plaza many times before. Experience teaches that it is the way of megacorporations to become annoyed with those who evade their guards, and so they commit more resources each time he comes.

But Bandit is ready. He's prepared. At a word, the round golden cover to a utility access shaft jerks from its recess in the tiled floor of the plaza. Bandit climbs down into the shaft, grips the sides of the ladder there with hands and feet, and drops at speed to the floor of the tunnel below.

"Uh-oh," his watcher whispers.

The tunnel is about two meters across, lit by panels in the ceiling and lined with conduits and pipes. As Bandit steps back from the ladder, he turns and faces a squad of waiting guards, orks, massive and heavily armed. There are five of them and they stand in a semicircle that backs him against the tunnel wall.

"Gotcha," says one.

Bandit nods, and says, "Don't shoot."

The magic triggers instantly. A cloud of blazing white boils up around him and expands to fill the tunnel. Guards shout. Bandit ducks beneath grasping hands and dodges around turning, stumbling bodies. He slips free and runs.

Raccoon would be pleased.

"Where is he?"

"There! *There!*"

"GET'IM!"

Guards emerge from the cloud and charge along in pursuit. Bandit turns a corner and runs into a secondary tunnel. Barely three meters ahead waits a corp mage in a long black robe marked with mystic insignia. The mage lifts her arms in a posture of spellcasting. Bandit points a finger at her and shoots. The mage sneezes, her magic misfires. Bandit ducks and lunges forward, past the mage's side. An explosion roars at his back. Someone screams in agony. Bandit feels the heat of the blast on the back of his neck, but keeps on running.

Magic both simple and fast has advantages over complex sorcery. That is something the mages from the high towers of the corporate over-world never seem to grasp.

The guards keep on coming.

Bandit darts around another corner. The new tunnel ends suddenly, three meters in, blocked off by a panel marked with red and yellow warning stripes. This was not here before.

Bandit puzzles.

The new panel looks made of steel. It is marked with the logo of Villiers' security forces, Bandit notes. On the astral plane, magic swirls around it incessantly. The panel is warded and the ward is powerful. It is probably impenetrable in the time Bandit has left, and that is rather annoying.

"Master, behind you!"

Boot heels ring loudly, charging near. Bandit looks back to see three massive ork guards rounding the corner behind him. They stop just a meter or two away and point their weapons at him.

"You're under arrest, spellboy," one says, grinning.

"Mage," says another, sneering.

Bandit nods understanding. He is no mage, but mundanes rarely see the distinction. He is a *shaman*. He follows *Raccoon*. He has about as much in common with mages as artists have with scientists. He could try to explain that, but would rather not waste the time. "Be one with the world."

"Huh?" the leading ork grunts.

Bandit turns and steps to his right. The eyes of a mundane

would see him stepping through the wall of the tunnel and disappearing from sight. That is a sort of illusion. The guards gape and exclaim, but hesitate to follow. By the time they figure out what happened Bandit will be long gone.

Once again, the guards have been outwitted by guileful Raccoon. That, too, is in the way of things. Only now Bandit's little secret, his secret opening, has been compromised. He compresses his lips and frowns.

"Damn."

3

The sun is long gone when vision returns.

Tikki's fur is caked with dried blood, and the snow around her is splashed with her own gore, but her hide is whole once more, and her bones mended. Her musculature comes to life twitching and flexing. With a rumbling breath that threatens to explode into a ferocious roar, Tikki bolts to her feet, charges the cabin, and smashes through the cabin door. Then no doubt can remain. The cub is gone.

She roars with the fury burning inside her, but abruptly stops. Experience warns her. She has been in this position before—opposed by two-legs, assaulted by humans, crossed by orks and elves. Confronted by treachery and guile and forced to deal with it. With the rising moon, instinct cries for vengeance, and yet she knows that this is not the way.

To succeed, to prevail in the world of two-legs, she must face down the savagery of her instincts and use her mind. She must think. Analyze. Consider. Decide what is the best course to follow and what paths to avoid.

She steps outside, stares into the gray dark of the night. The air is thick with the stink of the Mostrans. The ACV's fans have blasted a clear trail through the snow. The smells and the trail will linger for many hours, perhaps even days. She will follow; but, first she steps back into the cabin. There are things she must examine and things she must decide.

The cabin is ancient: rough-hewn walls of seasoned wood, a scattering of leaves, and the needles of pines. The stench of elves hangs in the air. Tikki drinks it in, draws the scents all the way into her lungs, for she wants them burned into her memory, remembered so clearly that she will recognize the faintest trace wafting past her on a fleeting zephyr of air. She walks to the low mound of dog hides in one corner and buries her nose in it, smelling the traces her cub has left behind. She will remember that, too.

She will hunt the elves, hunt them till either she is dead or the cub is again at her side. Should she find the cub dead, she will maul the elves, destroy them, tear them to pieces, then leave their meat for the crows.

She will repay these elves one way or another.

Now, to decisions. Raman's departure has left her without transportation. Tikki had not minded that until now. She had not planned to go anywhere till the cub was old enough to travel and to understand about two-legs. So she has a problem. She has guns and other tools that might be useful in her hunt, but no way to carry them, no hands with which to hold, no shoulders with which to bear, unless she assumes her human guise and travels on two legs.

Nature designed her four-legged form with all the weapons and tools she might ever need for life in the wild built right into her body.

And in the world of metahumans . . . ?

It does not matter. Guns and other tools can be gotten anywhere. Time is the essential element now. She must begin the hunt at once, before the elves have gone too far, their trail grown too cold. Before scents fade and traces in the snow dwindle away.

She must move quickly. Go on four legs.

Her thoughts are interrupted by quiet noises, distant snarlings and yappings. Smells come with the sounds and together give rise to new thoughts, reminders about certain things, certain basic truths. They tell her of her next move, the very next move she must make. Her belly is gnawing. She burned much in the way of resources in charging the elves. Before she does anything, goes anywhere, she must eat.

There is nothing in the cabin she needs. She lopes into the forest, charges up icy slopes, races between tall trees. This time it is wolves, large ones with dark fur. Five of them surround her kill. The largest male and the largest female tear at the carcass and snap and snarl at any of the other three that dare to draw too near.

As one, they turn their heads and meet Tikki's eyes.

She roars and charges. The smaller three wolves scatter, smelling of fear and surprise. The largest male and female hold their ground, snarling, baring fangs, displaying all the savagery they can muster till Tikki is nearly on top of them. Abruptly, they bolt away.

Tikki comes slipping and skidding to a halt at the butt-end of the dead elk, and now the battle begins in earnest. The pack circles. They slaver with the need for meat and fill the air with desperate anger. The largest female darts back and forth, snarling, menacing. Tikki roars her warning to the female even as the largest male circles in on her rear. Tikki spins, bounding up high on her hind legs, forelegs splayed, fangs and claws bared and flashing, and the largest male darts away while others circle in.

Again and again, the wolves close in, scratching and biting, harrying her flanks and hind-quarters. They are swift and powerful creatures, and they are many while she is only one, but she is large and strong and her weapons are unforgiving.

And her bloodied body heals even as she turns and strikes.

Three times her claws connect and three times a bloodied wolf bolts away howling in terror and pain. The third time, it is the largest male, and that is the end. The pack retreats into the trees till they are nearly out of sight. There they stop and there they wait. Tikki tears at the elk carcass and eats, watching, always watching, ready for a new assault.

The battle for survival is simple. It is one against all others and it ends only with death. There is predator and prey and nothing else that really matters. This is the lesson her mother taught her and the way of thinking she brought with her to the world of two-legs.

There is no other way to approach living in the wild, living as her ancestors lived, but she is not sure how well this way of thinking applies to the peculiar world of two-legs. The times she has spent in the human cities have given her much to wonder about. She has even considered whether the dual nature of her own form might not imply that she is somehow something more—better, stronger, standing higher than ordinary creatures—though what this might mean, if true, she has only half-imagined guesses.

But the elves make everything simple again. The time for idle thoughts is ended.

Now, she hunts.

4

The subway train thunders into the Tremont Avenue station, rattling and shaking, brakes screaming. Bandit watches the crowds struggling to get into and out of the train. When the battle is almost finished, he thrusts his way through the tightly packed bodies and manages to push through the door to the platform before the air brakes gush and the doors battle the pressure of bodies, and haltingly—jamming, unjamming—slide shut.

The gray concrete of the platform is as tightly packed as the train. People shove against Bandit's side and back, forcing him ahead or left or right, or they come right at him, right up against his front. The crush only gets worse as he nears the exit. It becomes an inexorable tide propelling him up the grimy graffiti-covered stairwell to the street.

The heart of the Bronx is like Newark's Sector 3, only worse. The streets are lined with crumbling concrete and flimsy duraplas structures. Signs and display screens flicker and gleam, but the products advertised are strictly grunge rate: soybran, soykaf, plastiwear, body filler, StreetDocs, Ramboic 14. Most of the people living here are SINless and poor. They live like sardines, packed into plastic tins called coffin hotels and apartments consisting of single rooms. The streets are jammed night and day with those seeking work, seeking food, seeking shelter, seeking all the thousand things they need and the means to get them. Some nights it seems that every person Bandit sees is either a criminal on the prowl, ready to maim or even kill for an easy nuyen, or a victim, soon to be robbed and perhaps bludgeoned to death, stripped of his or her meager possessions. The criminals here are as poor as everyone else. The yakuza and others all have their outposts, their little scams, their gaming parlors, their BTL labs, but the streets are ruled by gangers: elf gangers, Asian gangers, troll gangers. The trolls are the worst. The worst of the worst call themselves the Kong Destroyers and are best avoided at all times.

Along the fronts the buildings, in front of the scamshops and stores and simsense theaters, sit those too poor to afford personal living space, the beggars.

Bandit pauses and selects one of the beggars, apparently an ork, wrapped in many layers of raggedy threadbare clothes and so blanketed with filth Bandit is at first uncertain whether it's a male or female. Its aura shows it to be a male. Bandit steps near and holds out a piece of corporate scrip in the amount of five nuyen. The beggar grabs it, seizes Bandit's wrist with one trembling hand, then both hands, and begins crying out for more, pleading, sobbing, wailing. The beggar's two nearest neighbors join in, also grabbing. Bandit shows them his empty hands. All three beggars lose interest. They sit back against the building front and stare off into nothing. And that, it seems, is the way of beggars. Most of them, anyway. No matter what they are given, they always seek more. When nothing more is forthcoming, they turn their attention elsewhere. Most do not say thank you.

They are not grateful.

Perhaps they are degraded.

Two blocks further on, Bandit turns down a long dark alleyway lined with shelters made of plastic cartons and crates. The people living here seem almost dead. They lie in their poor shelters unmoving. Many do not even look up. They are thin and dressed in rags. Their auras are subdued. Bandit pauses to talk to one or two, but receives no reply. It seems they are waiting to die.

The alley leads into another, broader alleyway, choked with garbage and junk, cast-off appliances, bits and pieces of anonymous scrap. Devil rats scurry wherever he turns, but only in the periphery of his vision. They are quick to dart out of sight. A cat the size of a small dog lies atop the rusting shell of an automobile, and hisses, baring its fangs as Bandit draws near and walks by.

A doorway leads into the dark of a stairwell.

Bandit glances around, checking both the astral and the mundane, then quickly passes inside.

Things got uncomfortably warm for him over in Newark. Certain corporations have objections to certain things he has done, or participated in, and would like to see him dead; if not dead, then "neutralized." A change of scenery seemed in order. Too many people knew his name and had ideas about where he might be found. Here in the Bronx he is all but unknown. For the time being, it should stay that way. For the moment, he has little or no interest in megacorps or their divers holdings. More important things concern him.

The stairway down ends at a doorway. The door suddenly bursts open and a small horde of young kids comes through yelling and shouting, surrounding him. They jump up and down and pull at his sleeves and scream, *"Make the ball! make the ball! make the BALL!"*

"Wait."

And suddenly they are silent, standing there all around him with eyes wide and round and gazing up at him expectantly. It is a strange thing, the way they seem to respect him, the way they heed his words. As if even a softly spoken word somehow assumes the power of an imperious command. Bandit does not understand it. These children know nothing of magic. They know nothing of Raccoon and the things he can do. Mostly, they only seem to care about the ball.

Making the ball is a simple thing, trivial magic, but he's tired now and must concentrate. He cups his hands before him. Momentarily, the energy gathers, slowly coalescing into a softly glowing yellow globe that sits comfortably in the palm of one hand.

When he lifts that hand, the globe floats upward, and drifts.

And suddenly the kids are all screaming again, jumping up and down, reaching for the ball, batting it back and forth like a balloon.

And then through the rickety door comes Shell.

"Hoi," she says, with a smile.

She is young, younger than Bandit, anyway. She weaves her hair into dozens of skinny braids that scatter across her shoulders like twisting vines. Her body is slim and curved in a feminine manner. Bandit supposes she is attractive. In the dark of the stairwell, her skin looks as black as night. In truth, it is like the color of soykaf, light brown. She dresses for the street: jeans, synthleather, and sneaks. Shock gloves dangle from her belt. Tucked into the belt is a Narcoject needlegun. Bandit does not care for guns, but he understands why Shell keeps one. The kids are young and Shell has no magic, or so little it hardly matters, and these spaces around them, hidden in the sub-basement, are worth their cubic space in gold. They have it all to themselves, just him, Shell, and the kids. They must be careful. Were the space discovered, they would have a small army of streetlife fighting to get inside.

"Jozzie, bolt the door!" Shell says, lifting her voice above the noise of the kids, and one of the older girls run up the stairs toward the door to the outside. They keep the door bolted except when someone goes out. Often, they post a guard.

Shell smiles and turns and she and Bandit step into the apartment. The main room is nearly four meters on a side. For the Bronx, that's enormous. The couch faces a Tifun DX-2 telecom with a video screen that plays incessantly. Cushions, pillows, and blankets for the kids to sleep on fills most of the rest of the floor.

Shell takes a light hold of Bandit's arm and rises on her toes to kiss his cheek. "Did the zonies freak again?"

"They chased me."

"But you slot away." Shell smiles. "You're the best."

"How do you know?"

"I know." Shell crosses her arms, smiling all the more broadly. "You follow Raccoon and Raccoon is too clever to get caught, right?"

Bandit supposes that's so. At least in theory. The point is that Raccoon has many tricks. That is his edge. The greater truth is that Raccoon is clever enough to always go prepared. The right preparations take up the slack when simple tricks and cleverness fail, as occasionally they do.

"Right?"

Bandit nods, hands his begging bowl to Shell, then empties his pockets of credsticks and scrip. Shell's smile spreads wide as the bowl fills, and that is her way. Money is important to her. Raccoon would not really approve of him giving Shell all the cred, but this is a special circumstance. Sharing space with Shell and the kids is a special circumstance, too.

When his pockets are empty, Shell takes his hand and leads him through a beaded doorway to the cranny just beyond, their kitchen. The space is just large enough for a cabinet, a wave, a narrow fridge, and a table just barely big enough for two, if the two don't mind rubbing knees. Bandit sits. Shell brings him a glass of water and then starts counting the money, credsticks in one pile, corporate scrip in the other. When she finishes, she hides it all in the secret compartment in the base of the cabinet. Shell has plans for all the money they've collected. One day, she hopes to have enough to buy a condo in the burbs and to send all the kids to school. How she'll manage that without a SIN, or SINs for the kids, Bandit can only wonder. He supposes System Identification Numbers can be purchased. He's never tried it himself, but the way some people talk it's done all the time.

Shell steps around behind him, rings his neck with her arms, kisses his cheek and says, "Are you going to your room tonight?"

She means his alone place, his place of long magic, his medicine lodge. Shell knows where that is and that troubles him. Since his first taste of the higher mysteries, Bandit has kept this most important place, wherever it happened to be, a secret from everyone. He keeps many valuable things there, items of great interest and power. His lodge is protected by magic and in other ways besides, but no place is immune to theft. The fact that he himself showed the place to Shell troubles him most of all. It was a very un-Raccoon sort of thing to do.

Or maybe not. Knowing what path is right and what is wrong can be difficult. He lets Shell and her tribe of children share this sub-basement apartment because they have nowhere else to go, because he must attune himself with people, because people are part of nature. But what of the risk he runs? There's so much he could lose.

"Bandit?"

He turns his head to look at her. She's watching him with a funny expression. She smiles, then blinks her eyes and frowns.

"What's wrong?"

"Wrong?"

"Is something bothering you?"

How can he possibly answer that? If he told her of his thoughts concerning his alone place, she wouldn't understand. When he's tried in the past she got hurt and offered to leave. She tells him she may be a thief but would never steal from him because of all that he's done for her and the kids. She tells him that she cares for him too much to scarp him—ever. Whatever that means. The point seems to be that he should trust her, but that is easier to say than do. Shell may be a thief but she is no shaman. She may recite his words back to him, but she does not understood Raccoon.

Which brings him back to a familiar question. How can he succeed in his magic, succeed in attuning himself with people, and therefore with nature, if he cannot decide what to do in regard to just this one woman? Perhaps he has reached the limit of his understanding. Perhaps the greater secrets of the world are to be forever hidden from him.

How can he know? How can he answer?

"Bandit?"

"I'm tired." He rubs at his eyes. He has a headache. He wishes he knew a spell to cure headaches. He knows of someone who does, but asking for the spell would be an insult. Like asking Raccoon for a favor. "I'm hungry."

"I'll fix something."

"Okay."

The stuff she brings him is an odd assortment: beans, soybran, parts of frozen meals stolen from various stores. Seven Hexes spiral pizzas. Shell hoards money the way he guards items of interest. She never buys anything unless it's impossible to steal it. That's because money is hard to come by, hard to steal, or was, till Bandit figured out how.

Of course, he could always contact some fixer and get into a shadowrun, but that would waste time, and, worse, it would force him to shift his mental focus. Attuning himself to people is what matters now. As for money, he'll make do with donations to his begging bowl and whatever Shell happens to snatch.

"You seem really zoned tonight."

"Yeah?"

Shell nods, smiles, sits in the other small chair, and pulls out a wallet. "I got this on the concourse today. Isn't it wiz?"

"Is it?"

To tell the truth, it doesn't look like much. Just a burgundy-colored wallet like some exec might carry. There isn't a trace of magic about it. Shell opens it to display the interior. The trio of silver credsticks couched there could be sold to dealers in stolen sticks, but that's about it. Shell draws a card from a fold in the wallet and smiles. It's some kind of ID card, corporate. Useless trinket. There are big black letters identifying some corp Bandit's never heard of. There's also a hologram of some woman.

Bandit takes the card in hand and examines it closely, then searches through every flap and fold of the wallet. There's another card, more stylish than the first. It's the kind of thing a man or woman of the elite might pass someone at a party. The address that shows is for the office. But squeeze the ends of the card and another address appears. Residence. Complete with matrix address and telecom code.

"Bandit?"

Bandit stares at the card, incredulous.

5

The broad window panes crossing the rear of Amy Berman's office provide a panoramic view of New Bronx Plaza, including the riverfront, the fountains, the condoplexes, the still unfinished Villiers Arcology. In the distance rise the tall towers of Manhattan.

The day came up bright and unusually sunny. The sky appears an almost bluish shade of gray.

On any other day, Amy might have paused there before the windows merely to take in the view and enjoy a few moments' quiet contemplation. Today, she sees only her own image, reflected faintly in the panes. Today, she wears her sleekest dark gray suit of faux gabardine and matching shoes, her Cartier watch, and a single onyx ring. Her makeup is designed to subtly emphasize her eyes and cheeks while minimizing her mouth. She'd intended to look like pure executive juice, wired with so much voltage she's near to overloading, but she doesn't, and she has only herself to blame.

She should have drawn her hair back this morning, made it every bit as severe as she could. What the hell had she been thinking? With her bushy mop of curling brown dangling all around her face and scattering across her shoulders, she looks nothing if not warm and fuzzy, overtly and overly feminine.

She'll probably be mistaken for someone's personal aide.

She closes her eyes and shakes her head, then taps her brow with the palm of her hand. A woman in her position ought not to be making mistakes like this. It's just incredible.

But in fact, it's this morning's meeting. She slept little last night, thinking about it. What the devil is someone like Enoshi Ken doing here anyway? It can only mean trouble. The man is rumored to have a direct line to the board room in Tokyo, and Tokyo always means trouble. People like Enoshi Ken talk endlessly of wanting only the greater good for all, but what they say and what they mean . . . What they really mean . . . If you can tell . . . If you ever really find out . . . If by then it isn't too late . . .

Her telecom bleeps.

It's Laurena, her executive aide, saying, "They're ready to begin upstairs."

"Right," Amy replies. "Grab your pad."

Time for one last look at her hair, but no time to do anything about it. She steps through the door to her outer office. Laurena hops up out of her chair, palmtop in hand, and they head into the hallway. They're both so blatantly Anglo it's almost scary. If that weren't enough, Laurena's a natural blonde, and a brilliant gold-hued shade of blonde at that. How much more non-Asian could a person get?

It won't help.

The elevator chimes. They get on. The doors slide closed and the car rises. Laurena smooths back her hair and says, "What's this meeting supposed to be about, anyway?"

"I suspect it began somewhere in Tokyo."

"Oh, god."

It's just two syllables, but the anxiety comes through clearly. Amy turns her head just enough to meet Laurena's eyes, and says, "Remember your mask."

"I'm sorry, boss." Laurena makes a visible effort to compose herself. She's new to the higher echelons and not used to dealing with upper-rank Japanese. She'll be all right, though, as long as she remembers her mask.

The mask is an essential part of corporate life, at least when Tokyo comes calling. Think or feel anything you want, but keep it safely hidden. The Japanese model for the efficient corporate executive places an emphasis on business, getting the job done and done right and to hell with everything else. That poses a problem for Laurena because, simply, she has heart. She cares about people and has no natural reserve. That's one of the main reasons why Amy picked her for an aide. She's very un-Japanese: open, expressive, empathic. She's very human, very warm, and she cares, and not just about the organization. She cares about people. To Amy's mind, the corporate world in general and Hurley-Cooper Laboratories in particular need as much of those sorts of qualities as it can possibly acquire.

Impersonal robot employees may be all right for automated factories, but when people enter the equation, something more than simple nuyen, mere efficiency, and the fabled bottom line must be taken into account.

This morning, of course, such views should be carefully shrouded. Tokyo won't want to hear it.

The elevator chimes, the doors slip apart.

Amy steps ahead briskly, Laurena at her side, into the richly appointed reception area for the executive "manor", as it's called. It's one of the few places where Hurley-Cooper Labs has invested any significant money in what amounts to mere window dressing. To the left and right are the office suites of Hurley-Cooper's CEO and executive VP. Directly ahead, to the rear of the circular reception counter, are the gleaming rosewood doors to the executive conference room.

Flanking the conference room doors this morning are a pair of distinctly Asian men with distinctly impassive features and trim physiques. The pins on the lapels of their dark blue suits bear the green willow insignia of Kono-Furata-Ko International, parent corporation of Hurley-Cooper Labs. Amy guesses these men are security agents, escorts for the Tokyo bunch. She understands that KFK has a large covert security organization, but knows little about it. Officially, it does not exist. If it has a name, she's never heard it.

One of the agents gives her a nod. She passes through the open doors and into the conference room. It's large enough to be ridiculous, and lavishly decorated: simwood paneling, gilt-framed portraits of various corporate heavyweights, a full range of electronics, including a wall-sized video screen. The conference table, apparently made of mahogany, is easily long and broad enough to seat a small multitude. Each place at the table comes with miniterms jacked into the headquarters computer network. The chairs look like mahogany, too, though upholstered in dark burgundy leather or synthleather.

Laurena takes a seat along one wall and jacks her palmtop

into the network, then lifts a second platinum lead to her temple. Amy walks to the head of the room to join the group there. The minor luminaries are already present: the VPs for Systems Engineering, Information Management, Marketing and Patents, Research, Product Development, Finance. Amy herself holds the post of VP for Corporate Resources. Her specific domain includes personnel, purchasing, and consumption control. She and Chang, the money man—finance and accounting—interface frequently. Usually concerning nuyen.

Chang gives her a nervous flicker of a glance.

Amy replies with a quick, questioning flick of an eyebrow.

But then the doors at the head of the room swing open and the meeting's as good as begun. In comes the executive VP and some Asian man Amy doesn't recognize. Behind them come Hurley-Cooper's CEO Vernon Janasova and KFK's VP for Corporate Liaison-North America, Enoshi Ken. Enoshi looks very much the proper Asian executive, immaculate in a dark blue suit bearing a KFK lapel pin. Janasova looks exactly his usual self: checked sports coat and slacks, powder blue tie over a pastel yellow shirt. One collar of the shirt is neatly secured by a platinum tab. The other tab is open, the collar protruding at a burlesque angle. By comparison to that, the bedlam of the man's thin gray hair is hardly noticeable. Amy forces herself to suppress an unseemly reaction, such as a roll of the eyes or a sigh of dismay.

Janasova immediately begins introducing Enoshi around.

"Yes, I remember," Enoshi says, briefly clasping Amy's hand. "A pleasure, Ms. Berman."

"Likewise," Amy replies.

And then, abruptly, Enoshi smiles.

Amy mutes her response, struggles to appear composed, like nothing untoward has occurred.

During his rapid rise from obscurity, Enoshi Ken has become well known as something of a sphinx. He never smiles, except as an afterthought, and even then the smiles are so ill-timed that they seem deliberately indicative of something other than mere good humor. Amy gains a sense of foreboding, in addition to a sudden chill and a nervous something that rises into her stomach. She feels confirmed in her suspicion that nothing good will come of this meeting. Nothing good at all.

They're invited to sit. Janasova begins the meeting in his usual jocular fashion, saying that Enoshi is touring the North American subsidiaries of KFK "to see what we're up to," and to ensure that "we're all being good boys and girls." Amy lifts a hand to screen the lower half of her face, to hide the tug of a cringing smile, and, she hopes, to distract from the exasperated flush she feels rising into her cheeks. Janasova is a smart man, an excellent science-administrator and a good CEO for an organization like Hurley-Cooper. Amy just wishes he would stop joking around. This is not the time and place for his lighthearted avuncular routine.

A man like Enoshi Ken isn't the type to approve of comedy in the boardroom, or any other room. He's as straight a suit as one might find. With him, it's all business all the time, right on down the line.

Enoshi takes the floor. His opening remarks address the concept of *daikazoku,* the oneness of the corporation and all its subsidiaries, like one big family. Amy's heard this spiel before. It's part of Hurley-Cooper's own orientation program for new employees. And in Amy's view, the analogy is flawed. Any family she's ever known could be characterized by diversity both in attitudes and objectives, whereas the point of a corporation is to get everyone pulling in the same direction. Doing that takes a lot more than morning anthems, more than group exercise, more than lectures on the "oneness of being," or zen and the art of successful corping, and more than cute analogies. Making a corp successful means getting people to feel like they're an integral part of something bigger than themselves. It means addressing people's concerns, their frustrations, their complaints, their objections. It means trying to improve their lives, both off and on the job. It also means getting personal, and that's what people like Enoshi Ken and other Tokyo suits never seem to comprehend.

Or maybe they do understand it, but simply refuse to practice what they preach when dealing with non-Asians.

Or maybe they don't know how.

Enoshi quotes the American editor and critic H.L. Mencken. "Nine times out of ten," he says, "in the arts as in life, there is actually nothing to be discovered. There is only error to be exposed."

Amy considers that in light of the fact that Hurley-Cooper Laboratories specializes in biomedical research.

Just what is his point?

"Allow me to now introduce to you Mr. Kurushima Jussai. Mr. Kurushima has been appointed by the board of KFK, North American Division, to assist us with the survey of North American subsidiaries. Mr. Kurushima is a graduate of Tokyo University and he and his staff are very highly qualified."

Kurushima, of course, turns out to be the Asian who accompanied Hurley-Cooper's executive VP into the room. His suit is as black as his hair. He takes the floor and rambles on for nearly an hour, but the point of him being here is soon clear. Kurushima is an auditor. His staff is composed of auditors. They are here to examine the accounts of Hurley-Cooper, everything from income and expenditures to interdepartmental transfers, and no record anywhere will be excluded from examination.

Janasova merely smiles paternally and nods as if pleased to accommodate the least request Kurushima might make. Amy glances across the table at Chang. The man's brow is gleaming with perspiration.

"It is our objective to complete this audit within two weeks," Kurushima continues. "I have assigned the senior members of my staff to coordinate the work with each of your areas of responsibility . . ."

"How extensive do you expect this audit will be?"

Janasova looks down the table. "Amy—"

"This is important, Vernon." Amy puts up a hand to Janasova to forestall any further objections, then looks to Kurushima. The man does not seem at all perturbed at being interrupted. The emotionless mask of his face is without flaw.

"I'm primarily concerned," Amy explains, "with the potential for disruptions and discord in our research groups. We have many highly regarded people on the research staff, and they are very devoted to their work. They don't appreciate interruptions. Hurley-Cooper management has made a deliberate, continuing effort to minimize the impact of business practices on our research groups. Research," Amy continues, as no one else is speaking up, "is not at all like manufacturing. It's a process that relies at least in part on creativity and imagination. As one of our leading scientists has remarked, research is half art, half guesswork. Untimely distractions can damage that process, and have the potential to cause irreparable harm."

Kurushima gazes impassively at Amy for several moments, then consults a palmtop. "Perhaps you refer to Dr. Liron Phalen of the Metascience Research Group?"

Amy hesitates just for an instant. Kurushima has apparently not come ill-prepared. She wonders why he would name any one scientist. As it happens, his guess is right, but what is his point?

What is Tokyo really after?

"Dr. Phalen is an excellent example of what I am referring to," Amy replies. "He has been cited by the Noble Commission for his work in metaserology. His group has provided Hurley-Cooper with some of its most significant patents. Quite frankly, his value to Hurley-Cooper is inestimable. However, he is both a brilliant man and an eccentric man. He could easily triple his salary should he choose to seek employment elsewhere. He stays with Hurley-Cooper because he holds his colleagues here in high regard and he likes the way we do business."

At the head-end of the table, Janasova fiddles with his necktie, still smiling, but looking uncomfortable.

Across the table, Greg Vanderlinde, VP for Research and Development, gives Amy a quick glance and adds a quick nod, as if to confirm what she just said. What he should have said. Greg's a good man, with a strong science background and an incredible imagination, but he hasn't got the nerve to stand up to anyone, much less a Tokyo-appointed auditor. How he got the VP post for R&D is really a mystery. Amy suspects he was promoted one step beyond his level of competency.

Chang's sweaty sheen has spread to his cheeks.

Kurushima gazes at Amy impassively, and opens his mouth to reply, but then Enoshi Ken is on his feet, talking about *daikazoku* again and how everything can be worked out to the greater benefit of the whole corporation.

Amy doesn't believe that for a second. She can see there's a collision coming. The Tokyo cadre is driving straight at her, whether they know it or not, regardless of what they really want, and she's put too much effort into her work, and into this corporation, to tug on the wheel and veer off.

She just hopes her seatbelt holds.

6

It's a little past noon when Brian Guerney eases his battered brown and green Mitsubishi Sunset Runner through the intersection and onto some street in Manhattan's Lower East Side. Brian's heard this part of the city referred to as The Pit, and it's easy to see why. The buildings are pretty decrepit, the streets are strewn with crap, and the streetlife has the look of chiller thriller go-go-go gangbangers.

There are no street signs. The building numbers are either hidden somewhere behind steel grilles or mesh gratings or buried beneath about forty gazillion layers of multicolored and mostly illegible graffiti. Brian's supervisor told him what to look for, but the only thing he really recognizes, as he turns onto the street, is the small group of Sisters Sinister gangers on the corner to his right, and the group of Blood Monkeys on the corner to his left. He's seen them before on Staten Island and in Brooklyn, though what they're doing here, in the shadow of the Manhattan Bridge, maybe two blocks from the elevated FDR Drive, he couldn't guess. And he wouldn't try to even if he could. The gangers look ugly as usual and they're carrying submachine guns and machine pistols in addition to their usual ordnance. Most of the surrounding streetlife seems intent on getting as far away as possible with no delay.

About halfway up the block is a DocWagon clinic with metal bars arrayed across its facade of graffiti-covered windows. Brian wonders how the graffitoists got their paintguns in through the bars. Directly across from the clinic, jammed in between slum-rent apartment buildings, is a small structure that looks like it was carved out of a block of grayish bedrock. Brian guesses that's where he's supposed to go, based on his super's descriptions, and pulls his car into an empty space at curbside.

As he switches off the ignition, the clatter of autofire weapons erupts. Brian leans down across the front seat, covers the back of his head with his sky blue Department of Water and Wastewater Management hard hat, then waits.

The opening fusillade is followed by a thunderous discharge of guns, like the whole First UCAS Marine had just opened up. That's followed by a bang and a boom that could be from any one of a number of offensive or defensive explosives, possibly grenades. More bangs, thumps, wumps, and clatterings follow. Brian risks lifting a hand to flip down the sun visor on the passenger side, just to show his orange florescent Department of Water & Wastewater Management Official-Use-Only permit, allowing him to park anywhere in direct violation of law. That's to show he's a noncombatant. Just a guy with the D.W.W.M. The "Water" Department. He doesn't bother anybody, nobody bothers him. Most of the time, anyway.

A few minutes pass. The gunfire subsides. Brian carefully sits up, looking all around and rearranging his hard hat. Good thing he popped the extra cred for the special Kevlar-3 insulated hard hat, just in case. If his super keeps on dispatching him to neighborhoods like this, he'll spring for the matching body armor and face shield, too.

The quiet holds. Streetlife returns to the sidewalks. A few cars pass by. There's a bunch of bodies sprawled near the corner, but nobody looks on the verge of punching any more tickets.

Brian pulls his utility belt from the passenger-side floor and gets out. In addition to the hard hat, he's wearing his sky blue D.W.W.M. jumpsuit. Nobody passing by more than glances in his direction. He's invisible, or nearly so. Just another grunt for the city making his daily rounds. Too bad he's not bullet-proof as well.

He steps across the sidewalk to the rough-faced gray stone building. He's never been to this particular site before, but that's no surprise. The D.W.W.M. has literally thousands of sites scattered around the metroplex, everything from management offices in Midtown to sewers out in Queens. Brian notes that the building before him is certainly plain enough, workmanlike enough, to be a D.W.W.M. outpost. There's a vehicle-sized bay door and a human-sized door, both black. Beside the latter is a black stud like for a doorbell. Immediately above the stud is a mesh-covered speaker and, above that, the lens of a security cam.

Brian lifts a finger to touch the black stud, but a metallic-toned voice says from the speaker, "Let's see your ID, kid."

Must be some automated voice program, maybe coupled

with proximity sensors. Cute. You wouldn't think that anyone would ever bother breaking into buildings devoted exclusively to either the water supply or the sewers, but, hey,
there's buttonheads everywhere, so security's routine. Brian
holds his D.W.W.M. ID up toward the security cam lens.

"Okay, kid," says the voice from the speaker.

The door buzzes and clicks. There are no handles or door-
knobs, so Brian steps forward and pushes and the door
swings inward. He's two or three steps beyond the doorway
before he realizes that the shadowy interior is not just a lot
dimmer than the sunlight outside, or that his eyes are not
just taking an extra moment or two to adjust. The door slams
shut behind him and he's enveloped in pitch blackness, a
dark so complete he can't see a fragging thing.

"Uh . . . hello?"

"Who're you?" a gruff voice asks.

"Hit the lights, willya?"

"I asked you a question, kid."

So much for automated security systems. Confirm name,
rank, and ID: nothing new about that. "Guerney. Brian.
From Metro Two. My super told me to report—"

"Who's the Deputy Director for Metro Operations?"

"What?"

"Answer the question!"

"Uh . . ." What the frag's the name? "I guess that'd be
Orly. Michele Orly, I think."

A match flares so near Brian's face he jerks back involuntarily. In the light of that small flame, he sees a man's round
face, a face with a balding pate, a thick black mustache,
heavy black brows, and eyes that gaze at him intently.
"Close enough," the slag says.

"Who the hell are you?" Brian asks.

The guy lowers the match. He's wearing a black vest, like
an armored vest. On the left breast is an oval patch with broken block capitals that read, "Art".

"You the site manager here?" Brian asks.

"You ask too many questions, kid."

What's with this "kid" scag? And what the hell's going on
here, anyway? This guy "Art" is starting to look kind of
lu-lu. "Hey, if it's a problem, I can head back to Metro Two.
It's lunch break anyway. *Art*."

Art sneers. "Union man."

"You ever meet a D.W.W.M. worker who ain't?"

"I'm a G-67. What does that tell you?"

Brian frowns, uncertain. He's a G-8, himself. His super is a G-12. "Nobody's got a tech rating that high."

"You got a lot to learn, kid."

Without warning, the lights snap on. Brian covers his eyes briefly, then gets his first clear look at his surroundings and "Art." They're standing in a narrow hallway that leads toward the back of the building. Art is about as tall as Brian, which makes him about average height, but he's chunky, stout. There's a kind of pitbull-something in his expression that hints he could be a dangerous man in a fight. Beneath the vest, he wears black fatigues stuffed into the tops of milstyle boots.

They watch each other a moment, then Art reaches behind his back and takes out what Brian recognizes as an Israeli heavy automatic. "Know how to use one of these?"

"What the frag are you talking about?"

Art flips the pistol to him. Brian has the choice of catching it with his hands or with his face. He uses his hands. Art immediately puts his back to the wall on the left and points toward the end of the hallway, lost in blackness. "There's your target!"

Something comes rushing out of the darkness. It looks like a gangbanger, maybe one of the Blood Monkeys, outfitted in gleaming synthleather and studs and spikes and chains. The ganger points a submachine gun at Brian's face. Brian's reaction is nearly automatic. He drops into a combat crouch and snaps off three quick rounds: two to the chest, one at the face.

"Bingo," Art says. "We *have* a bingo."

In that instant, the figure rushing up the hallway comes fully into the light. It's a dummy, like a clothing store mannequin, hung on a wire from the ceiling. The dummy's weapon, though, looks as real as they come, a Sandler TMP.

"I'll take that," Art says, extending a hand.

Brian considers the heavy automatic in his hand, and the man before him. Definitely lu-lu-land. Brian pops the ammo clip and ejects the one shell in the firing chamber, hands Art the pistol, but keeps the clip. "I'll hang onto this if it's all the same to you."

"Suit yourself." Art doesn't looked pleased, but then he reaches into a pocket of his vest, pulls out another clip and slots it into the pistol, and goes on to cock the slide and return the weapon from where it came, somewhere behind his back.

"Not bad," he says, then turns toward the dummy. "Chest shots're okay, but the head shot's dead on. I guess you gotta be good to make Commando One."

"Say what?"

Art turns and looks at him, nodding. "Sure, kid. You wanna play dumb, that's fine. Null sweat. We'll pretend you never heard of Commando One. You were never in the UCAS Marines, First Division. You weren't first in on that little dustup in Morocco. You didn't see your CO's intestines blown out and that's got nothing to do with you coming back to the plex and joining a peaceable organization like the D.W.W.M. If that's how you want it, that's fine."

Brian says, slowly, "Who the frag are you?"

"You ask too many questions."

"You're not Water Department."

"Oh, no?" Art steps up real close, close enough for Brian to smell his spearmint-flavored breath. His eyes get very intense, his expression like granite. If this is his imitation of a Marine drill instructor, it ain't half-bad. "Lemme ask you something," he says, quietly. "Why do you think you're here?"

"I got no idea."

Art stares, then says, "I'll tell you a little story, kid. There's maybe twenty million people in this megaplex, Jersey included. What do you think those people depend on more than anything else just to survive? What do you think would happen if some nasty little Sixth World virus got into the water supply? Do you have any concept of how fast this whole plex could go down the drain?"

This is unreal. Brian wonders if he's hallucinating. No one outside the military knows about his involvement with Commando One, or Morocco, or any of the rest. Art must have some heavyweight federal connections, and yet with all that talk about water . . .

"What are you talking about?"

"You heard me."

"So what're you telling me? You're running some kind of security op to protect the water supply?"

"We do what we have to do, kid."

Brian holds back a sudden flaring of temper. Enough with

the "kid" squat, already! He'll be fragging thirty next week. "What'd you mean 'we'? Who is 'we'?"

"You. Me. Anybody the Department needs."

"The *Water* Department?"

Art nods. "D.W.W.M."

"And you're looping me in."

"Yeah."

"To do what?"

"Whatever's necessary."

"This is novacrap."

Art stares at him a few moments, then says, "How does triple time and a half sound to you?"

Brian gapes. "You ain't serious."

"I'm damn serious."

"Nobody gets pay like that."

"Maybe you think the lives of twenty million people aren't worth a few extra nuyen."

"I can't believe the Water Department—"

"Kid, you don't know the half of it."

"And maybe I don't wanna know—"

"Good. You ask too many damn questions."

Art turns and heads down the hall toward the back of the building. The lighting panels overhead light up before him and fall dark to his rear. Brian considers making a break for the door, but wonders if he'd live to see the street.

"You coming?" Art asks from the distant end of the hall.

"I'm thinking about it," Brian replies. Triple time and a half? That's tempting even if Art is lu-lu.

"Don't think too long, kid."

"There ain't nothing in the union contract about squat like this."

Art nods. "You're right. Forget it, kid. It's not your job. I'm sure there must be some other slag with your qualifications somewhere in the Department. Lose yourself. I'm not gonna trust my life to some candy-ass punk who can't hack it—"

"Now wait one fragging second!"

"Kid, you either got balls or you don't."

"Who the frag do you think you're—!" Brian begins, so hot he thinks he might pop, but then Art steps through a doorway and out of sight. The lighting panels above wink out and the hallway goes dark.

Fragging great.

7

Churning storm clouds turn the day into twilight. Sweat washes the blood from her fur and then freezes. The cold crisp air burns her throat and lungs, but the burning soon subsides. Her limbs ache with fatigue, but the aches fade as well. Tikki lopes and runs. The trail is clear before her—the scents, the signs in the snow—drawing her onward. She will never stop, never pause, till she has her cub again and the elves have been repaid.

The trail of the elves' ACV follows the old road through the forest, around the foot of a mountain, upslope and down, through dense copses of woods and across half-frozen rivers of broken rock. Every running step, every breath, every current of air slipping past her nose and ruffling her thick fur reminds her of the winters of eastern Siberia and Manchuria. She and her mother once traveled for weeks in search of prey, constantly on the move, testing the air, watching the ground for signs, battling other creatures to prove their right to the prey they hunted. That was when she learned of the strength nature had granted her, that she could push herself to the point of exhaustion again and again, and still continue the hunt.

Now, she plows over a snowbank two meters tall and suddenly descends to the point where the snow-covered track through the forest meets a narrow, icy strip of pavement called the Road to Nowhere.

The locals gave it that name, but Tikki knows that every road goes somewhere, and she's seen and smelled and heard enough to know what goes on. In the summer, the Road to Nowhere leads directly north to the border between the United Canadian and American States and the Republic of Québec. The runners who ride this road in every kind of armed and armored vehicle carry cyberware and chips and simsense rigs into Québec. Such things are taxed very heavily there, enough to make smuggling a lucrative trade. In the night, when the air grows still and hearths glow with heat and liquor paints the air, she has heard two-legs boasting of the fortunes to be made along the Road to Nowhere.

Two kilometers further on stands the last waystation on the Road: a rickety wooden structure that might once have been a barn or a home, but now serves as a watering hole, an oasis amid the trees and snow.

A dog begins barking as Tikki approaches, but she knows the dog is chained to a small house at the rear of the tavern and poses no threat. A soft rumble of warning rises out of her throat and the beast abruptly goes silent, smelling like fear.

Between the tavern and the ice-covered road wait a collection of vehicles, a Sikorsky-Bell Red Ranger, small and swift and heavily armed, a Chrysler-Nissan G12A, and others, vans, pickups, all with custom mounts and oversized tires. Among them sits a boxy Mostrans KVP-14T Air-Cushion Vehicle. It has a weapons pod over the cab. Tikki slips through the shadows to the side of the vehicle and sniffs at the cargo door. At first, she isn't sure what she's smelling, but then something changes in the air and she catches the scent of her cub. The scent comes from inside the truck, she's sure of it. But it's old. Her cub was here, but now it's gone. Gone where? She glances around, sniffs the air, then waits.

Darker clouds boil across the sky. Lightning flashes in the distance. The door at the front of the tavern creaks open and bangs shut. A male approaches, a human male, clad in natural fibers and odd bits of jewelry and smelling of alcohol. A large knife and a sawed-off shotgun hang from the belts slashing across his hips. He slips on the hard-packed snow in front of the tavern and staggers drunkenly. He pulls open the driver's door of the Mostrans. Tikki steps out from the vehicle's rear.

"Hoi."

The male jerks as if startled, and grunts, and turns to look at her. She is in her human guise now, and she is nude. She steps nearer. A faint sheen of melted ice gleams from her skin. The male stares at her, then smiles. He says something in some unknown tongue, then switches to English, oddly accented. "Where you come from?"

"Looking for friends."

"Here I am."

Tikki shakes her head. "Elves."

"Don't need no fragging elves."

The ploy is not working, Tikki realizes, and that is very aggravating. It's what she gets for trying to get subtle. She's seen this kind of thing work in practically every actionvid she's ever watched: the female offers her body, the male gives the female whatever she wants. Yet this stupid fragging two-leg male sees her nude and thinks only of sex—right here, right now. She smells it in his scent. And she's too short of time to try and take the tease any further.

She hurls herself at him, using her hands like bludgeons, slamming into his face and head, only her hands are massive paws and her arms are covered with fur, and she's driving him down, down, into the snow.

The male's struggles grow frantic. Words of fear burst from his mouth. Tikki straddles his chest and pins his arms and leans down till her face is just a breath away from his. As she speaks, fangs gleam from among her teeth. She feels a sudden urge to seize his neck in her jaws and squeeze the life out of him, but she resists. "The elves are where?"

The male stammers, straining to squirm away. His eyes are huge with terror. "Don't know! Headed south . . ."

That is no news. Two-legs on the Road to Nowhere head in only two directions and she already knows the elves did not go north. "Their names."

"T-Tang . . . *called one Tang!*"

Streetname. Assumed name. Runner? corporate? criminal? what? "There were three."

"Don't know the slitches' names!"

Then Tang is the name of the male. "They paid you how?"

"Cred. Credstick."

"Give it."

"My pocket!"

Tikki tugs and tears. A credstick falls into the snow. She snatches it up, then lowers her face to the male's face, breath rumbling in her throat. She can feel the fur coming out on her face, her fangs lengthening, her arms and shoulders swelling with power. "The elves used your truck," she growls in a voice inhumanly deep. "What did they tell you?"

"Hunting . . . going hunting!"

"Hunting what?"

"Moose! I don't know!"

That is a lie, but it does not smell like a lie. The male is too scared to lie, so the elves must have told him lies. No animal would wait while a hunter stalked near in a noisy ACV. Except a cub too young and too weak to run. Or a cub who thought to hide.

Tikki drives one paw across the male's face, hitting hard enough to hurt. That is the payment the male deserves for helping the elves. He slumps, unconscious. Lucky to be alive. Tikki stands.

The credstick in her hand gleams softly. It looks like a certified credstick. Such sticks may be used by anyone. Unlike normal credsticks, they carry no electronic codes to identify the bearer. They do, however, carry codes that identify the bank or corp that issued them, and that may lead her to the elf called Tang and the two females.

Tikki considers the male at her feet, and the Mostrans ACV, dismisses both and walks to the door of the tavern. A cloud smelling of two-leg sweat, stale beer, and cigarettes meets her nose long before she puts out a hand and pushes inside.

The main room is small and rustic and, like the outside, seems made of wood. The music keening quietly from the neon-stroked box in the corner is nearly a decade behind the mode. The two-legged humans seated on stools at the bar and at tables scattered around are dressed in ragged natural fibers and cheap plastiwear. One or two wear feathers and other ornaments suggestive of Amerinds.

Beside the door is a payfone. Tikki turns to that, slots the credstick from her friend outside, and keys a telecom code. The other end rings once. The voice that answers is like two voices, one male, one female, speaking in synch.

"Your number?"

Tikki keys in a number. This is a previously established code that ID's her as the owner of an account possessing much nuyen. As the next several moments pass, Tikki watches the payfone's small viewscreen. The normal calling screen is gradually replaced by a stylized face, a sort of cartoon animation, far too large to fit on the screen. Only the eyes are visible. They seem to glare.

"This is Oracle," the voice says.

"I want a trace."

"Identify."

"The credstick in this telecom. Who bought it? Where are they now? Everything."

"Scanning."

A few seconds pass.

"Report in five hours."

The call ends. Tikki hangs up and turns from the wall. The neon-stroked box in the corner has fallen silent. Every two-leg in the room is gazing at her. Several are showing their teeth, smiling. She realizes why as a female steps toward her, pointing at her front. "Wuss," the female says, "you look like you're missing something."

Tikki nods understanding. "Give me your clothes."

The female frowns and stares, then throws back her head and laughs. This is not to show amusement. It is to show ridicule, disdain, dominance. Tikki seizes the female's throat, jerks her around in a half-circle, and flings her against the wall.

"Give me your clothes."

Everything changes. The female blubbers incoherently, cowering, slumping to the floor. A large male rises from a nearby table and comes toward Tikki from the left. He smells like anger and makes a fist and that is a mistake. Before he can strike, Tikki drives the heel of her foot into his chest, then lunges, smashing her head into his jaw.

The male topples, but others arise. Two males come at her together and then it's too late to stop. The smells of violence speak to instinct. Black-striped fur the color of blood sweeps up from her waist and over her face and down both her arms. Her hands grow claws and her upper body swells with muscle. She hurls one male through a window and smashes another to the floor. Others scream and shout and the stink of fear draws back her lips to bare her lengthening fangs. A shotgun roars and something impacts her left hip. The gore streaming from the wound slows to a trickle and then stops. A female screams loud and shrill with terror. The male behind the bar hastens to reload. Tikki charges, flings herself over the bar and hits the male dead on, and drives him down to the floor, pounding his head and chest.

When she gets up, the two-leg female who started it all is frantically wrenching off clothes; she runs naked for the door, shrieking. Tikki dresses, then turns to face the few who remain.

Now she needs a vehicle.

8

"You're making too much of this."

"I'm standing up for what I believe."

The office is plush and paneled. Artificial trees stand in the corners. A ninety-year-old bonsai sits on a special table off to one side. Vernon Janasova sits behind his gleaming onyx desk. Amy sits facing the desk. She looks to the ceiling when Janasova smiles. It's not quite a condescending smile, but it's close enough to be mildly infuriating.

"Amy," he says, folding his hands on his desktop, "we're a wholly owned corporation. These people are our bosses. We can't tell them no, you can't do an audit. It's unreasonable to even consider a tack like that."

"So you think I'm being unreasonable."

Janasova's expression turns warm and earnest. "I think you're a very dedicated executive. You've worked very hard to streamline your part of the operation. Personally, I think you've done a fabulous job. The science staff loves your modifications to the purchasing system. All I'm saying is that realistically we have to cooperate with the auditors. If the research people get a little wroth about it . . . well, we'll do what can to smooth things over."

Amy finds it difficult to argue with someone so obviously determined to be so *reasonable*. Clearly, Janasova is not going to fight the auditors about anything. All the more reason for Amy to be adamant now. Insistent and demanding. Even a self-righteous bitch. She declares, "I will not lie down and let Kurushima and his crowd walk all over me and this organization."

"Amy, please . . ." The infuriating smile returns. "No one's asking you to do that. You know that."

"I don't want Kurushima thinking he can walk in anywhere he wants and start scrolling through people's records."

"He has every right to do—"

Before Janasova can finish, Amy raises her voice, exclaiming, "*If I have to cooperate, I will!* But I want to know exactly what's going on every step of the way, what Kurushima's looking at and what he wants."

Janasova stares at his desktop. His face has reddened a little. He does not handle confrontations very well. Angry people disturb him. "I really don't understand why this has you so upset," he says quietly. "The audit staff seems to be very organized. I'm sure any disruptions will be very minimal."

"Vernon, what's minimal to you or me is not necessarily minimal to someone conducting research."

"But, Amy, you have no authority over the research groups."

"Don't tell me about authority! I'm a vice president of this corporation. I give a damn about what goes on here."

"Amy, please . . ."

She stares at the ceiling again.

"Mr. Enoshi strikes me as a very reasonable person. And I'm sure Mr. Kurushima will be glad to keep you informed of everything regarding your groups."

"Yes, I'm sure."

"Let's not argue about this. Really, I consider you one of my top people. We've always had such a good relationship. But you must understand . . . We have to get along with the audit staff. Think of how it might seem if word gets back to Tokyo that we're not cooperating."

"I'm sure it would look very bad."

"Then you see my point."

"Oh, of course."

Amy rises and takes her leave of Vernon Janasova. Her stomach's in knots and her blood pressure's rising, and there's no point in talking further with the man. She's just wasting her time.

In reception, she pauses, looking across the room to the office suite of the executive VP. Talking to that woman might or might not accomplish something; unfortunately, Amy's already been to the top. Janasova would certainly object if he got the idea that Amy had tried to undercut his authority. He might even accuse the two women of the senior staff of ganging up on him. Janasova is sensitive about things like that.

A little too fragging sensitive in some ways.

What she would give right now to have a CEO with an iron hand, rather than lily-wristed, spineless Vernon

Janasova. In the ordinary course of business, he handles
Hurley-Cooper so well, always striving for consensus.
Against their parent corp he's a nothing, spineless.

One of the receptionists looks up from behind the circular
reception counter, meets Amy's eyes, smiles, then stands.
His name is Bryce and he speaks English with a distinctive
British accent. He's also quite attractive, if you like the wiry
type. He was the executive VP's answer to Janasova's selec-
tion of a pretty female receptionist who just happens to be
of Japanese extraction, a point that is probably irrelevant,
except in considering Vernon Janasova's attitude toward
Tokyo.

"Mr. Kurushima just asked me to ring you," Bryce says,
smiling sweetly. "If you have a minute . . ."

Amy points to the executive conference room doors. "In
there?"

Bryce nods, and says, "Yes, that's audit HQ."

9

The truckstop is a hundred kilometers north of Bangor. Rain
and sleet cut through the gloomy day like small daggers. A
rocky layer of hard-packed snow and ice covers the ground.
Tikki steps from her stolen pickup truck and slots the
credstick into a public phone.

Oracle reports.

"Credstick purchased Bayerische Vereinsbank, Boston, by
officer of Union Affiliates Corporation. Acting as agent for
Swiss registry Solothurn Trading. Front for Brussels registry
Anderlecht Travel Associates. Dummy subsidiary for Free-
Cal registry Vonnegut Athletics. Dummy subsidiary for New
York registry NewMan Management Systems, principal offi-
cer Elgin O'Keefe, alias Ogin, alias Pointman, alias Tang.
Former Ares Fire Force NCO. Experience in Desert Wars.
Expertise in weapons, demolitions, interrogation, mantrack-
ing, air-cushion vehicles. Freelance specialist in fugitive re-
covery."

Yes. This is the kind of information Tikki had hoped for.
Paydata. The elf who stole her cub is called Tang. His real

name is O'Keefe and he is a bounty hunter. That is the essential data in Oracle's report. The rest are the lies and half-truths that O'Keefe uses to keep his identity hidden.

"Recent credstick disbursements in Massachusetts, New Hampshire, Maine. Queries?"

"Largest payment made by credstick."

"Boston. Two hundred-kay nuyen. Paid to Boston registry Dynamic Enterprises, principal officer Charles Kant, alias Spinner, alias Clutch."

Tikki's upper lip curls back into a sneer. She knows this two-leg called Clutch through personal experience. "O'Keefe associates."

"No current listings."

"Address."

The address Oracle gives is old, somewhere north of New York City. Tikki feels instinct urging her to go straight to that address, smash through any obstacles and drag O'Keefe to the ground, but she knows that would be stupid. That is the wild in her talking. O'Keefe is no amateur from a gutterpunk sleazehole. First, she must learn more. She must prepare. She must visit Boston and question the lowlife piece of scag who told O'Keefe where to find her.

She must interrogate a dead man.

10

The room is outfitted like an armory. Brian spots a rack of Colt M22A2 assault rifles, an FN-MAG 5 medium machine gun, an Ares portable laser, a strap-on gyro mount for heavy weapons, grenade launchers, mortars, a Vindicator minigun, fragmentation grenades. Crates of high-velocity ammunition line an entire wall.

"What is this drek?"

"Tools of the trade," Art replies. "You oughta know that."

"Are we protecting the water supply, or staging for a war?"

"Call it what you want."

Art passes him a full set of Kelmar Tech body armor, complete with helmet and face mask, then begins suiting up.

Art straps holdout pistols to both his ankles and a third to his inside left arm. He holsters a Scorpion machine pistol at his right hip and the Israeli heavy auto beneath his left shoulder. He loads up with knives. After that comes a shoulder rig slung with shotgun shells, a couple of grenades, and a flare gun.

"We'll leave the heavy hardware for another run," Art says.

"Yeah?" Brian replies. That's just what he needs to hear. Like maybe this'll be a milk-run, with Art loading five handguns just for starters. "You expecting some opposition?"

"That's always a possibility."

"So what's the plan?"

"We'll make a quick sweep."

"A sweep of what?"

"We'll start with the old Seventh Avenue main. The three-five conduit. After that, who knows? See where it leads us."

"I thought all those old three-meter pipes were wiped out by the quake back in '05."

Art stops, gazes at him with eyes like a viper, coiled and ready to strike. "Kid," he says, in a menacing undertone, "you got a lot to learn."

11

The club near the heart of Boston is called Blind Puppies. Angst rocks roars and thunders through the cavernous main room, but the apartment upstairs is quiet, insulated. Cherry pauses to check her hair and sparkling neomonochrome dress in the mirrored panels of the entryway, then goes into the living room. She's got a body like simsense star Taffy Lee, except for her light brown skin—full breasts, flaring hips, nails as long as you like—a body built for pleasure and lots of it, but that doesn't stop her from standing up for her man and saying what has to be said.

"Slot and run, you halfer. You're giving my stud a brainache."

The man and the dwarf sit on the blue marbleized sofa in

the living room, hardcopy spread all over the low table before them. Clutch leans back and smiles, looking her over,
obviously enjoying the view. The halfer sitting beside him
looks at Cherry and glares, but that doesn't scare her. Cherry
takes guano from nobody. Especially nobody with a datajack
in his skull and a handcomp on his belt.

Fragging dirteater C.P.A.

"Why don't you go calc some digits somewhere."

Clutch grins and reaches for her. He pulls her close, kisses
her hard on the mouth. A hand slips between her smooth
round thighs. Chills of pleasure rush up her spine. She shivers. Clutch chuckles, and says, "You shouldn't be talking
drek to Mr. Numbers. He just found me some nuyen we
didn't even know I had."

Cherry smiles. "Enough to buy me something real ice?"

"As ice as you like," Clutch croons. "Two hundred cool
ones."

"Two hundred-kay nuyen?"

Clutch nods. Cherry marvels. Imagine him making so
much money he can't even keep track of it all. She always
knew life with Clutch would either shine like gold or sparkle
like diamonds.

Cherry laughs, delighted.

Clutch laughs, too.

12

In the few hours since the morning meeting, the executive
conference room has been transformed into a local office for
Kono-Furata-Ko International. The long table is now filled
by Tokyo's audit staff, all in black blazers, all wearing KFK
identification. Many have palmtops and full-sized cyberdecks jacked into the conference table's dataterms. Several
carts filled with additional equipment, what Amy takes to be
mass memory modules, stand along the walls.

Up at the head of the room, there is now a trio of black
desks. The center desk is nearly surrounded by a small
crowd of people, more black blazers with KFK I.D. Amy
walks as far as the desk on the left and sees Kurushima

Jussai seated at the center desk, apparently giving orders to the troops. His Japanese is far too fast and fluent for her to catch more than a few scattered words, and nothing whatsoever of content.

Abruptly, Kurushima glances aside, sees her, and, for a moment, his impassive mask dissolves. His eyebrows jump, as with surprise. He stands up. The troops disperse. Amy meets Kurushima beside his desk and bows, then shakes his hand. Someone brings her a chair. Two other someones bring tall lacquered screens of Asian design. These are placed, apparently, with the idea of casting an illusion of privacy around them.

"Thank you for coming, Ms. Berman," Kurushima begins. "Before we begin our formal business, I would like to explain. Naturally, for the purposes of the audit, we and our respective staffs will be working closely together. It would seem most desirable that we understand one another."

Amy nods. "I agree."

"Thank you," Kurushima says, also nodding. "As an auditor, I am accustomed to dealing with facts, primarily accounting data, which, as you undoubtedly know, must necessarily be very precise."

"Of course."

"As a result of this, my experience and my training, I sometimes demonstrate less acumen in dealing with people. It has come to my attention that such might be the case with regard to this morning's meeting, specifically my remarks to the senior executives, yourself included, concerning this audit. I hope you were not offended."

This is almost a disappointment. Amy had been expecting a fight. It will be hard to get that fight going if Kurushima insists on being so polite, nearly as *reasonable* as Vernon Janasova.

"I'm from New York, Mr. Kurushima," Amy says. "I'm used to offensive people saying offensive things. But I did not conceive of you or anything you said this morning as being offensive."

For a moment, as she pauses between one sentence and the next, deliberately, Kurushima's eyes widen, but then the impassive mask returns. "I had hoped that such would be the case, Ms. Berman," Kurushima says. "It was my intention to disseminate information in as clear a manner as possible. Perhaps I sought to say too much, to convey too many specifics, rather than elaborate in general terms the reasoning inherent in our audit methodology. What I am saying, Ms. Berman, is that perhaps I was too blunt."

"Maybe I was blunt."

Kurushima hesitates. "It would be difficult for me to say, Ms. Berman. Certainly, you expressed you views very clearly. As Hurley-Cooper Laboratories is located in New York, I would naturally expect its executives to assume a Western style of management."

Amy has little trouble imagining what Kurushima thinks of "Western-style" management. The same thing his superiors probably think. Hence, the audit. "I see your point," Amy replies. "My point was that scientific research can be very sensitive to bureaucratic disruptions."

"Indeed," Kurushima says, "I did understand this very clearly, Ms. Berman. Please be assured that we will be making every effort to minimize any intrusions the audit plan may cause us to make. Further, I have instructed my staff to deal exclusively with Hurley-Cooper's administrative and support staff, in so far as this is possible, so as to leave the scientists undisturbed."

"I'm glad to hear it." This really is turning out to be a disappointment, if Amy dares believe him. She has trouble doing that. She's met too many Tokyo-bred execs who seemed deserving of the typical streeter description of elves: six-faced and three-hearted. Impossible to know. Difficult if not impossible to predict. Dangerous to trust.

"Of course, this may have the unfortunate effect of placing a greater burden on the administrative and support staff."

"Mr. Kurushima," Amy replies, definitely, "it's always been my belief that the job of the administrative staff is to support the science staff. Hurley-Cooper is in the business of research. Everything else is secondary. Therefore, anything I can do to further the research is exactly what I should be doing. If my people and I have to work a little harder to prevent research being interrupted by this audit, then that's exactly what we're going to do."

If Kurushima's genuinely pleased to hear it, he gives no clue. He merely says, "Such views are very commendable, speaking as they do of the strategic goals of Hurley-Cooper, rather than the objectives of your specific areas of responsibility."

"I'm glad you see it that way."

"Indeed I do. And in fact this comes as no surprise to me. I am aware of your efforts to make Hurley-Cooper a more efficient organization. Here, I speak specifically of the Purchasing Department and purchasing procedures as these affect the research groups."

"Oh?"

"With your permission, I would like to discuss certain matters concerning the Purchasing Department and its procedures."

For a moment, Amy says nothing. They've been all around the world and exchanged any number of compliments, or near-compliments. Maybe now the gloves are actually coming off. "Go ahead."

"Typically, in KFK subsidiaries," Kurushima says, "purchasing requests rise through the executive hierarchy. They originate with the group or department-level supervisor and are eventually validated by the division director or vice president."

Amy nods quickly. She's not hearing anything new. "We've adopted a decentralized budgeting program in order to speed up the purchasing process, especially in regard to the research groups. The Resource Committee assigns each group a budget based on a variety of factors, including the likelihood of a particular group's research eventually yielding a return on monies invested. From that point on, it's largely up to the specific group leader to decide how his or her budget should be spent."

"Might this decentralization be subject to abuses?"

"Any program can be abused. We have confidence in the integrity of our people."

"I am sure your confidence is entirely justified. Certainly, I did not mean to imply that your purchasing system has been abused or that any employees of Hurley-Cooper are lacking in integrity. Please excuse me if you took this as my meaning."

"I didn't. Please go on."

"Naturally, in my role as an auditor, it is my task to ask questions, and to seek answers, even where the answers may seem obvious or of trivial import. This is so our superiors can be assured that business is proceeding in a profitable and efficient manner."

"I understand."

"As regards the purchasing system, I would like to ask

certain questions concerning the Metascience Group led by Dr. Liron Phalen. My preliminary inquiries have indicated that Dr. Phalen is the group director. It would seem then that all purchasing requests from this group should originate with Dr. Phalen, or be validated by him."

Amy shakes her head. "The Metascience Group is a special case. You're correct. Technically, Dr. Phalen is the group director. As I mentioned this morning, he's also a brilliant scientist and somewhat eccentric. He prefers to devote his time to research and we accord him the latitude to do it. Dr. Phalen's chief assistant, Dr. Benjamin Hill, has been authorized by the senior executive board to originate purchasing requests on Dr. Phalen's behalf."

"In the normal course of business, who would countervalidate these requests by Dr. Hill?"

"That would depend on the value in nuyen of the request."

"You, of course, do not countervalidate all requests personally."

"That's why we have purchasing agents."

"Yes, most certainly, that is correct. However, it would appear, Ms. Berman, that the Vice President for Research does not countervalidate these requests either."

An obvious point. Kurushima is apparently trying to make something out of nothing. Amy replies, "It's a question of value. In a case where the request involves trivial sums, such as for office supplies, the purchasing req is validated by one of my purchasing agents and the VP for Research is simply informed of the request by memo. Where larger sums are involved, my chief purchasing agent or I myself will countervalidate."

"Is it not true, Ms. Berman, that the VP for Research is out of the loop, so to speak, until the monies involved reach a figure in excess of a million nuyen?"

"No, that's not true. The VP is informed every step of the way. The purchasing process is simply not kept waiting pending the VP's validation."

"In other words, if I understand you correctly, the purchasing process might be described as forward-looking. It continues ahead, presuming that validation will be given, where required, until such time as a senior executive rejects the purchasing request."

That is a twisted way of looking at things and Amy does

not like it. She replies, forcefully, "There are only two presumptions being made: one, that the Resource Committee knows what it's doing in allocating the research budget, and, two, that the individual research group leaders know best how to spend the funds given them."

"And yet, all of the group leaders do not themselves originate all purchase requests."

"Didn't we just discuss that?"

"Most certainly, Ms. Berman. However, from the standpoint of the auditor, this remains a point of concern. I am especially concerned in regard to the Metascience Research Group, because of the considerable sums of money allocated to that group."

"I assume you're not suggesting that Doctors Phalen or Hill have made any illicit use of funds."

"Indeed I am not, Ms. Berman. Forgive me if I gave such an erroneous impression. My concern, rather, is whether such funds are being used in a manner that best reflects the objectives of Hurley-Cooper Laboratories. My concern is that the Metascience Group leader's assistant rather than the group leader himself appears to be determining how funds will be spent."

Amy forestalls an angry retort, then says, pointedly, "Dr. Hill is not merely an assistant. He's a brilliant scientist in his own right. And he works side by side with Dr. Phalen."

"I accept this, of course," Kurushima says. "I would assume this was the case or Dr. Hill would not be the group leader's senior assistant. I would also assume that there are reasons why Dr. Phalen, rather than Dr. Hill, has charge of this group."

Amy shakes her head. Kurushima is playing with words, and those words carry obvious implications. "That is not a fair assessment. Dr. Phalen's standing as a scientist is exceptional. He's considered a genius, whereas most of our other science staff are merely brilliant. Were Dr. Phalen to leave Hurley-Cooper tomorrow, Dr. Hill would succeed him as director of the Metascience Group."

"But Dr. Hill is not in fact in charge of that group."

Amy resists the urge to exclaim, and instead, asks, "Why are you making such a point of this?"

"It has come to my attention, Ms. Berman, that the Metascience Group consumes a significant portion of Hurley-Cooper's research budget. I do not have detailed figures as of yet, but the Metascience portion of the overall budget appears to approach thirty percent. That is a very significant amount of money."

Amy nods. Another obvious point. She replies with obvious points of her own. "Metascience research is not cheap. Many of the devices used by the group have to be custom-designed and manufactured. And naturally the group makes extensive use of materials that are of an arcane nature and are therefore extremely expensive."

"Yes, I see," Kurushima says. "Thank you, I understand. Allow me to explain, Ms. Berman, that as an auditor, it is part of my responsibility to assure my superiors that these monies are being allocated with all due care. The fact that the Metascience Group leader leaves his administrative responsibilities to his assistant is not necessarily a circumstance that will inspire my superiors with confidence."

"I believe I already mentioned that the executive board of Hurley-Cooper has specifically authorized Dr. Hill to act on Dr. Phalen's behalf."

"Yes, certainly," Kurushima replies. "I am quite certain that the board was entirely justified in doing so. However, I am equally certain that the board has not seen fit to appoint Dr. Hill leader of the Metascience Group."

"A few moments ago I asked you why you're making such a point about this. I would like an answer to that question."

"Yes, of course. Excuse me if I seem to belabor certain topics." Kurushima consults his palmtop. "A preliminary survey of certain purchasing records has brought certain matters to my attention."

Apparently, the audit staff has carte blanche to investigate anything they want without asking permission of anyone. Obviously, Amy's conversation with Vernon Janasova was a complete waste of time. "Go on," she replies.

"Several months ago, a purchase order originating with Dr. Hill was issued for an item, a certain appendage of a dragon. This appendage was valued at five hundred thousand nuyen."

"May I see that?"

"Certainly."

A glance at Kurushima's palmtop refreshes her memory. This particular purchase order had struck her as odd when it crossed her desktop. Many things involving metascience research at least seem that way. That is probably because she is no scientist, and, certainly, no magician. "There should be a supplemental report hypered to this purchase order which explains the need for this particular item. The 'appendage' referred to was a scale from the tail of a live dragon. As you can probably imagine, dragons are rather fond of their scales and are not generally inclined toward giving them away for nothing. It had to be purchased. Five hundred-kay was the price."

"Was this the best price?"

"It was the only price. My chief purchasing agent investigated this req personally. Only one dragon of the few we could contact would even discuss the matter. Five hundred-kay was his price."

"Do you know if this item was ever used?"

"That would be in the supplemental report."

"I have examined this report, Ms. Berman, and see no indication that the item was ever used. This compels me to ask if perhaps the item was purchased prematurely. You would certainly agree that five hundred-kay nuyen is a considerable sum to invest before an item is actually needed."

"Obviously."

"My preliminary inquiry has turned up several other items of a similar nature. Items purchased but apparently never used. Together, they amount to a fairly sizable investment of monies."

"Give me a list. I'll investigate the disposition."

"Your willingness to cooperate is most appreciated, Ms. Berman. May I say that I have every expectation that by working together we will conclude this audit satisfactorily and on schedule."

Amy nods and forces a smile, saying. "Let's hope so."

13

There should be nothing but comfort here in this room, Bandit tells himself. The slow, steady whisper of Shell's breathing, her warmth, the soft pressure of her body, leaning lightly against his chest. The atmosphere of privacy. The shadowy dark. And on the astral, the pulsing rhythms of life, the subtle colorations, the quiet intensity of a living being now deeply asleep.

He could cast a spell on himself, lure himself to sleep, if he knew such a spell, if he really wanted to sleep. But he does not. He decided to spend the afternoon in contemplation. Shell decided to keep him company, then decided to take a nap. The kids are all out. It should be easy to think, but it isn't.

Carefully, he mouths the words to a small spell, a sort of trick. He has used it on shadowruns many times. It has many uses. Now he uses it to erect a kind of shield around Shell, so she will not feel him moving, hear him rising from the couch, or stepping carefully across the room. He does not wish to disturb her. She has problems enough of her own and would be troubled if she got the idea that something was troubling him.

Shell is an amazing person, like few he has met. Learning about her, getting to know her, perhaps to understand her a little, has done more to help him attune himself with people, hence with all of nature, than anything he has tried since leaving Newark. She does things for people without ever asking anything in return. The kids are not really even her own children. They're orphans, abandoned to the streets, of no importance to anyone but Shell. She calls them her family, her little tribe. There were only six when Bandit first met her. Now there are eight. Shell picks them up where she sees them, when she thinks she can help them. She is teaching some of the older ones the hard lessons of the sprawl, how to survive, how to get what they need, but she insists on feeding and clothing them herself, or with what she and Bandit snatch. She takes nothing of what the kids get on their own. She wants nothing from anyone, nothing . . . except maybe love.

That is another thing that troubles him. His feelings for Shell are hard to define. He's not sure if his feelings for her are what she would call love. He hasn't spent much time considering love. Before leaving Newark, before meeting Shell, he didn't think about it at all. He never imagined it might really matter.

Raccoon is a loner, but must he always be alone? Could there not also be room for another in his life?

It is difficult to know what path is right.

Quietly, Bandit closes the door leading into the stairwell. Beneath the stairs, the stairs to the outside door, is a small cranny about the size of a large closet. Shell's kids play here sometimes. It is a good place for hiding and for having secret talks. The back wall of the space appears solid, but it is no more solid than a cloud. Behind the cloud is another wall with a solid metal door and many locks. Bandit silently says the words to lower the wards defending the door, then tends to the locks. To his surprise, he suddenly finds himself facing a spirit, a spirit of Nature, of Man.

In form, the spirit looks kind of like a dwarf, with rough-hewn features and a heavy beard, but it wears clothing that seems ancient and fine, adorned with ruffles and lace. In a voice as deep as the earth, the spirit says, "You are welcome in my hearth."

Bandit replies, "I thank you."

The spirit bows, then says, "It has been many years since the sounds of frolicking children have carried through my vestibules and halls. I am old. The years have taken the color from my brick and the vigor from my mortar. Soon, the time will come when only memories will inhabit my domain, and that will be very sad. For what am I if I give no refuge? I would have no purpose. I would have no more ties to the plane of my own substance." The spirit pauses, and smiles. "I am grateful to hear the joyful noise of children again. They are welcome here. She who brings them is welcome most of all."

"I thank you."

The spirit bows and fades from view. Bandit takes one step further and enters his lodge. And then he is alone.

Alone in his alone place, his place of long magic.

The space is not large, just tall enough for him to stand, just large enough for him to do magic, and to store what must be stored in a safe and secret place. The lodge, like the apartment, is contained within a portion of the sub-basement no longer used by anyone but him, Shell, and the kids. Before making any changes, before making this private den, he took the unusual step of consulting with the spirit of this place. The spirit had welcomed him, invited him to make his den, to do his magic here. It had seemed gladdened to provide a sort of refuge. It has since manifested many times to speak with him, to tell him of the ways of spirits like himself, and of the ways of Man.

But it is not Man or men that trouble him tonight. It is the wallet Shell snatched yesterday, the ID card in that wallet, the image of the woman on that card. The woman's image resembles someone he once knew. He wonders if that is co-incidence, or if it is not, and what he should do about it.

For a time, he sits cross-legged, facing the small trunk that serves as his ritual altar. The candle glowing there gives him light to see the many artifacts of his lodge, the contain-ers of colored sand and minerals, boxes of crystals, pelts, bones, drums, rattles. What the candle's light does not show him is the answer he desires.

He lifts his flute, fingers the carefully engraved wood, watches the sheen of light from the candle coursing over the flute's waxy finish. When he lifts the flute to his lips, he does not play any particular arrangement of notes, no set melody. He lets the music flow from within. He lets his spirit make the song.

Before long, the light of the candles wavers. Bandit real-izes he is no longer alone.

The figure at the rear of his lodge looks like an old man. Bandit calls him Old Man. That is the name that seems right. He once thought that Old Man looked kind of Asian, but he was wrong. Old Man looks Amerind. His thin gray hair flows down past his shoulders. He wears clothes of natural leather, tan and dark brown, and necklaces and beads like native peoples wore long before the Awakening. Bandit once thought that Old Man might be Raccoon wearing a human mask, or some sort of spirit guide. In this, too, he was wrong.

"I guess you want something," Old Man says. "You called."

Bandit nods. He considers turning to face Old Man, but decides against it. He faces the front of his lodge, the focal point of his magic. That is as it should be. That is the way of the shaman. "I'm troubled."

"I figured that. What about it?"

Bandit draws a breath, and says, "The shaman's path can be hard to know. I began by learning magic and ignoring people. I tried to do what cannot be done. The shaman must be one with nature. People are part of nature and cannot be ignored. I tried to know nature, but not all of it, and so my magic was flawed, and I could go no further."

"I know all that," Old Man says. "What's your point?"

"Now I'm trying to learn about people. I've opened myself to people, I guess. I'm learning again. Discovering new things."

"And?" Old Man sounded impatient.

"My thoughts trouble me."

"That's nothing new."

"These thoughts are new. I think Shell gave them to me. She makes me wonder. About people. It's not enough to learn only about people you meet in the streets. That's just the beginning. People are individuals. They have different personalities and moods, and . . ."

"Yes."

"They have different relationships."

"Nobody would argue that."

"Some people are mothers and fathers. Some are just friends. Some are good friends and nearly as important as sisters or brothers."

A long silence passes, then Old Man says, "I don't know why you're telling me this. I'm just an old man. I don't have any answers. If I did, I probably forgot them. And what good would they be to you? You're a shaman. You know some things about the world. You have to decide. You have to find your own answers."

"I know that."

"One time, I heard a man say to another: what's it all about? The other man went on and on trying to explain, but he never did get his point across. He didn't understand the question. He couldn't. The man who asked the question was the only one who really knew what the question meant. How could anybody else explain when they didn't understand the question?"

"You don't understand what I'm talking about?"

"Do you?"

"I think I do."

"Then let's hear you explain it."

"I'm not sure I can."

"That's no answer. You know better. You're a shaman. You've been through the ordeals. You didn't attain the power of an initiate without being able to face the pain. You won't get anywhere if you can't face the pain. You know that. Pain is part of the world and you have to face it at its worst. That's why attuning yourself to people is so important. The pain of mother earth is great, but what's that compared to the pain of people, and the pain inside yourself? What greater pain is there than the pain you're feeling right now?"

"You're right."

Old Man is right, Bandit tells himself again. The pain he's feeling now is worse than anything. It's fear and guilt and a sorrow so intense, so pure and so focused he can't keep the tears out of his eyes. Can't hardly breathe without choking. "I ignored so many people . . . spent so much time with only magic . . . I almost killed myself . . . I see that now . . . I cut away part of myself . . . I guess . . . I guess . . . I have to get it back . . ."

"What was your first clue?"

"It was Shell . . . something she said. She called me . . . she said . . . She said I'm a private person . . . I never thought of it that way . . . I'm a shaman . . . follow Raccoon . . . That's all . . ."

"You're a person, too."

Bandit nods. "I need to become whole again. A whole person."

"I guess you know what you have to do."

Bandit nods, wipes at his eyes. The image of that woman on the card Shell snatched makes it a certainty.

"I guess you're ready now."

Bandit nods.

Ready for anything.

14

The road is a wavering phantom streaming toward her, white lines blurring, gleaming in the brilliant headlights of the truck. She is somewhere south of Bangor with Portland coming up fast. The truck engine whines, telltales pegging max. The hunt for her cub leads her now to Boston. That is where she will find the only living person who knew she would be at the cabin along the Road to Nowhere.

That person has betrayed her. Whether the betrayal was deliberate or the result of some foolish error is irrelevant. The betrayal has cost her and she will see the debt repaid.

Doing that should tell her more about the bounty hunter O'Keefe and the other elves who stole her cub, such as where they might be found.

In Boston? That would be too easy.

Abruptly, a siren wails. Tikki looks to the rear scanner to see strobe lights flashing behind her. Some form of patrol vehicle, a cruiser perhaps, is just thirty meters away and closing in fast. The speed of closure makes Tikki wish she had a vehicle quicker than this pickup truck.

She tugs at the wheel, yanking the trunk into the right-hand lane, but the cruiser abruptly slows, rather than passing by, and veers into the lane close in on her backside.

The siren whoops and screams.

A voice booms, *"PULL IT OVER!"*

And now she must make a decision. Possibly, these police want her to stop for something as trivial as speeding. They may know nothing more than that, but they will swiftly realize the truck is stolen, even if they're just hick backwoods cops or corporate zonies. She could ignore them, go on driving, but more two-legs would come and they would force a confrontation. She could abandon the truck and run, but that would cost her time, and every passing instant is a rising fury threatening to supplant rational thinking with instinct's most savage urgings. She can no more afford the inevitable costs of instinct than the loss of more time. She really has only one option.

She puts on the right-turn blinker, slows the truck, and steers onto the shoulder. The cruiser follows closely. When she stops, the cruiser halts about five meters behind her truck. She counts to three, watching the flashing strobes, and then, with the tranny in reverse, rams the accelerator to the floor.

The truck engine roars. Tires shriek and whine and tear at the earth. Acceleration is rapid, but fleeting. The rear of the truck impacts the front of the cruiser. Plasteel crashes and the impact hurls Tikki against the back of her seat. The shock of that costs her half a second, but then she's like a road train slamming out through the driver's door, turning, charging the cruiser, lunging into the air and across the cruiser's rumpled front hood.

As she lunges, her body swells and stretches. Clothing bursts and tears. Black-striped fur the color of blood rushes over her skin. Jaws swell immense. Hands become massive paws sprouting claws and smashing the cruiser's windshield into fragments.

The cops are shouting in alarm and stinking of terror, but by then she's inside the car—twisting, turning, tearing belts off uniforms and commlinks from the dash.

In the frenzy of those moments, a gun roars beside her ear, but she hardly feels the sting of fur and flesh being torn from the side of her skull. She drives a paw against a head and the head hits the passenger-side window and one of the cops goes limp, alive, but unconscious. The other one is disabled as quickly.

That leaves her with another problem, one becoming too familiar. What does she do for clothes?

She eyes the cops' blue uniforms.

15

"Amy? . . . *Amy!*"

Startled, Amy looks up and around.

Tonight, she's wearing her newest, most costly evening gown, her Armante Starlight gown, clinging cloth-of-gold speckled with faux diamonds that cast a subtle golden halo all around her. The gown really belongs on someone with a figure far more stellar than her own, but she felt persuaded to make the investment, and to take the incumbent risk, on account of the man sitting opposite her.

Just across the glittering crystal table sits Harman Franck-Natali, wearing the Saville Nights suit that makes him seem so much the successful exec. Amy notices that Harman's looking at her like he's either puzzled or angry, and that's odd. Harman is usually the picture of self-control. What's going-on?

Beside the table stands an older, gray-haired man, a waiter in a tuxedo, the very picture of Old World elegance and dignity. He fits his background perfectly. The main dining room of Avant Tout is lit subtly by the suffused light sifting up through the crystal tables. Rainbows shine softly against the ceiling. Whalesong plays discreetly from hidden speakers. The atmosphere is one of understated opulence.

"Would you care to order?" Harman asks.

On the table before her is a sparking *haut ton* menu. Of course, she's barely glanced at the listings and now everyone's waiting for her decision. Harman's waiting again. She kept him waiting almost half an hour, earlier this evening, while she finished dressing. "What are you having?" she asks.

"We'll be a few minutes," Harman tells the waiter.

"Of course, sir. Madame." The waiter bows and goes off.

Harman turns his right hand palm up as if to ask what's going on, and says, "Am I putting you to sleep?"

"I'm sorry," Amy says, suddenly recognizing the disappointment in his eyes. She barely suppresses a moan. "I'm spoiling it all."

"I don't understand."

"It's work. I can't get it off my mind."

Harman hesitates a moment, watching her, then says, "Why don't we forget dinner? It's been a long day for me, too. We can grab some food somewhere, and I'll drive you home. We can talk on the way."

Amy nods, grateful, and sad and disappointed, but resigned.

Harman had wanted this to be a special evening. They've been seeing each other for exactly a year, and it seems like their relationship is really heading somewhere. Lately, they'd begun talking about the future in terms of "we" and "us". Amy likes that. She's been a long time getting around to meeting someone with whom she could talk like that. She has a definite feeling that this could be the one, a someone she might spend the rest of her life with. She hopes so. She hopes he understands that her problems tonight have nothing to do with her feelings for him.

They head for the door. Harman rescues her shawl from the checkroom and drapes it carefully about her shoulders. She manages a smile of thanks. A tuxedoed doorman escorts them outside, to the broad semicircular walk embracing the sparkling fountain before the restaurant's main entrance. A black-suited valet brings Harman's stately Mitsubishi Patrician. The doorman opens Amy's door.

"Au revoir, Madame."

"Yes. Thank you. Good night."

Harman turns the car onto Seventh, heading downtown. Just a few blocks north of Times Square is one of the city's

small treasures: The Second Avenue Deli. Tourists look for
it over by Turtle Bay, but it's actually right at the heart of
things, just off Duffy Square. Harman goes in alone, gets
them hot pastrami sandwiches, a carafe of wine, and two
cups of dessert coffee. They eat in the car, parked right there
at curbside, accompanied by classical melodies from Harman's extensive stereo collection.

"Picnic in Midtown," Harman says.

"It's fine."

What better place to eat than so near the theater district,
where scripter's dramas strive to illuminate the melodrama
of life? It's safe enough. Cars marked for NYPD Inc. pass
by nearly every time the traffic lights change. A pair of uniformed officers from Winter Systems stand right outside the
deli, keeping a watchful eye on things.

"It must be your Tokyo auditors," Harman says. "They're
stirring things up?"

Amy nods. She supposes it's time for the talk Harman
mentioned. She doesn't want to burden him with her work
problems, but neither does she want to shut him out. She
struggles with that minor dilemma, and finally decides it's
important that he should know. He's become as important to
her as her career, perhaps even more so. She shouldn't keep
secrets. But where should she start? "You know what a mess
things were when I joined HC. It was taking some departments months just to order software prepacks."

Harman nods, smiles. "You did a hell of a job straighten-
ing that out."

"I did what I could," Amy agrees, "but I'm only one person.
The purchasing process seemed like the obvious priority. Unfortunately, I still have lots to do on the other side of the equation,
and that's what the auditors are looking at."

"Resource consumption?"

"Tracking, consumption . . ." Amy nods, recalling her
"discussion" with Kurushima Jussai. "We bought a dragon's
hangnail for some metascience experiment. Did we ever use
it? Well, it cost us half a million nuyen. Why don't you have
any answers?"

"I wasn't aware that dragons could get hangnails."

"I'm being facetious."

"As am I." Harman's smile turns from apologetic to warm
and sympathetic. "I'm sorry. I don't mean to belittle your
situation. It's just rather surprising . . . half a million nuyen.

Sometimes it seems that my people spend that much on drinks in a week."

"I know." Amy watches the play of emotions across Harman's face, then leans near enough to kiss his cheek. "I know exactly what you mean."

And, in truth, Harman's reaction is perfectly natural. He is Managing Director of Sales for Mitsuhama Systems Engineering, a division of Mitsuhama UCAS, part of one of the world's most powerful megacorps. Hurley-Cooper's parent corp, KFK International, is pretty big too, but comparing HC to Harman's division is simply ridiculous. Harman's sales force spans the globe and brings in billions. Hurley-Cooper Laboratories does important work, and turns a tidy profit, but in terms of nuyen it's strictly small-time.

"Don't you have a resource director?" Harman asks.

"Yes, Bob Ganz," Amy replies. "He's Director of Resource Management. That's another problem."

"Tell me about it."

A year ago she might have looked at Harman and wondered why the Director of Sales for Mitsuhama Systems Engineering was so interested in her problems. She doesn't suffer from doubts like that anymore. Harman's voice is soft, his expression is concerned. He wouldn't waste a second over a little corp like Hurley-Cooper except that it's her little corp and that makes all the difference. She trusts him to keep this just between him and her.

"Bob isn't a very imaginative person."

"That's not good."

"And he uses BTLs."

Both of them know what that means. Through the miracle of virtual experience, BTLs give thrills even *Better Than Life*. They're a variety of high-gain, mega-output simsense chip, perfectly addictive. "Then he should go," Harman says softly.

"It's not that easy."

"Chipheads aren't going to do you or HC any good."

"Bob's been with HC almost thirty years. He worked his way up from nothing. He's one of those people who always worked twice as hard as everyone else because he knows he has limitations. I think that's how he got hooked on BTLs, trying to take up the slack, pushing himself."

"He'll burn out sooner or later."

"Maybe. I gave him a pep talk and an ultimatum. You're

a good man and you do good work, but get into a program.
Get clean or you're out. I think he's making progress."

"And you believe he deserves the chance to redeem himself."

"Yes, I do."

"So, meanwhile, your resource group is limping along and
now you're personally in a hole."

Amy looks at him and nods.

"Is it worth it?"

That's a question Amy's asked herself at least a few million times. Somehow, she always comes up with the same
answer. She forces herself to say it now with conviction. "If
I'm not prepared to back up my beliefs, then I shouldn't be
in the game."

"I admire your pertinacity."

"You'd do the same thing."

"In your position? I like to think so. I hope I'd have your
courage. There are changes I'd like to make right now, only
I'm surrounded by sharks."

"Harman, you don't have to apologize."

"I want you to understand."

"I do understand. I do."

Harman's situation is really quite different from hers. People don't matter at Mitsuhama, not in Harman's division.
The only issue there is "product" or "sales." Harman seems
to spend most of his time fighting defensive battles against
superiors who want to kick him down a few notches, or sub-
ordinates who want to cut his legs out from under him, pref-
erably with as much gore as possible. Harman can't take the
time to address human issues. He'd be a fool to even try. It's
that brutal an environment.

"Have you thought any more about getting out?"

"I'm thinking about it very seriously," Harman says, definitely. "I really envy your position. That's what gets to me,
you know. Here you are, a vice president for a little group
of labs, but your work makes you feel like you're contributing something to the world. I've got people all over hell's
creation and I feel like I'm swimming through a pool of pi-
ranha, and accomplishing nothing."

"Do you want my opinion?"

"I already know it." He smiles, reaches over and takes her
hand. Their fingers intertwine. "You know, I wanted to talk
about us tonight."

"I'm so sorry."

"It's all right. We're both having an off day, I think. Maybe we can try this again next week, when you get those auditors out of your hair. In the meantime, I'd like you to think about us, and what you want. You know what I'm talking about."

Amy nods. "I love you."

"And I love you, darling." Harman stops and smiles, and says, softly, "Should we leave it at that?"

Amy nods, smiles. "Yes. Let's."

The drive home begins with the ride uptown. Traffic slows to a stop-and-go crawl at the entrance to the Triborough Bridge. Amy gazes out the side window at the night. Her concerns about Hurley-Cooper and KFK and, above all, Kurushima Jussai come seeping back into her mind.

By late this afternoon, the chief auditor's list of unaccounted-for resources—materials, equipment, arcane supplies—had grown very long, to crisis proportions, for all practical purposes. On the one hand, Amy can't believe that more than a hundred separate items could have slipped through the cracks; on the other, her worst expectations about the arrival of the Tokyo staff seem to be coming true.

"Amy. Hon?"

Harman touches her shoulder. She finds him gazing at her expectantly. So is the uniformed Port Authority officer looking in through Harman's window.

"Sometime tonight, lady," the officer says tartly.

Abruptly, Amy realizes what's happening. It's one of the more charming aspects of a visit to Manhattan. One must have the proper pass to get in or out, or expect a great big hassle from the police. Amy got her pass through Hurley-Cooper, along with the other senior execs, one result of HC taking office space on New Bronx Plaza. She digs the gray card out of her purse. Before she so much as looks up, card in hand, the Port Authority officer is waving them ahead.

Harman takes them across the bridge to the Bruckner Expressway, then on toward Scarsdale, the corporate side of town. Amy has her resident pass already in hand as they slow before the gatehouse to her highrise condoplex.

"Have a better tomorrow," the guard says cheerfully.

Harman replies, drolly, "Echo that."

16

The van's tires scream as they round the corner, nearly rising onto two wheels. Monk grabs at the door and puts a hand out to the dash and manages to stay mostly upright in his seat. Flashing signs, traffic lights, the lights of other vehicles and crowds of people on crosswalks, sidewalks, and other kinds of walks all zip by in a blur.

Minx shoots him a glance and grins. "Hang on, *you booty!*" she cries. And the tires scream again.

Monk sways across the center console, and sways back the other way. He takes a final deep drag on his cigarette, then drops the butt out the window. Just an ordinary Millennium Red, but it's made him feel like he's flying, flying high, right into orbit.

Zoom! zoom! *and away he goes!*

And here they are, he and Minx, flying through the streets of Sector 10, the cramped, dingy, crud-encrusted commercial part of the Newark plex called the Stacks. Warehouses and factories rush by. Big rigs roar, air horns blatting. Corners swerve past. Null sheen, no persp. No chance of him wetting his shorts. The van veers through a slalom course of cars and cycles stopped all over the street, up on the sidewalks, some lying on their roofs, and comes to a sudden halt. No problemo, omae.

"Let's go, you booty!" Minx exclaims.

They hop out, wearing their face masks and gloves, their dark gray coveralls marked CORONER'S ASST., and their big black ooze-proof boots. A cop in battle dress complete with face shield, heavy armor, and submachine gun motions at the street, and says, in a metallic remodulated voice, "There's the beef. Take your pick."

"Wiz," Minx replies. "Six two and even."

"Over and out," Monk adds.

Minx jabs his ribs and giggles.

Monk grins.

The street looks like a combat zone. Aside from the cars and cycles all over the place, and the various tow trucks, meat trucks, fire trucks, and cop-mobiles, there are three buildings with smashed-out windows and one smaller structure, a simsense parlor, that's now missing most of its second floor, said floor having fallen into the pile of crud spreading halfway across the street. Bodies are everywhere, sprawled in the gutters, hanging out of burnt, turned-over cars, lying beneath various chunks of rumble.

So which stiffs do they want? Monk wonders. It's obvious. The best ones.

The best can be hard to spot. They don't look all that different from the ones that are really dead—just as dead as they could get. All bloody and gory, with bones sticking out, and eyes drooling out of sockets, and squat like that. Maximum slimy and definitely yarfland. The best ones might be just as mashed and mutilated, but there's a difference. What Minx calls the "subtle radiance of life" still lingers. Like an aura. Very subtle. Seeing that faint radiance against the bright reddish haze of daylight isn't easy. Fortunately, they work the night shift. The faint reddish glow of life stands out pretty plainly against the dull, brooding, reddish haze of night.

"That one," Minx says, pointing. "And that one."

Minx has had lots of practice.

The cop shrugs. "Move 'em out."

They grab the gurney from the rear of the van and hustle to the corpses. The first one looks like a ganger in synthleather, spikes and lots of body color and tats. The second one looks like a regular citizen, some suit. Cause of death isn't exactly obvious and Monk for one doesn't much care. After you've seen your first hundred bodies—munched and crunched and smashed, shot up, chopped up, shredded like for a meal—it gets to be pretty routine. They slam one gurney, then the other into the van, then fling the doors shut.

On impulse, Monk waves to the cop, and says, simply, "Bye."

"Next time," the cop replies.

Minx giggles.

Five blocks away, Minx parks the van in front of a Voodoo Chili and cuts the engine. They go into the rear of the van. The corpses lie there on the gurneys, lie there like the dead. The lingering traces of life are getting fainter by the minute, but that's all right because now everything's set. Nobody'll interrupt them because the sides, front, and rear of the van are marked: City of Newark. Coroner. Most people know that means "icky flatlines inside." And nobody likes icky flatlines.

Well . . . Almost.

"I want the suit," Minx says.

Minx pulls out her Sony Budcam and snaps pictures of the corpses for her collection. Monk lifts the ganger's limp arms and waves them at Minx's face. "I'm coming to get you, Jessica," Monk groans.

"Eeek!" Minx squeals. "Okay, *let's do it, booty!*"

Monk leans down and puts his mouth over the ganger's mouth, then slowly inhales. It's kind of like giving mouth-to-mouth resuscitation, only in reverse. The breath of life? Getting it just right is tricky. It's easy to give life instead of just taking it, and doing that can have really weird results. This time it goes good, though. The rush that fills his lungs spreads a tingling throughout his body and rises up into his head, till he's swaying, dizzy, with a bliss better than sex.

He sits down heavily, sighing, grinning, sated, pleased. Minx pulls her hand from the suit's pants pocket and holds up a pair of silver credsticks.

"Look what I found," she says softly.

In the dark reddish twilight in the rear of the van, Minx's eyes blaze like Vulcan's furnace, which was really fiery and hot, or so it's said. "Nova."

Monk grins.

17

It's after four A.M. when Amy exhales heavily and finally gives up on the idea of getting back to sleep. She dropped off like a rock the moment her head touched the pillow, thanks to a cap, but the caplet didn't hold. She drifted in and out of sleep for a while, but has spent the last hour just lying here, staring into the dark. It's one of those times when she's glad to be single. No one to disturb.

Why can't she sleep? She knows why. And there's no point putting it off any longer.

She dials Harman's home code, breathes a sigh of relief

when his recording answers. It's early yet. She didn't want to wake him.

"Darling," she says softly, "I'm going in early and I'll be out of the office all day. Most of it, anyway. I'm not sure when I'll be home, so I'll talk to you tomorrow."

After a moment's hesitation, she adds, "Why don't we try dinner again on Friday? Maybe out on Long Island? You decide. Love you. Bye."

A shower washes some of the cobwebs from her brain. She dresses, swallows vitamins and juice, grabs her briefcase, and stops off at the closet by the front door, staring at jackets and coats. The obvious choice, her black Zoé trench, won't cut it today. That's too much like a straight suit, the good corporate girl fitting into the fashionable corporate mode. Too much like something people from Tokyo would expect her to wear.

She let the auditors get to her yesterday, get her down and depressed, and so she ended up ruining what should have been a lovely evening on the town.

Enough.

Today she's going to take the initiative and make things go right. She wants answers, she'll get answers, or be damned trying.

She pulls on her florescent yellow synthleather jacket, grabs the matching gloves and helmet, then exchanges her briefcase and pumps for a backpack, also florescent yellow, and low-heeled ankle boots.

The elevator delivers her to the condoplex sublevel garage. In the space beside her Toyota Arbiter GX is a Harley Roadraider. The Toyo is silver-gray and dignified, pure executive juice. The Harley is florescent yellow, bright enough to burn, to burst into flames, and has about as much in common with a straight suit as, well . . . she doesn't know what.

She pulls on the backpack and helmet. The Harley rumbles to life. She makes it whine, then rides up the ramp. It's not quite five a.m. The tall silvery lamps along the curving tree-lined lanes of the condoplex cast an orangey light into the mist. Amy heads for the main condoplex entrance.

Coming in or heading out, IDs must be shown. Amy stops, flips up her mirrored face shield, and shows her pass. The guard grins. The guard's name is Mo—"Mo" *Rasheen.* Quite a name. In a voice that lilts up and down like a song, he says, "I see you are feeling in the mood for making the trouble today, Ms. Amy."

Amy smiles, and says, "We'll see about that."

"Well, I am wishing you to having a good day!"

"Thanks."

A kilometer's worth of local roadways puts her onto the ramp and gliding swiftly onto the Hutchinson River Parkway—five lanes of pavement as smooth as glass, and, to her surprise, nearly empty of traffic. She's no harem-scarem go-ganger, but she decides that today's the day to let the Harley open up. She's never seen the highway this empty. She cranks up the throttle till the engine's starting to whine, and she's hitting one-ten, one-twenty. Fast enough to be worth a hefty fine, though not quite fast enough to be insane.

The Cross County Parkway brings her to the Thruway. She flies past a police car parked on the shoulder at something well above the limit, but nothing happens. Maybe it's karma. Maybe this is her day.

She crosses into the Bronx and cruises down onto the exit ramp to the Van Cortlandt Industrial Park, a sprawling site encompassing everything from chemical plants to office towers to little bitty companies that design subprocessor chips and servo-devices for cyberware. The end of the exit ramp is flanked by dark blue cars and vans marked for Apollo Services, a Yamatetsu corp subsidiary specializing in site security.

Amy pauses at the park entrance to show her ID, then heads for the northeast quad. A tall hedge backed by a cyclone fence lines the curb before the Hurley-Cooper metascience installation. Amy slows to a halt at the entrance. Two red and black-uniformed guards emerge from their booth, looking at her like *who's this slitch? and where does she think she's going?*

Their attitude changes radically when she shows her ID, the card with her holo and the big VP in bold black letters. "Ms. Berman!" The sergeant grins, chuckles weakly. "Didn't know you rode a screamer."

"This is a Harley, Sergeant."

"That's a *Harley*? It looks like—" The sergeant stops himself short, looks at her, and says, "I mean . . . well . . ."

Amy nods. "You're right."

For some odd reason, when people think Harley, many of them seem to imagine something resembling a Honda Viking: big, clumsy, powerful enough to propel a troll. Her Roadraider looks even less like that, less a "Harley," than the Harley Scorpion. That is simply to say that it looks like speed, like screaming down side streets at insane velocities, and taking curves that would make simsense star Holly Brighton look as straight-lined as a boy.

It has a certain *je ne sais quoi.*

Call it style.

The gates slide open. Amy rides up the lane, past the parking lot, nearly empty, to the building's main entrance. The building is two-story brick, parts of it cloaked in ivy. It makes up in depth what it lacks in height.

At the reception counter in the lobby is another guard instead of the usual receptionist, who doesn't show up till later in the morning. As Amy enters, the guard is standing like a sentry, gazing fixedly at something, security monitors, located behind the counter. He looks up as Amy's heel first hits the lobby floor. He smiles, and says, "Welcome to Hurley-Cooper Laboratories, ma'am. May I see your identification?"

It's hard to resist a smile.

"Thank you, Ms. Berman. Have a good day."

"Same to you ... Officer Frank-o ... "

"That's Frankavello, ma'am."

"Officer Frankavello."

"Yes, ma'am. Thank you, ma'am."

Enough like Harman's last name to catch her off-guard. Frankavello, Franck-Natali. She smiles. The guard smiles and nods, and Amy steps through the double doors and turns down the hall.

COMP OPS says the little sign projecting out from the hallway wall. Amy's ID opens the fireproof door. She enters a room constructed like a bank vault.

Filling the wall on the left is the rack containing the mass memory modules to a Renraku System 80. To the right is the main console, about the size of an ordinary desk, and, beside it, the big green box containing processors, slaves, random access memory, and associated hardware. The woman in the pink sweats and orange sneaks, with her feet up on the main console, would be the graveyard shift sysop. She twitches, looks back, and nearly falls out of her chair as Amy enters.

"Morning!" the sysop exclaims, catching herself, then switching off a throbbing boombox. "Uh, what's tox?"

Amy pulls up a chair, takes out her palmtop, and passes the sysop a cable. "Plug me in. And get rid of that pizza, please."

"Yes sir! ma'am! I mean . . ."

Right.

The Renraku System 80 is essentially a network server, an immense bank of data archives. It provides for term-to-term interfaces between the Metascience Group's users and network-wide operations, primarily administrative, such as Resource Consumption Control. Unfortunately, the RCC software's glitchy. It misses things if the entries into the science databases aren't made just so. There are protocols and formats for data entry, but they aren't foolproof, and scientists researching blood plasma, for example, do not necessarily make good data-entry clerks. The various sections of the Metascience Group have administrative aides who should look after chores like that, but most of the aides are science-people with science-oriented aspirations, rather than people with specializations in computers or administration.

The experts in Hurley-Cooper's own computer unit have made any number of fixes to the RCC software, and improved things somewhat, but there are only so many experts and they can only fix so many megapulses of code at any one time. And the software's complex enough for even minor fixes to give rise to unforeseen bugs. Amy's looked at possible upgrades, whole new replacement packages, including some from Mitsuhama, which is how she met Harman, but so far nothing she's seen will quite do the job in quite the way she wants.

It's also a fact that Renraku computers run on Renraku computer code, which is idiosyncratic and interacts best, when it interacts, with code written by Renraku and no one else.

To really fix the resource-tracking system Amy may have to convince Vernon Janasova to replace a lot of machines and a lot of software, which, in general terms, will take a great deal of money. Unfortunately, she hasn't had time to do a proper evaluation and estimate. She hasn't had time to make more than a few pages of notes on how, ultimately, she would like the fully upgraded/replaced system to work. And until she gets those jobs done, she's stuck. They're all stuck with what they've got.

Would the people in Tokyo like to donate the money to fix

things up right? That's one idea she'll have to wave in Kurushima's face when she gives him his answers.

Getting the auditor his answers will take some time. The first step is jacking in. Amy's palmtop does what it couldn't have done from her office at New Bronx Plaza: establish itself as a priority terminal with unlimited access to the System 80's resources, including its many terminals, scattered throughout the building. The Metascience Group computer net utilizes an unusual technique to defend against unauthorized intrusions: complete isolation. No comm lines in or out of the network. A prospective datathief, or accomplice, would have to physically enter the building before a theft could be attempted from the group's proprietary data.

Step two is initializing a data-sifting program called Sniffer that will search the entire system for references to the list of 148 items she's compiled from Kurushima's list of things purchased but apparently never used. Has she done this kind of thing before? Yes, she has. Her special search prog was written by one of Hurley-Cooper's software gurus. It will do what the RCC prog on the net doesn't do right all the time, and much, much more. It will likely return with a few megapulses worth of references for her to review. A distinctly unsatisfactory case of more being less, since she'll have to sort through the references manually, but that's life. That's when the real fun will begin.

But the thing that keeps her mood in a positive mode is the thought of giving a definitive answer to every last one of Kurushima Jussai's inquiries.

That she's going to enjoy.

18

The moment the rain begins, Tikki knows she's somewhere near Boston. The smell of the sprawl comes through clearly with every drop. It reminds her of her first visit to a two-leg city, the smells from that night so long ago when she walked into Seoul with her mother. She thought the smells of the plex must be the most exciting scent in the world. She lusted for it. Even when she quietly stalked through the shadows of

Hong Kong, and, later, in Seattle, she relished it. She's since grown weary of the reek.

It's become a smell that tastes of scag, two-leg machinery, chemicals, and waste. Of guileful predators in high towers pointing fingers and making bad things happen. Of razorguys and every form of animal fighting and dying in dark alleys and rotting in gutters. Most of all it tastes of two-legs and their monstrous magic and their inevitable treachery. It reminds her that the two-leg world is a lie, and that human or metahuman, elf, ork, or troll, they are all cheats, deceptions, betrayals just waiting to happen.

Almost all. A rare few rise above the standard set by the rest of the herd. Tikki can count them on the fingers of one hand. One of them will shortly aid her in her hunt.

Dawn is an hour past and the sky is nearly as dark as night. Lightning flashes in the distance. Thunder rumbles. The hairs on the back of her neck are constantly rising. Tingling with the power in the air. It reminds her of magic. The two powers on earth that cannot be touched by fang and claw, the powers of nature and of magic. Tikki mistrusts them both, resents them. Such power should not exist. It makes her nervous. It brings questions and doubts back to mind. It makes her wonder if her place in the world, in the hierarchy of creatures, is quite as high as she's often supposed.

The dark rain splatters against the windshield. The wipers smear the plas with dust and dirt till some foamy stuff sprays from the wiper arms and washes it all away.

Finally, an exit appears. Tikki ignores the sign and turns down the ramp. It's time to make a call.

She's now driving a multifuel Jackrabbit running on petrochem. Nearly every third or fourth car on the road is a Jackrabbit. That is its advantage. It's good cover, good camouflage.

Two kilometers further on, she finds a NewPac station. The credstick she took from the Amerind back in Maine buys her food and fuel and time on a telecom. The attendants in the store and at the pumps sit in armored booths. She's near the sprawl, all right. Very near.

An advert for Fuchi cybernetic systems plays on the telecom screen while her call goes through.

A male voices answers. "Word."

"Steel."

"Who wants him?"

"Who asks?"

Minutes pass. Tikki waits. She knows why the delay stretches out long, and has to work at containing her impatience. The voice that finally comes on the line is a breathy whisper, a rasp, inhumanly hoarse. "You're breaking protocols."

"Eat it," Tikki snarls.

The male at the other end of the line is known as Steel. His real name is Castillano. He was once a serious figure in the Seattle underworld. He is now serious in more places than one, and he does not like being snarled at.

"Problem?" he rasps.

"Your man gave me up."

Another silence. "Then I owe you."

"You owe me much." The theft of her cub will not be reconciled so easily. "Something's been taken from me. I'm taking it back. I'm hunting again. *Man.*"

Yet another silence ensues. Doubtless, Castillano understands what she means by hunting. In their last conversation, she had talked about getting out of the biz. Two-legs make things too complicated, and she had things to think about: her cub, her life. What it all means. But the elves have changed that. She may be out of the biz for good once this is all over, but until then she's in, just as far and as deep as she needs to go.

Castillano says, "What do you want?"

"A name. I need things."

"What area?"

"Boston."

A name is forthcoming, a source for what she needs. Castillano says the source will be told to expect her. That is not worth even half of what he owes her, but it will do for a start.

Two hours later, she parks in a slum near Norwood Airport and walks through the door of a place called Vung Tau. The smell is shrimp and spices. The interior is dim, the floor worn. A counter with stools runs down the right wall, booths on the left. The ork behind the counter hardly gives Tikki a glance. The small gang of five in the booth at the rear of the place pretend to ignore her: two males, three females. They smell discontent. They're wearing sateen and synthleather and they look Vietnamese.

"Who's Thuy?" Tikki asks.

One of the females answers. The reply is brief and could be Vietnamese. The tone is aggressive. Arrogant. The female herself looks strong, willful, ready to fight. Tikki isn't impressed.

She tries Korean. "Who's Thuy?"

The female says, tersely, "Who sent you?"

"Steel."

"How you know Steel?"

A very presumptuous question. This two-leg, this person, Thuy, obviously has no conception of who she is facing. She proves this a moment later by looking to one of the males, who rises and turns to Tikki. This is not to be a greeting. Tikki smells it. The male steps toward her. Cyberspurs slide out of the ends of his arms and snick softly into position. That is annoying enough to bring instinct raging to the fore. In the next instant, Tikki is pounding the male with her fists and driving her knee into his stomach.

The male sags, falls bleeding and wheezing to the floor, and vomits.

The others come to their feet. Tikki seizes Thuy by the throat, shoves her back into the booth against two of her friends, and leans in nose to nose. "You smell bad," Tikki growls. "Maybe I tear out your throat."

Thuy is wide-eyed. Her smell is now like fear. The others smell like fear, too. They're looking at her differently. Maybe they're impressed. Maybe one or two of them saw the quick change in her hands, their size and shape, fur, claws.

"You know Steel, you're wiz. Primo," Thuy yammers.

Tikki lets the slitch feel the tip of a claw that pierces flesh like a razor, then disappears. A trickle of blood runs down the side of Thuy's neck.

"You want hardware?"

Tikki lets go, steps back and nods. Thuy rises, warily, like prey, turns and walks swiftly to a door at the rear. Tikki follows. A narrow hallway turns to the top of old wooden stairs that lead down into a basement. The floor is concrete and scattered with macroplas crates. The smell is pure machine.

"Anything you want."

Tikki opens a crate. What she wants is a Kang automag, heavy, powerful, simple, reliable. The closest she can get is a Merlin Viper A12, a big, heavy black gun with integral laser sighting and a silencer. As a substitute for the Kang, it's not bad. It will select-fire two or three-round bursts. She finds ammunition and loads. She also finds a few tools that might prove useful, such as a Magna 2 electronic passkey.

Two hours later, Viper in hand, Tikki steps into a bedroom paneled in some black shiny stuff like sateen. Little motes like stars twinkle on the ceiling. Music like an ethereal chorus plays softly from around the room. Lying asleep in the big red-hued bed is a large two-leg male with dark brown skin and black hair. His name is Clutch. He became one of Castillano's Boston contacts only recently. He was thought to be reliable. Beside him lies a two-leg female with blue razor-cut hair and light brown skin. This female lifts her head and looks, lunges up, and, snarling, comes charging straight at Tikki.

This is no surprise. It may be daylight outside, but the moon is waxing full. Primitive instincts are on the rise. As the two-leg female comes off the end of the bed, Tikki swings the Viper automag like a club, and the female drops.

"What the frag!" Clutch growls, suddenly sitting up.

The Viper thumps and bucks. Clutch twitches and shouts, and suddenly the smell of his anger turns sour with fear. There is a big black hole in the pillow beside him. He looks at that sharply and immediately looks back at Tikki, eyes going wide.

"What the frag *are you doing*!"

"On your belly."

"Are you crazy!"

The Viper thumps again. This time the hole in the pillow is only a centimeter or two from Clutch's left hand. The man shouts and jerks away, now stinking of fear.

"Don't do this!"

"On your belly."

The male turns onto his belly. Tikki steps onto the bed and straddles his back. She grabs his left wrist and flattens his hand against the mattress. She puts the muzzle of the Viper against his small finger, where the finger meets the hand. She knows what the loss of this finger might mean to a human. When humans lose limbs, the limbs do not grow back. Humans sometimes die because they heal so slowly that all their blood leaks away. They are really very fragile.

"Three elves came to me at the cabin."

Clutch shouts. "I don't know nothing about this!"

"You are the only one who knew. You told them where to find me. You took their cred, two hundred-kay. Now you will tell me their names."

"I don't—!"

The Viper thumps. Clutch screams. The screams give way to nearly incoherent pleas for mercy. Maybe now Clutch understands that she is not playing gutterpunk games. She will do anything and everything to get the information she wants. "Tell me their names."

"Tang!"

And that is the third time she has heard this name, that of the male elf who helped steal her cub. The elf also known as O'Keefe. "Where is Tang?"

"I don't know!"

"Where does he live?"

"I don't know!"

"How do you know him?"

"New York connection!"

"Give me a name."

"I can't—"

The Viper thumps again. This two-leg does not learn quickly. His screams go on long enough for Tikki to wonder if someone might get curious and come to investigate. It is unlikely that anyone in the neighborhood will summon police. It is even more unlikely, if her guess is correct, that police would actually respond to this neighborhood. It is a place where scagmen like Clutch make their dens.

Clutch's joygirl wakes. Her smell gives her away. She remains where she is, however, lying on the floor as if unconscious. She is a fast learner.

"The name," Tikki growls.

Clutch groans, *"Sabot . . . !"*

That smells like truth.

Tikki asks more questions. She learns more about Sabot, such as how he might be found. That's all Clutch has to contribute.

As for his betrayal, there is only one just repayment.

She seizes his throat in a hand like an enormous paw and squeezes till cartilage is snapping and her arm's shaking with the effort. Her lips are curling and her fangs are coming out by the time the man's eyes roll back into his head.

That's one score evened up.

19

"The pigeon has been aced."

"Any police involvement?"

"Not as yet."

That's good to hear. O'Keefe returns the handset to the heavily armored payfone, then pauses to light a Platinum Select. The first drag is smooth and flavorful, hinting of cloves, and adds substance to his sense that everything is going as it should. An interesting perception, he reflects, considering where he now stands. A quick glance around assures him that Hartford may be the only place in the world more disreputable than Newark.

Everywhere, traffic rumbles, from the elevated lanes of the interstate, barely a block away, as well as from the street immediately before him. Trucks and buses rumble; motorcycles whine and blare. Everyone is on the move and none of them are stopping here. He can understand that. The street is lined with garbage, some of it burning. The buildings rising five and six stories into the dirty sienna glow of the morning look like burned-out derelicts, well beyond salvaging. At one end of the block, synthleather-clad orks are beating on someone whose shrill screams briefly rise above the rapid thudding of fists and clubs. At the street's other end, a Lone Star special tactics team lines gangers up against a wall, and, when one steps out of place, opens fire with autoweapons.

O'Keefe turns and heads into an alley cluttered with garbage and junk. Devil rats peer at him from dark corners. A pair of troll-sized legs protrudes from under the rusted remains of a stripped-down refrigerator. O'Keefe slides one hand through the pocket of his black duster to the butt of the Luger SPv3 holstered at his hip. The weight of the parabellum is as reassuring as the Kelmar Tech utility vest covering his chest. When real trouble comes, and it is already on the way, he will be ready.

Three blocks further on is the Kuritomo Motel. It's the kind of streeter hole where joyboys and girls jack their clients, then leave them to die. O'Keefe is not worried about the pair of biffs he left waiting here. They can handle most common sorts of trouble. That is why he uses them.

O'Keefe crosses the narrow strip of parking lot to his rented Leyland-Rover van, grabs his duffel, and goes to find room 12 and his "partners."

The room is a moderately squalid rectangle of stained wallcoverings, scratched and mismatched plastic furnishings, and worn carpeting. There are two narrow beds and one chair. In the chair sits Shaver, cleaning her Ingram 20t SMG. On one of the beds sits Whistle, watching her wristwatch. Beside her, in a large gray case made of a macroplast composite, lies about seventy kilograms of bait, now slumped, prone, unmoving.

"You fed it first?" O'Keefe asks.

Whistle nods, then whistles to confirm it. Keeping the bait well-fed is essential to delivering it intact. Testing the effectiveness of tranquilizers on it is essential to events soon to come.

"I don't like sharing space with Weres," Shaver grumbles.

"You'll adjust," O'Keefe replies.

Shaver is a former Sister Sinister. She knows many deceitful little tricks that turn a female's natural deficiencies into edges as deadly as any gun, and she is deadly with guns. She conceives of herself as enticingly voluptuous and dresses in tight-fitting black synthleather, though now stripped down to underwear, revealing her many tattoos and scars. Whistle always dresses in white. She's young for a mage and has only a limited repertoire of spells, but she comes from the streets and has a temperament as solid as granite. No sniveling suburban slitches, either one of them, though they do complain. They are a team unto themselves. For the moment, they make advantageous allies.

Whistle the White and Shaver the Black.

Curious . . . a curious pair.

But, O'Keefe understands Shaver's sentiment. Having a Were, even a young one in the room only recalls the risks they face, and hunting creatures like Weres is about as risky as it gets. They're unpredictable, some little more than animals with the power to assume a human form. They're difficult to snare because they recover so quickly from almost any sort of injury. O'Keefe's tried fifty different brands of tranquilizers, with dosages strong enough to bring down a behemoth, yet the best results tranqs ever yield is a fleeting stillness, perhaps as little as a minute or so of unconsciousness. Repeat exposures sometimes yield no effect whatsoever, as if the body, once exposed, immediately develops a natural tolerance.

And snaring them is just part of the problem. Holding them can be even more difficult. Ordinary chains and manacles are not always effective. Nor are cages and cells. The beasts can be slippery. For one thing, they're not limited by metahumanal preconceptions about how the world should work, and therefore how it "must" work. They're quick to make use of an opportunity a metahuman might not notice. The classic story of the beast that gnaws through its own leg to escape a trap is just the beginning, as far as Weres are concerned.

"You better have this zoned out frozen," Shaver says.

"Things seem to be evolving properly."

"So says another one of your contacts?"

O'Keefe nods. "Quite."

The small red and black figure in the dark gray cage lifts its head, growling hoarsely, and begins slapping angrily at the bars of the cage. Whistle whistles soft and long, as if favorably impressed. "Hey, Tang," she says, looking to O'Keefe. "Forty-five seconds this time."

Unfortunate. O'Keefe had been hoping that this latest mixture of barbiturates and opiates might provide a longer-lasting effect. He'll have to try something else. If worse comes to worse, he knows of a gas that can be used, though only under controlled conditions.

"Good going," Whistle says. "With tranqs like this, taking Striper'll be a glide."

O'Keefe shakes his head. From what he's learned of Striper he knows better than to joke. "You'll remember my instructions," he says pointedly, "and you'll follow them to the last decimal."

Whistle whistles.

"You said you'd have a tranq that would work," Shaver growls.

"Focus on your own concerns, and leave my problems to me."

"Sure, Tang. Whatever."

"Good." O'Keefe turns to check his bed. The coming days will be trying. If his plans unfold properly, the payoff will make his efforts worthwhile, but in the meantime he needs some rest.

Nights spent on the road are long and tiring, and sharing space with two biffs, even a pair like this, soon gets rather old.

20

Amy slips the lead into the jack behind her right ear, and spends a moment hanging in the nothingness of interface wash, then finds herself sitting in the virtual node of her palmtop.

The node looks more or less like a regular office, complete with pictures and plants, except that everything's yellow or gold. Amy rolls her iconic hiback armchair in against the back of her virtual desk and the touch-sensitive keyboard of the desktop comes glowing to life. To her left and right are racks of microcassettes containing various programs. On the walls facing her are three large display screens. The screens themselves are a pastel shade of canary yellow. Data displayed on the screens comes up a bright, distinctive shade of gold.

Amy glances down at herself, then grunts with wry disbelief. She's spent odd moments playing with different master persona control programs, changing her persona icon in an attempt to make herself more comfortable with the virtual world of the Matrix. Today, her iconic self, one of the less likely ones she's tried, takes the form of the Voluptuous Swede. She's got long blonde hair down to there, a swimsuit smaller than heck, and a golden-tan body with dimensions way out of proportion to anything approaching reality.

Her breasts are the size of . . . of . . .

Well, forget it.

The Sniffer program has unearthed something like 400 megapulses of data with enmeshed references to the 148 items Mr. Audit-Kurushima Jussai is questioning. Marvelous. Amy slots a scanner subroutine into her desktop and starts wading through the data, armed with a trio of language interpreters and a wordchecker boasting several thousand synonyms and buzzwords with any relationship to terms like used, consumed, expended, and so on. Unfortunately, most of the datafiles are proprietary research text files that can only be analyzed, and analyzed with some hope of accuracy, by the primitive art known as reading.

Thumbnail definitions pop up on the left-most display screen for words with more than six syllables or ten letters, or anything particularly obscure.

Hours pass like instants. Noon has come and gone by the time Amy's found definite indications that a mere twelve items have been consumed. It's almost five P.M. before she's reconciled the consumption records for a total of sixty-two items. At midnight, she's gone through every last record the Sniffer prog unearthed and she's still got twenty-seven items worth almost eight million nuyen unaccounted for.

It's impossible.

She jacks out.

Not impossible . . . nothing's impossible. She tells herself that, popping a cap for her headache, sitting for five minutes with her eyes closed and the throbbing behind her eyes slowly subsiding. She'll just have to extend her search. The Metascience Group's databases are organized into clusters. Everything, both research and administrative records, revolves around specific group sections and research tracks. Obviously, the Sniffer prog missed some dark, dusty corners in the datastores where the missing twenty-seven items are mentioned.

Again, Amy jacks into her virtual office. She compares the list of datastore directories the Sniffer prog checked against a swiftly compiled list of all the directories on the network, and—ah-hah!—several small ones were indeed bypassed.

One of them isn't regular.

Datastore directories are named to identify the specific group section and research track of the data they contain. One directory isn't named like that. It's called, "Special."

What the frag is that?

Special?

Some administrative aide's idea of a joke, most likely. Someone's been using the network for playing electronic games again, or for viewing *Live! Action! Porno!* or God knows what else. Still, she should check it out, leave no byte unturned. Amy taps her desktop to bring up the Special di-

rectory and suddenly her virtual office disappears. She finds
herself standing, not sitting, all but surrounded by utter
blackness, and facing a massively constructed oval-shaped
door. The door is orange. Standing before it, facing her, is a
blazing red man, tall as an elf, but equipped with enormous
wings. Above him, in bold red caps, sizzles the word, SPE-
CIAL.

Great. A glitch in her palmtop? No. You idiot. She realizes she hit the wrong key. She's autoexeced herself right
into the electron fantasy of the network, apparently right to
the address of the directory she wanted to examine. Usually,
she leaves this kind of thing to the people who really know
what they're doing, the gurus in Systems Engineering. Tonight, though . . .

Oh, what the hell.

"You. Open up," she tells the Winged Man, wondering if
that will work. That is what you do on the inside, right? Talk
like it's real? She's done this before, enough to be practiced
at it, but it always seems so foolish.

"Identify," the Winged Man replies.

"Amy H. Berman, Resource VP, Priority Five."

"Your SecCode."

"Four-eight-two-nine-nine-one."

"Executing."

The Winged Man turns and flies away, right through the
big orange door, which immediately clanks like a bank vault
clanks, and swings open, revealing the broad panorama just
beyond . . .

Amy steps onto a sun-drenched beach, like something
from a Carib League travel promo: golden sun overhead,
powder-blue sky, near-transparent water stretching away to
an infinite horizon, virgin white sand extending off to her
left and right as far as the eye can see. She feels something
wobbling and shaking and looks down and realizes it's her
big bouncy-breasts—not hers, the Voluptuous Swede's.

To her rear, a sun-bronzed, muscle-bound giant with an
enormous bulge in a too-brief g-string is pointing a camera
at her and snapping pictures. Naturally, she must turn, lift
her hair up atop her head and smile, posing.

This is what she gets for fiddling with persona programs.
Enough.

Two steps away lies another sun-bronzed-muscled monster with another giant bulge, sunning himself on the sand.

Amy steps over and pulls off his mirrorshades. There's a viewscreen where his eyes ought to be. A text file starts scrolling by even as she first looks. Nothing interesting there. She moves on to the next one, the next in the series of tanned, muscled superstuds lying there in the stand, and the next one and the one after that. The datafiles she's looking at seem no more significant than secretarial notes. She's onto her fortieth hunk when something stops her cold. When suddenly, she's looking at nuyen.

Or maybe . . .

No, the file has the format of an accounting spreadsheet. Rows and columns, titles and dates and amounts. She's seen enough spreadsheets to recognize one, even if all the entries in the file are scrambled, encoded in some way so that she can't read it. Which is ridiculous. One of the reasons the Metascience Group's computer network was originally isolated from the greater world of the global matrix was to negate any need for special codes and other security measures, all of which consume network resources and impair network performance.

She should be able to read this file! Unless it's written in Ztech programming code . . .

Amy pulls out her mirrorshades—from out of her cleavage of course. The shades bring her programming interpreters online. She takes another look at the file. It's not in Ztech, that's for sure. Still scrambled, encrypted. Still unreadable. But why?

The golden electron sun overhead begins seeming very hot, and Amy feels droplets of perspiration slipping down from her underarms, and a worried, queasy sensation rising into her stomach.

This is not right.

21

Ivar Grubner belches.

"You fragging *jack*!" Novangeline exclaims.

Ivar can't quite restrain a grin, or another belch, a real deep gargley one, like maybe came all the way up from his

lower intestinal track. Naturally, Novangeline shrieks and
hops off his hips, off the side of the bed, then leans toward
him to beat him on the chest.

"You're *so disgusting*! Why do I even try, *try* . . . !"

"Watch it. I got some wind coming."

Novangeline shouts and sobs, and storms out of the bedroom, but not quite in time to miss the bloated bombshell of
a fart Ivar realized was on the way. A real blockbuster of a
blubby bomb—smelly, too. But, hey, this is what the biff
gets for feeding him all her gaseous manufacturing food.

Abruptly, she's back, standing in the doorway, with a
weird look in her eyes and one hand at her mouth like she's
afraid of what might come out. She gonna belch, too?

"There's someone on the telecom . . ." she says, voice
trailing off.

Ivar grunts. "I didn't hear no bleep."

"I picked up and the call was just there. I guess before it
had a chance to bleep. It's a smoothie, some woman. She
says she's from work. Your work. Amy Berman?"

"Who?"

"Amy—"

The name hits home—hearing the first name threw him
off. "Fraggin' *squat*!" Ivar exclaims, tumbling out of bed,
then running for the bedroom door. They couldn't have a
bedroom extension like everybody else in the world! No,
he's gotta run on his stunty dwarf legs all the way to the living room, then grab the phone, and say, half out of breath,
"Yeah, uhh . . . Ms. Berman! Hi there! I mean, *hello*?"

A roundish smoothie of a norm face gazes at him from the
telecom display. That's Ms. Berman all right. Something
seems amiss, though. Her eyes are pointing kind of low.
"Heh . . ." Ivar glances down, grabs a pillow off the sofa and
covers his lower parts. "What, uh, *what a surprise, Ms.
Berman!* Caught me just outta the shi . . . er, shower. Sorry
'bout that. Kinda forgot the ole clothes, you know!"

The round eyes in the face on the display blink a few
times, then Ms. Berman says, "No, I'm sorry, Ivar. Excuse
me for calling so late. I need to ask you a favor. It's important."

"Sure, whatever," Ivar says eagerly. Ms. Berman's one of
the movers and shakers at Hurley-Cooper, where Ivar works.
VP of some fragging thing or other. Got to keep people like
that singing your praises all right, all the time, as loudly as

possible, especially with chipface Tokyo auditors on site, snooping around.

"Always aim to please, Ms. Berman," Ivar adds hastily, just so it won't seem pretentious. "Something to do with the comps?"

Ms. Berman nods. "Yes, in fact it's a small datafile. It's encrypted, but I'm not sure how. I'm hoping you can decode it for me."

"Sure. Pipe it through."

"Oh, umm . . . hold one moment." Ms. Berman leans out of sight, moves around, then says, "All right, I'm ready to transmit."

"Fire away."

The file's in his queue in no time. Not even a megapulse of data. Should be no problem. The really dangerous encryption progs that wipe your deck bone clean, and maybe your brain besides, all take at least a few pulses of code to . . . well, to execute their code. To do whatever. This file ain't big enough.

"Got it. Hang on."

Ivar hustles into the kitchen to get his cyberdeck, the Cruncher, which he created from Fuchi and Fairlight spares and so can call any damn thing he wants. It's got combat-hardening, more memory than elephants, an IO rate like the speed of light, and a master persona control program that just can't be beat, or at least not very often, unless he really pushes his luck.

He jacks the Cruncher into the telecom, but not into his head. Why waste the time? One touch of a key and he's got the datafile in memory. One more touch and the file's de-coded. Nothing to it.

Kid stuff.

"All set, Ms. Berman. I'll shoot it back to you."

"Oh, you're . . . you're done?" she says, sounding sur-prised. "I didn't realize you could do it so quickly. Go . . . go ahead."

One tap of a key. "Got it?"

Ms. Berman spends a few moments leaning out of sight, checking things, Ivar guesses. Smart lady, but no comp jockey. "Yes, it's here," she says, then she leans back into the screen and looks out at him. "There's just one thing, Ivar," she says in a sober sort of way. "This file is rather proprietary. I . . . probably shouldn't have transmitted it over an unsecured line. Can we keep this just between you and me?"

"Hey, null sheen, Ms. Berman. You know that."

"Yes, I know," Ms. Berman replies, in a real serious sort of way. "And I'm very grateful, Ivar. If I can ever help you in any way, I want you to let me know. Don't hesitate. I mean that."

"Well, hey ... thanks a load, Ms. Berman."

"You're very welcome."

And then they close the call. Ivar scratches his beard, then scratches the itchy spot on his butt, then taps a key on the Cruncher to clear Ms. Berman's file from memory like it was never there.

"What was that all about?" Novangeline asks.

Ivar grunts. "Can't tell ya ... It's proprietary."

Novangeline curses.

But, hey, that's life in the corps.

22

A trio of spotlights casts a murky orange glow over the parking lot of the Van Cortlandt Industrial Park's one and only Nathan's Gourmet Express restaurant. Amy switches on her Harley Roadraider, then stares blindly through the technical readouts that briefly appear on the inside of her helmet's visor. Unfortunately, staring blindly doesn't help. Worrying won't help. And sitting here like a statue won't get her closer to home or to bed.

She puts the Harley in gear and drives to the Thruway. She's tempted to go straight to New Bronx Plaza, jack into the headquarters mainframes, and check things out further, but it's too late, and she's too tired. Her brain feels like mush.

Out on the highway, she stays to the right-hand lanes and keeps her speed down. She's not used to riding the cycle at night, and her mind's so full of questions she can hardly focus on driving. She keeps trying to tell herself that there must be some absurdly simple explanation for the file she found on the Metascience Group network, but something deep inside rebels every time. She knows the kinds of files the group keeps and how those files are organized. The group's master budget is clearly labeled "MASTER BUDGET" and it resides in its own directory along with related datafiles, and none of those files are encrypted because there's no reason for them to be. The group's two ranking scientists, Dr. Liron Phalen and Dr. Benjamin Hill, have their own sets of files related to the budget in their own personal datastores, clearly labeled.

The mystery file, by contrast, was hidden away and encrypted. To Amy, that suggests something improper, perhaps even illicit. It demands her attention. Calling on her favorite guru from Hurley-Cooper's Computer Engineering Department was simply the quickest way of getting the file decoded.

One look at the decoded file was about all she could take.

The file has no proper headings or anything to identify who created the file or made the various entries, but the rest seems obvious. One column contains a list of names, probably corporate names. The next column contains dates, some going back as far as five years. The column after that contains numbers, all with two digits to the right of the decimal place. It looks like a record of payments.

Amy did all the standard Management Science courses in school. She knows that numbers can be deceptive. She also knows that implicit assumptions can play games with one's perceptions. Still, there are two points she can't get past no matter how she tries to rationalize: there's a nuyen amount in the mystery file that corresponds exactly with each of the twenty-seven items she's been trying to account for; and, the date for each of those figures corresponds with payment dates in her purchasing records.

What do not correspond are the names, and that is the point that worries her. If this file is a record of payments, the names aligned with the dates and nuyen amounts represent payees. Yet, those payees do not agree with the payees in her purchasing records, and that at least suggests the misdirection of funds, which suggests the possibility of fraud.

Worse, the mystery file includes more than twenty-seven items. The bottom line total approaches thirteen million nuyen.

Is this file part of someone's online game? Or is an employee using the Metascience Group network to evaluate their personal finances? Amy can't accept that. Two columns out of three in the file could have been copied directly from her own records. The correspondence between dates and nuyen amounts is exact. Why do the payee names differ? There must be a reason. Why can't she think of any legitimate explanation that makes sense? In fact, the more Amy mulls it over the more worried she becomes that her Purchasing records may be wrong, that someone in Metascience is making fraudulent use of Hurley-Cooper funds, possibly by diverting payments to the payees named in the mystery file.

This could be very bad. And not just for Hurley-Cooper.

If it really is fraud, and if the people from Tokyo should decide that Amy shares the responsibility for fraud, she could lose not just her job, but her career. And of course she would be held fully responsible. The entire executive board would be held responsible, and her most of all, because Purchasing is her area.

She's got to find out what's going on, who created this file and why. If it is fraud, she's got to expose the culprit, present the auditors with a fait accompli—the whole story—proof as to what happened and who did it and maybe a signed confession as well. Otherwise, her career and everything she's worked to accomplish will turn to so much static.

By the time she gets home, she's considering going to the Executive VP first thing in the morning in hopes of getting the power of that woman's office behind the investigation.

That makes sense, doesn't it?

Still wondering, Amy turns toward her bedroom, but stops abruptly, looking into the living room. The room is dark and Harman's sitting in there on the sofa, and what's he doing sitting there in the dark? She steps toward him and he stands up and suddenly it's not Harman . . .

"It's . . . It's . . .

"Scottie? *Oh, my god!*"

It's a shock, a slap in the face, a brutal punch to her stomach. Her helmet and backpack drop from her hands. Something clutches at her chest, squeezing the breath right out of her. Suddenly she feels weak enough to faint and her head's pounding and her throat's gone dry.

The figure rising from the couch is her younger brother, Scottie, the first she's seen of him in years, the first proof she's had that he's still alive. He comes a step toward her. She hesitates a moment, then takes three quick steps toward him and wraps her arms around his neck. "Scottie," she gasps, struggling to breath. "Huh . . . how . . ."

She's so close to breaking down she can't get the words out of her mouth. She draws back to look at him and can hardly see for the tears washing through her eyes. She knows it's him, though. He looks just as she remembers: just a little taller than her, trim build, narrow face. The impassive features that always made him seem like he's a million kilometers away, or just not paying attention. He's cut his hair very short in one of those slash-cut styles. He's wearing a long dark duster and has something, a flute, slung behind his shoulders.

He presses something into her hand.

"You lost this," he says.

It's a burgundy wallet, just like the one she misplaced earlier in the week. No, it *is* the one she misplaced! How could Scottie have found it? And who cares! With everything that's been happening . . . and now this . . .

She throws her arms around his neck and sobs.

Her little brother . . . she can't believe it.

23

Meddler.

From her office window on the second floor of the Metascience lab building, Germaine Olsson watches the skinny figure in the bright yellow jacket and helmet mount the bright yellow motorcycle down by the front lobby, and, after a moment, ride off. Germaine had been wondering if the slitch was ever going to leave. Amy Berman. The big deal VP. The meddler. Good riddance.

Germaine shakes her arms to loosen the fists her hands have bunched into, and grunts, exasperated.

Just what everyone needs: another meddling corporate bureaucrat, another suit. Another smoothie who can't mind her own business. As if Hurley-Cooper hasn't got enough of them already. And Berman's one of the worst. Always sticking her nose where it doesn't belong. She isn't happy diddling data in her nice, shiny headquarters office. Oh, no. She has to come around here and jack into the research network, too. If she isn't changing things just to change things, or inventing new ways to make more work for everybody, she's just snooping, trying to get things on people, if only to impress them with her authority and make herself look good. As if she hasn't got better things to do. And probably she doesn't.

She ought to get a real job. Something productive.

Grunting again, Germaine turns to her desktop terminal to check on Doctors Phalen and Hill, now in Metaserology Lab 12, she sees. She better go tell the doctors that the headquarters busybody has finally left the building. She's sure they'll be glad to hear it.

24

The voice that answers the phone at NewMan Management Systems is just a computer simulation or a recording. The phone itself is located in a grim brick building in a seedy section of Yonkers. Tikki pauses in the dim hallway before the door with the NewMan log, listens, tests the air with her nose, then applies a Magna 2 passkey to the doorlock. The door clicks and opens.

Tikki steps into a bare one-room office. There's no furniture, nothing on the walls, one grime-smeared window. The telecom sits on the floor, jacked into the wall on the right. Tikki crouches over it, sniffs it, considers what to do.

What she would like to do is smash the device into pieces, then fire a hundred or more explosive rounds into the debris, but that won't do. That is instinct talking. The wild. Maybe the moon, too. Oracle's information has led her to this place, this front run by O'Keefe, probably a phone drop for clients wanting to speak to O'Keefe the bounty hunter. Now she must get to O'Keefe himself. Faint traces in the air speak of elves, but her nose will help little now. She needs more definite clues.

Clutch the betrayer met O'Keefe through a fixer called Sabot. She could go and question Sabot, and maybe she will, but first she considers the telecom before her. Interesting devices, telecoms. Many function as complete entertainment and communication systems. Some perform all the functions of computers, televisions, simsense decks, and more. Even the plainest models have many sophisticated functions, and in order to perform those functions they must have sophisticated internals: chips, circuitry, parts. Some parts perform specific functions, while other parts merely remember things that the user has keyed in.

What devices remember, technicians can reveal. And what this device remembers might be useful.

Tikki rips the telecom cord from the wall and takes the device under her arm. She will find herself a local technician, one she can trust, and have this device analyzed.

In the hallway, she puts the telecom down, then hurls herself against the closed office door, smashing it inward.

Smash and grab.

This close to New York City such things should seem routine. Maybe it will keep O'Keefe guessing, wondering when she will come.

25

They sit on the sofa in the shadowy dark, holding each other. Amy keeps her arms wrapped around her brother's middle, her head to his shoulder, and Scottie . . . well . . . He has one arm around her shoulders, and that's enough. More than she would have expected of the brother she once knew. Having him here in the same room with her is all she could ask for. It's probably more than she deserves.

She's a while calming down enough to speak. When she finally lifts her head to look at him, something so stupid and utterly senseless comes to mind that she can't help smiling. Smiling and nearly crying. She brushes her fingers over his cheek. "Where's your mask?" she asks softly.

In a hushed voice, Scottie says, "I don't need it anymore."

And then he looks away, down toward the floor, up toward the ceiling. It's so typical of the way he always used to act that Amy feels her smile spreading wide, till she sees the darkish tint to his neck, slowly rising into his face. He's upset. His eyes look wet. That's such a shock, Amy feels another tug at her insides and hugs herself to him again.

"I'm a shaman now," Scottie says quietly. "An initiate. I've come far. But now I need ... I need to ..."

When he hesitates a second time, Amy lifts her head, looks, and realizes he's almost crying. The emotion's twisting up his face and making him shake. The sight nearly makes her cry, too. She draws his head to her shoulder and holds him.

"It's all right," she murmurs. "We'll work it out. We'll work everything out. I just want you back in my life again. That's all. You're my *brother. I missed you.*" She has to pause, cling to him even as she holds him, regain some composure, but she manages to blurt, "Scottie, I love you. Don't go away again."

Scottie collects himself. He draws back and wipes at his eyes; then, to Amy's amazement, he reaches out, and, tentatively, brushes at the tears still slipping from her eyes. It's a gesture of affection she would never have imagined him capable of. Scottie was always so distant, so far away. She takes his hand in hers, holds it, folds their fingers together.

"I don't use that name anymore," he says. "You can use it, if you want. People call me Bandit."

Amy shakes her head. "What do you mean? Why?"

"It's safer."

It's too much is what it really is: his sudden reappearance, the warm, affectionate way he's acting. Amy remembers too clearly how he used to be, how it all began, and she's too aware of how much time has passed, time they've lost forever.

That stupid mask of Scottie's comes back to mind. Bandit. Yes, of course. The mask he used to wear was just like a cartoon bandit might wear, surrounding just his eyes in black. When he started wearing that all the time she decided her brother wasn't just weird, he was crazy, beyond hope, and there was no point in worrying about it. She was fifteen and he was twelve, and suddenly, all he ever talked about was raccoons. Raccoon-this, raccoon-that. She heard about raccoons till the word made her sick. He read books about raccoons. He went to zoos and museums. He got himself a raccoon hat and started wearing it at the dinner table every night; till, one night, she grabbed it while he slept and threw it into the trash. When an imitation raccoon pelt appeared on his door; she threw that out, too. She just couldn't accept that her little brother wasn't going to grow up and act like a normal person. When he started wearing that stupid little black mask that outlined his eyes like the "mask" of a raccoon, and not just all day, but wearing it to bed as well, that was it. That was all she could take. That was when she gave up.

And she's never stopped regretting it. Not since the time when she started growing up herself.

"I'm so sorry."

Scottie looks at her like he's puzzled. "What?"

Amy puts her arms around his neck and hugs him. How can she explain the guilt she's felt? She can hardly believe he's here. She has at least a million questions, things she needs and wants to know.

"Scottie . . . Oh, god, where do I start?" she says, voice wavering. "There's so much . . . so much I want to know. About you. Where you've been, what you've been doing. Make me understand, your magic. What it means. What it means to you."

She wants that more than anything.

26

"It's just no good, Ben. No good at all."

Dr. Liron Phalen shakes his head sadly as his friend and colleague Dr. Benjamin Hill returns the last of the *draco minimalis* plasma to the cryogenic cooler. The small chore is soon complete. There are only a few samples left, little more than a hundred milliliters in each macroplast container. An incalculable wealth of meta-microbiotic data, but futile, without any relevant application to the current track of research.

"This subset just isn't bearing fruit. I must say, as you postulated, that it did look very promising at the outset. I'm afraid we'll have to forbear until the new matrix arrives."

"Yes," Ben replies. "Yes, I agree."

"That will be soon, I trust."

Ben's face sags, and that is just like him, poor fellow. Every failing of theoretical application, every wasted effort, every delay, is somehow the result of his own lack of insight. He takes his work far too personally. Perhaps he expects too much too quickly. Liron smiles and lays a hand on his shoulder to reassure him, as Ben says, "I expect it should be here within the week. Certainly, no later than that."

"That's fine, Ben. I'm sure we'll find some way to keep ourselves occupied until then."

"Yes, well . . . the delay's unfortunate."

"I'm quite sure it can't be helped."

Someone, some female person coughs, and Liron turns to find Germaine Olsson waiting just a few steps away. Germaine is the Metascience Group's ranking aide, and a very competent one at that. Her job description is an immense understatement.

Liron smiles. "And what does our good Girl Friday desire of us now? Have we broken too many specimen tabs perhaps?"

"Umm . . . well, excuse me," Germaine says, pausing to clear her throat a second time. She's rather self-conscious, poor girl, though hardly a girl. "I just wanted to tell Dr. Hill that she's gone."

"Oh? Has Nettie slipped free of the bonds of perdition again?"

Nettie first came to the group as a test matrix, but has since become something of the group mascot. She's quite tame for a novopossum. Unfortunately, her rather corrosive saliva interacts with a wide range of compounds, hydrocarbons, metals, even ceramics, nearly everything they've used, in fact, in an attempt to keep her safely caged.

Germaine hesitates, looking fidgety. Liron looks to Ben, but Ben looks back at him with a blank expression. The silence grows over-long, and rather awkward, in Liron's view.

"Was it something I said, my dear?" he inquires.

Abruptly, Germaine smiles, quite broadly in fact, though she's usually hesitant to display her ork incisors. Perhaps she's a little embarrassed. "Um . . . well, no," she says. "I was really talking about Amy Berman. She's gone."

"Oh, I'm sorry," Liron says. "I didn't realize our Ms. Berman was in the building. Was there something she wanted?"

"I . . . didn't actually talk to her," Germaine replies. "She's been on the network all day and all night."

"Always busy," Liron says, smiling, glancing aside to Ben. "I don't think I've ever met a more dedicated administrator. Her energy astounds me. You really must let me know, Germaine, when our Resource VP comes for a visit. I would have liked to say hello."

"Of course, Dr. Phalen."

With that settled, Liron has a look at his watch. "Well, we've gone on quite late. I expect I'll be in somewhat past my usual time tomorrow, Ben."

"I'll handle things, boss," Ben replies.

Liron smiles, nods, and heads out. His ancient Mercedes awaits him in the parking lot, and, ever faithful, rattles quickly to life. Brahms pours from the stereo-deck, or whatever it's called, and soon he's gliding along the highway, humming, heading north, over the Bronx border, through Yonkers and on to Dobb's Ferry. The music of the old master makes the trip soothing, smoothing over the bumps, distancing him from the ever-rushing traffic.

As he turns down Ford Lane, a faint luminescent rippling of air manifests in front of the car, then inside it, slightly above the passenger seat. The voice that emerges from the shimmering air is bell-tone clear, but soft and lush. *"You have tarried long, Master."*

Liron smiles. "Yes, I know. Forgive me."

"I forgive you all things, Master. Am I not obliged to do so?"

"That is for you to say, dear Vorteria."

The words are barely out of his mouth when Vorteria manifests, comes fully to the physical plane, as fully as she is able. The form she takes is rather ghostly—white, all white—like that of a mature young woman in the full flower of her beauty, long flowing hair, soft eyes, a tender smile, glittering robes that call attention to her fine womanly figure but without tainting the purity of her presence. She is delightful in appearance, endearing, and quite chaste.

"Have you kept busy?" Liron asks.

"I have guarded my master's land," Vorteria replies, smiling warmly. *"And my master's house, and all of his household. And I have given much thought to my master's great work."*

"And have you reached any conclusions in regard to that work?"

"I believe that my master must do more research."

"Do you not believe that we are on the verge of a break-through?"

"My master has bound me to this world. If only I could travel beyond the walls of this temporal plane I might repay my master's generosity with an answer."

Liron smiles and softly sighs. Vorteria hints that if freed from his service, freed to do as she wishes, she might somehow look beyond the limits of time and so tell him of what might come in days hence. It is her one form of protest, often repeated, against being bound to Liron's will. Vorteria says she would always serve him, for she is pleased to do so, and Liron believes her, but still she must protest. In an odd way, it makes her seem almost human, more womanly, capable of a woman's natural and charming contradictions.

"Will you work tonight, Master?"

"Yes," Liron replies. "Presently."

His house comes along on the right, old and rather large, two stories tall, with steep mansard roofs and soaring chimneys, windows glowing despite the hour. The winding gravel drive leads past the broad front walk. Liron leaves the Mercedes there. He's just old-fashioned enough to prefer to enter through the front door, rather than through the garage like a chauffeur or stable boy.

His wife's nurse, Gwyna, opens the door as he climbs the stone steps to the porch. Gwyna is tall and slender, obviously an elf, even at a distance. She greets him with an uncertain smile.

"How is Mrs. Phalen this evening?" Liron asks.

"Feeling some discomfort earlier," Gwyna replies. "I gave her five c.c.'s of Tukenol."

"You must be very sparing," Liron says with quiet emphasis.

"Yes, Dr. Phalen. I know."

"Of course, you do." Liron smiles apologetically. "I always seem to be repeating myself unnecessarily. It's very difficult, my dear, to maintain a professional detachment where the one involved is so close."

Gwyna seems moved to sympathy. "Of course," she says softly. "I understand. I must say . . ."

"Yes, dear?"

Gwyna hesitates, looking at him, then says, "I admire your courage. Mrs. Phalen's, too. I admire it very much."

Liron takes her hand, gently pats it. A smile of understanding is all the answer he has to give. It seems sufficient. "Would you please tell Mrs. Phalen that I'll be in shortly."

"Certainly."

"Thank you, my dear."

In the bedroom, his bedroom, Liron pauses to clip and light a cigar, an uncivilized habit, his wife used to say, but his one and only indulgence. Vorteria comes through the physical plane of the door like a ghost, assuming her womanly manifestation as she crosses the threshold. Oddly, Liron does not mind her being present while he undresses, changing from his lab clothes to his ritual robes. Vorteria has seen too much of his soul for the sight of his blighted physical substance to have much significance.

"You did not visit me at the lab today."

"Spirits spoke against it," Vorteria replies. *"There is a darkness, Master. It troubles me."*

Not the first time Vorteria has spoken this way. Precognition? Liron knows of no documented cases. None which could survive even the sometimes fuzzy lens of metascience. He is aware, however, that the many planes of the astral are home to myriad entities of which men have incomplete knowledge at best. "What spirits were these who spoke? Do they have names?"

"None I could express to you, Master."

A familiar reply.

Liron turns to the mirror and carefully removes the mask and hairpiece that cover his face and head, and then too the theatrical appliances and the lenses that complete the deception necessary to his work. Anyone who could view him as he truly is would see only a horror, a skull shorn clean of any hair, a face laid bare of even the most trivial human features. His nose a hideous blackened pit, his mouth a grisly skeletal grimace, his brow and cheeks covered only be a slender layer of epidermis, stretched tight across his bones.

His trip to the Middle East, taken many years ago, supported by a foundation long defunct, brought him to this. The affliction is called *metamycobacterium leprosis,* the Sixth World form of leprosy. It's quite virulent. His tissues deteriorated rapidly, his wife's even more rapidly. Now he searches for a cure. He has long since affected a means of holding his ground, and of stabilizing his wife as well, but a cure ... *The cure still eludes him!* He must go to his li-

brary, filled with all the ancient and arcane tomes of a lifetime of research, and continue his work on the cure.

"Victoria calls," Vorteria says softly.

"Oh, of course." How inconsiderate of him to forget.
First, he must visit his wife. "Thank you, my dear."

Vorteria replies, *"I am pleased to serve you, Master."*

27

"It's complicated," he says.

Amy shakes her head. "I don't care."

"I need to become a person again."

Amy waits, and listens. Scottie's explanations start and
stop, and trail away into silence, but there's always more
that needs to be said, and somehow he just keeps on going,
finding the words and saying them, till she's heard more
from him in one night than she heard or listened to or ignored up to the day he disappeared.

Then, despite splashing herself with cold water, and all
the willpower she can summon, her eyes are closing and
won't reopen, and she feels herself slumping, nodding off.
When she wakes, she's lying on the sofa with her head in
Scottie's lap, and he's gazing down at her, and saying, "I
have to go."

"Stay. Please."

"I'll come back tomorrow. I promise."

"I don't want to lose you again." The fear of that wakes
her up. She forces herself to sit up. She takes his hands, remembers things he said. Despite all that he's told her, she
feels like he's been here only moments, and she hasn't had
time to explain anything about herself.

"Scottie, I'm living here by myself, and I make good
money. Shell could come, and the kids, too. They're important to you and I want to meet them anyway. You could all
stay here. There's plenty of room."

"I have to go my own way."

"But . . ." Of course. That's the point. It's always been the
point and until now she was never mature enough to accept
that. What did he say? The shaman's way is hard. He has to

do what he thinks is best, and *she must accept that*! She must! She should be trying to understand, not telling him what to do. She has to face the fact that she doesn't know what's best for him. She can't know. She barely knows who he is, the man he's become, the shaman, or anything else. If she wants him to play a part in her life, she's going to have to stop being the older sister and start being the woman with enough maturity to love her brother without conditions.

"I'm sorry," she says, struggling to smile. "You're right. I'm just so afraid you'll go away—"

Her breath catches.

Scottie takes her hands in his.

"I can't believe you're really here again."

"I'm here."

"Mom and Dad'll be—"

"Don't tell them."

"Why not?"

"It's too soon. I need time."

Time to adjust, or maybe the time to come fully out of his shell. Maybe it's got to do with his magic. Many of the things he's said make it seem like he's at a crossroads, a point of transition, important in more ways than she can imagine.

"All right," Amy says. "But I want you to remember that I love you and I care about you. I always have. Even when I was stealing your things and throwing them away. I'll do anything I can to help you, if you need help. If you want anything. Anything. I really mean that."

"I know."

At the door, she hugs him one last time and kisses his cheek, and then he's walking down the hall to the elevator, and she's forcing herself to smile, to wave, like he's never really been away.

She's sitting on her bed in her underwear, still wiping at her eyes, when the first dusky rays of dawn comes sifting in through the drapes, and then her alarm clock starts bleeping. Oh, god no . . .

How can she possibly get ready for work?

And . . . how can she not?

28

In the shadows of the pre-dawn dark, the security car rolls slowly along the tree-lined lane winding through the condoplex grounds. Brake lights flare, but then the car rolls on. Bandit watches from among the bushes leading away from Tower D. He has no permits or passes allowing him to be on these grounds. Raccoon has no need of such things.

He turns his head to look back at Tower D reaching high into the dark gray sky, and, for a moment, he shifts his perceptions to the astral. The spell he casts is fleeting. He gains a brief sense for his sister, up there in the tower, at a window, now turning away. She seems upset, happy and sad, like she's crying and also smiling. She did that a lot tonight. It's almost frightening.

When they were kids, Amy walked the narrow course. She was always very popular. Her grades at school were upper bracket. She had corporate sponsorship and a place awaiting her at university before she reached her sixteenth birthday. He'd always taken it for granted that Amy would turn into just another faceless clerical or executive level wageslave, another straight suit, just like their parents. Now he finds that she's become as whole a person as he's ever known, every bit as whole as Shell. It's amazing.

The way she talks, how she acts . . . she got right inside him without even trying, enough to move him pretty deeply. To hurt. To make him regret things. Like how they've lived totally separate lives.

Maybe now that can change.

There's so much he has to learn.

In among the trees by the condoplex main entrance, he finds the Hyundai ActionScoot he borrowed and walks it out to the road. The scooter doesn't go very fast, but it'll get him back to the subway a lot faster than walking. Assuming nobody notices the scooter's missing.

When he gets home, he finds Shell slumped in a plastic chair by the door at the top of the stairs. He told her to go ahead and bolt the door because he'd probably be gone all night. But here she is, sleeping, with the needlegun in her lap. Waiting for him? He gives her shoulder a squeeze and she comes around, moaning, then hugs him around the hips.

"Did you find your sister?"

"Yeah."

"So, do I lose you now?"

Lose him? "Why would you lose anything?"

Shell looks up at him with eyes that seem wet. "She's a suit, right? She could set you up. She must have lots of money."

Bandit puzzles, then sighs inwardly.

People are always talking about money, even when money makes no difference, no difference whatsoever. It's in the way of things, it seems. An inescapable part of nature.

It makes him tired.

29

"Okay, kid. Let's *move out!*"

Brian Guerney forces his eyes to open. How long has he been asleep? Two, three hours, his watch indicates. He rubs a hand over his face, feels the stubble grown thick around his cheeks and jaw, and grunts. When he agreed to triple-time and a half, he figured he'd be getting into action. What he didn't figure on was spending twenty-four hours plus in tunnels underground. What he didn't foresee was getting so deep into the tunnels that he'd have to wait for Art to show him the way out.

Somewhere above his head, it's morning. Wonderful.

He drags himself up, suits up, gets ready for action. The tunnel is over three meters across and perfectly round and dank, real dank. A trickle of water forms dark, dingy-looking puddles every couple of steps. The air smells foul.

There's a ghostly feel to it all. Maybe the ghost of water that used to pass this way. Brian wonders if maybe he should have become a Buddhist. Don't Buddhists believe that everything has a soul?

Up ahead, forty or fifty meters on, there's a junction, a pair of secondary tunnels coming in from the right and left.

That's about as far as Brian can see. His Nightfighter visor casts a grayish image of the tunnel in front of his eyes, but there ain't much light for the visor to gather, and the only IR sources of any significance are him and Art.

They're both ready for Ragnarok, armed to the nines, assault rifles, machine pistols, handguns, grenades, flares, knives, body armor, helmets, visors. Brian wouldn't mind so much, not at triple time and a half, if only he had some idea of what they might be going up against.

"So, if all these tunnels weren't destroyed by the quake in '05, how come nobody I ever talked to knows these tunnels are still—?"

"What, are you kidding?" Art interrupts.

"Kidding about what?"

"You never heard of security?"

"Art. Listen." How can he put this? without slotting Art off yet again. "This is a water main. We work for the New York City Department of Water and Wastewater Manage—"

Abruptly, Art drops into a crouch, signaling halt with a quick mil-style gesture. "You hear something?"

"Just the sound of my own—"

"Jam it!" Art whispers harshly, edging ahead. "Look! *right there! LET'EM HAVE IT, KID!*"

Art's rifle stammers on full auto. The discharges echo like thunder. Fire flashes from the weapon's muzzle, streaming straight up the tunnel. Maybe twenty meters ahead, beyond Art's left shoulder, Brian spots a shadowy figure big enough to be an ork, only it isn't an ork like any Brian's ever seen. "What the frag!"

The figure darts out of sight, across the junction and into a secondary tunnel.

"Art! *Art!*"

Art charges ahead. Brian wonders if maybe he should've taken the day off, but then runs to catch up. Art stops at the junction, looking down the tunnel to the left. Five meters along, a water-tight door in the tunnel wall stands wide open, only blackness beyond.

A water-tight door .. ? like on a submarine . . . ?

"What's the frag is a door like that—"

"Ain't you never heard of flow valves?"

"Sure, but I never seen one like that."

Art grunts. "This is where the fun starts. You ready?"

Brian stares at the door and the blackness beyond, then

says in a low, angry voice, "Just what are we facing here? Orks? Does that *door* lead into the ork underground?"

Art turns to face him, jabs a finger at his armor-insulated chest. In a voice low, angry and menacing, Art says, "Some of them look like orks, but they ain't orks. Not anymore."

"Then what are they?"

"You don't wanna know."

"Yes, I fragging do."

"No, you don't."

"Do I have to repeat myself?"

"You're slotting me off, kid."

"Not likely."

"Oh, no?"

"You got too big a sense of humor."

"Hah-hah. Funny, kid. Real funny." Art nods, sharply. "We'll see how funny you are when those scummers come straight at you. You know what they do when they catch you? Do you have any idea what those things are capable of?"

Brian hesitates. "You're telling me there's more than one of them?"

Art leans into his face, and whispers, "Good guess."

30

The street is just a hairbreadth beyond the border of the Bronx, in a crumbling district called Pelham. The shop located at midblock looks like a rat hole, crammed into a narrow space between a burnt-out warehouse and a rotting tenement building. Tikki pushes the door of the shop inward. It creaks. The shop's interior is dim and dusty and crowded with every kind of electronic device: everything from telecoms to comp decks, kitchen appliances, and security devices. Mounted up near the water-stained ceiling, also veined with cracks, is a pair of Ingram SMGs mated with vidcams. One gun silently turns, tracking with Tikki as she walks toward the rear of the shop. The other stays pointed at the front door. The shop owner must be a careful person.

At the rear of the shop, behind a wooden-tone counter, sits

a small male with thin gray hair. A magnifying device hangs before his eyes from the metal band ringing the crown of his head. He wears a white shirt, black suit jacket, and blue felt tie. His right hand holds something that looks like a circuit board. His left hand is pure cyber, some kind of multifunction tool, now a drill, faintly whirring, now some kind of soldering iron, sending a faint trail of smoke drifting up.

As Tikki approaches the counter, the man lifts the magnifying device from in front of his eyes and lays the circuit board aside. He looks at Tikki blankly.

"Langkafel," she says.

The man nods, and, rising from his stool, lays his hands, such as they are, against his side of the counter. He speaks in an undertone, an almost timid murmur. "I am Heinrich Langkafel. Good morning. How may I help you?"

Tikki puts the telecom from NewMan Management Systems on the counter. "Tell me everything it knows."

Langkafel nods vaguely, eyebrows rising. He smells less of anxious uncertainty than simple indecision. "An unusual request," he says in his sheep-like murmur. "May I ask . . . is this your device?"

"Who carried it in?"

Langkafel nods again, seeming willing to accept that as his answer, but then says, "You will understand, I think, if I remark that a businessman must be mindful of his reputation. How is it, if I may ask, that you happened to come to my shop with this request?"

"Number four-two-six."

A nervous, sweaty scent enters the air. Langkafel hesitates, watching her. That is a sensible reaction. Number 426 refers to Lau Tsang, a ranking member of the triad organization known as the Large Circle League. Lau Tsang is the "Red Pole" in charge of enforcement for the New York metroplex. Lau Tsang does not hesitate to kill or brutalize people who displease him. Lau Tsang is a dangerous person.

And powerful.

"Yes . . . yes, of course." Langkafel nods. He takes the telecom in hand and looks it over. "Naturally, I'm happy to assist the friend of a friend. What you ask will not be difficult. A few simple tools. I would ask in return only a modest fee."

Tikki's been to the bank, tapped one of her accounts. She lays five fifty-nuyen notes in Fuchi scrip on the counter.

This close to Fuchi-town, the corp's scrip is as good as certified cred.

Langkafel picks up the notes. "That will be quite adequate," he says. "The work will take a few minutes. Do you wish to wait?"

"I'm waiting now."

"Yes . . . yes, of course."

Ten minutes later, Tikki's walking out with five sheets of densely packed information, a hardcopy direct from the telecom's memory. Included in that info is a list of telecom codes. Those codes identify the originating telecoms used to make the last one hundred calls to NewMan Management Systems. Only one code appears more than once and it's in the local telecommunications grid.

The question, then, is this: could O'Keefe have called the telecom at his NewMan Management office, presumably to get his messages—not once, but five times—from the same telecom, such as the telecom in his home?

And is O'Keefe that stupid?

31

The DocWagon Crisis Response Team drops from their CRT twin-engine VTOL on rappelling lines to the roof of some grungy squatzone building, and opens up with SMGs. Dr. "Hoot" Hoganoff leads the charge to the fire escape. There are fifteen orks and a dozen yakuza killers all trying to cut him down with autofire and grenades, but nobody keeps Dr. "Hoot" from the scene of a medical emergency.

Abruptly, the channel changes.

CyberRider appears, somewhere in the sprawl, racing through a gauntlet of howling, blood-drenched vampires and groaning gore-splattered ghouls on his Harley Magnum Express, fitted with quad-mounted machine guns and rocket launchers.

Again, the channel changes.

This time it's Taffy Lee, swaying in time to a slow, languorous rhythm and smiling, and opening the front of her neomonochrome dress and baring her fabulous quivering boobies with their thick, jutting . . .

The telecom screen goes black.

"Yo," Monk says.

"Hoi, yo," Minx says, lying down beside him on his lounge of cushions, blankets, and pillows. She smiles and cozies up against his side and lays her head on his shoulder. "You still awake?"

"Is it late?"

"It's morning."

"Yeah?"

"You booty." Minx giggles. "You make me so wiz happy."

"Yeah?"

The idea makes Monk tingle. Minx is the most gorgeous stunning beautiful woman he's ever known, from her wild frizzled hair, changing from red to reddish orange to reddish gold and back again, to her gleaming eyes and pert nose, her slim, luscious body, and her little girlie feet. He still can't believe that she actually likes him, much less that she *loves* him, or wants to be with him all the time. Yet, she lifts her head to nod at him and smile, then kisses him full on the mouth, and briefly exhales into his mouth, his throat, his lungs. They breathe into each other's mouth a couple of times. It makes him hotter than sex.

And then they're tearing at each other's clothes and jerking around, tussling, twitching, shivering, gasping, lunging together. It's like a fight, but every move sends them flying closer to climax, and when it's all over they're both winners.

"Are you happy?" Minx whispers.

"Sure," Monk replies. "With you."

"Me too."

It's hard to believe how his life has changed since he met Minx. She got him a SIN, not a SIN with his name, but a SIN's a SIN. Some of her friends got them whole new identities and the jobs with the Newark Coroner's office, and even keyed them on this new apartment. The apartment's not very big—not here in Newark's Sector 3—but it's their space and now they've got the nuyen to do what they want with it.

Mostly, they've just thrown down a few mattresses and lots of cushions and pillows, installed a big mother-fragging telecom, and tacked some of the Minx's pictures to the walls.

The pictures are jewel. They come from all over the sprawl, pictures of bodies, corpses, hanging out of wrecked cars, lying in streets, on stretchers, some missing body parts, or with holes in their heads or other places, drooling blood and gore and various internal organs. One of the best ones shows this slag's decapitated head sitting in the middle of a transitway lane with its eyes wide open and an expression like, *Is this for real?*

Monk chuckles, just thinking about it.

When he finally gets around to writing his TV/3V script or simsense treatment, the one that's going to make him famous and rich, so rich he'll make money just moving his bowels, he's going to have to write in a big part for Minx, just to thank her.

He'll make her a novastar, as big as Taffy Lee.

Even bigger.

Brobdingnagian.

Nude, and gorgeously lovely, Minx leans down over him, smiles, and kisses him. "Listen, booty," she says. "If I told you we had to go do something, would you do it? without asking why? Do you trust me that much? Do you?"

Monk ponders. "Sure."

Minx smiles and nuzzles his cheek, and strokes his neck, making his nerves tingle all the way down to his feet. "We have to go see somebody," Minx says.

"Wiz," Monk replies.

"He's kind of different. You might think he's strange."

"Uh-huh."

"We call him the Master."

"Yeah?"

Minx smiles and nods.

"Nova." The Master.

Why not?

32

The morning is hell. The Human Genome Group fires off a batch of priority reqs for some rush project that absolutely requires her personal attention, and Mr. Audit, Kurushima Jussai, requires her personal explanations for any number of trivial matters that any ordinary wageslave could understand.

On top of that, she can't keep her composure. Wildly emotional thoughts keep popping into her head. Scottie's back! He's *alive*! Amy's forced to run off to the lav or take refuge in her office to grin like an idiot and brush tears from her eyes.

When she thinks of all the times she worried that Scottie might have succumbed to the dangers of some dark corner of the sprawl, gotten mixed up with shadowrunners, or worse . . .

All she can do is shake her head and moan.

Harman calls, and immediately notices the conflicting emotions on her face. She's hardly begun explaining when he says, "I didn't know you had a brother."

Trying to explain about that brings her back to earth. She stalls by talking about her and Scottie as kids. That gives her time to try to understand why she's never mentioned her brother to Harman. It's more than just a lapse of memory. It's a deliberate omission that she's considered at least in passing dozens, if not hundreds, of times, and it disturbs her.

Having a shaman for a brother, if that's what Scottie really is, isn't something a straight suit should brag about. Shamans don't make good suits; corps and corporates mistrust them. That fact has influenced her in the past, when Scottie wasn't around, when she and Harman were new, but she won't let that affect her anymore. If Harman really cares about her, and wants to forge a future with her, this is something he'll have to accept.

He seems to take the news all right. Before she's finished, he smiles oddly, and says, "Does this mean you've got magic genes?"

"Oh god, no . . ." What a joke. "I'm as mundane as they come."

"Suppose you have children?"

Now that's a sudden, frightening turn-about. Amy hesitates. The thought holds her speechless, if only because she can't honestly answer it with a definite no. Science has yet to determine exactly what is the genetic difference between a magician and a mundane. There's no way she can be absolutely certain that any child she might have would *not* turn out to be magically active.

"Amy, I'm just kidding."

"I'm sorry. I just—"

"No, *I'm sorry,*" Harman insists. "Of course you don't see anything funny in this. It was a foolish thing to say. I apologize."

Amy draws a deep breath, and says, "Does this change anything?"

"What, your brother? I'd like to meet him. But this certainly doesn't change how I feel about you."

"I'm so glad you said that."

"Well . . ." Harman smiles warmly, but that fades into a matter-of-fact expression, sincere but sober. "I won't say I'm not surprised. In fact, I may be more surprised than I realize, if you know what I mean. As far as anything else goes . . . well, why don't we talk this out over dinner?"

"Yes, you're right. Let's do that."

This is all very new; they both need time to adjust. Better they should leave thoughts about children and magic till they've had their dinner and that talk about the future.

Once they've disconnected, Amy turns to the serious business awaiting her: the mystery datafile from the Metascience comp network. Getting focused takes a real effort.

The mystery file, apparently a record of payments, contains an entry for every one fo the twenty-seven items the Resource Consumption Control program failed to note as consumed. The entries in the file also include a total of thirty-three names, apparently names of corporations.

Amy keys her desktop term into Hurley-Cooper's accounts payable database. Whenever something is purchased, an entry is made into the payables database to provide a record of the monetary transaction. For each of the twenty-seven unaccounted-for items, there should be a record of payment including specific information on where the money went and how it got there. And, she soon determines, the records are there for every last transaction.

According to the payables records, the money for the twenty-seven items went to the same corps named in her Purchasing records. There's absolutely nothing indicative of fraud or even sloppy record-keeping.

Next step.

Amy keys her desktop into the LTG and calls TransUnion Intercorp. She selects the TUI Corporate Profile database. TUI has general business information on everyone, practically every last corp in the world, large and small. If the corp's registered anywhere, TUI has a profile. Within ten minutes, Amy's downloaded profiles for every name in both the Payables database and the Metascience mystery file. After just a brief look-through, she closes her eyes.

She is in a nightmare with no way out.

Another twenty, twenty-five minutes of sorting through text windows confirms her fear. The names in the Metascience file are not part of someone's online fantasy. They are the names of corporations or the divisions of corporations, and every one of them is related in some way to the corps in the Accounts Payable database.

What does that tell her? For a moment, she can't figure it out. She sits back in her chair and stares at the ceiling and tries not to think of Scottie or the newly arisen implications for her relationship with Harman. So someone at the Metascience Group is keeping separate track of payments made to Hurley-Cooper's vendors. So what?

But that's not the issue.

The names—that's the point. Why bother keeping a record of payments if you only have to dial into Purchasing or Payables to find out who got paid what, and when? There is no real point unless the actual payee does not go by the name emblazoned on the Hurley-Cooper electronic draft.

And so what? The corps in the Metascience file are all related to the corps in the Purchasing and Payables records. Corporate divisions and subsidiaries swap funds every day of the week. It's a perfectly legitimate and integral part of doing business. What's the issue?

Amy knows the answer to that too well. The issue is that you don't take merchandise from one organization and pay someone else. You pay the people who deliver the goods. Because whoever made it and got paid for it is going to be held liable if the merchandise doesn't perform to spec. In a case where limited partnerships or joint ventures complicate matters, you make damn sure the path of liability is blindingly clear, and in any event you get everything fully documented.

The implication then, if Amy can believe it, is that the vendors in the Purchasing and Payables Records are not really the organizations that made and sold the twenty-seven items she's been trying to account for. The real vendors are named in the Metascience mystery file. Or are they?

Amy looks at the corporate profiles again, and starts keying telecom codes. She starts with the corps listed in her Purchasing records, then goes on to those from the Metascience file.

"We're sorry, the number you dialed has been disconnected . . ."

"We're sorry, the number you dialed is not in service . . ."

"For directory assistance, please dial . . ."

Not one call goes through.

Maybe the telecom codes are old. TUI's profiles aren't always up to date. A common problem with the database. Amy tries Telecom Directory Assistance. No luck. No listings for any of the corps on either of her lists. Maybe the corps were absorbed by other corps and the telecom codes all changed. Happens every day. She tries the TUI Special Service Bureau. Her answers are not long in coming. There's no record of any of the corps having been acquired by anyone. So either the corps no longer use telecoms, or they're defunct. Or they were never anything more than registration papers and bank accounts and descriptions in databases like TUI.

Fronts, in other words. Phony corps.

Prospective vendors are routinely checked out in order to prove that they're more than electronic shills, but that doesn't mean the checks are foolproof, and the growing likelihood that Hurley-Cooper has been scammed makes Amy angry enough to want to shout.

Instead, she pounds her fist against the desktop, hard enough to hurt herself, then sits back in her chair again and covers her eyes with her hand. Never mind whether or not the twenty-seven unaccounted-for items were ever used. *Were they ever received?* Did Hurley-Cooper actually get anything for the money it spent, or did the nuyen end up in someone's private account?

And what the hell does she do now?

33

Afternoon fades into evening. Tikki watches and waits. The street before her is a side street and it's almost suffocating, crammed on both sides by jammed-together three-story brownstones, sidewalks glutted with people, curb lanes packed with parked and abandoned cars. Everything is stone and metal and plastic and pushing, jostling meat. Tikki wonders how she could ever have seen anything appealing in this choking crush of metahumanity. The smells, the sights, and the sounds all speak of the two-leg infatuation with things, machines, ornaments, trinkets. Nothing that really means anything. Nothing of significance.

Her cub has meaning. She isn't entirely sure what the meaning is, or what words might be used to describe it, but the meaning's there. She can feel it, smell it. Waiting somewhere, in some corner of her mind. She feels like finding her cub might be the most significant thing she'll ever do. Instinct reminds her of it with nearly every breath.

She sits in the driver's seat of a Eurovan parked at curbside, around mid-block. Eurovans are made in New Jersey, very common. This one is dented and rusted. The windows are darkly tinted. It blends well with the street. Tikki sits and waits because waiting is part of stalking. She's undercover, using cover, not merely in her human guise, but in a costume that no one would readily associate with her Striper identity.

Gold-blonde synthhair cascades over her shoulders and halfway down her back. Scenes from Taffy Lee's latest simsense production wash across the gleaming black macrotech of her jacket. Black lace gloves cover her hands. A skirt clings to her hips like a second skin. Crimson LED roaches dart up and down the webwork of her stockings, disappearing beneath her skirt and into the black synthleather booties strapped for her feet. Facepaint, earrings, chains, and bangles complete the image. She's just another lowlife gutterpunk waiting for tomorrow's high to come along and find her, like most of the two-legs she's seeing on the street.

Hours pass. Twilight settles in and the two-legs prowling by assume a darker cast. The predators are coming out. None give Tikki anything to worry about. She keeps her attention focused on a particular house just across the street. No lights, no sign of movement. No one's gone in or out since she arrived. The telecom that called the office of NewMan Management Systems on five separate occasions is supposed to be inside that house.

Is this O'Keefe's house? or just another deceptive front? Time she found out for certain.

She leaves the van and crosses the street. Her Magna 2 passkey cycles the lock on the front door. She steps inside.

Nearly every living thing leaves traces in the places they inhabit. The traces build up till they color the air, giving the place a definite character. This particular place stinks of elves.

Nobody's home. She knows that even before the door swings open. The background stench of elves doesn't confuse that recognition, no more than a profusion of potted plants might fool her into thinking that she's stepped into a forest somewhere. Live bodies give off fresh scents that are unmistakably distinct from the stamp of smells impressed on a place over time, and the smells here are all old. Exactly how old she isn't sure: a few days or so. Her human-shaped nose isn't quite as acute as the real thing.

She takes a look around.

The house is narrow and deep. There arc five levels, including a basement workshop and an attic for storage. Ground floor: living room, kitchen, dining room. Second floor: bedroom, den. Third floor: more bedrooms. Stairs connect the main floors. A pull-down ladder connects to the attic. The furnishings are dark and heavy and seem of a masculine character.

The smells carry her back to the Road to Nowhere, a memory of cool air, trees, snow and ice, then an image of the tall lanky figure that stood before the Mostrans hovertruck in front of the cabin. She remembers his gray and white camo, his rifle, his scent. Before another moment has passed, she's certain that she's come to the right place—his place—his home. She finds some documents to confirm it in the second-floor bedroom, made out to the name of Elgin O'Keefe.

Bounty hunter. Former mercenary. The question Tikki asks herself is what a two-leg like that would want with her cub? Did someone offer him a bounty for her cub? That seems unlikely. Tikki doubts that anyone but her and the cub's sire even knew the cub existed. Could this be some enemy's way of taking revenge against her? She feels forced to acknowledge the possibility, but she's not comfortable with it. Anyone wanting revenge should have just ordered her killed.

O'Keefe obviously knows some things about Weres. He knew enough to be waiting with enough firepower to knock her down and keep her down while he and his partners made off with the cub. What else might he know? What might he expect?

None of this really makes sense.

If he knows that Weres begin life on four legs, not two, he might assume she has more in common with so-called animals than metahumans. In that case, he should expect her to come after the cub, but not very far. No ordinary four-leg would come chasing all this way after a cub. The ordinary female would follow only until scents dwindled and disappeared, then forget it. Look ahead to another season, another mating, another litter. In the wild, the dangers are many and the young are easy targets. Losses are inevitable. Four-legs know that. They're too concerned with survival, with hunting down the next meal, to go much beyond their territory and waste time on fading memories, dwindling like fleeting scents.

Of course, if O'Keefe knows her rep as Striper he might expect her to seek revenge at any cost, if only to repay those who shot her up.

Maybe that's part of the plan, inciting her anger, inspiring her to seek revenge, in order to lure her somewhere. But why bother taking the cub? Shooting her and killing the cub would be the most effective way of rousing her rage. She might have gone completely wild. She might have gone so crazy that she'd walk willingly into a trap.

Maybe some collector of exotic creatures hired O'Keefe to capture something really special. Maybe O'Keefe began by targeting Tikki, but then, discovering her cub, opted for the easier target. That seems logical, but most likely it's all part of some scheme that no one but an elf could understand. A conspiracy that ultimately has nothing to do with Tikki or anything she cares about. She and the cub are simply being used. That's what elves do.

She's in the process of deciding what to do next when she hears noises: the click of a lock, the thump of a door.

The smell that comes into the air stands out starkly. A female elf has just entered the ground floor hall. The elf grunts and says, "Where's your fragging telecom, Tang?"

Tang is O'Keefe.

Tikki draws the Viper automag from under her jacket and moves into position near the top of the stairs. Footsteps sound, still on the ground floor, moving around, but Tikki hears only one set of feet. The elf female grunts again, and says, "Fuchi, of course. Piece a squat."

Is she talking to herself?

Beeps follow, like beeps from telecom keys; then several bleepings, like the far end of a telecom line bleeping. A voice that sounds computer-generated says, *"We're sorry . . . the number you dialed is out of service . . ."*

The elf grunts.

More beeps, more bleepings.

"Answer the freaking phone!" the elf snarls.

The line clicks, a male answers. The male's voice is middle-pitched and sounds odd, oddly inflected. He speaks his English like he learned it in Britain. "Ah, it's you," he says. "Any sign of our quarry yet?"

"Of course not! It's too fragging soon!"

Brief silence. "I warned you about the danger of underrating this individual."

"We haven't been in town a fraggin' day, Tang," the female elf growls. "No way this slitch is gonna come on this fast! I don't care what she is. Or who!"

"Nonetheless, stay alert. We're about to make delivery. We'll be with you shortly."

The elf female grunts. "By the way," she says, "the telecom at NewMan is out of service."

"What? You *dialed that number*—!"

A loud thump interrupts. The telecom screen bursts into a shower of sparking fragments. The elf whirls. Tikki's standing on the threshold of the living room with the Viper automag pointed right at her. "Hands up," Tikki says.

The elf is a piece of work, tall and dark, all black

synthleather and tats, with a long black curling mane of hair. As she turns, her eyes are so huge they seem round. She smells of a shocked surprise bordering on terror, but that lasts only an instant, just long enough for her to look and see Tikki and the Viper.

"Shick!" the elf snarls.

In the next instant, she's diving for the sofa and the Ingram smartgun lying there in a hip holster. Tikki lunges. The elf's not the type to be impressed by guns pointed at her. She's made that clear. So, it's shoot or get physical and Tikki wants this one alive.

They collide. The elf is very fast. She gets a hand on the smartgun. Tikki swings the Viper like a club. The elf falls onto her back on the sofa, bleeding from the head. She nearly seems out of the fight, but then she twitches strangely, up at the waist. Tikki feels something plunge into her belly. She staggers back from the sofa, looking down at the raw red wound streaming blood from just under her waist. She looks up to find the elf sneering, rising, standing up. The bloody blade protruding from the elf's midsection abruptly vanishes. A belly blade. Tikki should have expected that, something like it. The elf smells of metal.

"Come on, slitch!" the elf snarls. She flings the smartgun away and opens her arms in arrogant invitation. Cyberspurs appear at the ends of her fingers, from the backs of her hands, and from her forearms, too. "Let's *dance*!"

Tikki burns with fury.

A low rumbling growl rises into the back of her throat. Fur rushes up over her arms and face. Her upper body swells. Her clothes strain and split. Her hands become paws and the Viper automag drops to the floor, and then she's roaring, lunging ahead on two legs and hurling herself bodily into the elf.

Metal slices and tears, claws rend and rake. The cyberblades move too quickly to be avoided. Tikki doesn't try. The elf has the advantage of speed; Tikki has power. She uses her paws like mallets, then rams the elf into a wall and drives her down to the floor. The belly blade stabs again. Tikki staggers back, wounded in a dozen places, and then the elf staggers up onto her feet.

"You're good," the elf snarls. "Like a road train. Now you're good-*bye*!"

The elf is a whirlwind rushing in with flashing, slashing

razors. Tikki sees her arm laid open to the bone before she glimpses the spur that does it. But the pain hardly touches her. The water washing through her eyes blurs her vision, but that affects nothing. She pounds the elf in the face. The elf staggers back. Tikki seizes her about the body and hurls her across the room. The elf goes crashing over a table and tumbling to the floor.

Now, they're both hurting, drenched in blood, clothes shredded, but one of them has already healed and is ready for more.

Tikki roars and charges.

The elf is slow to respond, only halfway to her feet when Tikki impacts. The elf spits and something like a string lashes out from under her tongue, but it misses. Tikki smashes the elf back off her feet, into a glass-faced cabinet, a pair of walls, then down again to the floor on her belly. The elf struggles to rise, but Tikki pounds the elf's head till she slumps, unconscious. She is fast and tough for an elf, but metal, cyberware, can accomplish only so much.

By the time the elf wakes, she is manacled at wrists and ankles and lying in the rear of Tikki's stolen Eurovan. Tikki touches a handful of claws to the elf's cheek. "Soon, we talk," Tikki growls. "I ask questions. You answer. Or you *die*."

The elf groans feebly, then curses.

Curses will not help her.

34

It's well past the usual quitting time when Max Chernick puts a hand to the wall to find the old sensor pad that switches on the lights. Not very high-tech, but then a corp like Hurley-Cooper usually puts its money where it matters. Stock rooms don't have much need for fancy automated lighting. Max glances around at the shelving, the bins, the stacks of macroplast crates, the refrigerated cabinets, and slips his hands into his sweater pockets.

Things are pretty quiet right now. A lot of the Metascience Group's scientists have closed up shop and headed home. A few of them work odd hours, monitoring experiments, taking advantage of resources they'd have to wait to use during the day, but most are gone somewhere around sundown. Max would be gone too, except this evening he's got a special coming in.

Since it's after normal hours and he's got the stock room to himself, he decides to indulge. He pulls his old briar pipe from his sweater pocket, strikes a match, and lights up. Technically, there's no smoking anywhere in the building, or near any of the building exits, but no one'll mind as long as he doesn't start blowing clouds that threaten to asphyxiate people.

Abruptly, the door behind him rattles.

Max turns to find Ms. Suhree coming in, stepping briskly along in her blue guard uniform. "How late we are working, Mr. Max," she says in a voice that lilts up and down melodically. She has a brother that talks the same way, she says. Works at some condoplex. "You must be having a late delivery tonight, I should be guessing."

Max nods. "That's a fact."

Suhree goes straight on to the black box by the freight doors. That's where she keys in her security code to prove he came through here on her rounds. "Would it be that you are receiving something of specialty interest this evening, Mr. Max?"

"Can't say for sure," Max replies. "Have to check the receiving schedule. I imagine it's some arcane thing. Mystic substance. Probably coming on some special courier service."

"That is sounding like business as usually."

Max nods. "That's a fact."

"Be having a good night for yourself, Mr. Max."

"You too, Suhree."

Suhree goes out and Max steps over to his counter by the freight doors. He keys his desktop comp and brings up the receiving schedule. Before he can more than glance at that, the exterior alarm dings. The monitors ranged across the rear of his counter show a streamlined van pulling onto the apron behind the building, then turning, preparing to back up to the loading dock. Max taps a few keys to get a close-up view, but the van's got no exterior markings. He'd be suspicious if it did. Special couriers don't advertise except in the Corporate Pages.

Max accesses his desktop intercom to call upstairs. That cranky ork girl Germaine answers Dr. Hill's line. "What do you want?"

"Looks like the doc's delivery just pulled up."

"No squat."

Germaine breaks the connection. Max shakes his head, wondering what it is that makes young women want to talk like gangers and gutterpunks. Seems like they're always demanding respect and yet the words they use show no respect for anyone, including themselves. Talk like a beebo, expect to be treated like one.

The exterior alarm dings again. The side doors of the van are open. Two people get out. The monitors zoom in close. It's two elves, a man and a woman, dressed in dark clothes, armed. They've been here before. Max recalls their faces. These two use aliases on account of the business they're in. Apparently, transporting expensive, arcane merchandise can be a dangerous occupation.

The alarm dings again as the two elves come up onto the loading dock and slot their IDs into the exterior checker. The one comes up as Roger Thorstin; the other, the woman, as Aphrodite Zolde. Both employed by NewMan Management Systems.

Max grins, restrains a chuckle, then keys the exterior intercom, and says, "Be right with you."

Thorstin says, "No hurry."

He sounds English. Real polite.

Security regulations prohibit Max from opening the freight doors after normal hours till one of the bosses shows up and says okay. That's just a precaution. Dr. Hill comes along in a minute or so, still in his shirt and tie and white lab coat, ready as usual with a smile and a friendly greeting.

Max asks, "What would we be receiving tonight, Doc? More of that unicorn powder?"

"This is a special shipment, Max," Dr. Hill says in all seriousness. Dr. Hill's a very serious fellow, maybe too serious for a relatively young man. Serious and kind of sad. "I think the records show we're accepting several containers of snake venom."

Max nods. The receiving schedule refers to something like that. "Can't be too careful, I guess."

"No, Max. I'm afraid that's so."

What the records say and what actually comes through the

freight door are not necessarily the same thing, and, unfortunately, it just has to be that way. It's like the doc explained some time ago. People can be real ignorant. Count on those who are most ignorant of all to carry their views to extremes. People like the Humane League or the eco-terrorists. As ignorant as pus, or, say, medieval peasants. Give them half an excuse and they'd be crashing through the front gates and planting bombs and God knows what else. They just have no understanding.

The Good Book says that the beasts were put on this earth to be used as people see fit, and Max figures that covers it. Of course that doesn't give people a right to turn furry little creatures into things as frivolous as coats, but coats aren't the real issue.

The kind of research Dr. Hill and the other scientists are doing here is for the betterment of people. Work that might eventually save people's lives. Max figures that's about the best possible use any animal could ever be put to. The life of an animal should be respected, and no animal should ever be made to suffer, but compared to the life of a person ... well, there's just no arguing that animals are expendable, and people aren't. Without animals for use in experiments, research comes to a halt and that's pretty much the whole story.

Max keys in his code to open the smaller of the two freight doors. Dr. Hill adds his code; then, while the door rumbles upward, Dr. Hill makes the entry to show the delivery of "snake venom" accepted.

"Anything I need to know?" Max asks.

"No, I don't think so," Dr. Hill replies. "This one should be relatively safe."

They've had a few close calls in the past. Wild animals, especially the Awakened species, can be full of surprises. They once had a sort of human-looking chimp that busted free of its cage and ran all over the place, breaking things up. Made one hell of a mess.

Max wheels his flat-bed wagon onto the loading dock. Roger and Aphrodite, the elves, muscle a large gray case with bars along the sides out of the rear of the van. Max lends a hand getting the case onto his wagon. Fifty kilograms easy. The dark shape inside doesn't seem happy. It growls and snarls kind of like a dog with a sore throat and bangs the sides of the case. Max catches a quick glimpse of long, dark, gleaming claws. They look real sharp.

"Be seeing you," Thorstin says to Dr. Hill.
"Part two of two?" Dr. Hill asks.
The elf nods. "Yes. Presently."

35

To honor the Tokyo auditors, the usual Wednesday dinner meeting is moved to Ginza House, on New Bronx Plaza. Amy's suffered through tatami-style dining—sitting on cushions on the floor—often enough to take it in stride.

The private dining room could have come straight from Japan. Everything looks like genuine wood or paper or ceramics: the long low table, the lanterns, pots and cups and bowls. Flower arrangements just so, as if designed by an artist. The maître d' wears traditional costume and gestures with a small fan. Women in pastel-shaded kimonos hasten hither and yon, without ever seeming to rush, delivering things, removing things.

The menu includes shrimp tempura, platters of raw fish, shabu-shabu, sukiyaki, and a northern Japanese specialty called *robata*, like shish-kebab. And of course Atami beer and sake, lots of sake.

Tonight, no one sits at the head of the table. There is no head. Rather, things are concentrated at the middles, where Vernon Janasova and the executive VP sit opposite Enoshi Ken and Kurushima Jussai.

Vernon fumbles constantly with his chopsticks and jokes about it. Amy tries not to notice.

The meal begins at six P.M. Enoshi Ken talks a bit about archery and kendo, then passes some idle comments about KFK International's evolving global strategies. "Diversification is the key element," he says. "We must be moving in many directions simultaneously if we are to meet the challenges of the future. We must take care to avoid redundancies, as well."

That last remark concerning redundancies turns Amy's beer sour. What it brings to mind is Richmond Research Associates located over on Staten Island. Richmond is another KFK subsidiary, much larger than Hurley-Cooper and far less a pure research facility than a commercial lab. It has a largely Asian staff and a CEO straight from Japan. What little true research the corp does almost always leads to highly lucrative patents. Richmond's bottom line usually makes Hurley-Cooper look a weak sister.

Richmond also enjoys a reputation for absolute adherence to corporate protocol and bureaucratic procedure, whereas Hurley-Cooper has been described in trade publications and elsewhere as "informal."

Another word for sloppy, in executive parlance.

When Enoshi starts talking about meat being fatty or lean, and what that may lead to, from a corporate perspective, Amy swallows an orange-flavored bit of sushi whole.

Looking up the table, she says, "Of course, it is difficult for a scientist to accurately predict where the creative process integral to all research may eventually lead. Leonardo Da Vinci claimed that nature is full of infinite causes that have never formed part of anyone's experience. We limit our chances of discovering these causes, these scientific unknowns, if we as executives attempt to micromanage the course of pure research."

Several blank looks turn her way, but the quote from Da Vinci seems to grab Enoshi Ken's attention. Amy hopes it goes further than that. The man's fondness for quotes is well known. Enough that Amy had her aide Laurena searching databases all afternoon for any "wise words" that might be flung at Enoshi to make a point.

Enoshi replies, "Perhaps you are suggesting, Ms. Berman, that many details make up perfection, and perfection is no detail?"

If perfection is seeking truth, searching for real answers, not merely commercial success, then Mr. Enoshi Ken has a point. True research is no minor detail. Trying to better the world is no trivial effort. For what it's worth, Amy agrees.

Dinner ends at eight. Vernon makes noises about adjourning to one of the glitzy nighthowls on the Plaza: Twelve Chrome Spikes. Tonight featuring ME-109. Amy decides to make her exit.

But before she can quite complete her escape, the executive VP touches her elbow, and says, "You asked to see me this afternoon."

Amy nods, admits it. She feels like she's way out on a limb. It would probably be smart to tell the executive VP everything she's learned about the Metascience mystery file, so if and when she gets around to making any incriminating disclosures she's got someone firmly in her camp.

"I'm sorry," Amy says. "Tomorrow would be better. I'm really not feeling very well tonight. Excuse me, won't you?"

"Certainly."

The Plaza monorail ferries Amy back to her office tower. Escalators carry her down to the first level of the Plaza's underground parking garage. She gets into her sedate, silver-gray Toyota Arbiter GX, closes the door, sits back and shuts her eyes.

It's going on eight-thirty. She shouldn't be wasting time. Scottie promised to visit her tonight. She keys the ignition and puts the Toyo in reverse, and then her cellphone bleeps.

It's Harman, reduced in size to fit on a twelve-centimeter screen, seen against a background of flaring strobes and blazing laserlight. As the Managing Director of Sales for Mitsuhama Systems Engineering, Harman has no choice but to participate in after-hours business meetings and affairs. It's written right into his contract.

"I have only a few moments, darling," he says, "but something came to my attention. I felt you should know. Well, what I mean is, I feel I have to tell you . . ."

Why is he acting so ambivalent? It isn't like him. "Does this have to do with business?"

"Yes, it does."

"If you're uncomfortable, don't tell me anything."

"No, that's wrong," Harman insists. "I mean, you're correct. I do feel uncomfortable. I suppose I'm not used to trusting people like this."

The smile he adds only makes him seem more uncomfortable. Amy struggles to conjure up some sort of appropriate response. They usually don't discuss business, except in general terms, simply to avoid any conflicts that their relevant corps might use against them. They know for a fact that on a few occasions Mitsuhama spies have followed them around on dates. That's yet another reason why Harman is considering getting away from Mitsuhama.

Can Harman trust her? That seems to be what he's asking for, without actually putting the question to her in so many words. "It might be better if you say nothing," Amy replies. "But if you're telling me something in confidence, it goes no further. It's your decision, Harman."

"Yes, I know," Harman says. "Of course I trust you. It's just that .. well, you're aware of the risks we both face."

"Of course."

"I don't know if this means something or nothing, but I know what you've told me about recent events at your corp. That makes it seem possibly of significance."

Amy says nothing, waits. It's his choice. If he wants to tell her . . .

"A Mr. Enoshi Ken of Kono-Furata-Ko International dropped by the tower this morning. He was in conference with Bobinek and El-Gabri for about three hours. One of our senior attorneys attended as well."

Bobinek is exec VP of Mitsuhama UCAS. "Who's El-Gabri?" Amy blurts.

"He's the exec VP for the Biotech division."

"Oh, my god."

That's all Harman knows, but it's enough. Amy tries to keep her expression neutral till she and Harman are off the phone. There's no point in upsetting him, too.

His information brings back everything Enoshi Ken said at dinner, about meat being lean or fatty, and the need to avoid redundancies, and her own thoughts about Hurley-Cooper's rival subsidiary over on Staten Island. The obvious implication is that KFK International is considering or possibly already arranging for the sale of Hurley-Cooper Laboratories.

It can't be.

If KFK divests Hurley-Cooper . . . if MCT buys . . . If anything like that happens, Amy's career is as good as over. Any career that she cares about is finished. She'd rather spend the rest of her life cleaning toilets than find herself thrust into a brutal environment like MCT. Unfortunately, she might not have even that option. Hurley-Cooper owns her contract just as surely as any other asset. MCT would have every legal right to insist that every last employee of Hurley-Cooper be part of the buy-out agreement. She could be compelled tomorrow to work for MCT in whatever capacity the predators might want.

But . . . thoughts like that won't help.

What does it mean? *What should she do?* If her guesses are correct and a sale really is in the works, maybe she should blow the lid on the discrepancies she's discovered in hopes that MCT will take one look and say, "Thanks for the offer, but forget it."

No, that's crazy. She really would end up cleaning toilets if she blows a sale desired by KFK's Tokyo office. She'd regret that for the rest of her life. All she can do is hope, hope that her guesses are wrong. But, no—that's no good. She can't just sit and wait and hope for the best. She's got to do something and do it now. Somehow, she must get to the bottom of the mysteries she's uncovered and find a way to cast Hurley-Cooper in a positive light. She must see to it that in the end Tokyo will be too content with its little research subsidiary in downstate New York to consider divesting it.

Maybe it's time she tried something a little extreme.

Everything's on the line.

36

The warehouse stands in the shadow of the elevated Cross Bronx Expressway, not far from the Throgs Neck Bridge. The warehouse loading bay is large and strewn with the garbage of uncounted squatters, no longer present.

Across the broad ceiling run the rails of a small crane. From this crane dangle several loops of thick cable that run through a large pulley. At the bottom of the pulley is a hook. Hanging from that hook by her wrists is the elf razorgirl Tikki fought and captured inside O'Keefe's brownstone. In addition to being bloody and bruised, the elf is now nude, and her tattooed hide bears several small burns from the head of a slim Sumatran cigarro. The tips of her toes brush the gritty concrete floor.

Tikki walks around to her rear.

The elf has a shapely rear end for a ganger: full and round. Pear-shaped. This is good. Such behinds are full of fatty tissue and tissue like that is mostly water. Salty water. That sort of water is an especially good conductor of electric energy.

Tikki places the head of a Defiance AZ-S shock baton against the elf's body, touches the key marked 7, and pulls the trigger. The baton's lithium capacitors deliver a jolt that makes the elf jerk as if kicked by a horse. For a moment, she is rigid—then, she screams. The scream is loud and raw and, combined with scents in the air, bears witness to her pain. It is intense. She goes on grunting and gasping for minutes.

"What is your name?" Tikki asks.

The elf moans. "Shaver . . ."

Finally, an answer, a streetname, essentially meaningless, but a place to start. Instinct urges Tikki to threaten the elf with immediate death or dismemberment, but she knows better. Interrogations cannot be rushed. They must be carefully executed.

"Who is your leader?"

Shaver shakes her head and snarls something vicious. Tikki triggers the baton. The elf's scream rises high and shrill and goes on longer than before. The pain is more intense. Shaver's resistance appears to be wearing thin.

"Who is your leader?"

Shaver grunts. "Tang."

Tang is O'Keefe by another name. The former mercenary. The bounty hunter. The elf with many names and many dummy corporations. "Who is the other elf female?"

Shaver mutters, "Frag you."

Tikki applies the stun baton again, this time to Shaver's front, to her groin. When the screaming finally ends, Shaver is pale and shuddering. Weakly, she murmurs, "Whistle . . ."

Another streetname. "Why does Tang want my cub?"

"Bounty . . ."

"Who offered bounty?"

"Don't know . . . Tang's client . . ."

"Why was the bounty offered?"

Shaver sneers. "Ask Tang . . ."

Tikki applies the stun baton to each of Shaver's thighs, with the power level set to 9. This time, when the screaming ends, Shaver's eyes seem about to roll back into her head. Her head lolls.

"Why was the bounty offered?"

"Ree . . . research . . ."

Tikki frowns.

Research? Shaver does not smell like she's lying and yet her answer is one that Tikki had not anticipated. Research? What possible use could her cub be for that? What kind of elf scheme could O'Keefe be involved with? Tikki abruptly realizes it doesn't matter. She doesn't care. It's irrelevant.

She has a cub to retrieve or a cub to avenge and scores waiting to be settled. Get to the point.

"Where is my cub?"

Shaver mutters, "Frag . . ."

Another jolt of the shock baton. More screams. More time wasted. "Answer. Where is my cub?"

"Tang . . ."

"Address."

The address is not long in coming. It takes the form of a street name and a building description, right here in the Bronx. Tikki sheaths the stun baton and walks to the rear of the warehouse.

There wait two dark blue synthleather-clad members of the Kong Destroyers: Baka and Dogmeat. They are here because the Kong gangleader owes favors to certain individuals who command his respect. Baka and Dogmeat are each well over two meters tall and as massive as mountains. One is hairy; the other bald. Both have horns and huge fangs and great quantities of spikes and studs distributed about their clothing. Both wear smartguns.

"I'm leaving the weedeater here," Tikki tells them. "Make sure she's alive when I come back."

Dogmeat grins. "No shick, chummer."

"We'll be real gentle," says Baka.

Tikki lights a slim Dannemann Lonja cigarro, takes a drag, then walks out. Even if she hadn't understood what the trolls meant by their words and leering grins, she would have guessed it by their smell.

She should have warned them about the elf's belly knife.

37

The living room is in ruins. A table is overturned. Several plants are smashed right out of their pots. Lamps and pictures lay scattered about, some in pieces. There are dents, gashes, and holes in the walls and smears of blood on the walls, furniture, and carpet. By all that he sees, a pair of trolls might have done battle here.

"Shaver?" Whistle blurts.

"Wait."

But too late. Whistle is already darting ahead, down the hallway toward the kitchen and dining room. O'Keefe waits, listening, his Luger SPv3 in hand. He turns to open the panel beside the front door and check the household security system. Whistle comes running back up the hallway and dashes up the stairs to the second floor, shouting Shaver's name. O'Keefe wonders why she goes through this exercise. It would be far more efficient and cautious of her to simply use her mage's ability and survey the house from the astral.

The security system informs him that only two live bodies are present.

It's still early evening, but for Shaver it's obviously too late. Shaver arrived per O'Keefe's instructions to watch for Striper, but Striper was perhaps already here and lying in ambush. Obviously, they fought. Obviously, Shaver was not the victor or the pair would still be present. That presumption adds to O'Keefe's awareness that he has made the serious error of underestimating his quarry, the time Striper would need to track him down. He will not make that mistake again. Next time it could mean his life.

Of course, in this case he has every reason to suspect that Shaver played a vital role contributing to Striper's early arrival. "The phone at NewMan is out of service," Shaver said. O'Keefe can hardly believe that Shaver could have been so incredibly lax as to call the NewMan number from here in this very house. His house. How many times, he wonders, has Shaver committed similar breaches of security?

Why not simply put up a sign: Here I am. Kill me.

O'Keefe had expected Striper to follow the trail leading from Maine, from a certain Amerind with a certain ACV and a certain credstick, from that to Boston and a slag named Clutch, and then to New York and Sabot. And thence into O'Keefe's carefully prepared trap. Shaver seems to have helped shorten the trail.

Striper must have found a path leading to the NewMan Management office. That would explain the telecom there suddenly going out of service. It would be a relatively simple matter to download the telecom's onboard record of incoming calls. That record would likely provide sufficient data, thanks to Shaver, to lead Striper straight to this house.

Just what is the full extent of the damage? O'Keefe goes

down the hall to the stairs and descends to his basement workshop. His plan had not called for Striper to enter the house, but rather to pick up his trail here and follow him elsewhere. Now he sees another result of his miscalculation. A quick survey of the workshop reveals that his SPAS-22 combat gun and a Colt Cobra SMG are both missing, along with several smoke and concussion grenades and a sizable quantity of ammunition. Perhaps most significant of all is the disappearance of his Dragunov Drake-1 heavy-caliber sniping rifle. This is one of the few rifles in the world designed specifically for sniping, and, hence, the trade of the professional assassin. Much as the name suggests, a single shot from the Dragunov can knock down a metahuman as easily as the paw of a western dragon, and an angry western dragon at that.

O'Keefe finds these thefts rather curious. Certainly, Striper would have the resources to obtain weapons on her own. Unless . . . Perhaps she has been so intent on moving swiftly that she has been forced to pick up weapons where and when they become available. O'Keefe hopes that means Striper is tracking him with the same reckless spontaneity with which she charged into his guns at the cabin in Maine. It would make his task all the easier. He will not rely on that, however.

"Tang!" Whistle cries. *"Tang!"*

O'Keefe climbs the stairs to the ground-floor hallway. Whistle meets him there, all in a frenzy about her missing Sister Sinister. So much for the temperament that seemed as solid as granite. Solid until something happens to her chummer.

"Shaver's gone! We *have to find her*!"

"Of course," O'Keefe agrees.

Aside from any questions regarding loyalty or ethics, O'Keefe wants very much to find out what Shaver has told Striper of his plans. She'll certainly have told Striper something, possibly everything. Striper has experience with interrogations, O'Keefe assumes, and in her current frame of mind she will probably be quite brutal, not unlike an animal. The only real question is whether or not Striper will leave Shaver alive. O'Keefe has doubts in that regard.

He takes his SecLink from a vest pocket. This small device is utilitarian in appearance, about the size of a pack of cigs. Push a key and it warns him when a person, such as

Shaver, comes near. Push another key and it indicates with near ComSat precision where someone, such as Shaver, happens to be.

Whistle looks at him sharply. "What the frag's that?"

"I took the precaution of bugging Shaver before she came here," O'Keefe explains. "Just on the chance that something like the current situation might arise."

"Bugged her when?"

"You recall our discussion of Asahi beer?"

"You dropped a bug in her beer?"

"A very small and sophisticated device designed to lodge temporarily in the intestines."

"You don't trust either of us."

O'Keefe restrains a wry smile. In his book, trust is earned over the course of many years and he has not been working with Shaver and Whistle for anywhere near that amount of time. In his view, they are both very much on probation. "Former gangers are not known for their loyalty, and you will admit that your friend is not the type to let a little treachery stand in the way of an easy profit."

"You don't know her," Whistle says adamantly. "She's not as savage as you think."

"I think she is as heavily chromed as anyone I would care to meet, and chrome exacts a price that goes beyond nuyen."

O'Keefe knows for a fact that Shaver has a number of implanted weapons, replacement muscle tissue providing heightened strength, augmented reflexes, and other cybernetic enhancements. She is about as close to becoming the magnum vatjob warrior as one can get without losing every last trace of metahuman sentiment. She is walking the razor-fine monowire of sanity. That makes her extremely dangerous, potentially unstable. Precautions are therefore essential.

"What did you put in my drink?"

"Bug a mage? You must think me mad."

"If I had a truth spell—"

"It would bear me out." O'Keefe checks his SecLink. "Shaver is within range. Shall we go?"

They take O'Keefe's Isuzu Metrovan down to the southeast tip of the Bronx, beneath the Cross Bronx Expressway, nearly as far as Locust Point. O'Keefe's SecLink points them down streets lined with ancient brownstones and then through blocks of commercial-zoned properties, many large brick and concrete structures. At length, they come to a warehouse bearing the sign: Edgewater Shipping. The place is dark, no lights showing inside or out. O'Keefe drives past and parks just up the block at curbside. A passing semi sounds its airhorns.

"Survey the building."

Whistle nods. "Don't move me."

"No, of course not."

Mages traveling in the astral plane are quite vulnerable. They apparently have no intrinsic sense for where their meat body might be located. If the body is moved, they might never find it, which would mean death. A gradual fading away into the neverland of the astral. Whistle's body slumps, but only for moments. As her eyes snap open, she curses and blurts, *"They're jacking her!"*

"Who?"

"Two trolls!" Whistle grabs at the passenger door handle. O'Keefe seizes her elbow and tugs her back to face him.

"I lead."

"Well, *come on!*"

"How many in the building?"

"Just her and the trolls!"

O'Keefe readies his Luger, exchanging a twelve-round clip for a fifty-round drum, then adding the laser sight and wire-frame shoulder stock. Whistle is frantic to get moving. An unfortunate result of her relationship with Shaver, which is rather close. O'Keefe keeps a hand on her elbow till they've rounded to the rear of the warehouse and he steps firmly into the lead.

The door there is unlocked. A narrow hallway leads to a large dusty area occupied by only a few scattered macroplas crates. A large freight door, standing open, provides access to a truck loading bay.

And there they are, near the center of the bay. Shaver is hung from the hook of a ceiling crane. She looks unconscious. The two trolls with her both look like gangers. Kong Destroyers by their colors. One holds Shaver's legs bent back and is jamming her from behind. His tool is quite large. The other one stands and watches, grinning ferociously. He appears to have taken some minor wound in the stomach region.

Whistle brushes past, darting through the doorway and into the loading bay, shrieking with banshee abandon. The bluish light swirling around her hands abruptly jumps across fifteen meters of open air and erupts into a coruscating haze that surrounds the troll at Shaver's back and crackles like roaring flames.

This leaves O'Keefe little choice.

As the troll enveloped by Whistle's magic staggers back screaming, O'Keefe steps into the open doorway and points his Luger at the troll's partner. "Stop!" O'Keefe barks.

But this troll does not stop. Barely glancing at O'Keefe, he tugs a smartgun from a side-draw holster and lifts it toward Whistle. He is obviously about to fire and O'Keefe cannot permit that. Despite his best efforts, Whistle remains the one essential variable in the whole of his equation, so he absolutely must defend her.

The Luger rattles, spitting explosive slugs at a rather stately fourteen rounds per second. O'Keefe grits his teeth and struggles to keep the burst on target. The troll's size aids in that regard.

The troll's smartgun stammers, but the burst goes high, toward the ceiling, and the troll joins his partner on the floor. O'Keefe joins Whistle in freeing Shaver, who is in fact unconscious, and a bloody mess besides.

"Wake her."

"She needs a doc!" Whistle declares.

"Don't make me force the issue."

"You fragging bastard." Obviously furious, Whistle presses back Shaver's hair and softly whistles one note. A reddish light radiates from beneath her open hand, stroking across Shaver's face. Shaver stirs, head lolling.

O'Keefe kneels down, asks, "What did you tell Striper?"

Shaver is several moments working up to an answer. She draws a deep breath, moans, and murmurs, "Your name . . ."

"What else?"

"The cub . . . It's at Brogan's . . ."

O'Keefe hesitates, then smiles.

Impressive.

38

The subway runs him straight across the Bronx to the Pelham Bay Projects, a crowded cluster of concrete blocks each rising up forty stories. A mini mall leads directly from the subway station to the Projects' entrance. Ivar cools his heels and stares into space while the crowd ahead of him moves slowly inside. Must be evening shift change. A couple of uniformed trolls from NitroSec, gripping SMGs and grinning, keep watchful eyes out for anyone with ideas about cutting ahead of the queue.

When Ivar's turn finally comes, he puts his palm to the printscanner at the entrance, then steps briskly ahead. Door Number Six gushes open half a step before him and gushes shut at his back. That puts him in a mantrap—door ahead, door behind, both closed. Blank walls to left and right. Mirrored ceiling above probably concealing a bank of security scanners, not to mention the things those scanners ignite if the wrong sort of personal goods are detected.

"Identify," says a honey-toned female voice.

"Ivar Grubner." He recites his ID code, then adds his personal password, "Hurry up."

The door ahead snaps open, and Ivar steps into a wonderland free of offensive weapons, theoretically, not to mention a lobby unmarked by laser burns or bullet holes: simulated marble flooring, pastel-colored walls, and a couple of simplas decorative plants. It ain't much, but it's better than most places one might find in the killzone known as the Bronx. A consortium of corps, including KFK International, owns the place.

The elevator runs him up seven stories. Two doors down the pastel-shaded hallway, he steps into the chrome and mirror-plated haven of his living room. Novangeline's sitting on the black neovuelite sofa in a silver Mercurial tee and shorts. She looks kind of anxious. Sitting next to her in a dark gray executive suit is Amy Berman.

Ivar stops, staring, almost gaping.

"It was very nice meeting you," Novangeline says to Ms.

Berman, and then she's up and walking briskly to the bedroom, just flicking a glance at Ivar before disappearing behind the bedroom door, which, for once, closes without a sound.

Ms. Berman looks back and forth.

"Uh ... heh," Ivar says. "Want a beer?"

"Thank you, no," Ms. Berman replies. "Novangeline made tea."

"Ah." Ivar nods. "Good."

"I apologize for intruding like this—"

"No, no," Ivar interrupts. "No, it's ... nothing like that. Not at all. I mean, *what a pleasant surprise!* What's tox? Well ..."

"Ivar, I need your help again."

"Hey, sure. Whatever. You name it."

Whatever it is, it must be serious. Berman's got that kind of look on her smoothie face. She opens her executive briefcase and takes out a sheet of hardcopy, and says, "I need to check on some people. I can't tell you why, but I wouldn't ask something like this if it weren't very important."

"Sure." Whatever. "Check 'em how?"

"Well, I need as detailed a credit history as I can get." Ms. Berman seems really determined. "In particular, I need to know if any of the people listed here have recently come into large sums of money. There may be illicit activity involved, so the money, if it's there, may be in hidden accounts. That's why I need an expert like you."

"Null sheen. Of course, it could be kinda risky."

"In what way?"

"You know. Running the Matrix."

"I thought—" Abruptly, Berman stops, stares, then turns her head and looks away. "No, you're right. I *didn't* think ..."

"Hey, it's no big deal."

"Yes, it is a big deal!" Berman insists, looking back at him. Abruptly, she's on her feet. "I was wrong to approach you about this. I don't know—"

"It's not like I never ran the Matrix before."

"No," Berman says adamantly. "I will not allow it. This is my problem. There's no reason why you should risk, risk anything. I'll have to go to some other quarter—"

Ivar hesitates a moment; then, with one quick hop he's near enough to snatch the hardcopy from Berman's hand.

She sways back, wide-eyed with obvious surprise, then glares at him angrily, but by then of course he's got the sheet. "Give me that."

"You got a problem, I can help."

"Ivar—"

"You gave me a job when no one else would, Ms. Berman. I don't forget squat like that."

Frag, he made his first run when he was just a kid, just for the chuckle of penetrating system security. He used a Sony deck that's ancient history these days, and he didn't even snatch any data. When he got his first Fuchi deck . . . well, then he snatched data. In fact, he went a little nutty. Busting code-red mainframes. Scamming the P's, paydata, the kind of proprietary yak that corps and even the military get all kinds of stroked about. He made maybe a couple of million nuyen and was living high in the trons, only then Telecom Security came down on him like a high-yield nuclear weapon—with multiple warheads, of course—and he spent a few years digging graves at the Dannemora graybar hotel.

But, hey, nobody has to hit him twice with a mallet. He learned his lesson. The corps always win. Why fight 'em if joining works out just as well? Once he got out of slam, he made about a thousand applications, only none of the corps were interested in ramjammers unless they came up through the corporate system. Too much of a risk. He got just one call and that was from Berman. She took a chance. Sure, he had to go through all the usual tests and interviews, pledge his allegiance to the corporate logo, but that was just a formality. Berman made the decision. She sat him down in her office one afternoon for almost two hours and just talked and listened. Like she really wanted to know this fraggin' dwarf halfer, know more than if he was just "reformed."

It's time he paid some more of his tab.

"Ivar, I'm *ordering* you to give me that sheet."

"You're just being considerate, Ms. Berman, and that's wiz. I know what I'm doing. Probably better than you do. Have a seat."

"I don't believe this," she says, but then she sits again on the sofa. Definitely not the type to try making a grab for the hardcopy. In fact, she leans forward and cups her face in her hands. She seems a little upset. "Ivar, please don't take any risks."

"I know what I'm doing."

"Yes, but this is on my conscience," she says quietly. "I know why you're doing this, and it's not necessary. You don't owe me or Hurley-Cooper anything."

Ivar doesn't doubt for an instant that she sees it that way, but there's another side to the chip that she's not mentioning. "Way I figure, Ms. Berman, if the names on this here list got you worried enough to come to me like this, on the sly, then it must be serious, and it must be a problem for ole HC, which means it's my problem, too."

"No." Berman shakes her head. "You're wrong."

"Maybe. Maybe not."

It's probably open to debate, but Ivar ain't debating. What's the point? He's got the list and a brainwave that's set in motion, and that's all he needs.

Ivar gets the semiplas toilet plunger from under the kitchen sink and uses that to suck a pair of tiles out of the kitchen floor. The hidden space below, now revealed, is where he hides the Cruncher and related hardware, such as his toolbox. He wouldn't bother hiding things except the parole board doesn't like him keeping cyberdecks around, and now and then they send somebody around to check. Of course, nobody glued his datajack shut, or, for that matter, messed with the tech inside his head, such as his expanded memory module and advanced data manager, so the parole board couldn't have been too serious about wanting him to "stay away from computers." More like, do what you have to, chummer, but don't do anything *bad*. Guy's gotta make a living, don't he? Well . . . anyway.

Comps is what he knows, that and not much else. Running the Matrix is probably not a good thing for him to do, but keeping Ms. Berman happy, repaying his debts, and doing what he can for good ole Hurley-Cooper, to which he pledged allegiance, seem like compensating factors.

He carries his tech back to the living room, to the SoloFendi recliner next to the telecom. As he starts hooking and plugging things up and in, Berman says, "I hope this won't encourage you to fall into old habits. You've earned a lot of respect. You've got a career now. A real future."

"Sure, I know that. Don't worry about it."

Hey, he's reformed already. He knows to stay outta trouble. And anyway he spends most of his time at Hurley-Cooper HQ inventing new and faster ways for the mainframe progs to chew on data. Maybe when he's got a

few minutes to spare, he pulls out the Cruncher and blasts
off into the trons just to see what's going on. Gotta keep
rubbing the ole iron or things get rusty, or develop kinks, or
whatever ... But he's a solid citizen now. No question. The
old days are gone for good.

"Any last-minute instructions?" he asks.

"I still don't want you to do this."

"Well ... I know that."

They've had that discussion already. Ivar slots his black
wire lead into the jack behind his right temple, gets comfortable in his SoloFendi, and punches INIT.

The Cruncher winds up.

He's suddenly in the gleaming rainbow cockpit of his
virtual Boeing-Federated Death Eagle 2, the *Iron Dog,*
streaming down the datalines, blasting through the Projects'
node, and going to afterburners, hurtling like lightning out
across the glaring starlit night of the LTG. Acceleration
keeps him nailed to his seat. The cyclone roar of his engines
rises to a banshee scream. It's, ahh ... heh. Quite a rush.

Ivar thrusts his joystick forward and plunges down, down,
down, into the infinite electron abyss between the soaring
cubes and towering towers of computer clusters. A certain
LTG address comes up quick. He jinks to his right.

The white wall of a node flashes around him and suddenly
he's standing in the blazing blue neon virtual office of
Nuyen Now! Mr. Service himself, chief bottlewasher of this
very legit but rinky-dink loan operation, is sitting right there
with his iconic feet up on his iconic desk. Mr. Service's
iconic self looks like an investment banker. Just another Matrix fantasy.

"Yo, Conan," Service says.

"Need to borrow the wire," Ivar says.

"Be my guest. Fifty cred."

Ivar, now two meters tall and built like a Viking barbarian, dressed like one too, greatsword and all, pulls a coin
from his belt pouch and tosses it to Mr. Service. The coin
winks "¥50." Service snatches it out of the air and slaps it
down on the desk. The coin bongs like a bell, slapping
down.

"Double or nothing."

"Ask me later."

"Sure thing."

Ivar turns and stalks like a real barbarian hunk to the door at the back of the office. The floor trembles beneath his massive stalking weight. At the center of the door, winking on and off, is the logo, TRW CredCorp. Beyond the door is the infinite black depth of a fiber optics dataline. Ivar draws his huge silver-gleaming ruby and dragonhead-adorned greatsword, and, with a shout, a war-cry—which is part of his style, not to mention this particular aspect of his master persona control program—he steps through the door.

A direct link to TRW CredCorp.

He's blasting down the line in the cockpit of the *Iron Dog,* then something flashes, a node, and he's standing in a brilliant gold reception room decorated with gleaming red plants and a purplish waterfall. A gray and white-framed window opens right in front of his face and the giant disembodied eyeball of a Watcher 7K stares at him, blinks once, and disappears.

Hey, he's a legitimate user coming in on a direct optical feed. Of course the eye disappears.

He stalks between a pair of glaring chrome knight-in-armor guards and pounds on an orange vault door. The door snaps aside. He stalks into a bare neon-yellow room. An androgynous figure in a pink and white kimono bows, "CUSTOMER SERVICE" winking above its head. The figure says, "How may I serve you, sir?"

Ivar pulls an amulet from his pouch and hands it over. Inscribed on the amulet, in binary code of course, are the names of Amy Berman's list. "Gimme everything you got."

"A complete credit history of these subject-attribute names?"

"And make it pronto."

"Certainly, sir."

A few nanoseconds pass, more or less. Ivar smoothes back his flaming yellow mane, brushes at his massive bulging biceps, then also at the barbarian hides he has for clothes. The customer service icon mostly just stands there, swirling hexadecimals racing across its face, then it holds out the amulet and says, "Search complete. Thank you for referencing TRW CredCorp."

Back to the *Iron Dog.*

While he's blazing back down the datalines, going nowhere in particular at a hellacious velocity, he offs his heads-up combat display and brings up the data from the TRW CredCorp scan. That shows him what he takes to be complete credit histories on the names from Amy Berman's list: names, SINs, addresses, salaries, loans, ratings, everything. All that really stands out, as far as Ivar can see, is that everyone on the list has their credit accounts with the First Corporate Trust of New York. But that's no surprise. F.C.T. of N.Y. is one of those cooperative ventures. KFK International is a principal shareholder. Probably every employee of every KFK subsidiary in the New York-New Jersey megaplex has their cred accounts at that particular institution.

Good corporate etiquette, you might say.

All except this one slag, who's got accounts elsewhere. Benjamin Alan Hill. Might as well follow that up.

So what has he got in his online storage that might sleaze him inside the local branch of the UCAS Bank?

Something good, of course.

39

Amy sits and waits for almost an hour. Ivar sits in his recliner like a corpse, cyberdeck across his lap. Once, his fingers come alive and tap rapidly at the deck's touch-sensitive keys, then nothing. Motionless. Amy hears a thump and a bang from beyond the bedroom door, but the door stays closed and Ivar's lady friend stays out of sight.

Abruptly, Ivar's eyes are open and he's pulling the jack out of his head. Amy exhales deeply with relief. "You're all right."

"Sure," Ivar says. "Just had to crash a bank or two."

"Please . . ." Amy lifts a hand—she'd rather not know the details. It's bad enough that Ivar's violated his parole out of some misguided sense of loyalty. She'd never have forgiven herself if something had gone wrong. "Can you download what you . . . ?"

Ivar's already taking a datachip from a slot in his deck and bringing it to her. "Think I got what you need. Only unusual stuff involves this one guy Hill, so I tracked down everything I could without getting crazy."

Amy frowns. "What kind of stuff?"

"Sort of like what you said. He's got a lot of cred *and* he

doesn't keep it at the First Corporate Trust." Ivar hesitates.
The sober look on his face shows that he is well aware of
the implications of what he just said. "It's, uhh . . . Well, it's
all on the chip. What I got. I can go a whole freak of a lot
further if you want . . ."

Shaking her head, Amy takes the chip. "No, absolutely
not. You've done enough, Ivar. Too much. You mustn't ever
do this again."

"Course not."

Amy forces a smile, and says, "It would be best if you
keep everything about this strictly confidential."

"Hey, null sheen. It never happened."

Five minutes later, Amy's sitting in her Toyo Arbiter GX.
Orange floodlights fill the parking field with a hazy glow.
Rain patters against the windshield. Amy slots the chip from
Ivar into her palmtop and quickly scans through the data.

There's a fairly extensive datafile on Dr. Benjamin Hill
and it shows that he not only has an account hidden away at
the UCAS Bank, but that he has nearly three million nuyen
in that account, and the account record shows large infusions
of cash going back several years. The deposits do not coin-
cide exactly with the dates and nuyen amounts of payments
made by Hurley-Cooper on behalf of the Metascience
Group, but of course that doesn't really mean a thing.

Surely, someone embezzling money would be careful to
muddy their tracks, to confuse dates and amounts; and he or
she would certainly have expenses, such as to pay accomplices, or to maintain phony shell corporations, or just to
transfer money, and so on.

Groaning, Amy switches off her palmtop and stares into
her lap. She tells herself that the money in Dr. Hill's account
could have come from anywhere, but she has trouble believing that. Every employee of a KFK subsidiary is told very
clearly from day one where they're expected to do their
banking, and there's no reason to disregard corporate expectations. Employees of Hurley-Cooper get very favorable
rates at First Corporate Trust, and not just on interest-
bearing accounts, but on loans and all other services. And
there's an A.T.M. in the lobby of every HC facility that
banks direct to F.C.T. There's no reason in the world to use
any another financial institution, unless you've got something to hide.

Ivar didn't track down the source of the funds in Dr. Hill's account. Amy's glad he didn't. For one thing, the risk would be too great. For another, she'd never be able to look Dr. Hill in the face if she had obtained incontrovertible proof that the man was stealing.

She's gone too far. She sees that now. She let feelings of desperation get to her. She's approached this like she works for the despots of Fuchi or the iron-fisted masters of Mitsuhama, and that's wrong. If her beliefs mean anything, she should go to Dr. Hill openly, point out the irregularities she's discovered, and listen to whatever explanations he might offer. That's what someone who really cares about people would do, and that's what she's going to do, first thing tomorrow morning.

She sits back and closes her eyes. Her watch bleeps. Ten p.m. Time for Corporate Diary on News Network 42.

And then she realizes Scottie should be waiting for her.

"Oh, *slot!*"

She keys the Toyo's ignition, then taps her cellphone, and calls home. Her telecom answers. It would be like Scottie to ignore an incoming call. She can't actually remember ever seeing him talking on a telecom. Thank god her telecoms at home are set for auto call screening. "Scottie, it's me," she says, hoping he'll hear. "If you're there, please wait. I'm coming right now."

No answer.

She hangs up and puts the Toyo in Drive.

The ride to Scarsdale seems to take forever. She's barely onto the Bruckner Expressway when she comes onto the scene of a massive accident involving two trucks and at least a dozen cars, and, seemingly, half the emergency vehicles in the city. Between glaring, almost blinding emergency strobes and suddenly flaring brake lights, there are uniformed officers stepping in and out of the lanes waving lighted batons, stopping traffic, waving it on. Five lanes jam down to one in the space of fifty meters. Amy's fifteen minutes getting past the crash, another fifteen getting to Scarsdale, another five getting to her tower, parking, and riding the elevator up to her condo.

The living room's dark and empty. "Scottie?"

No answer. Not a sound. She walks to the bedroom door. The lights come up softly as she crosses the threshold, but show her nothing. She turns back to the hall with the idea of checking the kitchen, as if there's any hope remaining, and bangs square into someone's front.

"YAGH!" she exclaims, staggering back.

"It's me," Scottie says.

Yes, obviously. Now that she's nearly wet herself. Gasping, catching her breath, she says, "I think . . . now I understand . . . that name. Bandit. Please don't ever do that again."

"Sorry."

"It's okay." Amy reaches for him to hug him. "Have you been here long?"

"Not so long."

"I called, but you didn't pick up."

"No." Almost apologetically, Scottie adds, "I don't like phones. They can be tapped."

Amy hesitates. "You don't think my phone . . ."

Scottie shrugs.

Amy waits a moment, puzzling, then starts explaining why she's so late, how it couldn't be helped, only to realize that she's just rationalizing. Making excuses. She should have been here sooner. Been here for Scottie. Her career is important, yes, but now, tonight, when her brother's just come back into her life, Scottie should be her highest priority.

What could she possibly have done to deserve the crisis at Hurley-Cooper now of all times, when she should be concentrating on her brother? Sometimes life is just plain cruel.

They go to the kitchen. Amy makes tea. She turns back from the wave to find Scottie examining a spoon, turning it over, holding it up to the light, like it might hold some mystic property. She nearly laughs, and some of the anxious tension in her stomach subsides. Scottie's always been doing things like that, like looking at spoons. Scrutinizing totally ordinary things that no ordinary person would more than glance at. Maybe that's part of being a shaman. Maybe there's more to an ordinary spoon than a mundane individual like her would normally expect.

She carries two cups of tea to the table and finds Scottie looking over a small plastic figurine. She recognizes it at once. It's a gift shop figurine, maybe from some museum, of a raccoon. It came from the vanity in her bedroom.

"You took this out of my room," Scottie says. "You left a flute in its place."

A long time ago. Amy nods, remembering. Feeling a twinge of embarrassment. But facing up to things, even embarrassing things, is important now. "Yes," she says. "I remember I had this idea that maybe you'd take up the flute and forget about magic. I saw the results of your aptitude tests. Mom and dad made you take so many. The tests indicated you had a strong aptitude for magic, music. I mean . . . You know what I mean."

"Mom wanted me to be a musician."

Amy smiles. "I did, too."

"It's the same thing."

"What is?"

"Music and magic. It's all one."

"How do you mean?"

"Nature."

Amy remembers. This is part of what he talked about just last night. Part of what brought him back. The need to understand nature, and people, to further his understanding, his development as a person. It's like, after concentrating on magic for so long, he wants to rejoin the human race. That's the essence of it, and Amy's overjoyed by the news. "Is that why you've got that flute? Is it part of attuning yourself to people?"

Scottie nods, slowly. "I guess it is."

"You must be learning things from your girlfriend, Shell."

Scottie nods, more definitely this time. "Things I didn't expect. That's valuable. That's why I try to help her. To keep things fair. A fair exchange."

It almost sounds like barter economics. "Well, you're lucky if things are fair. Relationships aren't always like that."

"It doesn't have to be that way," Scottie says. "Raccoon is kind of a thief. But with a sense of honor. I like things to seem fair." Scottie hesitates a moment, then says, "Maybe I can help you, too."

Amy can't help smiling. Is this really her brother talking? Some of it's so mystical and strange and yet *so human*. Amy feels almost giddy with delight. "I don't need any help."

"You said you're having a problem."

"Yes, but that's just part of having a job and a regular career. Having problems is part of being a suit."

"Maybe I can help."

"How could you help?"

"I can do things. Raccoon has many tricks. I've been walking the path a long time."

"Can you tell what people are thinking?"

Scottie seems to consider that, then says, "Sometimes I can tell what they're feeling."

"Can you tell when they lie?"

"Sometimes."

A thought pops into Amy mind, but it's crazy and she should just dismiss it. This is her brother here, right? her brother who she hasn't seen in years. She shouldn't be considering anything that would get him mixed up in her problems at work.

"People are lying to you?" Scottie asks.

"No, not really." She didn't say that, did she? "No, I've been looking into discrepancies in our records. It's not certain what's going on, so I haven't confronted anyone yet, so no one's really had the chance to lie. But let's talk about something else. About you."

"This is about me. You and me."

"Scottie, this is just some corporate intrigue. At worst, it's a case of fraud." Why is she arguing with him? She should be explaining. She reaches across the table for one of his hands, and says, smiling, "I'm so glad you made the offer. Thank you. You don't know how much it means to me. It's just that . . . well, this is my problem. It's got nothing to do with you or your magic."

"You don't understand," Scottie says. "I guess I didn't explain real well. It's all one. Magic. People. Corporate stuff. It's all got to do with magic because it's about people, nature, the universe. You and me. Everything."

Amy shakes her head. "All I'm talking about is someone stealing from a corp."

Scottie nods. "Tell me more."

40

"Enoshi-*sama* . . ."

The voice which quietly speaks his name comes as his

only warning. A yellowish light is suddenly glaring in his eyes.

Enoshi Ken brings a hand up in front of his face to ward off the glaring light, but not quite quickly enough. The headache that menaced him all evening, rising discreetly into his forehead, then fading, is suddenly back with a vengeance, throbbing with knife-edged brutality. He grunts, pressing a hand against his forehead, then squinting into the light.

An indistinct blur hovers over him. For a moment, he imagines it is Setsuko, his wife. What could be wrong? A tumult of vague possibilities races through his mind, only to be thrust aside by the realization that Setsuko is not here in New York, but at their home in Philadelphia, near the North American headquarters of Kono-Furata-Ko International.

"Forgive me," a honied voice whispers in elegant Japanese. Gentle hands slip his glasses on over his nose and ears. Lips as soft as butterfly wings graze his cheek, and by then his eyes adjust to the light and he sees the woman leaning toward him. A lustrous mane of golden blonde frames Frederique's face. She smiles tenderly, sitting on the edge of the bed, attired in a diaphanous rose-colored peignoir that makes her seem every bit the exotic dream-woman she is.

Enoshi clears his throat, and says, softly, "What is wrong?"

"Your aide called," Frederique whispers.

"I did not hear the phone."

"You were sleeping, my darling."

"I do not really approve of my aide speaking to you."

Frederique smiles. "He could not know who would answer."

No, obviously not, and this situation is really Enoshi's own fault. It comes about as a result of the natural difficulties of being away from home. Telecom calls cannot compensate for being deprived of one's usual surroundings, or daily contact with one's wife and children. Unfortunately, it is not possible to bring his wife along on his business trips, so he arranged for Frederique to join him here in New York. This was not the wisest course he might have followed. His staff might have previously assumed, for various reasons, that he has a mistress; now they know. His personal aide certainly knows, if no one else. Enoshi is not comfortable with that. He prefers that such things remain confidential.

"Usami Gek has asked to see you."

"Now?"

Frederique smiles, calmly accepting, serene. She is perhaps the most imperturbable person Enoshi has ever known. She is like the still waters of a lake. A dropped pebble may stir gentle ripples across her surface, but she remains forever calm, as if in touch with the infinite. It adds immeasurably to her mystique.

Enoshi exhales heavily. It is after three A.M. Usami Gek would not ask to see him at such an hour unless an important matter had arisen. His duty is clear. He arises and steps into his *uwabaki*. Frederique helps him into his robe.

In the lav, he takes a Nodol for his headache, then washes his face and hands and combs his hair. The corporate executive must maintain a meticulous appearance. All the more so for KFK International's Vice-President for Corporate Liaison. Were the matter awaiting him not of an urgent nature, as apparently it must be, he would take the time to put on a suit.

As he steps from the lav, Frederique meets him with a kiss, and then spends a moment retying the belt of his robe.

"You are becoming like a second wife."

Frederique smiles. "A wife must tend to home and family, my darling. A mistress is free to tend other matters."

"You are more to me than a mistress."

Smiling, Frederique bows, to the exact degree necessary to demonstrate humility, yet without detracting from her obvious pleasure. Remarkable, that a woman so obviously of European ancestry should have such command of Japanese ways. She becomes more of a mystery, and more delightful, with each new piece of the puzzle that Enoshi discovers.

Outside the bedroom door waits one of the security agents who accompany Enoshi everywhere. There are four such agents on his staff. At least one is near him at all times. In Enoshi's view, this is simply a reminder of the importance attached by others to his position. He is not himself a particularly important man. The work he performs, however, is of consequence to KFK's North American operations. For that reason, he is paid very well, and provided with a staff, guards, and chauffeured cars. For that reason, and that reason alone, he is able to fly his mistress in from Philadelphia merely because, in private moments, he had begun feeling rather lonely.

Now, though, he steps briskly along the hallway leading to the main sitting room of his suite.

The room is decorated like the other rooms of the suite, in the very flamboyant style for which the Waldorf Park East hotel is famous: oil paintings, lavish draperies, intricately carved wood furniture. The gold-framed windows at the end of the room, now streaked with rain, overlook Central Park. All in all, Enoshi considers it excessive for an executive of his station, more appropriate for a KFK boardmember, such as the board's Vice-Chairman Torakido Buntaro.

Enoshi takes a seat on a satin-upholstered couch. His aide brings a tray with coffee and a pack of his cigarettes. He lights up and then sips some coffee. His headache is subsiding somewhat.

"Please ask Usami-*san* to come in."

"*Hai, sugu,* Enoshi-*sama*," the aide hurriedly replies, bowing.

Momentarily, the aide returns with Usami Gek. Usami is ethnic Japanese. He is originally from Yodo, which is between Osaka and Kyoto. He is tall and slim and looks rather dangerous, enough to be a gangster. He wears a severe black suit with a dark blue knit shirt. Generally, it is for Usami to determine what form his own attire should take. Usami is a senior security operative, involved in clandestine activities, and so must sometimes modify his appearance to suit his tasks.

He comes forward, bows, and says, "Please excuse me for disturbing you at this late hour, Enoshi-*sama*."

"*Yosh,*" Enoshi replies. "I am sure you are doing as your duty requires. Please sit down. What do you wish to report?"

Usami bows again and sits. "Two significant events have occurred recently," he says. "I decided that you should be informed, now that certain information has been tentatively confirmed."

Enoshi nods. "Please proceed."

"This concerns our monitoring of Ms. Amy Berman."

"Yes, or course."

As Enoshi is well aware, the audit process is a twofold path, involving the close examination of a subsidiary's financial records and the selective monitoring of executive activity. The examination of records sometimes pressures disloyal executives into committing acts which reveal illicit activity. In this way, the two features of the audit process work in tandem to root out any elements of the corporation that may have grown corrupt.

"Go on."

Usami says, "Earlier this evening, a telecom surveillance team intercepted a call to Ms. Amy Berman's carphone. This call originated with a man who appears to be employed by a local arm of Mitsuhama Computer Technologies, though we are still working on identifying him. He informed Ms. Amy Berman that you visited Ms. Bobinek of Mitsuhama UCAS and were in conference for several hours with her and Mr. El-Gabri and an MCT attorney."

A surprising turn of events. Enoshi wonders what conclusions Ms. Amy Berman might draw based on this information. It can be difficult at times to guess what any woman might think, much less one with whom he has very little personal experience. "Did this unidentified man make any other comments regarding my visit to MCT?"

"He identified Mr. El-Gabri as executive vice president of MCT's local biotechnology division. He also said that he believed Ms. Amy Berman would want to know about the visit. He said it seemed of possible significance."

"Did he give any indication as to why he found this significant?"

"Yes, he made reference to events at Ms. Amy Berman's corporation, events she had previously described. He said that is why he felt your visit to MCT might be significant."

"Did he mention what events Ms. Berman had described?"

"No, he did not."

Fortunately, for Ms. Berman, such disclosures as she may have made are not necessarily grounds for punitive action. Ms. Berman might be guilty of nothing more than a trivial lack of discretion. The board of KFK, including Torakido-*sama,* has a fairly liberal attitude toward the behavior of its executives. That of course does not mean that executives should not be monitored, nor that an executive may do anything he or she wishes without fear of punishment. "Was there any indication as to the nature of Ms. Berman's relationship with this man?"

"Yes," Usami replies. "The man used the word 'darling' in referring to Ms. Amy Berman."

That would seem to be highly indicative. "This word 'darling' was used in a romantic sense?"

"Yes," Usami replies. "A member of the telecom surveillance team confirms it. This particular operative is native to New York and learned English as a primary language."

That would seem to clear up any doubt regarding the word's implications. Not a good sign. A close personal relationship between an executive of any KFK subsidiary and an executive of a corp like Mitsuhama would be a matter for great concern. It could also be quite useful, given the proper circumstances. "Inform me as soon as you have a tentative identification on this man who called Ms. Berman."

"Yes, Enoshi-*sama*," Usami replies. "It should not take long."

"Good." Enoshi sips his coffee and takes a drag on his cigarette, then says, "You wished to speak of a second incident?"

"Yes, Enoshi-*sama*. This incident also involves Ms. Amy Berman. Shortly after her conversation with the unidentified man, she returned home and met with a man who awaited her inside her condoplex."

"The same man she met with last night?"

"Yes, Enoshi-*sama*. We have tentatively identified this man as Ms. Amy Berman's brother, Mr. Scott Berman. In their conversation last night, Mr. Scott Berman spoke of using an alias, the name of Bandit. We have tentatively identified this Bandit as a wanted felon, a shadowrunner, active until recently in the nearby city named Newark."

"A shadowrunner?"

"Yes, Enoshi-*sama*."

Remarkable. Enoshi is fairly astounded. To think that a vice president of a KFK subsidiary should be so closely related to a known shadowrunner. Enoshi is unsure what to make of it. Nothing quite like this has ever come up before. Prospective executives of all KFK subsidiaries are all thoroughly investigated to ensure that nothing in their backgrounds could give rise to trouble. "It is very difficult for me to understand how this could be so. Is it possible that your sources are less than accurate?"

"Certainly, Enoshi-*sama*, that is possible. There could be many 'Bandits.' The connection we have drawn between Mr. Scott Berman and the shadowrunner named Bandit is very tentative, based primarily on photo-comparison technology, which is not absolutely reliable. However, I would be derelict in my duty if I did not bring certain other details to your attention which relate to this matter."

"Please continue."

"We have ascertained that Mr. Scott Berman has been living without use of a System Identification Number for approximately fifteen years. His official record simply ends. He apparently disappeared. The police conducted an investigation of his disappearance at the request of his parents, but learned nothing. The case was eventually closed. Mr. Scott Berman's SIN was classified as inactive. He was presumed dead."

Of course. The only possible explanation. Or the only one that immediately comes to mind. Ms. Berman's brother was presumed dead, his official record ended; therefore, any checks run on Ms. Berman when she joined Hurley-Cooper would have turned up no connections with anyone, much less a shadowrunner or felon.

Enoshi closes his eyes and rubs at his forehead. His headache is gaining strength again. "Is there any indication that Ms. Berman is personally involved in criminal activity?"

"She spoke of someone stealing from a corporation, but did not identify the parties involved. Surveillance was terminated shortly thereafter."

"You terminated surveillance?"

"No, Enoshi-*sama*. Our audio surveillance devices abruptly ceased to transmit any sounds. Prior to this, Mr. Scott Berman warned Ms. Amy Berman that telecoms may be tapped. I suspect he made use of some method to defeat the devices planted in Ms. Amy Berman's residence. Possibly an arcane method. Mr. Scott Berman appears to be a shaman."

"You're quite certain?"

"Yes, Enoshi-*sama*."

A most disturbing turn of events. Enoshi knows little of shamans, but everything he has ever heard about them suggests that, at best, they are very individualistic persons. The worst are eco-terrorists involved in ferocious anticorporate activity. Enoshi looks to Usami and says, "We know from Ms. Berman's previous meeting that she has been out of contact with this person, her brother. Was there any indication tonight as to the specific cause that brought them together?"

"Mr. Scott Berman spoke again of attuning himself with people. I do not know what real significance this may have for a shaman. However, I think it is conceivable that this is some form of criminal argot referring to specific persons whom Mr. Scott Berman plans to contact in connection with some illicit activity."

Enoshi massages his forehead. He reviewed portions of the transcript of last night's meeting between Ms. Berman and her brother. At face value, it had seemed like a simple reunion. Tonight's revelations cast the meeting in a new and potentially sinister light. The possibility that Ms. Berman may be involved with some criminal conspiracy, possibly involving agents of Mitsuhama Computer Technologies, or terrorist elements, demands that swift and decisive action be taken. Questions must be answered. The situation must be resolved.

Usami says, "I believe it would be expedient to request hermetic resources to assist in this operation."

"I agree," Enoshi replies. "I will make the request at once. Meanwhile, you must make every attempt to unveil the mystery surrounding Ms. Berman. It is imperative that we determine what is going on, and if Ms. Berman's activities represent a threat to our corporate organization."

"I understand, Enoshi-*sama*."

Enoshi nods, and rubs at his forehead.

Usami bows and departs.

41

The tunnel is damp and dripping. Pools of water cover the floor. Strange red-hued stuff like mold clings to the tunnel's curving walls and adds a peculiar reddish glow to the dim red haze suffusing the dark. The air, though, smells kind of lush. Sweet and spicy. The only sounds are the dripping of water from the tunnel walls and the sloshing of Monk and Minx's boots through the pools on the floor.

So what are they doing in this tunnel that seems to go on forever? Monk isn't sure. He'd ask, except Minx asked him if he trusts her enough to do what she says without asking a lot of questions. Of course he does. He trusts her enough to ask *none*. They went underground somewhere just north of the Newark sprawl. Monk thinks they must be passing under the Hudson River. Where are they going? They're going to see the Master, but who that is or why they have to go through the underground to meet the slag Monk can only guess.

His first guess is that for some reason they have to meet the Master in private. If the Master is like other of Minx's friends, he probably knows the underground real well and uses it to get around without being seen. His second guess . . .

Abruptly, Minx stops, looking up at the reddish crete of the ceiling. "Oh, my god," she says. "Oh, my *god*! OH, *MY GOD*!"

There's nothing wrong with the ceiling that Monk can see. He guesses that Minx is getting a call over her implanted headfone. Before the Change, her Change, she was a messenger. Her friends all have her telecom code.

She looks at him and smiles.

"What?"

"Oh, nothing," Minx says. "You'll never guess what I just heard. Novastar Maria Mercurial is pregnant."

"Wiz."

"By a troll."

"Yeah?"

"And a vampire."

"Huh?"

Minx nods like she means it.

"Vampires are real?"

"Ever see one?"

"No."

"Me, neither."

They walk on, and on and on, and then on a ways more. The pools on the tunnel floor dwindle. The dripping fades into silence. A big jagged hole appears in the tunnel wall, like something as tough as a troll punched a hole through the bricks. The passage on the other side of that hole is narrow and ends at a metal grating. Minx pushes the grating open and they step into another tunnel, big and squarish, with tracks, like tracks for subway trains.

"What's that rumbling noise?" Monk says.

Minx squeezes his elbow. "That's just a highway," she says, pointing up. "Don't worry, you booty. Trains don't come this way anymore."

The paired rails are kind of rusty red. Monk wonders

where this tunnel leads, and where he and Minx are standing right now. He guesses they're somewhere on the east side of the Hudson. Maybe Manhattan. Probably north of that. He's never spent much time in Manhattan so he's not really sure how far north of the island the subway tunnels go. He knows they go way over into Brooklyn and Queens and some cross into Jersey, but north of Manhattan? He's clueless.

They walk on and on a while. Monk decides to ask a question. "Uh ... what am I supposed to do when we meet this Master guy?"

Minx smiles. "I'll show you."

Well, okay.

They come to another grating in the tunnel wall. Minx pulls it open. The passage beyond it is small and squarish. They have to bend forward to get through it. That leads them into a maze of passages, some large enough for them to stand upright, some so small they have to get down on hands and knees. Monk is in the process of deciding to ask another question when, abruptly, the tunnel they're in comes to an end and Minx turns to face him.

"Boost me up, you booty."

Monk makes a cradle of his hands. Minx puts one foot there and half climbs up onto his shoulders. It's hard to see what she does then, as her groin is right in front of his face, pressing against his nose. The smell that greets his nose, that seems to come seeping out through the crotch of her jeans, is lush and sweet, and ...

Abruptly, she's got both feet on his shoulders and she's rising, climbing up through a squarish hole in the tunnel ceiling.

"Come on, booty," she whispers.

A rope hits him in the face. He gets hold of that and climbs up. That puts him in a dark, dry, dusty space like a basement. The walls look like wood, a reddish sort of wood. The floor's concrete. Reddish concrete. There are a lot of crates and boxes and shelves standing around, some rising in stacks to the ceiling, and dividing the place into narrow cobwebby aisles.

"Don't move," Minx whispers into his ear.

Monk shakes his head.

Little more than two meters away stands a tall figure wrapped in a dark cloak. A hood and mask cover his face

and head. Gloves cover his hands. A sort of hazy red corona
radiates from around him.

Monk guesses this is the Master.

He can't move.

"Come, my dear hunter," the Master says in a quiet, reassuring, fatherly sort of voice. "Come to me."

Monk feels his whole body tingling, trying to move forward, but his feet are locked in position, glued to the dusty
floor. Minx moves forward. She moves to face the Master
and lifts her hands to his shoulders. Something happens
then. The Master's cloak swings out, encompassing Minx,
and then ... Monk isn't sure. It's like the cloak becomes a
dark cloud hiding Minx and Master both. Monk stands there
watching, unable to move, and there's just this cloud of
darkness hanging there before him.

A while passes.

The cloud of darkness fades. The Master comes back into
sight. He lowers his cloak. Minx turns and comes to Monk,
lifts her hands to his shoulders, and smiles. "You booty," she
says softly. "Get it?"

"Huh?"

"Now it's your turn."

"My turn?"

"To feed the Master."

"Huh?"

"If you don't, he'll die," Minx whispers, "and if he dies,
we die."

That would be bad. If they died, Minx would die, and then
Monk couldn't stand living. "How do I ... ?"

"You know ..."

Minx thrusts her mouth against his and exhales deeply.
The warm gush of her breath brings him a rush. *The breath
of life* ... Their life. The Master's life. Monk nods. He gets
it now. Minx takes hold of his arm and leads him forward,
one step, then another, closer and closer, till the Master's
opening his cloak, growing larger and larger, infinite, and
the Master's saying, "Come to me, my hunter. Come ..."

And Monk goes.

42

The name of the place is Brogan Bail Bonds. It occupies a ground-level storefront in a five-story brick building that's almost lost amid the cheesy stroboscopic pandemonium of the street. Glaring neon signs and flashing laser adverts illuminate nearly every window of every building; some reach right over the street. Adstands along the curbs add their thumping, echoing, electronic syncopated soundtracks to the rhythmic humming and rumbling of passing traffic and the chaotic shouts, cries, and wails of two-legs pouring along the walkways.

Autofire weapons chatter in the distance. A siren whoops from somewhere nearby. The air smells of meat and sweat and the poisons of the sprawl. Tikki watches Brogan Bail Bonds from across the street. The crowds of two-legs provide cover and she's in disguise anyway: wig, facepaint, duster.

An Asian male steps up close.

"You wanna *sumara*?"

That's a Japanese word meaning "bare penis." A synonym for condomless sex. Evidently, this part of the Bronx is one of those where a female standing alone on the street for more than a nanosecond is assumed to be whoring. "You like it rough?" Tikki asks.

The male smiles, then looks down. Peering out through the front of Tikki's duster, pressing into the male's gut, is the muzzle of a TZ-115 Colt submachine gun.

"I'm a memory," the male says.

And the memory fades.

At just past three A.M., Tikki catches sight of a pair of tall figures: one with lots of white hair, the other with ears, elven ears. They go through the front door of Brogan Bail Bonds and out of sight. Tikki crosses the street and pauses on the walkway. Amid the stench of the passing two-legs is a smell, a collection of scents that she remembers from the cabin along the Road to Nowhere. It's the stink of the elf male she's identified as Elgin O'Keefe, alias Tang, and the other female accomplice, Whistle.

Instinct says go right in, take the front door, smash it in if need be, and Tikki's more than tempted, but she heads down the block and turns the corner. Along the cross-street, she finds an alley that leads down behind the rear of the buildings to the back door of Brogan Bail Bonds. The door is locked, but her Magna 2 passkey should take care of that. She puts the passkey to the lock, sheds her wig and duster, and brings up, in one hand, the Colt SMG, and, in the other, the Viper A-12 automag. The door clicks. She pushes inside.

That puts her in a narrow hallway leading toward the front of the building. There's a pair of doors along the right and one at the top of the hallway, through which comes a tall lanky figure with pointed ears, wearing a black armored vest and dark gray fatigues.

As he turns from closing the door, he stops and looks at Tikki and makes a face like he's surprised, but he doesn't smell surprised, not in the least.

"Hands," Tikki says.

"What's the meaning of this?" the elf says, lifting his hands. "There's no money here."

"We have biz, *man*."

"And what would that be?"

O'Keefe glances toward the floor and something in his scent changes. Tikki stops in mid-step, freezes. O'Keefe glances toward her left foot, now extended out before her. Just the tip of her shoe touches the floor. She presses downward with the tip of that shoe, just a little, then a little more. Abruptly, the entire section of flooring between her and O'Keefe falls away and crashes into the next level down.

A trap. She was expected, maybe baited into coming here. That means she is facing dangers she can only guess at.

Instinct rises—fur rushes over her face and a low animal snarl rises from the back of her throat. O'Keefe whistles. Tikki's index finger squeezes down on the trigger of the SMG, but then with a deafening roar the wall to her right explodes.

The Colt stammers. O'Keefe staggers back. Tikki sees a flash of blue light. She hears a roar that rises into an agony of static. She feels the impacts from shattered bits of the wall to her right and a second impact as she hits the wall on her left. She realizes she's being hurt in a hundred different places. She knows some of the injuries are serious, maybe serious enough to kill a two-leg outright, and she feels herself changing, her body swelling, her clothes bursting, even as she staggers and falls.

Then it's too late.

43

Amy brushes at her eyes and smiles. Bandit smiles back, then turns and heads down the hallway toward the elevators. The hallway's empty, quiet, still. It's getting on toward dawn now, definitely time for him to leave. He pauses to look back and wave, then goes through the door to the stairwell.

The details of Amy's problem are hard to keep straight, but the main point is simple enough. She thinks someone's skeeving her corp. Finding out if that's true will probably take more than just a few simple tricks. The major players are mages; mages make things strange. Bandit's last direct encounter with a mage, over in Newark, resulted in an violent eruption of uncontrolled magic that destroyed a limo and left a parking lot full of debris. He should probably keep in mind the thought, just in case, that it won't help Amy if her corp's labs are blown to bits.

Bandit pauses on the landing by the third floor. Something's shimmering in the air. When he shifts to his astral perceptions, he sees an aura like a muscular figure in fringed hides, feathers, and beads, clothes like an Amerind might wear. But this is no mere Amerind—it's a shaman, a powerful one. He calls himself Dark Rain Hunter and he wears many masks. Tonight, the mask of the eagle covers his head. This probably means trouble. Eagle is lord of the sky and sees all that occurs on the earth below, and despises all that is ignoble.

"Be wary," Dark Rain Hunter says. "Men watch."

"What men?"

The answer comes in images: a mountain lion creeping stealthily through heavy brush; a crow fanning its wings, hovering above treetops. Bandit pushes his spirit body onto the astral plane, steps out through the walls of the condoplex and looks around. Near the entrance to the tower sits a van. Inside this are two men with a lot of technical equipment. Far above hovers some device, maybe a surveillance drone. Are the men and the drone watching him? or are they watching Amy? or someone else entirely? Bandit doubts that Dark Rain Hunter would give him warnings unless the danger affected him specifically.

He returns to his body, then climbs the stairs to Amy's level. They will have to be very careful from now on.

Tomorrow, they will meet covertly.

44

As the dust from the explosion slowly settles, O'Keefe struggles up to his feet. He feels like he's been beaten about the chest with a mallet. Breathing is a minor agony. Fortunately, none of the shots from Striper's hurried burst seem to have penetrated his vest.

At the foot of the hall lies the beast, and she's *huge!* O'Keefe taps the remote on his belt to bring up the missing section of flooring, then walks down the hall to have a closer look at Striper in her natural form. The paranatural rants speak of shapeshifters' "dramatic coloration," but that does nothing to describe the effect of this tigress's black-striped, blood-red fur. It gives her the character of something out of a nightmare, a very primal, violent nightmare.

Surrounding the tigress is a faint blue-green aurora. Whistle stands in the new opening through the hallway wall, her hands uplifted, fingers bent arcanely. The magic she casts is their only reliable way of keeping Striper quiescent and therefore harmless until properly confined, but this is hardly a panacea. In fact, it's the only spell the mage knows that might be used in this regard, and it's very draining.

"How long can you hold her?"

"Are you kidding?" Whistle mutters, features intense with concentration. The rest of her answer comes through clenched teeth. "After blowing through that wall? Half an hour. Forty-five minutes at most. And by then you'll have to carry me out."

It will have to suffice. They'll have no second chance.

O'Keefe flips open the cover of his wristfone to call for the muscleboys he's engaged for the occasion. Striper looks to weigh even more than he had supposed, 300 kilos at the very least. Alone he'd never get the beast out of the building, much less to her destination.

Fortunately, they don't have far to go.

45

The roar of the minigrenade seems likely to shake the old brick walls of the tunnel into dust. Brian's Nightfighter visor shows the muzzle of Art's Ares combat gun spitting red fire. Twenty meters up the tunnel a figure nearly the size of a troll staggers, slumps to the ground, then explodes.

There's no other word for it, but it's like no explosion Brian's ever seen in his life, not even during the flame-up he attended in North Africa with Commando One. The figure on the floor of the tunnel glows like a lamp, then suddenly the grayish dark of the tunnel is filled with streaks of dazzling white, flashing outward in every direction, like headless comets going faster than light. Art shouts; Brian goes prone. The flashes of white vanish through the tunnel walls, ceiling, and floor, and then the real strangeness begins.

A greenish sort of haze, sparking and glinting like some high-tech energy shield, swells out of nothing to fill the tunnel like a barrier between the fallen body and Brian and Art.

"What the frag . . ." Brian feels the hairs standing up on the back of his neck. "Art?"

No answer.

Then an orangey sort of orb, semitransparent, like a bubble, but about the size of a melon, rises from out of the prone figure and floats up into the haze, then drifts up and down like it's bobbing gently on zephyrs of air.

A second orb rises, then a third, and a fourth . . .

"Watch it, kid," Art growls. "Don't shoot. You'll bring the whole tunnel down."

"What the . . . what are they?"

No reply.

Three of the orbs come floating nearer: one high, one low, one in between. They come through the sparking greenish haze like it isn't there. The lowest of the three comes drifting right toward Brian's visor, then slowly turns and disappears through the floor of the tunnel. The other two drift past Art. One pauses mere centimeters away from the muzzle of the combat gun, then slowly rises and disappears through the tunnel ceiling. The third and last drifts on by, down the tunnel and out of sight.

"Mother of Mercy." Brian crosses himself.

But then Art's moving ahead. Brian gets to his feet and follows. The greenish haze is gone. Twenty meters further on they pause beside the body. It's sure big enough to be a troll, but it looks like none Brian's ever seen. It's half melted into the floor of the tunnel. The chest is an empty cavity, like melted plastic, everything fused and congealed and scorched black, and it smells really bad.

"This is magic," Brian says. "This is fragging magic!"

Art turns to face him, lifts up the visor of his Kelmar helmet, scowls, and says, "You don't know the half of it, kid."

Brian rubs at the thick stubble swathing his face.

They've been down in these tunnels too fricking long.

46

At just past ten A.M., Amy steps into her outer office, palmtop in hand. "I have some business to attend to," she tells her aide Laurena. "I should be back around two."

Laurena lifts her eyebrows in question.

"Let's say I'm in conference."

"Is everything all right?"

"Ask me that sometime tomorrow."

Laurena clearly wants more info, but Amy turns and walks away. She takes the elevator down through the levels of the underground garage to the subway and takes the next train to the Bronx Terminal Market. There she finds a little shop, black drapes obscuring the interior, the front window marked, "Madam Ortiz." The front door lets into a small space swathed in more black drapes, centered around a small table with a crystal ball. A fat woman wearing a bandanna and masses of gaudy jewelry sits behind the table. She draws back the end of the drape hanging behind her, and says, hushedly, "Spirits are calling."

Is she serious? or overly melodramatic? Amy hasn't time to worry about it. She steps past the drape, into a dark space that leads to another door, which leads to stairs, which lead down to the parking garage beneath the market. There she spots a white Toyota Elite and walks straight to it. Scottie waits in the passenger seat, wearing a dark gray suit. Amy gets in behind the wheel.

"Are we in the clear?"

"So it seems," Scottie replies.

The car is rented. Amy ordered it this morning from a payfone. She did that for the same reason that she's meeting Scottie here, for the same reason that she left her Arbiter GX at New Bronx Plaza, and the same reason she bucked the crowds on the subway. Scottie said they have to be careful. When he left her condo last night, someone was watching, watching him or watching her, or maybe both of them.

She hands him a plastic laminated badge that ID's him as Scott Hatsumi, an auditor for Kono-Furata-Ko International.

"How did you get this?" he asks.

"I lied," Amy says bluntly. She didn't actually lie, but rather led someone to presume something that wasn't true, and that amounts to the same thing. She isn't happy about it, either. Unfortunately, she couldn't see any alternative. "Just clip it to your pocket and forget it. Don't plug it in anywhere or every alarm in the world will go off."

Scottie nods.

"You're sure you understand what we talked about?"

"I understand."

"Are you sure you want to go through with this?"

"Don't you believe me?"

Belief isn't the issue, at least not in the way Scottie means. She believes what he says, of course. What she finds hard to believe is that her head-in-the-clouds shaman brother has come down so close to earth that he actually wants to get involved with her problems. He's always seemed so completely detached from the corporate life that she used to wonder if he knew even corps existed. She can't help wondering now if he really understands what she's told him, the very pressing but starkly mundane problems afflicting her little slice of the corporate domain.

But of course that's unfair. She really should give him some credit. After all, Scottie's survived all these years without a single nuyen from her or their parents. He couldn't have managed that without being at least a little in tune with reality. No one could. Considering what he's said about some of his experiences, he's probably better equipped for this morning's adventure than she is.

"Keep to the local streets," Scottie says. "They might be watching the highways."

"Who . . . oh, never mind."

It's useless to ask.

Amy starts the car and drives them out the 150th Street ramp to River Avenue. It could be anyone watching them, if anyone is actually watching. It could be KFK, it could be some corp out of Scottie's past. Scottie's been very careful so far to mention none of the names of the people and corps he's been mixed up with since he disappeared, except for Shell, his girlfriend. That's how he wants it. Amy's not entirely comfortable with that, but she's trying to accept it. She's also trying to deal with the concept that Scottie, by his own admission, has not only worked with shadowrunners but has gone on clandestine and illegal forays against various unnamed corps.

It's enough to give her pangs of guilt, to make her feel like a criminal herself.

Evidently, she's about to become one.

She must be losing her mind.

Scottie says his involvement with shadowrunning was limited to instances where corps, while legally in the right, were morally in the wrong. Amy reminds herself of the similarities between cases like that and her present situation. What they're about to do is totally wrong and illegal, but they're doing it for the right reasons. Ultimately, embezzlement is a sort of treason, and a crime of that magnitude must be uncovered.

Letting the ends justify the means is arrogant and unethical and she hates it, but she's just desperate enough to give it a try.

Jerome Avenue brings them to the main entrance plaza of the Van Cortlandt Industrial Park. Dark blue cars and security vans marked for Apollo Services line both sides of the road. Amy slows the Elite to a stop at the guard booths crossing the plaza. She runs her window down to show an elven guard her ID. The guard looks across at Scottie.

Scottie holds up his card.

"Have a better tomorrow," the guard says, waving them past.

Amy drives ahead. Does she have any hope of succeeding at this? She supposes that if she's still got a job by this time tomorrow she'll have her answer. She has no doubt about what Enoshi Ken or anyone else with KFK International will do if they learn that she's bringing a known shadowrunner onto Hurley-Cooper property. She'd be lucky to simply lose her job. More likely she'd end up in jail.

Why the hell did she let Scottie cajole her into accepting his help? Only last night she'd made up her mind to approach Dr. Hill openly, and now here she is hoping her shaman brother will be able to finger anyone who lies. She isn't *losing* her mind—she's lost it!

Never mind about her career! If Scottie's caught ... if he's found on corporate property ...

They're both dead, dead and buried.

She turns the Elite into the hedge-lined entrance to the Hurley-Cooper Metascience labs. Two blue-uniformed guards stand flanking the lane. Amy stops the Elite between them, shows her ID, then lets the retina scanner confirm her identity.

Scottie whispers something. Amy hears it, not with her ears, but somewhere in the back of her head. She feels it raising the hairs all along her spine. She struggles to suppress a shiver, then sees both the guards looking at Scottie so oddly.

"I'm Mr. Hatsumi," Scottie says.

"Yes, sir," the guards reply.

"My ID checks."

"Yes, sir."

"Thank you, sir."

"You can go on ahead."

It's that easy—they're in, without another word said.

What is she really doing here? Why is she bringing Scottie? It's more than just fraud or her career or any of the other explanations she's been feeding herself. More than anything else, she wants to prove her fears wrong, her suspicions groundless. For that, she's willing to risk everything.

Maybe with Scottie's help, she's got a chance.

47

The suit doesn't fit very well and it hasn't got anything like the number of pockets he wants, but that figures. It's in the nature of suits. The corporate lifestyle is constricting and confining, so it's only natural that a suit should force him to make compromises. The problem with compromises is that they prevent him from bringing certain items that might be of use.

Security at the entrance to the Hurley-Cooper Metascience Group facility doesn't seem very extensive. Raccoon could get inside blindfolded. One simple spell and it's done.

The building at the end of the lane doesn't look like much: two stories of vine-encrusted brick. Bandit wonders if such a place could contain anything interesting, but then reminds himself that he's here to help his sister. Helping Amy. That's the only reason he's come. He'll have to keep that in mind.

A faint shimmering appears in the air. Bandit shifts to his astral perceptions. The raccoon-shaped figure of a watcher spirit sits facing him from the dashboard. *"All clear, Master."*

No one's following. *"Keep watch on the car."*

"Yes, Master."

In the background, the Metascience building glimmers and gleams with the reflected energy of life: swirling, coiling, winding all around the building like eddies in a pool, seeking the deepest point.

"If anything happens," Amy says, "if anything goes wrong . . . Scottie, I want you to get out. Do whatever you have to do but get away." She puts one hand on his arm. "You know what I'm saying, right?"

"I understand."

Amy's very nervous. The anxiety shows clearly in the turbulence of her aura. "You sure you want to do this?"

"Yes."

Amy parks the car before the main entrance to the building. They walk into the lobby. A uniformed guard and a dark-suited receptionist stand behind the reception counter along the rear wall. They do not even ask to inspect IDs. A glance at the cards is enough.

"Where would I find Dr. Hill?" Amy asks.

The receptionist looks at something behind the counter, and says, smiling, "Dr. Hill's in his office. Shall I ring him?"

"Just say Mr. Hatsumi and I are on our way."

They go through a set of double doors and down a long hallway lined in gray and yellow tiles. On the astral, energy pulses and flows in diverse directions, and something's not right about that. Bandit gains a vague sense unlike any he's felt before, a sense of being trapped, with no way out. The very life energy flowing around him seems to reverberate with vague, discordant emotion.

They go through a door marked Lab 16 and enter a large area, a laboratory. Innumerable devices and equipment, bubbling and humming, cover the many black-topped counters and tables that divide the room into aisles. All except for the circular space at the center of the room. The floor there is marked with circles. Hermetic circles, Bandit guesses. A metal rack holds numerous large tomes. On the astral, all are radiant with power.

The moment Bandit steps into the room, his sense for discord rises sharply. Despite the nexus of glowing life energy at the center of the room, nature at its purest, he feels that he's entered a vault of horrors, a killing ground. A mood like death presses at him from all around the periphery of the room. Tones and colors of thought conjure images in his mind of many living things, small and great alike, giving up their life energy here, dying, in fear and terror.

Something growls. For an instant, the growl seems directed specifically at him, but then he's back on the physical plane, looking around with his mundane eyes. To his mundane ears, the growl seems strange, kind of savage, but lacking in real menace.

Bandit turns down an aisle, stepping toward the far end of the lab. He sees a small cage with heavy bars. Inside it is a cat the size of a large dog—a tiger cub, Bandit realizes. He's seen creatures like it at zoos and museums. But this is an odd one. Maybe some Awakened species. Its fur is red with black stripes. Is astral form is that of a tiger cub. Much as one would expect.

"Mr. Hatsumi," Amy says.

Bandit turns around. Amy's waiting beside the door to an office. The man standing in the doorway looks middle-aged. He wears a shirt and tie beneath his white lab coat. A rather plain mage's wand made of some black material protrudes from the hip pocket of his lab coat. On the astral, he's obviously an initiate, glowing with arcane knowledge of the higher metaplanes, attuned with the energies of the etheric. Bandit wonders what sort of mage could harmonize with a place like this lab, where so much of nature has been twisted, afflicted, even tortured.

"This is Dr. Benjamin Hill," Amy says.

"How do you do?" Bandit says.

"Fine, thanks," Hill replies. "It's always a pleasure to meet a representative of our friends in Tokyo."

"I'm glad."

They go into Hill's office, which is like a small box. Another rack of tomes, this one rising to the ceiling, stands beside a chrome-hued desk. Hill offers coffee or tea. Amy refuses. Hill looks to Bandit and waits. Is he waiting for a reply on the question of drinks, or is he looking for something more than anyone has mentioned? Is he strong enough to see through the mask cloaking Bandit's aura? "I do not care for tea," Bandit says.

"Coffee then?"

"No, thank you."

Hill's aura changes subtly. He seems very slightly disturbed. He steps around behind his desk and sits down. He sneezes.

"Bless you," Amy says.

"Thanks."

"You use animals in research," Bandit says.

Hill looks at him blankly, but his aura remains disturbed. "Well, yes," he says, hesitantly. "Yes, that's true. But of course all the animals we use are bred specifically for research, with a few limited exceptions. Without them, we'd be severely handicapped."

That answer does not seem to justify the way nature has been tortured in this place, but Bandit recalls his reason for being here. He forces himself to keep silent.

Amy goes on to explain about the reason for this visit.

Outwardly, she seems matter-of-fact, sober, serious, resolute, the dedicated suit going about her business; on the astral plane, her anxiety is apparent in the slowly shifting, turning, blending colors of her aura.

"All this began," she says, "because the audit staff is questioning a number of items that were purchased but apparently never used. I conducted a survey of the Metascience databases, but twenty-seven items remain unaccounted for."

"That sounds like a clerical glitch," Hill remarks.

"Yes, it does," Amy agrees, "but that's just where it starts. I also discovered a hidden file on the Metascience network. It looks like a record of payments. The dates and nuyen amounts agree with the missing twenty-seven items, but the payee names shown in this file do not agree with the corps named on the Purchasing reqs or in the Payables records."

Hill gazes at Amy for several moments, then says, "I'm a little puzzled. What do you mean?"

Amy stares back for several moments, then says, "To the audit staff, it could suggest fraud."

Hill coughs, then sneezes. "I . . . I'm afraid I don't understand."

Bandit wonders if that's a lie. If he'd been able to bring certain items with him, he could probably find out. But he's forced to keep things simple. To watch. Observe. Like a suit. An auditor.

"The suggestion," Amy says, "is that the corps listed in the Purchasing and Payables datafiles are not actually the corps who sold us the twenty-seven items. Those corps merely channeled the money to the corps listed in the hidden files on the Metascience network. That in itself brings up the question of liability, if the items don't perform to spec, but I went a step further. I checked on the corps named in Purchasing and Payables records as well as those in the hidden file on the Metascience network. I discovered that all these are related, and all of them, both sets of corps, are no longer in business."

"Well," Hills says, "corporations do go out of business."

"Every corp that sold us one of the unaccounted-for items? That seems a bit coincidental."

Hill rubs at his brow. His aura shows that he's somewhat more disturbed than before. "Excuse me if I fail to grasp all the intricacies of this," he says. "But let me point out that, as you know, some of the materials we buy originate with, well . . . unusual sources. Some of the people and corps we buy from are only in business long enough to market a limited quantity of a particular substance, then they move on to other things."

"Perhaps you refer to shadowrunners," Bandit says.

Hill hesitates. "I'm not sure what you mean."

"Shadowrunners have been known to market limited quantities of merchandise, then move on to other things."

Hill's disturbance increases. His face seems paler than before. He sneezes, or coughs; one or possibly both. "Damn allergies," he says. He looks to Bandit, and says, "Well . . . I'm sure Ms. Berman's people make every effort to be sure we only buy from legal sources."

"Yes, we do," Amy says. "Prospective vendors are routinely investigated. What concerns me is the possibility that those investigations may have been a little too routine, and that we've paid out money to corps that exist only in name."

"But if we received the actual merchandise . . ."

"I'm not so certain that we did. If our records of payment are wrong, our receiving records could be inaccurate as well. And if something fraudulent is going on, it's entirely possible that whoever's responsible for collecting things off the loading dock is part of it, by which I mean a paid accomplice."

"Don't you think—" Abruptly, Hill turns aside in his chair, coughing harshly, like he might be choking. His face turns bright red. His aura is in turmoil.

"Dr. Hill, are you all right?" Amy asks.

"I'm fine," Hill says, recovering, nodding his head. "I was just going to say . . ."

"Perhaps you should explain," Bandit says, "why you have an account with UCAS Bank. A very large account. Totaling almost three million nuyen."

Hill's expression becomes composed. The reddish hue to his face fades into paleness. Yet, his aura churns with emotion. The dominant emotion seems like fear. Quietly, looking only at Amy, he says, "I wasn't aware that an audit of Hurley-Cooper includes a detailed probe into its employees' private finances."

"Ordinarily, it does not," Bandit says.

"Am I being accused of something, Ms. Berman?"

Amy stares at the floor, then at Hill. Her aura shows almost as much turmoil as Hill's. "No," she says. "Let me apologize for Mr. Hatsumi's abrupt manner. No, you're not being accused of anything. All I'm hoping is that you can shed some light on what we've been talking about."

"Including my personal finances?"

"It's your decision," Amy replies. Her aura reveals her conflict, the clash between feelings of determination and softer feelings, sadness, sorrow, sympathy. "As I said, no accusations have been made. I apologize if anything I've said or done gave you that impression. If you can tell me anything that would help clear things up I'd greatly appreciate it. So would Mr. Hatsumi."

"Yes," Bandit says.

Hill sneezes. "Well," he says, "as for the irregularities in the records, I don't know what I could say. I don't know anything about it. If you think there's been some misconduct on someone's part, then by all means it should be looked into. Personally, I find it hard to believe—"

"So do I," Amy says softly.

This is really hurting her, Bandit realizes.

Hill hesitates, glancing at Bandit, then says, "As for my account at the UCAS Bank, it's not really my account. It's my wife's account. My name is on it because, well ..." Hill's aura ripples with emotion. Fear, uncertainty. "My wife is very ill. She's not. . . . really capable of managing her own money. She inherited the money. It comes from a trust account that pays off in installments. My wife's family was very well off . . ."

Amy stares, blinks her eyes. She seems astonished.

Hill has another fit of coughing, then slowly gets to his feet. "Could we continue this later? I'm not ... feeling very well."

Bandit pushes his spiritual self onto the astral and follows Hill out of the lab, down the hall and into a lavatory. Hill stumbles into a booth, bends over a toilet, sneezes, grunts, and then vomits. He goes on coughing and choking for several minutes. Bandit returns to his body. Amy's shaking his shoulder and urgently whispering his name.

"My god!" she exclaims softly. "I thought—"

"Hill's yarfing up his guts."

"Oh, god."

Amy's very upset.

"Let's get the hell out of here."

Bandit supposes they might just as well. They've found

out what they most need to know. Hill's probably guilty. His astral response to questions about the UCAS Bank account more or less proves that. He's afraid of being revealed as a thief. Probably that stuff about his wife was a lie, too, an explanation invented on the spot, with no basis in reality. It's in the nature of most thieves to lie, when necessary. Thieves don't like to be caught.

Amy leads Bandit out of Hill's office and through the lab to the door to the hallway. "Oh . . . Dr. Phalen. Good morning."

"Good morning, my dear."

The slag who meets them at the doorway is tall and slim, gray-haired, and looks maybe sixty. He smiles in greeting Amy and seems very pleased to see her. Bandit takes a look at his aura. What he sees almost stops his heart.

The aura of a magician is distinctive, immediately distinguishable from the aura of a mundane. All the more so in the case of an initiate, but an initiate can veil his aura, conceal his arcane powers and so "appear" mundane. It becomes second-nature, keeping secrets, veiling the truth. It comes without effort. Only another initiate can see through the veil.

Bandit shifts to his astral perceptions and looks across the astral terrain at Phalen, and finds Phalen looking back at him. In that instant, Bandit sees through the veil and assenses an aura unlike any he's ever encountered. It's brilliant with power, more power than one man should be capable of possessing, and almost wholly devoid of emotion, like a chair or a rock or some other inanimate object. So great is Bandit's surprise that he hesitates, captivated, before catching himself and casting a deliberate mask about his own aura.

Almost simultaneously, Phalen's aura is also deliberately masked, shrouded in a mundane guise that would take strong magic to penetrate. Bandit shifts back to his mundane senses. He finds Phalen gazing at him and smiling.

"This is Mr. Hatsumi," Amy says. "He's with the KFK audit staff."

"Yes, of course," Phalen says, still smiling. "An auditor. I'm very pleased to meet you, sir."

"Yes," Bandit replies. "Very pleased."

The subtext is blatantly obvious. Phalen must know that he's looking at a magician, maybe his equal, maybe not. Bandit wonders what the game is. What does Phalen intend?

Phalen looks to Amy. "Is there anything I can do for you, my dear?" he asks.

"Later, perhaps," Amy says quickly. "But Dr. Hill may need some help. He ran off to the lavatory. I think he may be ill."

"Yes, you're quite right," Phalen replies. His smile turns sympathetic. "I was there when he came in. The poor man hasn't been feeling well all day. I think I may send him home."

Interesting.

Phalen wasn't there when Hill stumbled into the lavatory. Bandit was there and he saw that no one else was in the room. Why would Phalen lie about something of so little consequence?

Could he be hiding things, too?

48

They're back in the rented Toyota Elite and heading along Jerome Avenue before Amy's heart stops pounding. She was absolutely convinced that Dr. Phalen would see right through her stupid ruse and recognize Scottie as an intruder. She'll never do anything this risky ever again! Never!

"Hill was scared."

Amy glances across at Scottie. He looks as calm as a bowl of soysoup, completely unaffected. "You've done things like this before."

"It's in the nature of shadowrunning."

"I can't believe we actually got out through the gate."

"Raccoon can escape any danger. His paws are cunning, and he knows many tricks."

Just what she needs at a moment like this: shaman-talk. Amy hardly knows what to make of what he's saying. She thrusts it all out of mind because this isn't the moment for it. "You said Dr. Hill was scared. What do you mean?"

"I mean Hill was scared."

"Scared of what?"

"He started feeling fear or something like fear when I asked him about the UCAS Bank account. His aura was very turbulent. He seemed disturbed from the start. I think he's hiding things."

"Do you think he's guilty of fraud?"

"Probably."

"Well, was he lying?"

"Almost definitely."

"Scottie . . ." This is frustrating. "From the way you were talking about your abilities, I thought you'd be able to tell me definitely. All you're saying now is that Dr. Hill might be guilty of something or he might not. I knew that going in! If you can't tell me, if you don't know . . . why did we take this risk?"

"You're upset."

"Of course I'm upset!"

"You're shouting."

"I'm sorry! I'm sorry . . ."

"Magic isn't science," Scottie says. "Some people call it art. I could have done some things to Hill to make him give up his secrets, but that would have been dangerous."

"So what are you saying? Tell me again."

"I think Hill has things to hide. He was scared. He probably lied."

"So what do I do?"

"You're the suit. What would a suit do?"

"Hand everything I know to the executive VP."

"So do that."

"I don't want to do that, Scottie. I want to get to the bottom of this myself. At least I thought I did. I kept hoping that Dr. Hill would say something to clear everything up. Do you believe that story about his wife?"

"I don't know."

Amy exhales heavily, feeling not just frustrated but incredulous, too. "Well, I can clear that up for you right now. It's a lie, or a fantasy, or I don't know what, but it isn't the truth. Dr. Phalen's wife is terminally ill. Dr. Hill doesn't have a wife. He never married!"

"You're shouting again."

"I know, I know. I'm just . . ."

"How do you know Hill has no wife?"

"It's in the personnel files."

"Maybe the records are wrong."

Amy can't believe that. Prospective vendors might be investigated only routinely; prospective employees are investigated in depth. Dr. Hill never had a wife. He was lying. There's just no room for any doubt about it. "No," Amy says, shaking her head. "I just can't understand why Dr. Hill would say something like that, something so obviously false, when surely he must know that I could check it out in an instant if I didn't already know."

"Maybe he couldn't think of a better explanation."

What other answer could there be? The big account at the UCAS Bank is his guilty secret. He's been skimming off Hurley-Cooper and she's found out and now he knows that and so naturally he's scared. "I just can't believe he'd do something like this. He's such a nice man. He's a *respected scientist!*"

"What about Phalen?"

"What about him?"

"He lied, too. About being in the lavatory when Hill went there. Phalen wasn't in the room."

"How do you know that?"

Scottie's reply is almost incomprehensible—more shaman talk. Amy struggles to understand. From what Scottie says, it sounds like he traveled out of his body somehow and followed Dr. Hill into the lavatory. That must be what happened when Scottie went as limp as wet noodles. For a moment, Amy had feared that he'd had a stroke and gone into a coma. Now it sounds like some kind of trance ...

But what Scottie says about Dr. Phalen points out the one thing she knows for certain, the thing she's learned, her one small payment for the risks they've taken. People are lying to her. There has to be a reason for that and whatever the reason is, whatever the cause, it can't be good. Two very respectable scientists do not just start telling lies because they're in a mood. Scientists are at least as conscious of their reputations as bankers. Saying the sky is green when in fact it's gray or brown would only make them look foolish and that is the one thing no scientist wants.

"I've got no choice," Amy decides, at length. "I've got to tell what I know. I'm only hurting myself if I delay any further." The longer she waits, the more time she spends looking into this on her own, the greater the chance that she'll be seen as an accessory or just plain incompetent.

"Maybe I can do something," Scottie says.

Amy looks at him. "What do you mean?"

"Let me think about it."

49

The room is rectangular, a uniform platinum gray. There are no furnishings, no pictures, no decor. No windows, no way to tell if it's day or night, no way for Tikki to know for sure how long she's been here. She woke up here a while ago, at least a couple of hours ago. Outside, it must be getting on toward midday. Here in this room, nothing has changed.

The air coming in through the vent in the ceiling carries many scents. Tikki discerns the scents of many two-legs, vague and airy, as if from far away, but none that she can identify. The smell of her own frustration and outrage fills the air, gnawing at her. Like instinct gnaws at her. Battling to control her mind.

Again, on four legs, she walks around the periphery of the room, sniffing where walls meet floor, and wondering which of the panels dividing the walls might conceal a door. Every panel is about the size of a door. Every panel looks and smells about the same. She keeps thinking that she must have missed something, some subtle clue at the very limits of her perception, but she's been around the room more than a dozen times already and discovered nothing new.

One thing is clear: the elf O'Keefe was here. He and one of his female accomplices—not Shaver, Whistle. This tells her that O'Keefe played a part in bringing her here, as if she didn't already know. The thought brings a discontented rumbling into her breath. She would like to drag her claws through O'Keefe's face, down through his chest and belly, and keep tearing at him till only shredded meat remains. She would like to make him die very slowly. Slowly and with much pain.

How does she get out of this place, this cell? That thought has monopolized her attention. She tried the obvious approach. She hurled herself bodily at the walls till cartilage crackled and bones snapped and finally pain conquered instinct, persuading her that brute force alone would earn her nothing, not now, anyway. She managed to dent one of the wall panels and scraped shick out of the floor—that's all. Not worth the price in blood.

Now, she sits with her back to one of the shorter walls, and she thinks some more. Where is she? Why is she here? What comes next? Maybe the idea is to keep her here till she starves to death. That doesn't make much sense, but with two-legs, who knows? With two-legged elves involved, anything's possible.

There must be a way out of this.

Something above her hums. She looks. A voice comes from the ceiling, a strange computer-modulated voice, neither male nor female. "I know what you are," it says. "And I know who you are. And now you're going to pay."

What is this . . .

The words are hollow, a meaningless threat. It's the voice that incites Tikki to anger. The thought of some two-leg speaking to her from the safety of another room arouses her rage. She bares her fangs and roars and batters the walls with her paws. If the creature wants to speak to her, let it come and face her. She may be confined for the moment, but she is far from helpless and she will face any creature, two-leg or four, with just the weapons nature has provided her. What she will not do is listen to two-leg noise.

She fills the room with her own voice, her fury, her menace, her promise to exact a savage vengeance for this outrage—roaring louder and louder—till the voice from the ceiling finally stops.

The silence that follows is more easily endured.

50

The first indication Harman has that something is amiss comes when he feels a stinging at the nape of his neck.

He lifts a hand, and suddenly everything gets very dark.

Then, he's sitting in a chair, a very rigid, uncomfortable chair that seems to have no cushions. It's a macroplast chair with arms, and, for some reason, he can't move. He's several moments struggling with that, trying to lift his hands to rub his eyes. He feels like he's just woken up, but that cannot be. The morning's already past. He was just heading out to lunch when . . . when . . .

Harman pulls his head upright. He's sitting in a small, dark, sparsely furnished room with no windows. He can't move because his wrists and possibly his ankles too are wrapped with thick black straps and fastened tightly to the chair. Another strap rings his chest. What the hell is going on? This is intolerable.

A door opens on his right. A stocky Asian male with eyes like gleaming black marble enters, then steps around to face Harman directly. This man is accompanied by an Anglo male with facial features of a vulpine cast. The Asian looks young; the Anglo a well-kept middle-age. Both wear suits and cool expressions.

"Who the devil are you?" Harman inquires. "Release me!"

"That's not possible," the Anglo replies.

"What the frag do you think you're doing?"

"Only what's necessary," the Anglo says. "You may call me Neil, Mr. Franck-Natali. May I call you Harman?"

"I insist that you release me at once."

"That is not possible."

"You're making a serious mistake."

Several moments pass. Neither of the men seems the least bit impressed by Harman's statements. They are obviously professionals, security ops or specialists in black operations. Harman feels a queasy sensation enter his stomach. He is obviously in a bad situation.

"Neil" inclines one eyebrow, and says, "Let's forego the theatrics, Harman. I'll tell you very simply that you and I have certain similarities. You might say we're both corporate men. We have objectives to meet and superiors who rate us on our performance. In this particular case, I'm forced to be expedient. There are certain things I must know. If you co-operate, you'll soon be back at work and your masters will know nothing of what's transpired."

"And if I refuse?"

"That would be unwise."

"In other words, you'll compel me to speak."

"I'd prefer to have your cooperation, Harman, but if that's not forthcoming I'll be forced to resort to methods I think you'll find unpleasant. Ultimately, you'll tell me what I want to know. It's really just a question of time."

"I will not betray proprietary data."

"That's very commendable, Harman. However, from your perspective, the data I'm primarily interested in is personal, not proprietary. I don't give a damn what you can tell me about Mitsuhama."

Harman hesitates. Only two explanations for this abduction had occurred to him thus far: one, a corporate competitor of Mitsuhama wants to squeeze him for information; or, two, a rival of his at Mitsuhama, perhaps someone with an eye on his job, wants to provoke him into making compromising statements. Neil's remarks seem to indicate that a third possibility exists. "I don't understand."

Neil says, "I'd like you to begin by describing the nature of your relationship with Amy Berman."

Involuntarily, Harman gapes. "Why is that any of your business?"

"You're not here to ask questions, Harman."

"I fail to see what this has to do—" Harman stops abruptly. Another explanation has suddenly come to mind. "You're investigating Amy. You're with KFK International."

Neil shows no response. He glances aside. The Asian steps forward, lays a hand over Harman's left wrist, presses down with the tips of three fingers. For a moment, nothing happens. Harman frowns, perplexed. In the next moment, his left arm is being seared by a fire that streaks up through his shoulder and into his head like an incandescent spike. His whole body jerks with the shock. He shouts. Colors burst in front of his eyes and for what seems like a brief eternity he's quivering at the end of a high-voltage wire. The current radiating throughout his body is excruciating pain. Every nerve ending burns with it.

As the pain subsides at last, Harman gasps and grunts, breathing hard. Vision returns. His left arm is numb, then tingling as feeling returns. "That's merely a sample," Neil says impassively. "My friend understands pain. He can do that to you all night. Your arm may feel a bit tingly, but there's no physical damage. Not yet."

Harman catches his breath, says, "This is heinous."

"Expedient," Neil replies. "Metahumans can take only so much pain. Then the mind begins to rationalize. You've had no training in resistance techniques. I promise you that you'll soon break down. Save yourself the pain."

That would be a good thing to do, Harman supposes.

What Neil says is probably true. A person can take only so much. "What assurance do I have that I'll be released unharmed?"

"I'll leave that for you to decide," Neil replies. "In the meantime, let's get back to Amy Berman."

Yes, of course. That's the point. And the question is how much can he say without compromising Amy or himself? If Neil is in fact with KFK International, might it not be best to tell everything he knows? If Neil is connected in some way with the audit going on at Hurley-Cooper, might it not be best for Amy, for everyone, for him to expound at length on everything he knows about Amy's recent activities? to prove that she's doing everything in her power to further the interests of KFK International?

Of course, if Neil has been sent by Mitsuhama, then every word Harman says, everything he knows, his very relationship with Amy, could be construed or manipulated to appear treasonous.

The Asian steps forward and lays a hand on his left shoulder.

Agony pours through his body.

51

The creature on the display screen strikes Dr. Ben Hill as possibly the queen of all tigers, a dark queen, robed in crimson fur with black stripes. Her resemblance to *panthera tigris altaica,* the Siberian cat, is perhaps only superficial, for she is truly named *bestiaforma mutabilis,* shapeshifter. But these technical terms convey nothing of her majesty or power. She is larger than the Siberian cat and more massively muscled. Her eyes glint darkly in catching the light. She lies now at one end of the room reserved for her, head erect, eyes searching the dull gray space before her like a queen surveying the cell of a dungeon, with regal anger and . . . something more. A resolve.

Germaine asks, "You want me to tell Dr. Phalen we're ready?"

"Yes," Ben replies, "and warm Mr. Tang we'll be starting in a few minutes."

"Yes, Dr. Hill."

"Thank you."

Germaine goes out. Ben looks back across the console controls to the figure on the central display screen. His stomach churns uneasily. Coming face to face with primitive creatures can be disturbing. One always wonders just how great a degree of intelligence lies behind the feral mask. With a shapeshifter especially, that question nags. Does not the ability to transform into a humanlike appearance at least imply a human degree of intelligence? Is it possible that he's participating in the confinement and abuse of a creature that should be regarded as having a stature equivalent to metahumans? The possibility gnaws at him. It's been plaguing him ever since this most recent project of Dr. Phalen's began.

The Weretiger has kept her secrets well. Like her cub. If not for her remarkable crimson fur and reflective eyes, Ben might have wondered if the bountyman Tang had not brought in a mundane animal. She has remained in her four-legged form since arriving, and shown practically nothing of any intelligence she may possess. She's demonstrated primarily animalistic behaviors, making her displeasure with confinement quite apparent. The sheer ferocity of that displeasure was shocking to witness, and captivating, and served to apprise them all of just how dangerous a creature they're dealing with here.

Ben has no doubt that within moments this dark queen could reduce a man to shredded strands of flesh and bone.

They must be very careful.

The door to the control room slides open and Liron Phalen walks in. "Ah, Ben. How is the stomach, my dear fellow?"

"I'm managing."

"I do wish you'd take my advice and go home."

"Work's a better remedy. Did you speak to Amy Berman?"

"Ben, you're really worrying yourself to death. I'll speak to our Ms. Berman later this afternoon. I'm quite sure this little administrative problem will be swiftly rectified."

"She had an auditor with her."

"Yes, so you said." Phalen smiles, then leans against the control console, gazing at the central display. "What are we calling our new matrix?"

"Germaine suggested 'Striper.' "

"Alluding to the subject's eccentric coloration?"

"It seems appropriate."

"Oh, I quite agree. I'm particularly keen, Ben, to see how this Striper compares metagenetically to her offspring. This could have implications that extend far beyond the immediate focus of our work." Phalen pauses to smile, then says, "Shall we begin?"

Ben turns to the console keyboard and taps in several commands. On the display screen, the dark queen is up on her feet and roaring, as if she hears the tapping of the keys and somehow guesses their import. Above her, hidden ducts are now opening and discharging a gas that is both odorless and colorless.

Five seconds later, Striper lies on her side, unmoving except to breathe. Telltales on the control console indicate she is asleep. "No immunity," Phalen says. "Now we wonder whether the Were's fabled regenerative ability will foster the rise of a tolerance."

"Err on the side of caution, Doctor."

"Certainly, Ben."

Life signs remain stable. The dark queen sleeps. They set a research assistant to monitoring the console and go into the next room to prepare for the next step. A small metasurgical team is ready and waiting. A technician helps Ben into a gown and gloves and then an air mask. Phalen suits up similarly.

Ben turns to the two elves, the bountyman Tang and his female associate. "Dr. Phalen prefers that you wait here while we're conducting the procedure," he says.

"It's your show, Doctor," Tang replies. "I'll warn you again that the gas is not always effective, and the tigress is very fast. If she awakens, she could have you in seconds."

Ben's stomach churns some more. He doesn't want to be inside the dark queen's cell when she wakes. Tang's weapons seem feeble compared to Striper's massive fangs and claws. "You're sure you can control her?"

"We got her here, didn't we?" Tang says quietly.

Before Ben can decide how to answer that, Phalen announces he's ready, then they're all turning, moving through the door and into the dark queen's den.

"All right, my good people. Take your places. Quiet, please."

And then they're beginning the procedure to remove metaphysically preserved blood and tissue samples.

52

Candles gleam through a haze of incense slowly curling, rising into the dark. Bandit sits cross-legged, gazing into the astral from the center of his medicine lodge. He has been many hours considering what he will do, trying to anticipate what will come, and making preparations. The time has come for him to begin. He rises with the incense, drifting free of his physical flesh, beyond the boundaries of his lodge, then through the dark fabric of the building around him. He emerges, still seated cross-legged, hovering a few meters above the ground, into the astral twilight at the rear of the building.

People speak of cities as living organisms, but that is deceiving. On the astral plane, the energies of life are clearly perceptible, but the city itself—the crete, the structures—are all dead. The buildings look like computer-generated pics: flat, artificial, illusory.

Yet, every building gleams with the life energies of the thousands of people within it. The astral landscape pulses with that energy, sometimes brightly, sometimes only dimly. Even here, in the heart of the Bronx, amid all these concrete and plastic coffins, nature lives.

Bandit assenses a change in the flowing, fluctuating pulsations of energy, and turns.

A familiar figure emerges from the dark shade of an alleyway. No neophyte's idealized self-image, but rather the astral form of a portly man wearing a black beret and an old green army jacket with many pockets. He calls himself Pug. He follows Dog. He possesses great power. Bandit descends to face him.

"You go to confront a mage?" Pug says.

Bandit nods. "I seek no confrontation. Only information."

"And if you must fight?"

Bandit knows what answer he must give, but hesitates before one as knowing as Pug. Lion is the willing warrior, as is Wolf. Raccoon is not. Bandit forces the words out. "Raccoon fights when he must."

"For what purpose?"

"For blood. For my sister."

"You speak like Wolf."

Bandit shakes his head. "Even solitary Raccoon will turn and fight when his own are threatened. It is in the way of things."

Pug smiles, but the smile quickly fades. "You grow sure in your steps, young shaman. That is well. There is much evil in the plex and you walk a dangerous path. Take care."

"I will."

Pug nods and waits. It is Bandit who must turn to go. Dog never turns from a friend, or even the friend of a friend. It is part of Dog's nature.

Bandit turns and soars high across the skyline. The astral terrain becomes a blur, but he knows where his path leads. He notes the position of the Van Cortlandt Industrial Park and the Hurley-Cooper lab building, then the highway leading north through the sprawl, more or less parallel to the broad expanse of the Hudson River.

An instant passes and then he's hovering just above a dull gray road in front of a large dull gray building, reverberating with primitive violence, radiant and seething with colors of hatred, treachery, and death. Oddly, the sign in front of the building is pale with apathy and indifference. Bandit puzzles, and abruptly realizes he's hovering before the prison for the criminally insane, located in Ossining, just north of Tarrytown.

Too far.

Movement through the astral can be tricky.

The world blurs. Bandit streaks back along his path and stops a hundred meters above a highway interchange. This is where he went wrong. He zips down through the interchange to an exit ramp to local roads that stream toward him in a blur as he rushes ahead, then slow to show him the main entrance to the Riverside Corporate Community, located in Dobb's Ferry. Now he's got it right.

The complex is unusual, flush with the energies of life, an oasis of parkland amid the squalor of the sprawl. Tree-lined streets lead past large houses surrounded by lush lawns. The gleam of life from within the houses is so soft that no more than a very few could dwell within. Only a dean among scientists or a daimyo among suits could rate highly enough to live in a place like this. Amy says that Dr. Liron Phalen has been living here for many years. KFK International provided this place for him as part of the incentive bringing him to Hurley-Cooper Laboratories.

Bandit approaches Phalen's house carefully, finding cover among the trees surrounding the property. The house is big, two stories tall with steep roofs and tall chimneys. Watcher spirits wait at the corners of the roofs. These small creatures look a little like sprites, little elves with butterfly wings, but with horns. Bandit summons one of his own, a small spirit in the form of a raccoon that materializes in his lap, looking up at him with big round eyes.

Bandit gestures at the watchers. *"Distract them."*

"Yes, Master." The spirit streaks upward to nearly a hundred meters above the house and begins taunting the watchers, screaming insults, cursing, all the while making a noise like somebody banging with a hammer on an empty metal drum.

The watchers drift upward, exclaiming, gesticulating.

The astral blurs—Bandit reaches the side of the house in an instant. He slips in through the wall. There are alarms in the wall, sophisticated devices, but they have no life and so no significance to anyone on the astral plane. He enters a spacious room like a living room, so-called, filled with all the usual dead furnishings, but also a number of interesting objects. Vases and bowls and other artifacts, like from a museum, scattered across tables and shelves and the fireplace mantel. All show glimmers and gleamings of magical energies. Bandit considers these artifacts briefly. They are as much a part of the room as the many-paned windows and shaggy carpet, and yet, to him, perhaps only to his aesthetic sense, they seem alien, as if originally from some place unknown to him, a place very far away.

There is a strange character about the room, too. An alienness that goes beyond mere decor, beyond artifacts. A strangeness Bandit can't quite identify. It's like coming to a foreign land, a place beyond the world of the mundane. Maybe that has to do with the fact that the house is occupied by a mage—one of those hermetic types who try to reduce the magnificent of nature to ridiculous artificial abstractions. Or maybe it's something more.

Bandit settles down through the floor in search of a basement, but finds only dark, dusty spaces that may have been abandoned for years. He rises again to ground level, passes through an open doorway and enters a broad hall. A stairway leads to the second level. At the top of the stairs is another hallway, extending off to right and left. Directly across from the top of the stairs is a set of double doors that burn with the energy of a powerful ward.

Powerful wards protect great secrets. Here, Bandit decides, he will find Phalen's special place, his hermetic library, his spell books and scrolls and other arcana.

It's no surprise when a radiant white figure steps out through the doors. Wards are just one form of defense. This will be Phalen's familiar or some other allied spirit charged with guarding Phalen's secrets. Bandit expected this. At first, the spirit takes the form of a woman, a stunning woman in flowing robes, like from out of a fashion vid. Abruptly, though, it transforms into a creature of horror, a monstrous thing with wings and menacing claws, shrieking at him like a bird of prey.

"You do not belong here!"

And then, behind one monster rises a second, a grotesque manifestation like a simsense demon, formed of air and smoke. Bandit feels the force of its magic at once. An elemental spirit. It is clearly a powerful spirit. In fact, both familiar and elemental have much power. The danger is clear.

An ordinary intruder would be doomed.

Bandit draws a handful of herbs and twigs from his pocket and casts it across the hallway, murmuring a single word of power. There is a puff of smoke, a flash of light. The familiar shrieks and grows brighter than before. The elemental swells, expanding toward him like a thriving cloud. Bandit notices the air around him growing thick, constrictive, and then, an instant later, thicker still.

New spells do not always work quite right.

"Watch out, Master!" his watcher calls out, appearing suddenly at his shoulder. *"They're attacking!"*

No kidding.

The familiar screams. Perhaps this is some sort of arcane command. The elemental surges forward, swelling rapidly in size to fill most of the hallway. Bandit exerts his will, breaks free of the elemental's grip and drops down through the floor, into a broad groundfloor hallway.

Inanimate objects like floors and walls have no substance

on the astral, but they are an obstacle to vision and all the other senses, including the sixth sense of magically active beings. That makes them an effective barrier to all forms of magical attack.

Unfortunately, such beings as familiars and elementals are just as capable of penetrating floors and walls as the average shaman. They follow instantly, streaking down from the ceiling.

"Master! Above you!" the watcher cries.

Bandit darts aside, through a wall, into a room like a dining room. He casts a handful of sand across the astral terrain. The magic discharged with the sand attracts swirling streams of vibrant power that instantly coalesce, rising into five near-perfect images of Bandit's aura, his own astral form.

His pursuers come through the wall even as the phony auras arise.

"Master!"

"Quiet."

The watcher falls silent.

Familiar and elemental both hesitate.

Bandit thrusts his flute out before him like a baton, and says, "Go away."

And suddenly he's at the center of a swirling maelstrom of power, a power so potent he feels the hairs standing up along the back of his arms and neck. The familiar's astral form turns blinding with radiant energy. The elemental swells to fill the entire room. The watcher screams with terror. The familiar shrieks. The elemental wails. The magic swirling ever more furiously around Bandit discharges like a fusillade of thunderbolts crashing down from the heavens, and a howling arises that seems likely to rock the house from its foundations.

And, in another moment, all is silent.

The elemental is gone.

Some spells work as they should.

The familiar hovers near one side of the room, no longer looking like a monstrous bird of prey, but rather like an attractive woman garbed in flowing robes. Looking around the room a bit tentatively, as if maybe a little afraid that she is suddenly all alone.

Great power does not always equal skill in magical conflict.

Bandit has brought with him the Mask of Sassacus, which he now lifts in front of his face. As he speaks, the power of the Mask reaches out and wraps around the familiar like a snake, gripping her tightly, permeating her aura with its influence. The familiar resists, but in the end her struggle is useless. "You will obey me."

"Yes ..." the familiar says.

"What is your name?"

"I am ... called Vorteria."

Probably not a true name, but good enough. It doesn't always pay to be fussy. "You will come with me, Vorteria."

"Yes ..."

They rise through the ceiling to the second-floor hallway, to before the double doors that blaze with powerful wards. No doubt the walls around these doors are similarly protected. No doubt the wards were erected by the familiar. Now that Bandit has a moment to scrutinize things, he assenses the kinship between the sorcerous barriers and the familiar's aura. He raises the Mask of Sassacus. "Dispel the wards."

"It is forbidden ..."

"Do it anyway."

The familiar lifts a hand. Power swirls and spreads to cover the doors. The wards flicker and wink out.

"Now we go inside."

"No ..."

"Yes."

The room beyond the door is quite large. The walls are lined with many large impressive books that gleam with astral power and hint of secret knowledge. The bare floor looks made of wood and is marked with several circles used in the hermetic tradition. Bandit knows little of such circles and is careful to stay clear of them. He is far more interested in the large volume lying atop a wooden stand in one corner of the room. That dark secrets are hidden inside this tome becomes obvious to him long before he is near enough to extend a hand toward the volume's astral form. He stops just short of touching it.

The words on the tome's cover are of course illegible. Abstract symbols like letters are impossible to read from the astral plane. That hardly matters. The book is radiant with dark power, so dark that what Bandit assenses inspires him to horror. Images come to mind that twist the fabric of na-

ture, terrifying images, abominations. Rarely has he encountered anything that hinted so clearly of evil, an evil more ancient than humans, and many times more malign than the
most vile of metahumans.

He turns to Vorteria. "What knowledge does this book
contain?"

Vorteria replies, *"It is forbidden . . ."*

"Tell me anyway."

The words the familiar speaks, the things she describes,
are almost beyond comprehension. Bandit's sense of horror
only grows more acute. The watcher is soon clinging to the
back of Bandit's shoulder and whining hideously. *"We must
leave this place, Master!"*

"Yes." It is essential that they leave.

He must speak to They-Who-Watch.

53

The procedure goes quite well. The Weretiger remains suit-
ably unconscious throughout. The blood and tissue samples
are preserved so as to remain viable for a full suite of metabiological tests. Ben will oversee the first series of tests.
Liron Phalen pauses in the outer room to shed his air mask
and surgical garb. He smiles and nods at the pair of elves
specially engaged to serve as the Weretiger's guards.

"All is quiet," he tells them.

"That's fortuitous," says Tang.

The other one softly whistles.

Liron returns to his office. As he steps through the door,
a faint shimmering of the air evolves into the manifest physical form of his ally, Vorteria. *"Forgive me, Master,"* she
says. *"I have failed."*

Her tone is one of great sorrow and dismay. Her aura
shows signs of great disturbance. Liron wonders what could
be the matter. He has not given Vorteria any special tasks to
perform. "My dear . . . whatever are you talking about?"

Vorteria trembles visibly. *"An intruder has penetrated my
master's inner sanctum. He distracted watchful spirits and
banished my master's elemental guard. He compelled me to*

open the wards to my master's library and to describe the contents of my master's book."

Liron hesitates. "Which book?"

"The Roggoth'shoth."

This is a dire occurrence, one that requires a swift, judicious response. Liron steps around to the rear of his desk and sits and thinks. "What can you tell me of this intruder?"

"He has been to the other-planes, Master."

By this, Vorteria refers to the planes beyond the etheric, the higher planes of astral space: the metaplanes. Four correspond to the hermetic elements of air, fire, water, and earth; four others relate to shamanic magic, the realms of man, water, sky, and land. For a magician to reach even the most accessible of these planes, he or she must be an initiate, and no mere beginner. Clearly then, the magician who penetrated Liron's house and subdued his ally must be an initiate of some degree of accomplishment. "How did this man work his magic?"

"He used herbs and twigs, Master," Vorteria replies. *"And a flute."*

The flute could conceivably be used by a magician of any tradition, but the herbs and twigs speak of a shaman, and that is disturbing. It brings back to mind the alleged "auditor" who assisted Amy Berman in questioning Ben Hill. This auditor's aura was masked, something only an initiate can do, and Liron caught a glimpse of the truths the masking concealed. What he saw suggested the eccentricity of spirit that generally indicates a shaman. That made him wonder. Though he knows of a rare few shamans able to find a comfortable niche within the corporate bureaucracy, shamans as a breed usually seem too obsessed with their trinkets and totems to pay heed to anything else.

The question that occurs to Liron now is whether it is possible that this supposed auditor is the one who penetrated his sanctum sanctorum? He taps the keys on his desktop comp that will initiate the program to contact the Metascience Group's senior administrative aide, wherever she happens to be. Germaine's features appear on his screen a few moments later. "Yes, Dr. Phalen?"

"My dear, is it possible that our parent corporation has sent some people to look over our records?"

"Dr. Phalen, I told you," Germaine says, suddenly seeming rather flustered. "I mean, yes. Don't you remember? I told you that. I mean I thought I did. There's a whole army of KFK auditors over at headquarters. That's why Amy Berman's been snooping around—"

"Yes, of course," Liron says, smiling. He merely wanted confirmation. "You're sure they're KFK people?"

"Oh, definitely. I have a friend at headquarters."

"Thank you, dear."

The problem then is not one of Hurley-Cooper's senior executives embarking on a personal crusade, but rather KFK people, auditors, shamans, whatever they may be, stirring things up and becoming far too inquisitive. He will have to do something about this, and about the shaman. The work of half a lifetime depends on it.

Ms. Berman should be a good one to start with.

54

The desk is like polished black marble. The chrome nameplate on the front right corner is like a warning sign: Mercedes Feliz, Executive Vice President. The woman to whom that legend applies sits erectly behind the desk, shoulders back, hands folded on the desktop.

She does not look like a woman with heart. Her stark white hair, cut short in a polished Lectrowave style that pitches radically across her brow, only emphasizes the sharp angles of her narrow-featured face. The lenses of her Porsche datashades are always tuned to nebulon black or chrome-silver mirrors. The face beneath those shades rarely displays any but the faintest of reproving emotions. She wears cutting edge Dunhill UltraMana executive fashions: razor-edged collars, reflective lapels. Her fingernails are like ten little mirrors, honed to knife-like points. Her mouth seems forever set in a disapproving pucker.

But all that, Amy knows, is misleading. Mercedes Feliz is a special sort of suit. Unlike Hurley-Cooper's CEO, Feliz would not demean herself by fawning over the representatives of their parent corporation. She is no one's bootlick. She believes that, yes, the corp must come first, but *her part* of the corporate heirarchy must come first of all, and, given the right cause, she will fight for it tooth and nail.

She understands the importance of people. She knows that people work best for organizations that treat their employees like valued resources.

"You're equivocating," Feliz says. "Unintentionally, I'm sure."

"I'm sorry."

"Just say it, whatever you're trying to tell me."

Amy draws a deep breath, struggles with her conscience. She feels as if she's betraying not only herself, but the employees of Hurley-Cooper, only she can't let herself believe that, not after her visit with Scottie to the Metascience lab. She's been lied to—that's definite. Steps must be taken. "I've discovered evidence," she says, "suggesting that someone in the Metascience Group may be manipulating the Purchasing and Payables system."

"Are you talking about embezzlement?"

Another deep breath. "It's possible that we've been made part of a scheme to improperly purchase controlled materials, including substances of an arcane nature. It's also possible that we've been defrauded out of a lot of money."

"How much money?"

"Possibly as much as thirteen million nuyen."

"Whom do you suspect?"

Stop. Another breath. "First, I want to make it very clear that I'm not accusing anyone specifically. I have no definite proof."

Feliz's disapproving pucker grows more overt. "Amy," she says, "proof is never absolute, and you needn't remind me that you want to be equitable. I'm well aware. Now, get to the point. This is just you and me. Whom do you suspect?"

None of that makes saying it any easier. Amy struggles with her own reluctance, her uncertainties, and the purely selfish wish that this whole mess would just go away, never to arise again. She struggles with the awareness that once the words are spoken they can never be taken back.

"Dr. Hill is the most likely suspect. By which I mean it seems likely that Dr. Hill must be involved in some way. That's my guess, and at this point it's still a guess. As you're aware, Dr. Hill has full administrative authority to approve purchasing requests for the Metascience Group."

Feliz nods. "How did this begin?"

Amy explains about the items purchased but not accounted for, about the mystery file on the Metascience Group computer network, about the corporations paid but no longer extant. Too soon, she comes to what could be the most incriminating fact she's unearthed. "Also, I've learned that an employee of the Metascience Group has a special bank account amounting to about three million nuyen."

"You're referring to Hill?"

"I'd rather not confirm that at this point."

"What makes this account so suspicious?"

"It's a great deal of money, and it's not located with the First Corporate Trust."

"That in itself makes it questionable."

The location of the account would certainly be questionable from the perspective of a KFK auditor. "Yes, I know," Amy says, "and I questioned the person who owns it. The answers I received were less than truthful. Much less."

"That sounds incriminating, too."

"Perhaps it is. I'm still not convinced, and I won't make accusations until I'm convinced."

"Will that be before or after you receive a full confession?"

Amy feels her cheeks flushing with heat. She's being too soft, too compassionate, too determined to be fair—that's what Feliz is saying. Maybe she's right. "Scientists are made and broken on their reputations," Amy says adamantly. "I'm not going to risk ruining someone's career until I'm convinced they've committed illicit acts."

"Proof can never be absolute."

"Yes, I'm aware of that."

"Very well." Feliz lifts a hand to brush briefly at one arched eyebrow, then says, "How do you want to proceed?"

Amy hesitates, a bit anxious to be asked that by the executive VP, but of course obtaining Mercedes Feliz's approval of her tentative action plan is the main reason she's here. A half-hearted and in all probability vain attempt at self-preservation. Or so she tells herself. There's also a small voice in the back of her head that keeps telling her that it's wrong to keep things to herself, that her suspicions should be reported, just because, well . . . things should be reported. Because it's the responsible and even the ethical thing to do. Because she's an officer of Hurley-Cooper and it's her duty to keep her superiors informed. That sounds so much like the voice of a straight suit she hates it.

"You must have some plan," Feliz prompts.

Amy nods, says, "I want to meet with Dr. Phalen, lay it out, everything I've found, and ask his opinion."

"And if he claims ignorance?"

Amy feels a bead of sweat trickling down her side. She feels her heart thumping faster and harder in her chest. If Dr. Phalen can't provide some acceptable rationale for what she's discovered, she's finished. If Phalen's part of some conspiracy and he lies to her . . . "Then I guess I would have no choice but to put it all before Janasova."

"Who will immediately run to the audit staff."

"Yes. I know that."

"Have you considered your own culpability in this?"

Amy nods, then meets Feliz's gaze directly, or at least the glare of her shades. "If I've contributed to someone's effort to defraud Hurley-Cooper, I'll face the consequences, whatever they may be. I'm not going to try to cover this up. That's why I'm here, that's why I'm telling you all this. I want you to know that I made the discovery, and that I'm doing everything I can to get at the truth."

"Of course, if Tokyo decides you're to blame, I may not be able to save you."

"I know that."

Feliz nods, just slightly. "Then let's concentrate on what must be done. I agree, question Dr. Phalen. His is the responsibility, even if the routine administration of the Metascience Group falls to Dr. Hill. Insist on a meeting at once. Invoke my authority at your discretion. Meanwhile, I'll consider what I might do to research this matter further."

"Research it how?"

"Have you any suggestions?"

Amy hesitates, feeling a warm flush rising up the back of her neck. Only one thought comes to mind, the one thought she would never dare say aloud. She could talk to her brother. Scottie probably knows some shadowrunner who would eagerly dig up dirty secrets on anyone she might name. "I'm sorry, no," she says. "No suggestions."

Feliz nods.

Meeting concluded.

55

Once the door slips closed behind Amy Berman, Mercedes Feliz reaches under her desk to touch the print scanner beside her knee. The bottom right drawer to her desk slides open. The Fuchi-Dektron Admonisher set into the drawer informs her that no one is attempting to eavesdrop on her office, and, if they are, they're listening to the Brandenburg Concerto No. 1 by Bach, that or white noise. The display on her Sony palmtop confirms what it told her first thing this morning, that no one has attempted to compromise the Admonisher.

She has no absolute proof that Enoshi Ken or the KFK auditors have made any attempt to monitor her activities, but as she told Amy Berman just moments ago no proof is ever absolute.

How Amy Berman discovered that some employee is maintaining an account at a bank other than the First Corporate Trust is anyone's guess. She must have stumbled over it somehow. She's far too resolute in her own brand of ethics, too much the humanitarian, to ever engage in any flagrantly illicit activity such as might reveal hidden bank accounts. It's her greatest weakness. It's also the quality that makes her of special value to Hurley-Cooper Labs.

She's like glue—set and stubborn—determined to hold things together, to keep people moving in the same direction. She's a motivator and a negotiator and an efficient executive. She's too valuable an asset to risk losing because of some fool's attempt at petty larceny. This discovery indicative of fraud must be costing her.

It might well cost her a career.

Mercedes jacks into her palmtop and brings up her security files. Just as no proof is absolute, no person employed by Hurley-Cooper Labs or any other corporation is absolutely virginal. In the Sixth World, such people do not exist. Everyone has at least one small blemish somewhere in their record, and that includes not only herself but the people, both scientists and administrative staff, who work for the Metascience Group.

For the good of Hurley-Cooper, not to mention her own career, Mercedes has made use of such resources as she has to delve into the backgrounds of those who work in the most proprietary areas.

She scans her lists. Drs. Liron Phalen and Ben Hill are about as clean as the average person. Phalen changed corps once in violation of contract. Hill once got drunk and crashed his car into a neighbor's garage. A few other individuals in the Metascience Group are reputed to have various affiliations, through friends or family, that might be deemed questionable. Mercedes loads a select group of names including those of Phalen and Hill onto a datachip, then jacks out and keys her desktop.

Two minutes later, Zach Wanger comes in. His official title is Assistant Director for Site Security. His true responsibilities involve more than electronic surveillance, alarms, and uniformed guards. No one would guess it, at a glance. He looks rather like a good-time boy, grown up but still a child, always ready to party. Mercedes puts the datachip on her desk and gestures for Wanger to take it.

"What's this?"

"You'll find a list of people on that chip," Mercedes explains. "I need background information on every one of them. Pay particular attention to finances. I want to know what they're worth, where their assets are invested, and where their money comes from. I want any large inflows of funds tracked back to the point of origin."

"How large is large?"

"We'll say fifty thousand nuyen."

"How soon do you need all this?"

"Immediately."

"Crash priorities cost nuyen."

"You've got a budget. Use it."

56

As she wakes, Tikki hears a murmur of voices too vague and too distant for words to come through clearly, and a soft thump like that of a door slipping closed. The air she breathes stinks of two-legs and something else, some chemical, swiftly fading away.

Muscles twitch, one massive paw lashes out.

Someone shouts, "Get out! *GET OUT!*"

The bare room of platinum gray has changed. One of the wall panels has become a door and is waiting, not closed, but wide open. A pair of two-legs in long white coats are battling each other to get through the opening. Tikki lunges up and hurls herself across the room. Before she can strike, the two-legs have gone a step further and the door snaps shut in her face.

She rams it, staggers sideways, abruptly sits. Intense pain. Water floods her eyes. Her rasping breath rises into a throaty rumbling as the fractured bones in her chest knit back together. She sneezes violently. A little blood slips from her nose, splatters the floor. The pain is soon gone, like the water in her eyes.

The two-legs escaped her this time, but now she knows where the door is. She considers the door, then moves to sit beside it, her flank against the wall.

Time passes.

The voice from the ceiling speaks again. It's strange, metal-toned, computer-modulated, neither female nor male. "I know what you are and who you are," it says. "You're Striper. You're a killer. You get paid to kill people. You work for the yakuza and the triads. You're a real chiller thriller. How do you like your room so far?"

Tikki bares her fangs and roars.

More noise comes. "Sometimes you kill people for free. You must enjoy it. You must like killing. I bet it gives your life meaning. It's how you know you're alive, by killing people."

Tikki flicks her ears irritably. Listening to this noisy two-

leg is like having a cloud of flies buzzing incessantly around
her head. She'd stand up and roar again, but she realizes
there's no point. She's on a one-way comm line. She's totally in the blind. Nothing she does is going to have any dis-
cernible affect.

"I wonder if you know how many you've killed."

Tikki bares her fangs, mimicking a human smile.

57

As the subway roars out of the tunnel passing beneath the
East River, the world beyond the grime-smeared windows of
the train changes from black to colors of brown and gray.

Bandit watches the dark clouds, the passing buildings, the
throng jammed into the subway car around him. Everything
he sees and hears adds to his concerns. The afternoon has
turned dark. The landscape of the city bears the scars and
open wounds of decades of careless neglect and violent
abuse. The people immediately around him struggle to contain nervousness and fear.

There is danger ahead. Bandit can feel it waiting, lurking,
perhaps around the next corner. Amy's problem involves far
more than ordinary suits scagging their corporate benefactor.

The train comes to a thundering, shrieking halt at Smith
Street. A brief walk brings Bandit to the Brooklyn water-
front. He turns down an alleyway between two ancient brick
and mortar buildings. Halfway along, amid mounds of fes-
tering garbage and the cast-off remnants of generations past,
he comes to a doorway.

In the shadow of the doorway stands a large figure, an
ork. His name is Grinder. He follows Shark. His face is as
hard and expressionless as a nail. His coat is long and black.
The fetishes hidden in his pockets, but clearly visible on the
astral plane, burn with power. He speaks in a flat monotone.
"Why do you come?"

Bandit replies, "I must speak to the old one."

"There is danger."

"Yes."

A moment passes.

"You may enter."

The door swings inward on silent hinges grown black with grease and grit. The door and the walls around it are imbued with powerful wards. One step beyond the doorway is another door, and, to the left, a narrow stairway. To enter this place unasked, even for one like Bandit, is to invite certain death.

Bandit turns and heads up the stairs. He has been here only a few times before, but he knows the secrets of this place are many, the things of interest and of value innumerable. The temptation to investigate these secrets, perhaps take certain things back to his lodge, examine them, and learn what there is to learn is intense, but Bandit knows he must resist. They-Who-Watch would catch him at once, even as he reached out his hand. He will learn far more, in the long run, by practicing patience.

Four stories up, the stairway ends at a narrow door. Bandit reaches out for the knob, but the door swings open, untouched.

Beyond the door is the roof, maybe fifteen meters across and twice as deep. At the rear of the roof is a small shack that seems made of panels scavenged from macroplast crates. The shack has only half a roof and three walls. The interior glows with the soft orangey radiance of a small fire. A smoky trail of incense rises from the fire to the dark clouded sky above.

The interior walls of the shack are hung with hides, drums, knives, wands of bone, masks, and medicine bags. The chests and boxes positioned along the rear wall of the shack are filled with every manner of fetish: minerals, herbs, animal parts, bits of fur and feather and hair, small stones, twigs, crystals, and more.

Old Man sits cross-legged on a rug, facing the fire from the rear of the shack. His thin gray hair flows over his shoulders; his clothes seem made of natural leather. He wears necklaces and beads and bones and looks vaguely Amerind. The medallion at the base of his neck bears the likeness of a black bird. This is Raven, the transformer, the living contradiction. "You again," Old Man says in a voice as dry as sand, as creaky as old wooden boards, and yet vibrant with power. "Let an old man get some rest," he says. "Go away."

Bandit pauses at the edge of the rain- and grit-spattered

rug that marks the limits of the old one's medicine lodge. Quietly, he says, "I must speak with you."

"I'm just an old man. Don't come to me looking for answers. If I ever had any, I probably forgot them before you were born."

Old Man is sometimes cranky, especially when he wants to sleep. Like Raven, he can also be greedy and selfish. Bandit understands. The shaman must find his own path. It is not Old Man's path to do what another must do. He offers help where help is needed, but only when it is needed very badly, and only when he desires to offer help. When he thinks it's right to help. Bandit sits cross-legged at the edge of the rug and waits. He will wait as long as he must.

"Come into the lodge," the dry, creaky voice says.

By then, it seems like night. The sky is near-black and the dirty lights of Brooklyn gleam through the looming dark, and the fire inside the lodge glows a brooding red. Bandit crosses onto the threshold of the rug and sits facing Old Man from across the fire.

"You came here to tell me something," Old Man says. "What do you think you want to tell me?"

"I found something."

"What kind of something?"

Bandit hesitates, then says, "Monstrous evil."

The words seem to make the danger real, realer than before. Bandit isn't sure what danger the evil presents, but he knows it is threatening. He can feel it. Somewhere in the dark. A powerful presence that perhaps watches him at this very moment from beyond the boundaries of Old Man's medicine lodge. "What kind of evil?" Old Man says. "What do you think you've found?"

"It's a book."

"What book?"

"The *Roggoth'shoth*."

A long time passes. The red of the fire grows more intense. The column of incense curling upward swells to fill the lodge. Old Man begins softly chanting, rhythmically tapping a small drum clutched in his lap. Bandit feels the magic happening long before he has any idea of where it's leading. He feels the world of the medicine lodge changing. He feels the power rising like a tide.

"What do you know of *Roggoth'shoth*?" Old Man says.

"I know the book holds evil," Bandit says.

"You know nothing."

The smoky incense becomes thick, obscuring all from sight.

"Open your senses."

When Bandit looks, he is in another place, looking down on a large room lined with old books and radiating power. At the center of the room stands an old man with a long gray beard. He wears a hat shaped like a cone and a long dark robe inscribed with mystic symbols. With the glowing tip of a radiant wand, he writes symbols in the air. The symbols speak. *"I am the mage Penticlese . . . The phenomena described in this text, the knowledge that I now relate, comes to me from the Ancients . . . The dark ages of our forebears . . .*

"Know that we are doomed . . . That worlds upon worlds exist of which mortal man cannot conceive . . . That beyond the threshold of darkness lies the greatest horrors . . . The Vault of Roggoth'shoth."

"Do you know this place?" Old Man says.

"I have never been here," Bandit says.

"What do you see?"

Bandit describes what he sees.

"What do you see in the symbols?"

The symbols waver and blur, swell to fill his vision, and then form images. A passageway into darkness, greater and greater darkness, till finally all is black and a pinpoint of light appears somewhere far ahead. As this light comes nearer, it grows. It becomes a brilliant white figure, the image of his sister, Amy. "You shamed me," she says. "You and your shaman's ways. You embarrassed me in front of my friends, in front of our parents. You made me wish I could curl up and die. Sometimes I laid awake all night crying."

"I'm sorry."

"You never knew the truth. You didn't care."

"Now I know."

"Do you? Do you really? Can you say it?"

It is like the first test of an astral quest. He comes before the Dweller on the Threshold only to be confronted by some secret out of his past. Nothing can be hidden from the Dweller. Not even the most personal, most closely guarded secret.

What the Dweller speaks of is plain. Bandit knows to what it refers. He knows what answer he must speak. He struggles to get the words out through his mouth. "My sister . . . Amy . . . She loves me. *She has always loved me.* She wants only for me to return that love."

"And will you?"

"I will try."

The Dweller vanishes from sight.

Abruptly, Bandit feels himself moving forward, hurtling through places uncounted and unknown. Coming to a place where darkness rules and shadows lurk, where malignant shapes flicker at the corners of his eyes and danger looms from barely an arm's length away.

"Where are you?" Old Man says.

"I do not know," Bandit replies.

"What do you see?"

Bandit describes it.

"Look into the shadows."

When Bandit looks he sees a murky human shape moving toward him. At first, it seems all shadow and dark, but then Bandit sees deeper. He sees the power within, the dazzling power of a thousand souls, all burning with the radiant purity of life energy. And then he sees deeper still. Within the dazzling aura of life lurks a darkness blacker than black, a malignant core, feeding on life itself.

The horror comes nearer. Bandit feels himself shaking with fear. Abruptly, he's hurtling away from the core of darkness at a speed beyond comprehension, and still the horror comes, pursuing him to the very threshold of the metaplane, and beyond. Claws reaching out to snare him, tearing at him, reaching inside him . . .

Bandit's senses dim. He feels himself swaying. He finds himself sitting before Old Man's small fire, and his head aches, and his heart thumps in his chest. He feels the danger lurking beyond the boundaries of the medicine lodge, and he shivers.

"What do you know of evil?" Old Man says.

Bandit considers long, and says, "I know its name. I know it comes from beyond the threshold. That it preys on life. Feeds on life. Steals souls."

Old Man closes his eyes. "What will you do?"

"I don't know."

Old Man nods. "The shaman's path is hard to know. I remember a long time ago I heard two men talking. One claimed that Raccoon shared in the Eagle spirit, just as all men share in this spirit. The other man said that Raccoon is only a thief, just as all men are thieves. I remember my father once told me that nature is very powerful, but sometimes even nature needs help. You decide who's right. I'm just an old man. I don't have any answers."

Bandit considers, and says. "Good and evil are both part of nature."

"Maybe that's your answer."

Bandit ponders, and says, "It's in the nature of good to oppose evil. To fight it. Even to destroy it."

"If that's what you think," Old Man says, "maybe you're right."

Bandit wonders. Maybe this time Raccoon must bare his teeth and go for blood.

58

"Hey. Doobies."

Monk opens his eyes. A pair of orks are leaning down into his face and grinning. They have red glaring eyes and really big fangs and they seem kind of amused. Their names are Erin and Paige, two of Minx's friends. Monk gives her shoulder a squeeze. She lifts her head from his lap, looks up and says, "Oh! Wiz! How'd you find us?"

Erin says, "Poochie found you."

That's the other name for the Prince of Darkness, the big reddish-black Doberman Pinscher with the red glaring eyes, standing there beside Paige. At the mention of his name, Poochie snarls viciously, like he wants to tear something apart. Poochie makes Monk a little nervous.

Minx giggles. "Which way to the old subway tunnel?"

"This way."

Monk stands and stretches. He's stiff. He feels like he's slept for days. Maybe all day. He isn't exactly sure what happened. Things got kind of confusing after ... After ... something or other. He and Minx walked and crawled through a lot of tunnels and kind of got lost. He started feeling really tired and so did Minx, so they sat down to rest and fell asleep. Minx must've called Erin and Paige on her headfone.

Just down the tunnel a ways is a steel mesh that leads to another passage that ends in an old subway tunnel with reddish rusty rails. Erin and Paige stop abruptly. Paige motions with her head back the way they came. "We're going to feed the Master."

That's what it was: the Master.

"Oh, okay," Minx says. "Kintama, *omaes.*"

"Sure," Erin says.

They walk on, Erin and Paige and the Prince of Darkness in one direction, Monk and Minx on through the old subway tunnel. Once the orks' footsteps fade away, Monk says, "What does that mean? Kintama."

Minx smiles. "Oh that means 'balls.' "

"Balls?"

"Golden balls."

"Yeah?"

"You booty," Minx says, grinning at him. "Haven't you ever heard the old saying? Beware the golden balls."

"Who said that?"

"How should I know?"

Monk scratches behind his ear, wondering, then says, "It kinda sounds like this thing I read once. By this guy Mark Twain. Mr. Bloke's Item, it was called. It ended with this warning. 'Beware the golden bowl.' "

"What does that mean?"

"I don't know. Twain didn't know either."

Minx giggles. "It's just another mystery of our age."

"I guess."

They come to a rusty reddish door marked UTIL. It squeals as Minx pulls it open. The squarish passage beyond fades into a reddish haze. Maybe twenty meters into the haze, two figures appear. They look like they're wearing combat armor. Monk puzzles.

"Oh, no," Minx whispers.

"Blast 'em, kid!" one of the figures shouts.

Minx shrieks, *"Run, you booty! RUN!"*

They turn and run. Automatic weapons clatter and roar. Something explodes. Monk feels bits of things like maybe grit and dirt spraying the back of his head and jacket. Minx suddenly seizes his wrist and tugs him across the old subway rails, and the ground beneath them abruptly disappears.

They fall.

Maybe two or three meters. It's more of a surprise than anything else. Monk shouts. Minx clamps her hand over his mouth, tugs him up and pulls him ahead, running again. They're in a winding passage that seems chopped out of raw reddish rock.

"Who are those slags?" Monk asks.

"Killers!" Minx blurts. "Keeping running, booty!"

No drek.

59

Harman doesn't answer any of his phones. Amy supposes that he's in a meeting or some other place where he can't talk, and it's probably just as well. She sits back in her desk chair and exhales deeply. She needed a break, a moment that had nothing to do with Tokyo auditors and fears about fraud and ruined lives, such as her own, but she shouldn't be wasting time like that. She should be on the phone to Dr. Phalen, requesting an immediate interview, insisting on it, so she can present her discoveries and ask his opinion.

She swings around in her chair to look through the wall of windows spanning the rear of her office: the subtle grays of early evening, the golden wash of light filling New Bronx Plaza, the riverfront, the fountains, the condoplexes, the unfinished arcology. She must call Phalen now, like she told Mercedes Feliz she would. She'll need the Executive VP on her side if the wind doesn't blow her way.

"Stop vacillating," she tells herself.

Amy straightens up in her chair, but before she can turn back to her desk, something catches her eye.

For a moment, she isn't sure what she's seeing—a bird, a missile, a meteorite—a dark patch coming through her windows, coming straight for her nose. Involuntarily, she jerks back, feet thrusting at the floor. The back of her chair bangs against the back of her desk. She stiffens, gasping for air, then gapes.

The dark patch resolves into a hole, like a hole in the

ground, in bare earth, but hanging in the air perhaps a meter in front of her face.

For possibly the first time in her career, Amy remembers the PanicButton under her desk. She's hit it half a dozen times with her knee, completely by accident, only to look up in surprise when a squad of armed guards came bursting into her office. Now she wishes she could reach it, reach it without being obvious about it. She has no doubt that she's witnessing some sort of arcane phenomenon.

Her heart hammers.

A figure appears, head rising from the hole. It looks like an animal, dark and furry, kind of like a raccoon. It crosses its forelegs on the edge of the hole, and says in an oddly pitched voice, "Stay away from Phalen. He's dangerous."

Amy gapes. "W-what?" she stammers.

Her voice lilts upward about a thousand octaves. The figure gazes at her, scratches its head, then says, "Stay away from Phalen—"

"Who are you?" Amy blurts.

"Me?" The figure cocks its head to one side and scratches its brow, seeming puzzled. "I'm just another creature of quicksilver and shadow."

And then it's gone, vanished.

Quicksilver? Amy stares.

She's a good five minutes catching her breath and collecting her wits. She remembers Scottie's lifelong obsession with raccoons, and wonders. Is that just a coincidence? Does this apparition warning about Dr. Phalen have something to do with Scottie?

She remembers a trideo show called *The Shattergraves* from a few seasons past. It enjoyed a brief but intense popularity on account of its hero-magician, who might have stepped out of a Vashon Island catalogue. Even her aide Laurena was talking about him. Aragon, he was called. In the show, he had a helper, a kind of spirit. The spirit's name was Quicksilver. It wasn't very bright. Aragon would sometimes send Quicksilver to deliver messages. The spirit seemed able to find almost anyone, no matter where they might be, in just the wink of an eye.

If that bears any resemblance to the way magic really works, and the abilities of spirits, then Scottie might have sent this creature resembling a raccoon to warn her about Dr. Phalen.

But, why?

It doesn't make any sense. Dangerous? Dr. Phalen? Even if he's personally responsible for defrauding Hurley-Cooper, Amy can't believe that the man would make any attempt to harm her personally. This is not some violence-prone street-person with a long criminal history. This is a man who's devoted his life to science. A man who's always spoken to her, to everyone, in her experience, with the manners of an Old World gentleman: polite to a fault, kind and considerate, and rather charming. Dangerous? That's just not possible.

Amy remembers there were several *Shattergraves* episodes where Quicksilver got Aragon's messages confused. Maybe that's what's happened here. Scottie couldn't have meant that Dr. Phalen poses any real danger to her. He must have meant something else.

But what?

Phalen's in danger, so stay away? She's some minutes trying to work it out. The only thing she can think of is the possibility that she's being watched. Scottie seemed to think so. But if she's under surveillance by KFK operatives, then she should continue doing what she's doing. That's the only hope she has of saving her career. If the surveillance comes from other quarters ... she isn't sure what that could mean.

Her desktop bleeps.

"Dr. Phalen on One," Laurena says.

"Thank you."

Amy hesitates, shakes her head and taps the Connect key. Dr. Phalen's pale features appear on her display. He smiles and says, "Good afternoon, my dear. I hope I'm not interrupting some high-level executive function."

Amy can't help smiling, despite her worries. "No. In fact I was just getting ready to call you."

"Why, that's splendid," Dr. Phalen says, but then his smile turns sober. "Would I be correct in presuming that you wish to discuss the matter you brought before Ben this morning?"

"As a matter of fact," Amy replies. "I'm sorry, but I can't help thinking that Dr. Hill was not being entirely candid with me. At least that was my impression. He seemed, well ... you know how the meeting ended. And he seemed somewhat upset almost from the start."

"I'm certain it must have seemed that way," Dr. Phalen says in a quiet, almost intimate tone. "Ben's under a great deal of pressure, my dear. Stress. All stress related. I'm sure you noticed the coughing and sneezing. Entirely psychosomatic. He has such great hopes for our current track of research. I'm afraid of how he might react if things don't work out."

This is something Amy hadn't known about. If Dr. Hill really is ill ... "Is he receiving medical attention?"

"My dear, try to persuade a doctor to see a doctor. It's quite impossible. However, I'm keeping a close eye on our friend. You can be sure that I'll intervene before Ben approaches anything resembling a crisis situation."

Amy supposes she should feel reassured. Dr. Phalen does of course hold a medical diploma in addition to his many other credentials. But how does that affect her problem? "Well ... I'm sorry if I've made things worse for Dr. Hill. That wasn't my intention. I hope he'll be all right."

"Ben's stronger than he seems, my dear. He'll come around."

"I'm sure you're right."

Dr. Phalen smiles sympathetically.

"I'd like to come by and speak to you in your office."

"You're always welcome, dear. Unfortunately, I'm at home. My wife has taken a turn, a small one, but I feel I should stay at hand until this incident is resolved."

"Oh ... oh, of course."

It's well known that Dr. Phalen's wife is gravely ill, terminal. She's been lingering for years. Some slow, wasting illness. That's what made Dr. Hill's tale about his wife being ill and therefore incapable of managing her money—the three million in the hidden account—seem so incredible.

If you're going to lie at least be creative.

"However, if this is important, and I'm sure it must be, given what you've said already, you're certainly welcome to come by the house."

Amy hesitates. Visit Phalen at his private residence? Not a good idea. A meeting held that far beyond the normal bounds of the corporate milieu could be seen as conspiratorial, and therefore incriminating. There's also the fact that she would be intruding in the man's home, when, for all she knows, his wife could be in the process of dying.

"Oh, I couldn't possibly intrude like that," Amy says. "When do you expect you might be returning to your office?"

"Possibly later in the evening," Dr. Phalen says. "Why

don't I call you, my dear, when I'm sure my wife has stabilized."

Amy supposes she has no choice. Insisting on a meeting this instant would be outrageous, cruel and inhumane. She'll just have to wait. For what it's worth, her desktop will automatically save the voice-record of this phone call into her permanent database, which should at least justify the delay.

"That will be fine," she says, struggling to sound content. "And if there's anything I can do in regard to your wife, please don't hesitate to say so. I know she's very ill. I do hope that things work out for the best."

"You're too kind, my dear," Phalen replies. "Thank you."

They close the connection. Amy sits back and sighs.

Always another worry.

60

Tikki scratches the back of her neck, flicks her ears irritably, and abruptly comes to her feet. She's restless, she can't sleep. *She can't stand being trapped in this dull gray room anymore!* It's been hours and hours—at least a day. Thoughts of her cub keep coming to mind, and the voice from the ceiling is a plague, always returning, always droning. It speaks of killing and death and what a monster she is and what she deserves, and what she's going to get in payment for her crimes. The message is very clear. She's going to be held here and tortured with this noise, with her own unanswered questions, her doubts and uncertainties, until she's driven insane.

She sniffs at the floor. Nothing. Nothing she hasn't smelled before.

Things were simple in her youth. She was strong, gifted with nature's weapons, and everything that was not tiger or Weretiger was prey. Some prey was dangerous, some not, but she knew her place in the world, both in the wild and in the realm of two-legs. Who could possibly doubt it? Is she not obviously a predator? born to hunt? to kill? What difference could it make if the prey has two legs or four? Her mother taught her how to hunt on two legs as well as on four, and how to use guns, and how to beat locks and alarms, and other things—skills she would need to survive.

It came as a shock when she realized that two-legs would pay her money to hunt other two-legs, and it only went to prove what her mother had often told her. Two-legs prey on each other. They are betrayers, deceitful and vile, traitors to their own kind. They will do anything to save themselves, to advance themselves, or to earn themselves profit. They value little but their own lives, power, sex, and nuyen.

Tikki came to ask herself why should she suffer the deprivations of life in the wild when she could hunt two-legs in the city and enjoy an easy lifestyle?

The voice from the ceiling speaks. "He was in Philadelphia to visit some friends. In the evening, he went to a bar called Numero Uno. You were waiting there in the alley. You shot him once in the foot, then you shot him twice in the head and twice in the chest. Then you took his motorcycle."

The word "Philadelphia" snares Tikki's attention. Her visit to that city two years ago was not a pleasant one. She went there in search of a man, intending to repay him for trying to kill her. She ended up in the thrall of a powerful mage. She still isn't clear about how that happened, but she knows for a fact that the mage manipulated her perceptions, her thoughts, and many things she did. The experience persuaded her that she'd had enough of two-legs, maybe forever, and sent her north with Raman, her cub's sire, into the wilds of Maine.

Did she kill some slag in a Philadelphia alley, then take his chopper? She remembered something about a slag and an alley, possibly involving an ork, but she isn't sure what happened. She's certainly done things like what the voice is talking about. Many two-legs have paid her to do things like that.

And so what? Is there any difference between killing a deer for food to eat and killing a two-leg for a motorcycle to ride? One is obviously survival. The other?

"That was my son in that alley," the voice says. "When you killed him, you took everything from me that meant anything."

Tikki wonders what that's supposed to mean.

It almost sounds like grief.

61

"My point, Liron, is that this shapeshifter is a step up the intellectual scale from most other paranormal species. It isn't just that she looks human when she shifts. Her mind may be entirely alien to us, but I think she has an intelligence equivalent to any metahuman. And I think she should be regarded as having the same rights as metahumans."

As he finishes speaking, Ben forces himself to look back to the screen of his desktop. His stomach is churning and his nasal passages are nagging, and he already knows what Liron Phalen's going to say. They've had this discussion before, always with the same result. Liron gazes at him from the screen for a few moments, then says, quietly, "Our research requires that we make certain sacrifices, Ben."

Ben nods. "Yes, of course. I know."

"You shouldn't let yourself be troubled by questions like this. We have no definitive evidence that shapeshifters are intelligent. As of this moment, we have only our preliminary test results to indicate that our matrix—Striper?—may be more than an unusually large, oddly colored, but otherwise mundane tiger. You're upsetting yourself to no good purpose."

There's no arguing with the facts. The dark queen has kept her secrets well. Striper has said nothing intelligible, and has demonstrated nothing of the shapeshifter's abilities since arriving here at the labs. Ben struggles to develop a new thesis on the subject of Striper's intelligence, but with Liron facing him from the display screen his mind comes up a blank, as surely it must. He's in an untenable position. Why doesn't he just get out?

"Continue with the testing program as we discussed."

"Yes, of course." Ben nods.

The screen goes blank.

Ben takes a hypoinjector from his top left desk drawer, puts the unit's head to the side of his neck and fires. The solution that gushes into his bloodstream is part decongestant, part antacid, part tranq. It's all that keeps him going.

He taps the keys on his desktop to dial up the group's senior administrative aide. "Is the team assembled yet?"

"They're getting ready right now, Dr. Hill," Germaine replies.

"I'm on my way."

The walk to Lab 6E takes only moments. The prep room seems crowded with people, all looking to him, waiting for him to get started. In addition to colleagues and techs, there's the bountyman Tang and now, not one, but two associates, also elves, both of them women.

Tang gestures toward the inner room, once part of a sleep research lab. "Keep that room flooded with your gas, Doctor. And keep that door closed."

Ben nods. "Yes, that's the procedure."

"It was the procedure last time. Two of your people almost didn't make it out. If you don't keep the atmosphere saturated, the tigress is going to tear you apart."

Ben nods, stomach lurching. "We're all clear on that now."

"I do hope so."

Ben turns and steps into the central monitoring room. Germaine is there at the main console, facing the display screens. The dark queen displayed on the main screen looks not only awake, but keenly alert. She sits erect on her haunches, facing the room's only door from just beside that door. Her vital signs are strong. "Administer the gas," Ben says.

"What? Do what?"

Germaine gazes at him with an expression like astonishment. Ben realizes his error. He feels half asleep, like he's in a bad dream. "I'm sorry, Germaine," he says. He struggles to present a smile. "I guess I'm too used to you pushing all the buttons around here."

"Who, me?" Germaine slowly smiles. "I'm just a comp aide and a clerk."

"Dr. Phalen considers you indispensable."

"Well, he's the boss."

"Yes."

Ben taps the keys to flood the inner room with gas. When he looks again to the screen, the dark queen is gazing straight up at the ceiling as if she knows the gas is coming. She must smell it, of course. The tiger's olfactory sense is several magnitudes greater than that of any metahuman, greater than any metahuman could truly comprehend. Ben wonders what it must be like to be able to track prey through half a million acres of forest by sense of smell alone. He wonders how the world of metahumans would look to one with senses so keen? Could one ever lie to a creature with such insight?

Striper slumps to the floor.

"Want me to call Dr. Phalen?" Germaine asks.

"No," Ben replies. "Liron's attending to other matters."

"Oh, that's right," Germaine says. "He went home."

Ben nods. "Yes."

He steps into the prep room to suit up.

62

The stairs leading into the basement are dark and dusty, but Liron Phalen does not bother switching on the lights. His eyes have come to accommodate low levels of light. A benefit of his condition.

The basement is filled with boxes and crates, artifacts of expeditions made in his younger days, when he ranged far and wide in search of universal truths. How ironic that his search for truth should have led him, not to the essential nature of life or existence, but into a lifelong battle with the degenerative effects of *metamycobacterium leprosis,* a new and more virulent Sixth World form of leprosy. How sad that so much of his time should be spent, not seeking the greater truths of the arcane, but attempting to cure the small, dark truth eating away at his flesh.

He pauses near one end of the basement. From certain of the cases and crates around him come sibilant whispers and scratchings. They are like the words of the ancients, often so vague and faint as to be beyond comprehension, and yet taunting with the promise of secret knowledge. In this case, of course, the whispers only remind him of his early failures. He suppresses a sigh of sorrow and regret.

But now Vorteria draws near, rising through the basement floor, the faint shimmering of her physical presence resolving into the radiant splendor of her full physical manifestation. *"Two of the hunters approach, Master,"* she says. *"They are the ones called Erin and Paige."*

Hallowed vessels conveying the essence of life.

Liron bends and pulls open the heavy latch crossing the trap door set into the concrete floor. Momentarily, the door rises, swinging back. One, then another, of his hunters climb through the squarish opening and straighten up, turning to face him. They are not particularly attractive, these sturdy ork women, with their brutish fangs and black leather clothing, but they are strong and enduring, and among the most conscientious of his minions.

Liron opens his cloak, and with a brief movement of his fingers reinforces the enchantment affecting both of them.

"Come, my dear."

Erin comes forward, her smile almost girlish, coquettish. Liron envelops her with the enchantment of the cloak, an enchantment assuring privacy, and draws her mouth to his. The breath flows swift and lush from her lungs; he inhales deeply, eagerly. On the astral, she is a bright beacon of life gleaming against the dark. Her eyes burn with the light of souls uncounted. Now, the profusion of life energy she has assimilated flows to him. With it comes the essential force he requires to sustain himself, as well as the power to resist the *leprosis,* to hold any further deterioration in check.

As his reserve of energy swells, the whispers and rustlings from around the basement rise to a subtle crescendo. His failures sense the life he absorbs; they envy him his power. It is very sad. They are like Erin and Paige and the others, Changed, according to the principles of the great work of the *Roggoth'shoth,* only these early ones did not turn out so well. They are quite insane. Like the fiends of fabled Azzorloth, Bridge Between Worlds, so arcanely described by the ancient mage Penticlese in the *Roggoth'shoth.*

Erin sighs and sags. Liron releases her, then invites Paige forward, into his embrace. His power swells. His body tingles with pleasure. Once again, his hunters have saved him time, precious time, by bringing him life, thus allowing him to continue his great work, the search for a cure to the *leprosis.*

But now he must go to his wife, dear Victoria, to feed her, sustain her, as the hunters have sustained him. Tomorrow,

when he returns to the office, he will attend to Ms. Amy
Berman.

Dear child.

63

Ivar turns from the dark, crowded Bronx streets of
Morrisania to a lime-green door covered with black and red
graffiti. Beyond the door is a stairwell, a pretty dark one,
too. It goes down about two levels. At the bottom is a small
dark space, the bottom of the stairwell, and a pair of ugly
black-leathered dwarfs with the Trollhammer insignia tattooed onto their faces.

"What you want, squat?" one asks.

Ivar replies, "A piece of your mother's fat ass."

The one who spoke now grins. "You'll have to get in line.
Go on in, squat."

So much for passwords. The only door leads to a circular
stairway that circles down to the floor of a big room like a
natural cavern, but decorated in penthouse style, or something like that. The walls are rough-hewn stone, except for
the one covered by the three-meter-wide trideo screen. The
carpet looks like velvet. Soft as a pillow. Built into the corner of the room is a circular table and a curving bench seat
like a booth in a restaurant. Standing next to the booth is another Trollhammer slag. Now delivering a drink to the booth
is some skinny Asian biff in a smoky black bodysuit and
stilt-heeled shoes. At the rear of the booth sits a dwarf in a
multichrome reflective suit and matching shades, white
buzzcut hair, and a matching razorslash beard. His name is
Flint. He sits there stroking a rockworm, which is like a
snake, but with a mouth full of grinding teeth and horny
plates, not to mention corrosive spit.

"Hoi, Conan," Flint says. "What's tox, chummer?"

Ivar forces a smile, and says, "Heh."

"We looking for some dosspay?"

"In a manner of speaking."

Flint taps a remote. A small panel in the tabletop opens.
A slim cylinder rises. A panel in the cylinder opens and a

datachip comes into view. "You wanna cut some ice? Scan this."

"What's it pay?"

"It's negotiable, *omae*."

"Ain't it always?"

"This especially. Pick up tonight, download tomorrow. Silicon swift. Right up your jack."

"Sure, whatever." Ivar takes the chip and slots it into the datascanner on his belt and jacks the scanner into his head. A virtual protocol scrolls past his eyes.

The job Flint's offering looks pretty standard—deck into the Matrix, snatch some data, deep research—till Ivar catches some of the names involved. The first name is Phalen, the second is Hill. A few others look familiar too and all of a sudden he realizes he's scanning a run proposal involving Hurley-Cooper folks, various slags from HC's Metascience Group.

It starts him thinking, just a bit feverishly. Pixelated *squat*! Amy Berman must've set this up! She didn't want to risk him blowing his parole, so she passed the job through some shadowlink to a handy fixer, our slag Flint. That means Ivar's guess was right: *the problem's serious*! Ole HC is in trouble somehow. Maybe because of the effing auditors. Maybe not. Who knows? What matters is that Berman needs help, HC's in trouble, and Ivar's the slag for the job.

He jacks out. "Time to talk nuyen."

Flint grins. "Six fine."

"Double it."

Seven's as high as it goes."

"You mean eight."

"Give the halfer a cigar."

The Asian biff sashays over and hands Ivar a big fat smogger. Ivar accepts it just to be polite.

"Delivery in twenty-four hours."

"Sometime tomorrow."

Flint grins. "No liner."

"Heh."

It's a quick walk back to the street. Ivar catches the subway and rides the thundering tram back to the Pelham Bay Projects. The lift shoots him upstairs. In his apartment, Novangeline's sitting on the black neovuelite sofa, watching him as he comes through the door.

"How come you're so late?" she asks.

"Got a little work, that's all."

"What work? For that Ms. Berman?"

"Nah, it's got nothing to do with her."

"Then what's it got to do with?"

"Heh. Making a little extra money."

"In the Matrix?"

"Do I look like a BTL trader?"

That was supposed to be kind of a joke, but it doesn't go over. It flops. Novangeline gets to her feet, meets him beside his SoloFendi recliner and leans right into his face. "Ivar, you're on parole! You can't run the Matrix. They'll put you back in prison!"

"Have to catch me first."

"Ivar!" And suddenly Novangeline's eyes are spilling over with tears. "What—what are you doing this for? Are you glitched?"

Ivar hesitates, then blurts, "You want a kid, don't you?"

Stupid. Shouldn't have said that. Suddenly, Novangeline's face is all twisted up and she's sobbing. "That's not . . . you can't . . ."

"Go take a nap or something."

Hey, he's reformed, *all right*? He wouldn't be taking cred for a Matrix run if it wasn't important, and this is a special case. They *need* the money! Novangeline's got this problem getting foggled. She needs some kinda nova gene therapy. Not covered by the health plan. Eight fine'll cover it nice.

That HC and Berman're involved is an added incentive. In a manner of speaking.

Ten minutes later, he's sizzling with electrolytes and blasting down the datalines in the gleaming rainbow cockpit of his virtual Boeing-Federated Death Eagle 2, the *Iron Dog*. He flicks on the afterburners and slams like rocket-assisted lightning out across the glaring starlit night of the LTG.

Heh. As usual, quite a rush.

To start with, this slag named Hill. Where did he get all this money he's got cozied up in the UCAS Bank? Ivar steps through a portal into a blazing red node and comes face-to-face with the massively muscled icon of a Fuchi Centurion combat utility. That's chill, though, because Ivar tosses his flaming yellow barbarian hair and engages a special sleaze of a utility.

Two thousand iconic salarymen all wearing UCAS Bank ident codes come slamming into the node. The Centurion combat utility backs to the nearest wall and freezes. Gleep! Overload.

Ivar slips on by.

Somewhere back along the datalines, his stubby fingers are rapping touch-sensitive keys with silicon speed, but he's got no time for that now.

In another nanosecond or so, he's into the bank's datastore archives. He initializes his scanner: Karnik the Mystic. A hacked-up version of some Hacker House scanner prog that needed some custom upgrading. A burning chrome-spangled window opens. Karnik rises like a puff of smoke out of his multicolored bottle, extends a jeweled hand into the swirling streams of passing hexadecimal code, and removes a burning pink envelope winking with the logo: *And The Answer Is. . . . !*

"Newark Interbank Credit Corp," Karnik says.

"Where did Hill's nuyen come from?" Ivar intones, because it's traditional.

At his left, a burning pink window opens. A fat Irishman chuckles. The window vanishes. Thank you, Hacker House.

Ivar blasts through the regional telecommunications grid and goes streaming down into the Newark LTG, straight into the Vaux Hall Pirate Net. The node flashes around him. He's back in his barbarian persona, standing atop the quarterdeck of a Man-O-War flying the Jolly Roger high overhead and pitching and rolling through a smoke-shrouded sea. Iconic cannons roar. A shimmering silver Captain Blood goes swinging down from the yardarms to lead a party of iconic pirates boarding a nearby ship. Ivar turns to the slag at the wheel, the one with the knife clenched between his iconic teeth, and says, "I need to sleaze the Newark Interbank Credit Corp."

"ARRR, me hearty!" quirks the glaring green parrot on the slag's shoulder. "You'd be needing a code-red masking utility straight from Davy Jones' locker!"

Ivar flexes his massive barbarian biceps, and nods.

A nano or two later, he's into the Newark bank's archives and Karnik draws a burning pink envelope from the streams of hexidecimals. *And The Answer Is. . . . !* "First Corporate Trust of New York."

"Where did the money come from," Ivar intones, it's traditional, "that went into Hill's UCAS account?"

"Hurley-Cooper Corporation Materials and Supplies account."

"What specific account did the money come out of?"

The fat Irishman chuckles.

Heh.

So this slag named Hill got his three million nuyen, indirectly, from Hurley-Cooper bank accounts. Ivar wonders if that means anything. Who in hell is Hill anyway? Some labcoat, maybe.

He blasts back across the datalines.

A dozen more names to go.

64

The room is very much like the chamber where Striper is confined: dull gray walls, no windows. Furnishings are limited to a trio of cots, a table with chairs, and a large trideo-equipped telecom on a cart. The lone door is open, providing a view of the prep room and the door to the lab control room, as well as the door to Striper's room.

Whistle lies supine on her cot, drawing pictures in the air with her fingers. Shaver readies her weapons. O'Keefe keeps a wary eye on Shaver. Her experience with Striper and the trolls left her bruised, how badly is hard to discern, but O'Keefe suspects that the worst of the bruises show only very discreetly. She spends every spare moment working on her weapons. She mutters in her sleep. O'Keefe has little doubt that Striper figures prominently in Shaver's dreams.

Sitting at the table, O'Keefe looks back to the telecom. *Modern Merc* fades from the screen, replaced by a view of a troop of six-wheeled armored scout vehicles rolling through the hilly country of southeast Turkey, raising dust along some unimproved dirt road. The man standing before the road, looking right out of the screen, in urban gray camo no less, is Duke Baader, formerly a ranking commander with Germany's MET 2000 mercenary corp. This is the man who derailed the Russian offensive on Fortress Berlin back in 2032, and who later orchestrated the lightning assault on

Castle Sofia. Now he hosts trideo shows for the Arms and Armor Network. O'Keefe resists a sigh.

Time marches on and good men spiral downward, enticed by luxury, till they become parodies of themselves.

O'Keefe would rather take a bullet to the brain.

A metallic rattling arises. Germaine Olsson comes in from the prep room, pushing a commissary wagon. Whistle hops up to survey the food. Shaver glares, then returns to cleaning her Ingram 20t SMG. Olsson parks the wagon, then steps nearer O'Keefe, and says, "Dr. Hill feels we've got things under control, so if you'll just stay till the next procedure is finished we'll consider the contract complete."

O'Keefe hesitates, then nods. It won't be his funeral. "That will be fine."

"How should I contact you when the doctors have another contract?"

"You can use the same means as before."

"Oh, okay. Just checking."

O'Keefe smiles. Olsson turns and walks out. O'Keefe returns his attention to the telecom screen and ponders.

He'll be glad to be done with this contract. It's troubled him since the beginning. The doctors' interest in Weres seemed logical enough, but the insistence that he snatch a beast as powerful as a Weretiger had seemed unwise. All Weres change shape. They all have certain Awakened abilities, such as the ability to regenerate lost limbs, to heal injuries with remarkable speed. They are not, however, equally dangerous. Why pick one of the most menacing varieties?

Worse, in first discussing the contract, Olsson had insisted on a particular individual, rumored in certain quarters to be just such an Awakened beast, and, worse yet, a known assassin. O'Keefe would not have thought that someone like Olsson, or the doctors she represented, or any corporate for that matter, would have had occasion to hear a name like "Striper," much less have some concept of to whom the name referred.

O'Keefe supposes that one of the doctors must have some special interest in Striper. Likely, it's something personal.

What other explanation could there be?

65

The voice from the ceiling drones on endlessly about pain and killing and death, about the son killed in an alley in Philadelphia, and the millions of things all this is supposed to mean.

"I've lain awake in bed till dawn imagining what I'd do if you were ever caught," the voice says. "Thinking things I'd never tell anybody, they're so horrible. That's how I got around to wondering what would be the worst? the worst that could happen to you? You're an animal. You act like one. Being caged, that'd be bad. Real bad. Being used for research, now that'd be worse. Being caged and used for research. Like the animal you are. Now that'd be even worse than seeing you killed.

"I never thought you'd have a kid, too. I got lucky with that. I want you to think about it. What's going to happen to your kid. What would you do to get it back? What if you could never get it back? What's happening to it right now, and you can't do a thing about it."

Tikki lies beside the panel concealing the only door into the room, her flank pressed to the wall. Her hours confined in this room have taught her the futility of wasting energy on anger. But when the door opens again, she'll be ready. If she can just stay awake.

She's thought a great deal about her cub and decided it's probably already dead. The idea disturbs her, but it's not real. It won't be real until she can see it for herself, till she can smell it, rub her nose in it. If she ever gets out of this room, she'll exact a ruthless vengeance for that death. Lately, though, she's begun wondering if she'll ever get out of this room. She's also done some wondering about other things. One thought keeps returning.

The voice from the ceiling said, "You took everything from me that meant anything."

That's incredible. What is it supposed to mean? That some two-leg actually cares about its offspring? That by killing some ork in a Philadelphia alley Tikki took everything of

value from some two-leg's life? Tikki finds that hard to believe, harder still to comprehend. She's known two-leg females who left their cubs in garbage compactors rather than
bother feeding them. She's seen human sibs fight each other
to the death, the victor walk away laughing. Two-legs are
the great betrayers. They care about nothing but their own
survival.

"You took everything from me that meant anything."

Money, power, sexual gratification—that's what the
metahuman realm revolves around. The idea that some ork
could be damaged by the loss of a cub is obviously just stupid.

She remembers one of her earliest experiences with two-
legs. Humans came up the Nun Kiang River from Tsitsihar
and killed her sire. Why did they do this? Her mother explained that humans kill for the same reasons that all animals kill—to eat, to dominate, to survive. Killing is part of
the way of things, but two-legs make it personal. Sometimes
they kill for the fun of it, which is like saying for no reason
at all.

Her mother explained that by the end of the twentieth cen-
tury the semi-sentient creatures that are their ancestors were
hunted to the brink of extinction. If not for the Awakening
and the rise of ones like her and her mother—ones who
could really think, who could elude the two-leg hunters,
even destroy them—there would be no tigers, no Weretigers.
No Tikki. Their kind would be gone. Dead. Eliminated.

That scared Tikki and filled her with anger. It made a last-
ing impression. It convinced her that two-legs should be
seen as prey. Rival predators. As enemies to her and her
kind. As just waiting for the chance to kill her. That's probably why she's never had any problem with killing them.

Ruthless murderers. Every one of them.

Now she wonders if that's right.

If an ork could be hurt by the loss of its son, like she was
hurt by the death of her sire . . . Like she's been missing her
cub . . .

It seems almost impossible.

66

The clock on the wall shows just past eight A.M. as Amy strides into her outer office, and she immediately realizes she's just in time to get into a situation. A black-suited man wearing KFK ID is growling something about not having all day. Amy's personal aide Laurena is looking back and forth across her desk, brushing at her eyes first with one hand, then the other, then leaning forward, both hands abruptly covering her face.

Amy restrains a sudden rush of anger. She looks to the man, presumably from the audit staff, and says, tersely, "Thank you, that will be all."

The man frowns, abruptly bows. "Excuse me—"

"Get the hell out."

The man's face goes flush and he stiffens, but then he bows again, turns and goes out. Amy plucks a tissue from the pastel box on the desk, gently draws Laurena's hands down, and dabs carefully at her eyes. Her face is red and shiny and she's breathing fitfully, struggling to look composed. "He just ... just wanted the Materials Manual," she says in a pinched voice. "I don't know, know why ... he got so nasty. I—I guess somebody borrowed it."

"It's not your job," Amy says softly. "It's my job. If the auditors want something, you send them to me."

"I'm ... I'm supposed to be your a-aide."

"You are my aide. You work for me. No one else." Amy smoothes back Laurena's golden hair and smiles a little. "Take a walk to the lav and freshen up."

Laurena smiles, obviously embarrassed, and reaches for her handbag. Amy goes on into her inner office. Through the wall of windows at the rear of the office, the sun is a glowering dirty yellow ball rising above the horizon, casting the plaza below her, as well as the Harlem River, Manhattan isle, the Hudson, and the distant shores of New Jersey in morning shadow. One thing Amy is sure of. The day may have only just begun, but the shadows are growing longer.

Her desktop bleeps. She taps the key to answer the call.

Joey Chang, the Finance VP, appears on her desktop screen. His hair seems more gray than usual. "We're about to gut a trog."

Amy frowns. "What?"

"I just heard that the audit staff picked up on some problems with Vernon Janasova's office budget. About half a million nuyen in personal business expenses seem to have gone into his Manhattan condo."

Amy groans and slumps into her chair. The only good thing about this news is that it doesn't involve her specific area of responsibility. If it matters. And it doesn't. "How good are you with a mop and soapy water?"

"Don't even joke about it."

"I'm joking?"

If Hurley-Cooper's CEO has been skimming the corp, they're all likely to be out of a job: guilt through association. Maybe that's an exaggeration. And maybe not. In any event, the storm that's been brewing since the auditors arrived is obviously closing in quickly, complete with deafening blasts of thunder, dazzling bolts of lightning, and a sky as black as tar. "Does Mercedes Feliz know?"

"I couldn't tell you, Amy."

"You better fill her in."

The exec VP is about all they've got going for them.

Chang reluctantly agrees and signs off. The desktop bleeps again. This time it's Kurushima, Mr. Audit, requesting an explanation of events in the outer office.

Amy puts it simply. "No one is going to address my personal staff, or any other member of this organization, in a manner that is discourteous and abusive. Hurley-Cooper is a KFK subsidiary. That does not make us slaves or serfs. *That does not make my personal aide a dog your people can growl at!* If there are any more such incidents, I will call security and have the offending person removed from the premises."

And as a vice president of Hurley-Cooper Corporation, which pays the rent on these premises, Amy has all the authority she needs to do it.

Kurushima's eyes turn wide and rounded; his face gets a little pale. Doubtless, he considers such blunt talk impolite, perhaps even astonishing. It's probably suicidal, too, at least from a career-wise perspective.

Amy adds, "I demand an immediate apology."

Kurushima stares. He stammers several apologies. Amy waits for him to finish, then closes the connection. She sits back, stares at the ceiling, then shuts her eyes.

The desktop bleeps; it's Dr. Phalen.

"Whenever you're ready, my dear."

She's as ready as she'll ever be.

Once more, she tries to reach Harman, but no luck. Where the heck could he have gone? She tried calling him twice last night and once this morning before leaving for work, but with no success. It's not like him to be so long out of touch.

With a sigh, Amy grabs her briefcase and her Zoé trench and heads for her car. Traffic around the plaza is a nightmare, the streets jammed with cars and swarming with crowds of people crossing from corner to corner. She's a quarter of an hour or more just getting onto the Major Deegan Expressway, and most of the rest of that hour crawling along the highway as far north as the Van Cortlandt Industrial park.

Remembering Scottie's many warnings, she checks her rearviews several times, but spots no one who seems to be following her. Maybe Scottie's years in the shadows have made him overly suspicious, or cautious, or whatever. It probably doesn't matter.

If what Joey Chang said is true, then the auditors are going far beyond a simple examination of Hurley-Cooper records. In that event, they probably already know everything there is to know about the irregularities she's been tracking. The question then is why let her go through all she's been going through? If anyone's watching, she hopes they're enjoying the show, these the closing moments of her career.

It's well past nine when she gets to the Metascience facility. The parking lot is full of cars. Some members of the science staff never seem to go home. Amy's always admired their level of dedication, but today the recognition is tinged with pain. She's dedicated, too. Only it doesn't seem to be helping.

If this is her final curtain call, she'll play it out as well as she can. She owes herself that much. Anyone else would probably take a hint and just walk away. Too bad that's not her style.

She takes the lift to the second floor and finds Dr. Phalen in his dark little office, lined with books, an antique wooden desk, and an old synthleather sofa. Dr. Phalen, tall and quaintly elegant in a suit ten years out of fashion, comes out from behind his desk to greet her, shake her hand, pat it, and lead her to a chair. His manner is sweet and endearing. The thought that this man, or even his department, might be involved in fraud brings Amy feelings of acute dismay.

"Would you care for some tea, my dear?"

"That would be nice. Thank you."

"Oh, it's my pleasure," Dr. Phalen says, smiling. The tea is already prepared. There's an antique service on a small sideboard. Dr. Phalen begins pouring. "Let me just say, my dear, that I'm quite sure that whatever problem may have arisen can be cleared up to everyone's satisfaction, even our friends from Tokyo."

"I hope so," Amy replies. "But I have to tell you that what I've found doesn't look good. There are indications of activity that I can only describe as possibly being of a fraudulent nature."

Dr. Phalen brings her a cup of tea. "Well, I must say that I would be shocked if that suspicion turned out to be true. I wonder, though, if perhaps there might be information that has not yet been uncovered. I can tell you from personal experience that the smallest of datum can sometimes make a world of difference in how one views a particular circumstance."

"I'm sure you're right," Amy says. She pauses to sip her tea, which seems oddly flavored, and suddenly feels herself going limp, slumping in her seat, her chin dropping to her breast, the tea cup spilling across her lap. The tea soaks through her pantlegs and it's nearly hot enough to burn, but she can't do a thing about it. Her elbows slip from the arms of the chair; her hands fall limply to her sides. Her eyelids droop, nearly closing. Her head lolls.

"Oh, I am sorry, my dear." Dr. Phalen dabs at her pantlegs with a cloth napkin. "How clumsy. I should have realized. I do hope you'll forgive me."

Amy doesn't care about the tea or stained pantlegs. She feels so weak, so completely enervated, so distant from everything— including her own body—it's scary. Why can't she move? *Is she having a stroke? some sort of cerebral seizure?* She needs help. She needs help and she struggles to get a plea, a cry, anything out through her mouth, but nothing comes, nothing but a vague moan, formed by unresponsive lips and lungs that seem all but empty of air.

From the corners of her eyes, she catches sight of a reddish glimmer, like the reflected light of a gemstone, but magnified, growing stronger, piercing, overwhelming her vision, then, everything.

What's happening? *What is this?*

A voice murmurs into her right ear. It drones on for what seems like hours before she gains a sense of what it's saying. The things it tells her to do are wrong, outrageous, even immoral. No, she won't do it. She won't! she won't! She won't do what the voice wants. But the words the voice speaks are a tangible force—she can feel it—pressing her down, weighing down against mind and body, squeezing, crushing her down into the chair. It's like the weight of a planet, trying to mash her flat. She fights it, puts everything she has into an effort to hurl herself up, get out, get away, but she only manages to gulp a deep breath. Her heart thuds. Her resistance crumbles. She hasn't the strength to fight. She's too tired, too weak, barely able to cling to consciousness.

An image appears before her. It's the impassive features of the Tokyo auditor, Kurushima Jussai. She tells him what she must. "Dr. Phalen . . . can explain. Explain what's happened. He's available now. He has the data on his computer. He'd like to . . . like to meet with you in his office . . . here . . . at the Metascience facility."

Kurushima says, "This is very difficult, Ms. Berman . . . for an auditor. What you're asking . . . it is very irregular."

"It is . . . essential," Amy replies.

Kurushima says, "Very well."

And then everything slips away into blackness.

67

Incense curls and rises. Bandit fingers the smooth polished wood of his flute and moves his astral eyes around the confines of his medicine lodge, looking over the hides, the bones, the rattles, the drums, other arcana. He has searched his mind for some means of avoiding what must come, but the search has been fruitless.

The spell he has prepared is one of the few he knows that

has no purpose but to take a life. It is designed deliberately, specifically, meticulously to kill. He does not want to use it, but he knows that in all likelihood he will have no choice.

It is in the nature of evil to afflict that which is good. It is in the nature of good to oppose this. Though it may be wrong to ever take a life, it seems likely that, in some cases, special cases, that which is good must be defended and that which is evil must be vanquished, no matter what the cost.

Bandit reminds himself that even Raccoon will fight, and fight to the death, when left with no choice.

It is in the nature of things.

And there is one other thing he must not forget. Tonight, when he does what must be done, if he takes a life, he may also give it, give life, or at least return it to its natural state. That is, of course, if he has correctly grasped what he experienced at Old Man's medicine lodge. Let it be so, he hopes.

His watcher returns, materializing beside his left shoulder. *"He is there, Master. Just like you said."*

"Good."

He must confront the mage called Phalen, but he does not want that confrontation to occur at the mage's home, where the mage keeps his tomes and circles and that one item above all, the *Roggoth'shoth,* guarded over by the familiar Vorteria and other spirits. Rather, he wants the confrontation to occur where the mage is likely to be at his most vulnerable. The only other place Phalen has gone is to the Metascience labs of Hurley-Cooper, so, by default, that's the place. The watcher spirit's report means that Phalen is there.

So it's time to get going.

He stands up. The pockets of his long coat are filled with things he might need, everything he can think of. He steps through the door of his lodge and finds Shell waiting for him in the stairwell, sitting on the floor, huddled into a corner. As she looks at him, he sees something in her eyes, maybe an accusation. Her features are otherwise calm, but her aura is in turmoil. He goes down on one knee beside her. She slips her arms around him and hugs herself close.

"I must go now."

"Are you gonna come back?"

"Yes." One way or another, he'll be back. Maybe not in a physical body, maybe not for very long, but he'll be back. In death, the spirit is freed and spirits move very quickly. He could go almost anywhere as a dying heart beat its last. "Don't worry."

"How can I help it?" Shell draws back, looks at him. Emotion twists at her face. Tears stream from her eyes. "You won't tell me what's going on, what kind of run this is gonna be. What am I supposed to think?"

"Raccoon has clever paws and knows many tricks."

Shell grunts and then sobs, clinging to him. "I don't care about Raccoon! I care about *you!*"

"I am Raccoon."

Indeed, he must be, more now than ever.

"I'll be back."

"Hold me."

For a few moments, he holds her tightly, but then he gently disengages her arms and gets to his feet. Shell avoids looking at him then. She rubs and brushes at her eyes. She follows him up the stairs to the back-alley door, hugs him one last time, then lets go. Bandit steps into the morning shade. The door thunks closed behind him.

Bandit looks to his left.

In the shadows there waits Zetana. She is slim and small but has a look more menacing than any woman Bandit's ever seen. Her hair is a shaggy black mass that spills about her face and shoulders; her eyes are rimmed in koal, and her pupils are like ebony stones gleaming from the amid the hard, dark lines of her face. She is all in black: studded black synthleather vest and pants, boots, and a voluminous cloak that reaches nearly to her ankles. Necklaces and beads hang from her neck; a confusion of bangles and rings surround her wrists and fingers. Her voice is husky, soft and low, like a snarl.

"I'll watch the woman," she says.

"And the kids?"

Zetana nods.

That is reassuring, for Zetana follows Wolf. Once Wolf extends her protection to another, nothing will make her betray that responsibility. And there is one other thing, one special quality. It is said that Wolf wins every fight but her last, and in that fight she dies. Bandit does not doubt that when he returns, if he returns, he will find that either all is well, or that Zetana, Shell, and the kids are all dead.

It is in the nature of this day that things will either go very well, or very badly.

"Thank you," he says.
"Guard yourself, shaman," Zetana warns.
Bandit nods, and turns down the alleyway.

68

Brian swallows the last of the wintergreen-flavored nutrisoy crackers from his rations and washes it down with a quick gulp of water. All he's got left now are a couple of Nerps and the few ounces of Soyade swishing around in his canteen. He leans back against the tunnel wall, wishing he could sleep. "How long we been down here, anyway?" he says. "Seems like weeks."

"You hear something, kid?"

Brian opens his eyes to find Art already on his feet, bristling with weapons, looking back and forth along the old subway tunnel.

"Coming our way," Art whispers. "Mount up."

Art lowers his helmet visor. Brian pulls on his own helmet and lugs himself up. He's at the point where fear of the unknown isn't enough to overpower fatigue and recharge his batteries. It'll take a clear and imminent threat to do that. He's not looking forward to it.

They move up the tunnel, weapons at ready. Art pulls open a metal grille in the tunnel wall. They move into a maze of smaller passages. As they round a corner, two figures come into sight. In the grayish half-light of Brian's Nightfighter visor, they look like women, ork women, big and solid and clad in dark synthleather. Brian sees them suddenly halt, their eyes flaring wide with surprise, and the sight strikes him like a bullet to the bridge of the nose.

Against the twilight dark of the tunnel, the orks' eyes burn an infernal red.

"BLAST'EM, KID!" Art roars.

And then they're both blazing away on full auto. These aren't orks, not anymore. Brian isn't sure what the frag they are, but something about Art's cryptic warnings has helped persuade him that, whatever these beasties be, they're better dead than with eyes of burning red.

The tunnel vibrates with the thunderous stammering of weapons. The orks stagger around and collapse. Streaks of dazzling white like headless comets blast outward in every direction. A greenish haze, sparking and glinting like some arcane energy shield, swells out of nothing to fill the tunnel ahead. Then, from the fallen orks rise a half dozen semi-transparent orbs, orangey, like bubbles, but about the size of melons. The orbs float up like they're bobbing on currents of air and start drifting all around. A dozen more follow, then more and more. They float into the tunnel walls and ceiling and vanish.

"Okay, kid."

The bodies are half-melted into the floor of the tunnel. Hollowed out, like melted plastic, fused and congealed and scorched black. They smell like death.

"We're getting close now, kid," Art says. "Real close."

Brian looks at him, and says, "Close to what?"

Art puts up his visor, meets Brian's eyes, holds them for several moments, then scowls, turns and heads up the tunnel.

"I'm getting low on ammo, Art."

Art stops, and says, "Tell me about it."

69

Kurushima Jussai collects his briefcase, his aide, and a single KFK security operative and takes the lift to the parking garage beneath New Bronx Plaza. The car that awaits him there is a rather customary Toyota Elite. The driver is also a KFK International employee.

Once inside the rear compartment, Kurushima uses the intercom to inform the driver as to his destination. Kurushima's aide remarks, "It should be interesting, Kurushima-*san*, to hear how Dr. Liron Phalen will explain the inconsistencies in the Materials Records."

Kurushima nods. "Yes."

There is, however, a time and place for all things, and proper methods and proper channels. This morning meeting at the Metascience facility offends Kurushima's sense of propriety. What business has he, an auditor, meeting anyone anywhere but in the full and impartial light of his assigned station at Hurley-Cooper's administrative offices? He would not have agreed to this meeting had not Amy Berman been the one to request it, and he only agreed out of the fear that, if he refused, she might launch into yet another of her tirades. He has faced these astonishing outbursts more than once and once was more than enough. Amy Berman is certainly one of the most outspoken, aggressive, shrewish woman executives he's ever met, and he does not consider the acquaintance to be a pleasant one. There are ways in which one can make one's opinions known, and ways of being aggressive without leaving the finer traits of civilization behind. Amy Berman is obviously unskilled in any of these techniques. She gives weight to the arguments of those who consider all women to be chaotic bundles of hysterical emotion, and all non-Japanese—and especially all Anglos—to be little better than barbarians.

And there is also the matter of the brief confrontation between Amy Berman and one of Kurushima's junior auditors; specifically, Amy Berman's remarks concerning "slaves and serfs." Absolutely astonishing. Kurushima hopes that this trip to the Metascience facility—the fact that he is now going out of his way to accommodate a Hurley-Cooper executive—will serve in some part to dispel such ridiculous notions from Amy Berman's mind.

Slaves and serfs. Unbelievable.

Could anything be further from the truth?

Fortunately, before such thoughts can completely unsettle his mind, the car pulls to a stop at the entrance to the Metascience facility. Kurushima strides into the lobby and is met there by a tall, pale man in an odd suit that seems some years out of date. "I am Dr. Liron Phalen," the man says. "Allow me to welcome you, good sir, to our humble niche."

"It is my pleasure," Kurushima replies, briefly bowing, before he can quite stop himself. Being met by the eminent Dr. Phalen personally is something of a surprise. They shake hands. Kurushima hurries to say, "And it is my honor as well, Dr. Phalen. May I say that your standing as a scientist is well-known, both at the North American office of Kono-Furata-Ko, and at our home offices in Tokyo. It is regarded with great pride that a man of your reputation would serve as part of our corporate family, with our subsidiary, Hurley-Cooper Laboratories."

Dr. Phalen chuckles, seeming pleased. "My dear sir," he says, "you must forgive my humility if I say you flatter me over-much. I've had the good fortune to make a few small contributions to the metasciences, but please make no more of it than that. If you'll forgive the analogy, I am merely one bee in a hive of workers, nothing more. Shall we go on to my office?"

"I would be pleased to do so."

Naturally, in a facility such as this, security procedures must be observed. Kurushima presents his KFK identification to the guards behind the counter at the rear of the lobby. This is quite routine; however, a problem arises. The IDs of his aide and the security operative do not "check."

"There must be some mistake," Dr. Phalen says.

"These two gentlemen aren't in the computer," says one of the guards in a rather flat monotone. Blunt enough to seem somewhat less than polite. "We can't admit anyone unless they check out, Dr. Phalen."

"Why," Dr. Phalen replies, "that's absurd, surely."

"Can't be helped," the guard says. "That's procedure."

"My good fellow, you can see for yourself that these gentlemen have their cards."

"Can't admit anyone without verification. That's procedure."

Dr. Phalen hesitates.

Kurushima feels forced to intervene, rather than let this go any further and risk a man of Dr. Phalen's stature becoming embarrassed. "I am sure this is merely a computer error of some kind," Kurushima says. "It is of no consequence, however. My escorts can await me here."

Dr. Phalen smiles as if relieved. "I'm quite bewildered by all of this, this security business. You're quite sure you don't mind leaving your friends behind?"

"I am certain that I will be quite safe without them," Kurushima replies. "They are merely security escorts."

"Oh, I see," Dr. Phalen says. "Well, then . . . shall we proceed?"

"Most certainly."

"This way, my good sir."

They take the lift to the second floor and enter Dr. Phalen's small office, eccentrically furnished, much as one might expect, Kurushima supposes, of a mage and scientist. Such people are often a bit eccentric. "Our good Ms.

Berman will join us shortly," Dr. Phalen explains. "She had
to contact her office. In the meantime, may I interest you in
some tea?"

"A most hospitable offer," Kurushima says. "Thank you.
I would be most pleased to accept."

70

It's eleven A.M. when Shaver sits up, slides her legs over the
side of her cot, and rises to her feet.

Whistle whistles inquiringly.

"Where are you going?" asks Tang.

Shaver turns her glare across the room at the lone male.
She does not like this elf's constant close scrutiny, but she'll
take it this one last time. She resists a sneer, and says,
"Gotta take a wizz. Wanna help?"

"No, thank you," Tang replies. "I'm sure you're quite capable."

Arrogant shick.

Shaver walks on: through the open doorway, the prep
room, the corridor to the lav. Walking without limping takes
a deliberate effort. The pain starts in her thighs and runs up
through her groin and into her back. She has those fragging
trolls of the Kong Destroyers to thank for that, and she's going to thank them, just as soon as this job is finished. Her
friends with Sisters Sinister will help. It's gonna be a bang-
bang day. Like today.

Inside a booth in the lav, she pulls the Ingram SMG from
her hip holster and pops the clip. That clip goes into a
pocket. The new clip she fits to the gun is loaded with
thirty-two special slugs. Half are explosive. The other half
are pure silver. They are packed into the clip in alternating
fashion.

She has Striper to thank for the trolls, and she's going to
thank the slitch right now. The scientists have had the Were-
shick for long enough. Now it's her turn.

Frag Tang, frag the money.

She returns to the corridor. That ork biff Germaine who's
always hanging around passes by without a word. Just a ner-

vous glance aside. Shaver sneers a smile and walks on to the prep room door. She has the code to open it and walks right on through, then straight across the room to the door of the Were-slitch's room. She isn't supposed to have the code to that door, but getting it was no problem. Not for her.

"Shaver!" Tang calls.

She ignores that, taps in the code, draws the smartgun, and steps through the doorway.

71

The tea does its work. The man slumps. The burning red of power on the astral plane is soon swelling to the limits of the room, gathering, swirling, concentrating, focusing down into an intense pinpoint of power hanging before the man's forehead.

Influencing this man from Tokyo, this *Kurushima,* is not so much a matter of controlling his mind or thoughts, but rather the relatively simple matter of planting an idea, insinuating it into the mind, lodging it there, making it permanent. It is a sort of magic that Liron has practiced many times before, primarily to prevent others from disrupting his work. The cost to him in fatigue is negligible. He has grown strong since his metamorphosis, his transmutation into one of the Changed of the Roggoth'shoth. He has also advanced in the skills of the initiate. He has come quite far, all told. He yet has far to go.

Once the idea is securely lodged, Liron returns to his mundane perceptions, takes a datachip from his desk, and hands it to Kurushima. "This chip contains the verifications you require, my dear sir. You may introduce it to your computers, if you wish, so as to better relate matters to your superiors."

Kurushima rises from his chair like a man rising from sleep. He rubs at his forehead, his eyes. He shakes his head as if to clear it of the cobwebs of lingering dreams. "Yes," he says. "I understand ... what you mean. I will do this. Thank you."

"You're quite welcome," Liron replies.

"A most enlightening conference, Dr. Phalen," Kurushima adds. "I'm sure that appropriate measures will be taken . . . so that . . . that in the future your researches need not be disrupted by administrative matters."

"It was my pleasure, dear sir." Liron touches the intercom on his desk, which brings Germaine within moments. She is most helpful. Particularly in dealing with such matters as involve computers. "My dear, would you be so kind as to show Mr. Kurushima to his car? Forgive me, sir, if I do not show you out personally. A rather pressing matter already in progress demands my attention."

"Certainly," Kurushima replies. They shake hands. "Goodbye, Dr. Phalen. Thank you for your time."

"A pleasure, I assure you."

While Germaine is showing the Tokyo man out, Liron goes through the side door into the small conference room adjacent. Amy Berman waits there, slumped in a chair, completely pacified.

Liron says the words to gather the power of the etheric and brandishes the ring that serves to focus the magic. His objective now is to unveil the secrets of the mind, rather than plant secret thoughts into it. He surrounds Amy in the spell and begins with his questions. Again, he finds her remarkably willful for a mundane.

It is some minutes before she admits to any knowledge of a shaman and some minutes more before she admits to involving one in Liron's affairs. At length, she admits to bringing the shaman here to the Metascience lab, yet denies sending the shaman to Liron's house. Odd. Liron had thought the two events must certainly be linked. Could he be mistaken? First things first: what is the shaman's name? Where can he be found? Amy shakes her head, will not speak. Liron insists. He gathers more power and turns up the pressure on her mind. At long last, she gives in.

"Bandit," she whispers.

"That is no name."

"It is."

How curious. Surely, this must be some type of nickname. Yet, try as he might, Liron cannot compel Amy to admit to anything of the sort. Her aura is turbulent enough to suggest a lie, but her will is like a wall of stone, as if she speaks absolute truth. Bandit. She says that over and over. Bandit is his name. Bandit. Bandit. Bandit.

Liron sighs. "Oh, very well."
Where can this Bandit be found?
"I don't know."
Another wall of stone.

72

Tikki is lying with her flank to the wall and her nose about ten centimeters short of the doorway. She's been waiting for hours, maybe even days.

When the door gushes open, Tikki looks and springs, hurling herself up at the doorway. She knows who's coming before she can see more than just the edge of the doorframe. It's the female elf that stinks of metal. The slitch she left with trolls from the Kong Destroyers. One of the two-legs who took her cub. Shaver.

A male shouts—Tikki recognizes the voice.

Perfect.

As she springs, forelegs lifting to strike, hindlegs thrusting, propelling her forward, a slender hand appears before her eyes, pointing a submachine gun into the room. Tikki bats the gun down and away and in the next instant she's slamming bodily into the figure coming through the doorway. She sees that it's Shaver and Shaver opens her mouth as if to shout or scream, but the ambush is sprung, the trap is closed. Tikki seizes the elf with her forelegs, slams her into one side of the doorway, and flings her down to the floor.

The SMG skitters away.

Tikki straddles the elf, her jaws spread wide. With one lunge of her head she could put this slitch to death. Then she sees the elf's frenzy, smells the elf's desperate fury, and hesitates.

What if her mother was wrong? What if two-legs are not just insidious betrayers and murderers? What if they are more like her and her kind than she's ever imagined?

And what if the door slides shut?

Roaring, Tikki pounds the elf's shoulders into the floor, then turns and flings herself at the doorway.

The elf shrieks. "SLITCH! *I'LL KILL YOU!*"

The door is sliding shut. Tikki thrusts a paw between door and doorframe and, incredibly, the door bounces back, like the door to an elevator. Slipping, stumbling, banging off the doorway, Tikki shoves at the floor and lurches ahead.

The room beyond is lined with carts and cabinets and high-tech equipment. Tikki spots three doors. The ones ahead and to her left are closed. The one to her right is open. Her nose turns her to her right before she has time to consider which way might offer escape. Through the open door comes the elf O'Keefe and the other female, Whistle. O'Keefe's eyes grow enormous and the air suddenly stinks of fear as Tikki flattens her ears to her skull and charges.

"Whistle!"

O'Keefe tugs a machine pistol free of his belt. Tikki meets him nose-to-nose—fangs bared and roaring—using her chest like a battering ram and driving O'Keefe back three or four meters, right through the open door and into another room. Whistle cries out shrilly, driven back off her feet. O'Keefe's gun rattles on full automatic, but Tikki slaps the hand that holds it, like the elf connected to that hand, flat to the floor.

"FRAGGER!"

Tikki roars and tears at his chest. Here is a two-leg who deserves to be blooded if not destroyed. And she might have done that, too, only chills rush up her back. Her ears snap up. The air is suddenly electric. She jerks her head left and right. She's in another room like the room she was confined in—gray walls, no windows—just the one door. *What kind of place is this? What's happening?* She sees Whistle on her feet and making signs with her fingers like a magician might make. Tikki turns and lunges and batters the slitch to the floor. *How does she get out of this place!*

A gun stammers from behind. Tikki whirls. Gun in hand, Shaver's limping toward her from the room with the high-tech equipment. Tikki lunges aside, out of the line of fire. O'Keefe is rolling onto his side and reaching for his machine pistol. With a paw like a hand, Tikki grabs it, then spins toward the door and points the gun at Shaver's face.

Whistle screams, *"NOOOOO!"*

And then the world explodes.

73

"My ID checks."

"Yes, sir. Thank you, sir. You can go on ahead."

The guard behind the counter at the rear of the Metascience main lobby barely finishes saying that when the dull roar of an explosion rumbles through the building walls.

Bandit feels it vibrate through the lobby floor.

Has someone mixed the wrong chemicals together? or is there some more sinister explanation?

Alarm bells begin clanging. Amber strobes descend from the ceiling of the lobby and begin flaring rapidly. The guard blinks, shakes his head, rubs a hand down over his mouth, then grabs a telecom handset from the console behind the counter. "Sergeant on patrol," he says into the handset. "My board shows an incident at . . . at Lab Six. It sounded like an explosion. Yes, sir. Initiating security lockdown."

A klaxon blasts. Bandit turns to see heavy metal shutters descending over the front lobby doors. That could be a problem, but it could also work in his favor. The person he is here to see might be dissuaded from attempting to leave for a little while.

"Where do I find Dr. Phalen?"

Someone begins frantically shouting at the guard through an intercom. The guard speaks rapidly into the handset.

"Where is Lab Six?"

"Through those doors to the right!" the guard shouts.

Bandit steps through the doors beside the counter and turns right, and enters a scene of pandemonium.

Bells clang, klaxons blare, strobe lights flash. Dust and smoke billow through the hallway. People shout and shriek. Three people in white lab coats run past Bandit's left, one tripping, falling, and scrambling up in passing by. As Bandit moves ahead, the dust and smoke thickens, then clears a bit. He comes to a segment of hallway littered with debris. There's a huge, jagged hole in the hallway wall on the left. The hole flickers and flashes with arcane energy. Beyond the hole, Bandit sees a room littered with debris, an overturned table and chairs and the sprawled forms of several meta-humans.

Out through the hole in the wall steps an unusual figure. It is like that of a woman, but unlike any woman Bandit's seen before. She is slim below the waist—naked, too. Above the waist, she is massive and powerful, cloaked in a reddish fur marked by black stripes, and streaming blood. Her face is inhuman. Her eyes glint red in catching the light. A gun dangles from one hand.

This does not appear to be related to Bandit's reason for being here.

He frowns, puzzling, all the more so when he views the unusual being on the astral plane. Her aura is not that of a human. He is some moments realizing that he is looking at an aura like that of a tiger.

The being pauses, watching him, softly growling.

Is this a natural being? a dual-natured being? or is she the result of some terrible experiment, which might account for the warping of the fabric of nature of this place?

Something changes. The animal face suddenly seems more humanoidal. In a voice like a husky snarl, the being says, "My cub . . .

"Where is it?!"

Cub? What does she mean? That is an animal word, not a word for a human or humanoidal infant. Bandit stares, baffled, then suddenly an image comes to mind. He remembers his first visit to this place, the lab of Dr. Ben Hill, the small red and black-striped creature he saw in a cage. Could that be mere coincidence? "I saw a small . . . being, like a tiger, in Lab Sixteen. It had fur like you. The same color."

More shouts. Bandit looks to see a pair of uniformed guards coming up the hallway at a run. The mysterious striped being before him whirls, lifting her gun. The guards tug guns from holsters. Bandit murmurs words of power. The guards' arms leap upward. Their guns jerk free of their hands and go sailing back over their shoulders. Their pants drop to around their ankles and send them sprawling.

The striped being whirls again, pointing the gun.

"Don't shoot," Bandit says, lifting his hands.

"Where is Lab Sixteen?" the being snarls.

Bandit points. "That way."

74

What is it? Tikki scowls. The two-leg wears a long dark coat like a duster and holds a wooden flute. He smells like a magician and yet he does not attack her. Instead, he does something and then suddenly the approaching guards are disarmed and sprawling. When she turns back to face him, he lifts both hands in a gesture of surrender.

To judge by his smell, the magician has no feelings about her one way or another, except maybe a vague curiosity.

"Where is Lab Sixteen?"

He points down the corridor. "That way."

Does she dare turn her back on him? *Does she have any choice?* She must trust him or kill him and, incredibly, without really being threatened, he seems to be helping her.

Tikki turns and runs. The guards shout and stagger to their feet as she nears them, but do nothing to impede her. She grabs one of their guns from the floor and continues ahead. Now she's got two guns and that gives her odds to play with the next time some two-leg tries to get in her way. She needs odds like that because she's tired—her reserves are wearing thin. She needs sleep, real sleep, and enough meat to gorge herself. She's taken too many hits, too many explosions, in too little a time. She can't keep going like she's been going.

A door comes up marked by two big numbers: One-Six. She looks at the combination lock on the wall beside the door.

How does she get in?

Without warning, the door snaps aside. The human male who steps toward her abruptly stops. His eyes flare wide. His smell turns to fear. "No," he says.

Tikki thrusts the hard metal barrel of one of her guns across the male's throat, shoving him back through the doorway, then drops one gun to seize him by the throat and thrusts the other gun in his face.

She knows this two-leg. He's one of the humans who visited her in the room with no windows. He left his smell on her fur.

"Please!" he gasps.

Fear swells into terror. Tikki feels her fangs lengthening, fur rushing over her face, and then she smells the cub. "WHERE IS IT?"

The two-leg shouts, jerking as with surprise.

Tikki snarls, but by then she already has the answer to her question. The smell in the air turns her head toward the rear of the room. Beyond a sea of technical equipment and boiling, bubbling fluids is a cage. In that cage is a red and black-striped body, and it's pounding the cage's mesh, crying, snarling, desperate and afraid. Not dead, not even bleeding. *Alive!*

Tikki drives the barrel of the machine pistol across the two-leg's head, shoves him back off his feet, then turns— snarling her menace—toward the rear of the room. More two-legs in white coats shout and scream and rush frantically out of her way. She reaches the cage and smashes at the locking mechanism till the door pops outward.

The cub lunges into her grip.

75

For a moment, Ben Hill is conscious only of the pain throbbing through the left side of his head and the cool, flat hardness of the floor against his right temple.

When he lifts his head, the pain is intense. Colors strobe in front of his eyes. He hears people screaming and shouting, things crashing, a sudden rush of slapping, pounding footsteps. As his vision clears, he sees the brief stretch of off-white floor between him and the door to the hallway, and the black shape of a gun, lying barely two meters away.

It occurs to him that he might need that gun. Striper has escaped confinement. She is wild with animal fury. Fear motivates him forward, crawling, then up, on his hands and knees. The lab seems very quiet as he takes the gun in hand.

Shakily, he gets to his feet, leaning against a lab bench, then a table. He sees at a glance that his colleagues and lab assistants have all fled. The figure at the rear of the room looks only partly human, covered with fur about the head and shoulders.

When she turns, Ben sees that she holds a child in her arms, a human child, of four or five years of age.

But that can't be. It's Striper, it must be Striper and her cub. The sight is strangely fascinating. They've had both mother and cub for how long now, and, until now, neither has transformed into a human-like shape. Neither has shown the least hint of that ability. Why now? Striper presumably has some reason, but what of the cub? Does it simply take its cue from its mother?

Striper says, "Are you going to shoot me, *man*?"

"Mannnn!" the child echoes, growling.

And the small head turns, and the child's face comes into view. It looks half-animal, half-demon, lips curling, fangs bared.

Its eyes glint with the light.

Ben feels chills rush up his spine. He realizes now more than ever that he is facing a form of intelligence that bears only a superficial resemblance to the human kind. He is facing a born predator, a creature or creatures that perhaps assign no value to life, only to survival. The notion scares the hell out of him. He lifts the gun in his hand a little higher. Involuntarily, he sneezes. "I . . . I can't let you leave," he stammers. "You or your cub. I'm sorry."

Striper says, soft and low, "Get in my way and you die."

The child snarls, *"Diiieee!"*

"It's not . . . not my decision!"

Striper puts the child on its feet, takes its hand, and comes walking up the center aisle from the rear of the lab. Her eyes bore into Ben's eyes; the gun dangles at her side. The child glares and growls, its features twisted with vicious fury and hate. Mother and child pause barely two steps away. Both seem oblivious to the gun pointed at Striper's chest. Ben feels his arm growing weak, sagging, slumping downward. It's no good.

But suddenly someone's grabbing his wrist, twisting the gun out of his hand. To his astonishment, he sees it's Germaine, now shrieking, *"SHE KILLED MY SON!"*

"What? Germaine! NO!"

"MURDERER!"

It hardly takes a second. Ben does not see who fires first. He glimpses the feral violence gripping Germaine's features,

and the sudden vicious rage that possesses Striper's face. He
hears a series of reports: the barking of a handgun, a rapid
rattling like a machine gun. Germaine staggers, blood
splashing her chest, and topples over backwards. Striper
turns, twisting, crouching, sheltering the child, bending over
it, even as her head snaps toward her shoulder and the side
of her head becomes a gory mass streaming down her neck.

Striper crumbles. Germaine lies sprawled, unmoving. Ben
staggers back, slumps to his knees, bends forward, gags, and
vomits. Through it all, he hears Liron Phalen's voice, urging,
persuading, telling him what he must do.

76

The steps of the stairway are a dull muddy blue. The railing
is silvery chrome. The second-floor landing is empty. Bandit
pauses by the door on the landing to listen, then pulls the
door inward, and steps into a hallway much like the one on
the ground floor: lighting panels in the ceiling, gray and yellow tiles along the walls, muddy blue floor. Bandit pauses as
a faint shimmering appears in the air before him. On the astral, he sees the small raccoon-like form of his watcher.

"He's still in there, Master."

"Good."

In fact, there is quite a lot that's good about the situation.
The clanging alarm bells may pose a distraction to Phalen.
The alarm also seems to have sent people running for the
main lobby. There should be no bystanders hanging around
to get hurt.

A short way up the hall is a small sign that sticks out from
the wall. It reads, "Dr. Liron Phalen, Director." Bandit considers how to get past the printscanner, then watches as the
door clicks and slides open.

"Come in, my dear shaman," a voice says.

Not good. Not the way Bandit wanted to start things. He
surveys the hallway astrally, but perceives no way by which
he might have been detected. That's troubling. Is he about to
confront an initiate so far advanced that his skills exceed
anything Bandit can comprehend? Bandit supposes that's

possible, but there's no backing out now. He steps through the open doorway and immediately crouches, darting to his left, and pointing a finger.

The room is like a small study: bookshelves, chairs, a leather couch. Phalen stands at the rear of the room behind an old desk. He looks briefly to his right as a bang and a crash and the quick-razor snarl of an alley cat sounds from the corner of the room; but, then, Phalen merely smiles.

"Come, come," he says casually. "We have no need for artful ruses. I believe you're called Bandit. I'm Dr. Liron Phalen. We're both gentlemen, I'm certain. Let us discuss our differences like men who've devoted their lives to the pursuit of arcane knowledge. I'm sure there is much we can both learn. May I offer you a cup of tea?"

Bandit lifts the Mask of Sassacus to his face. "You will obey me."

The power of the Mask reaches out instantly, crossing the astral terrain to enwrap Phalen's aura, a blazing comet-head of power. The force of will Phalen immediately hurls against the power of the Mask comes back to Bandit in the form of a dull throbbing ache inside his head.

"Now ... Vorteria," Phalen says in a voice that sounds pained. "Quickly, my dear."

A radiant white figure descends out of the ceiling: Phalen's familiar. Vorteria. She settles between Bandit and Phalen, interposing a pulsing shield of life energy to divert the power of Bandit's spell. Divert it, then break it. The power flashes and fluctuates, splashing around the shield like water around rocks.

A clever strategy, but Raccoon is ready.

Phalen shrugs off the tendrils of the Mask's power and begins conjuring a spell, something that mounts slowly and steadily, gathering the power of the astral. Bandit snaps his fingers. The windows behind Phalen explode into fragments. Cups and saucers shatter. Books leap from their shelves. Books and window fragments and broken crockery rain across Phalen's end of the room, gathering into a whirlwind, bypassing the familiar completely, and forcing Phalen to cease spellmaking and hastily throw up another shield or risk being cut to pieces.

"Vorteria!" Phalen cries out sharply.

A confused expression crosses Vorteria's features; she

turns, looking behind her. Abruptly, she reaches across the astral to surround Phalen with her shield.

Bandit opens his palms, and whispers.

The figure that appears beside him is about the size and shape of a dwarf. It appears to wear natural tan leather, from its heavy, fringed shirt to its beaded moccasins. A raccoon cap sits on its head. Its long gray beard gives its face an aged character, which seems highly appropriate for a venerable being like a hearth spirit.

"Let spirits contest with spirits," Bandit murmurs.

"Yessireee." The hearth spirit thrusts out an arm, forefinger extended. Power surges across the astral.

"Master!" Vorteria exclaims.

But by then Vorteria has dropped the shield protecting Phalen in order to protect herself. Life energy flashes and crackles. Hearth spirit and familiar spirit wage war with the very life force of their own existence, and the contest promises to drag out long, for the two seem evenly matched.

Bandit darts around the familiar in order to face Phalen directly, and moves directly into the path of the spell Phalen has been preparing.

Not good.

The power hits him like a floodtide, surrounding him, weighing in on him, particularly in the area of his head. At once, his head begins to feel like it's being attacked by twelve mad dwarfs swinging warhammers. It's very distracting. The spell seems intended to confuse his mind or possibly to crush his will. It's powerful, too. Bandit guesses that Phalen isn't familiar with any of the explosive, fireballing, shock-wave-producing, pyrotechnical spells one sometimes encounters in the streets. Good thing.

Bandit staggers back a few steps. The weight of the spell is making it hard to think. Hard to figure what to do. He must know some way of countering this spell. Something clever. Quick.

Before time runs out.

77

The maze of tunnels comes to an end at a narrow passage that seems chopped out of bedrock, and that passage ends after about twenty meters. Brian exhales heavily, guessing this is finally the end, wondering if he and Art are lost, but then he notices Art looking up.

"Here we are, kid," Art says.

"Yeah? Where's here?"

"I'll give you one guess."

The rocky ceiling is less than a meter overhead. Directly above Art's head, chopped out of the rock, is a squarish recess containing a squarish door or hatch.

Art pulls something from his pack, and turns to face Brian. "Know how to set one of these?"

The item in Art's hand is saucer-shaped, twenty centimeters in diameter. The broken block lettering along the rim, reads, ARMTECH SAD-190. There's also a warning about explosives being the province of qualified personnel. Brian asks, "You got a detonator?"

Art pulls one from a pocket. It's about the size of a pack of cigs. Armtech DD-7 preset for thirty-second delay.

"Just lemme ask you one question."

Art compresses his lips, frowning, then says, "Sure, kid. One question. Shoot."

"These creatures we're blasting. I don't know what the frag they are, and maybe I don't wanna know. That's not my point. My point is that I'm working for the Department of Water and Wastewater Management, and I ain't seen a water main in at least a couple of hours. I'm not even sure if we're still in Manhattan. What I wanna know is ... how do you figure these things with the red monster eyes pose some kinda threat to the metroplex's water supply?"

Art scowls, then jabs a finger at Brian's face. "You got any idea, kid, how those creatures got the way they are?"

"Not a fraggin' clue."

Art jabs the finger a little closer. "Let's suppose they're infectious. Suppose they make new ones by infecting ordinary people. Now suppose they infected everybody in the plex? What then?"

Brian wonders about that, and says, "Then I guess it wouldn't matter if they fragged with the water supply or not."

"Exactly," Art says. "There'd be no water supply. There'd be nobody left to keep it running."

Brian hesitates. "Then we'd be out of a job."

Still scowling, Art nods.

"Does the union know about this?"

Art glares, hands Brian the Armtech shaped-charge and detonator, then makes a cradle of his hands. Brian slings his weapon, gives Art his foot and thrusts upward, lifting one knee onto Art's shoulder. The Armtech charge comes with a gelatin base that sticks to almost anything. Brian strips the plastic shield off the gelatin, positions the charge on the hatch just above his head, then presses the charge into place. The detonator sticks to the charge by a similar gelatin base.

"We ready to blow?"

"Do it," Art growls.

Brian pulls on the timer cord, then hops back to ground. He and Art jog back along the passage. The explosion is deafening.

When they return, there's a hole in the ceiling about a meter across and no sign of the hatch. Brian gives Art a boost up through the hole. Art turns back and pulls him up.

That puts them in a dark, dry, dusty place that looks like a basement. Lots of crates and boxes piled around in stacks. Cobweb-laden shelves divide the space into aisles. Brian gets a sort of hinky feeling creeping up the back of his neck that maybe he and Art aren't alone anymore. Is that rustling noise he hears the sound of his own breathing, or is something moving in here, moving all around the basement, maybe inside some of those crates?

Art signals mil-style. Grenades. There, there and there. Five-minute delay. Brian gestures in reply. Interrogative. *Negative!* Art answers with a stabbing motion of his hand. *Just do it!*

Well, all right.

Brian pulls three grenades from his web harness and sets them beside the crates Art indicated. Five-minute delay. When he looks up, Art's motioning him forward, across the basement, around a corner, then up a flight of stairs.

The stairs lead into the ground floor of a richly furnished house. Brian realizes it's a house and not a condo as he and Art move rapidly from room to room, as he gets glimpses through exterior windows, as he realizes the spaces here are bigger than in any condo he's ever seen, except on *Corporate Lifestyles*. Maybe the creatures they're hunting have infected some big wiz corporate exec. It'd have to be a real prime mover for the slag to afford an actual house.

Another flight of stairs leads them to a pair of ornate wooden doors. Art pauses in front of them, then turns down the upstairs hallway. He signals. *Action imminent!*

The door at the end of the hall swings open. They dart into a bedroom like a Victorian hologram: cascading drapes, onyx furnishings, huge canopied bed. Next to the bed stands a tall elf woman in a white medtech uniform. In the bed lies something inhuman.

It's like a dead man, or a dead woman. The skull is totally bare of hair and any of the fleshy features that make a human face. It's like a skull with sunken eyes, a hole for a nose, blackened teeth, no lips. The arms and hands lying on the bedcover are skeleton-thin and as white as bone. The sunken eyes glare a fiery red.

"Shick!" Brian shouts.

"NOW, KID!" Art hollers.

They open up on full auto. The elf medtech seems to faint. The thing in the bed twitches and jerks and screams and then everything flashes white.

78

The scream of terror and pain comes to him clearly across the astral terrain and instills in Liron Phalen a horror that shakes his consciousness to the core.

Watcher spirits come streaking toward him.

"Master!" they cry. *"Intruders!"*

"Vorteria!" Liron exclaims. "My wife! *GO!*"

Vorteria must rescue his wife. He himself must remain here in his office because the shaman must be defeated or everything will be lost. He must concentrate intensely, focus

all his power and skills. The intricate construct of his spell
is rapidly devolving, nearing the brink of collapse. He must
not permit that to happen.

79

Phalen's spell weakens. His familiar streaks out of sight.
Bandit isn't really sure why and he doesn't have time to
worry about it. His hearth spirit vanishes, its service complete, which leaves him facing Phalen by himself.

"Deezle," he blurts.

A watcher in raccoon-like form appears directly beside
Phalen's head and begins screaming, *screaming, SCREAM-
ING!* as loud as fire alarms and air horns and warning klaxons. Phalen twitches visibly. The force of Phalen's spell
shifts further off-center and Bandit rises from a crouch with
one hand extended, exerting his will, deflecting the blazing
energies of Phalen's magic.

Now, he must concentrate. He must become as completely
Raccoon as he has ever been. The spell he must use comes
to mind. He takes a step toward the rear of the room, toward
Phalen. He must get very near Phalen to do what must be
done and bring Phalen's evil to an end.

80

Amy lifts her head from the cradle of her crossed arms to
find herself sitting at a small rectangular table in a room
cluttered with filing cabinets, bookshelves, and what she
takes to be castoff computer equipment. She sits back,
pushes her hair out of her eyes, and wonders what's happened. She feels . . . Peculiar. Weak, a little shaky, like she
fainted or something. Her stomach feels strangely empty,
like she's just finished being sick, coughing up her lunch.
Only she doesn't remember having lunch or being sick.

What day is it? Where is she and what is she doing here? Her watch shows the hour's approaching noon. Why isn't she in her office?

She feels wrung out.

The room has two doors. She gets to her feet and steps toward the nearest one. It slips aside. She gets as far as the doorway before realizing where she is and seeing what's going on.

The room before her is Dr. Phalen's office. Phalen is standing behind his desk and making arcane gestures in the air. The desk and the floor around him are littered with window fragments and books. At the other end of the room, now looking at her, is someone resembling Scottie, wearing Scottie's long dark coat, carrying his flute, only his face and head look less like the face and head of a human being than that of an animal, like a raccoon.

Amy gapes. *"Scottie?"*

Patches of air shimmer and fade. Both men gesture arcanely. Dr. Phalen seems to straighten up, grow fuller, stronger. The other man seems diminished somehow, smaller, weaker. As if being forced back into a corner. For an instant, the resemblance to a raccoon diminishes and she sees that it really is Scottie facing off with Phalen, and she gasps.

What are they doing? What's happening?

"Go away, my dear," Dr. Phalen says. "You're in danger."

A voice whispers into her ear. It's Scottie's voice. "Do something," he says. "He's killing my will."

Amy exclaims, "What? *Do what?!*"

"Phalen's evil must be stopped."

The room wavers and blurs, her head pounds, and suddenly all Amy can see is Dr. Phalen, but he is not Dr. Phalen. He is a horror, a grotesque skeletal creature with a skull for a face and claws for fingers. Amy's first response is shock. She cries out, but even as the shock resounds, vibrating through her body, she remembers—the cup of tea, the crushing weight of Phalen's will. He tried to use her in some way, used his powers on her. Forced her to speak. To lure Kurushima here. She realizes that she must have been wrong about Scottie's warning, and wrong about Phalen right from the start.

The air shimmers around Scottie's head. The likeness of

the raccoon diminishes. "Oh, god!" Amy exclaims. "What should I do?"

Scottie whispers, "Distract him."

How? Amy looks around frantically.

How does she do that?

81

Amy's sudden appearance comes as a shock.

"Distract him," Bandit whispers, and by the time he says that the balance of power has shifted once again. Phalen's spell has gathered weight and power, now pressing him back like a tide of air too thick and heavy to stand against. The assault on his will becomes almost invincible. His hand and arm begin quaking with the effort of maintaining his shield. He strains to move another step forward, but finds his feet will not cooperate.

Phalen chuckles. His voice comes soft and complacent to Bandit's ears. "You are strong, my dear shaman, a worthy adversary, but I have gained too much through my fraternity with the transcendental."

Then, suddenly, Amy is beside Phalen, shouting, and swinging a large tome like a club, striking Phalen across the head.

Phalen sways and grunts. The cosmetic mask covering his face shifts and falls away, baring the horrific features below. Phalen shouts in outrage and the weight of his magic slackens. Bandit thrusts his flute up over his head and forces his foot ahead a whole step and the final contest begins. His special spell begins unfolding, gathering power, assuming the astral form of an enormous furry Raccoon, rising like a shadow to stand erect on two legs behind Phalen's back.

Phalen seems to assense the power gathering behind him and begins to turn around, but then the spell strikes.

The giant Raccoon claps its paws over Phalen's face, and tugs, and disappears. Phalen's shrill scream of agony rises high and loud. He lifts his hands to the bloody gashes of his eyes and staggers.

Bandit lunges forward, flicking a thumb. The antique desk

tumbles out of the way, banging onto its side and slamming
into the wall. Phalen screams, *"NOOOOOO!"* but by then
Bandit is chanting the last words of power and driving the
shaft of his flute into Phalen's body like a spear.

Phalen's scream rises into a thunderous roaring of agony.
The astral turns white—pure, brilliant dazzling white—with
the life energy escaping Phalen's body. A seething flood of
orange-hued globes surges forth, once-doomed souls now
free to seek their destiny, each according to its own nature.

Phalen drops to the floor, his body melting, caving in on
itself, seared and congealed by the power of life.

Then comes the Roggoth'shoth, the heart of darkness, the
evil. It is a black, malignant thing. Its astral form bears a
vague resemblance to a twisted sort of bat-monkey with
fangs and horns. It comes forth screaming, destined for the
hellish metaplanes from which it once emerged, but then
something goes wrong.

Something Bandit had not expected.

The entity manifests, assuming corporeal form. It flashes
past Bandit's nose, blurring with speed. He hears Amy
shriek. He turns to see her staggering backwards, collapsing,
the entity clinging to her face. As Bandit bends to tear the
creature free, Amy's eyes pop open, bulging, burning a fiery
red.

The evil has infected her aura.

"Drek." Bandit whispers.

82

The shaft is smooth and cool, lined in concrete. Metal rungs
serve like a ladder. Monk reaches up to catch hold of Minx's
ankle, holds on till she shakes it loose, then does it again,
then again, then ...

"Stop it, you booty!" Minx giggles. Then she stops climbing. Monk peers up past the delicious swells of her trim behind to see her shaking out her lavish curling hair, changing
in color from red to reddish orange to reddish gold and back
again. Maybe a hundred meters above the top of her gorgeous head is a faint glimmer of sunlight and the top of the

shaft. Monk remembers this shaft. It's on the Newark side of
the Hudson. Another hour or so and they'll be home.

Minx whispers, "Hoi . . . did you just hear something?"

"What kind of something?"

"I'm not sure."

"Yeah?" Monk says, gazing upward.

"You know what?" Minx says softly. "I'm getting this
weird feeling. Like something's happened to the Master.
Like maybe he's dead."

Monk puzzles. "I thought you said that if the Master died,
we'd die, too."

"Yeah, I did, didn't I?"

"Well?"

"I could've sworn, I mean . . . I thought . . ." Minx hesitates, then turns enough to look down at him, past the pert,
round, luscious swellings of her breasts; then, she giggles.
"You booty, maybe it was just something I ate."

Something she *ate*. Hah-hah-hah!

Monk grins. "Wiz."

As he lifts his head, wiping drool from his lips, Ben Hill
sees that, once again, he's missed the small miracle of
transformation.

Striper lies sprawled on her side. She has returned to her
natural form, the massive body so suggestive of the Siberian
tiger. The gore spilled from the savage wound in her head
stains red and black-striped fur. Her wound appears too terrible for even her remarkable Werebiology to heal.

Her child has already taken its cue. It stands on four legs
beside the unmoving body of its mother, looking back and
forth, growling mournfully, pitifully, now sniffing at the savage wound, licking at it. Ben can't stand to watch. He turns
his head, only to see Germaine, sprawled on her back hardly
an arm's length away. Her chest is drenched in blood and
gore, concentrated in dark patches around the half-dozen or
so bullet holes punctuating her blouse.

It's beyond comprehension, beyond belief, that things

could have taken such a terrible turn, that the search for a metabiological serum could end in death, a double homicide.

Two lives irretrievably lost, wasted ...

Liron Phalen was the motivating force, and Germaine played her role, but Ben knows too well where the responsibility truly lies, where it always lies. He's reminded of the words of Sir Thomas More. When asked for the sake of fellowship to join the nobles supporting an ancient king, More replied, "And when we die, and you are sent to heaven for heeding your conscience, and I to hell for disregarding mine, will you come with me for the sake of fellowship?"

It puts everything in perspective.

He allowed himself to be unduly influenced by Liron Phalen. He did not have the strength of will to insist, to demand, that the course of their research observe the moral and ethical principles he's tried to honor throughout his whole adult life. When it mattered, when it might even have saved a pair of lives, he failed. He failed himself by disregarding his own principles. He failed himself, science, all metahumanity. And this is just one more failing on top of a career plagued by shortcomings and outright failures.

He's never had a very strong sense of imagination. Maybe that's the greatest failing of all. Maybe that's what always limited him to positions assisting the person put in charge.

It's irrelevant now. Just one more task to perform. He must accept responsibility for what he's done. The slate must be cleaned. The final responsibility accepted.

Slowly, he reaches out for the gun lying beside him and lifts it to his mouth. The gleaming metal barrel feels hard and unforgiving against his teeth, and tastes of harsh chemicals. So, too, life.

It takes only a gentle squeeze of the trigger.

84

The end of the tunnel blazes with light. She feels it drawing her forward. In a way she doesn't really understand, she senses that somewhere beyond the blazing light lies a golden land of bounty and promise.

Abruptly, a figure rises before her, a dark four-legged shape, indisputably male, and massive enough to all but block out the light. The male's roar is like the thunder heralding the end of the world. His smell speaks clearly of possession and the violence he'll do to defend what he considers his own.

Go back! he tells her.

No ... She wants to go ahead.

You have no choice ...

A wave of dismay rises suddenly, cresting, overwhelming. She is to be denied the bounty and promise of the land beyond. The land belongs to the male. It is his territory. Fighting him for the right to enter would inevitably end in the complete eradication of her existence.

She must go back.

The blazing light fades into blackness, and suddenly Tikki hears a gunshot roaring. Involuntarily, she jerks, lifting her head. The lights of the laboratory glare, bringing water into her eyes. She wipes a paw at the itching afflicting the side of her head, then notices the cub, nosing into her neck, whining, growling with fear.

She surges up onto her feet, ears flicking, eyes darting all around. The floor is smeared with blood and gore. A pair of two-legs lie sprawled: a female ork in street clothes and a male human in a white coat. The ork is the one who tried to kill her and the male is the one who tried to stop her from leaving. Both look dead. They smell dead. They don't move. Tikki shakes her head, trying to understand how this could be, but thrusts the thoughts from mind. Dead is dead. She shot the ork to protect herself and to protect her cub. What happened to the human male isn't important now.

She wills the change: bones and muscles contract, fur fades into skin, paws form into hands and feet. The cub follows her lead and loops both arms around her right knee.

"Tik-*ki*!"

"Quiet," she snaps.

Tikki grabs the guns lying on the floor and leads the cub to the hallway door. They need clothes and money and soon they'll need food, but first they need to get out of this place. If any two-legs get in her way, she'll do what she has to do, and she'll do it for the only reason that seems beyond questioning.

The cub is what matters now.

85

Enoshi Ken watches the droplets of rain slipping down the outsides of the windows overlooking Central Park. They are all just currents in a stream, wavelets on the surface of a vast, incomprehensible ocean. He takes a drag of his cigarette and a sip of his coffee and wonders what his wife is doing. He feels very far away from their home in Philadelphia. With each new development, he feels more distant.

Earlier this afternoon, he received a call from his chief auditor, Kurushima Jussai, reporting that evidence amassed from Hurley-Cooper records now strongly indicates that several persons, including the firm's CEO, Vernon Janasova, have appropriated corporate funds to enrich their personal accounts. Kurushima also mentioned that certain matters involving Amy Berman's departments had been satisfactorily resolved, with the aid of the Metascience Group director, Dr. Liron Phalen.

Enoshi wonders how it is that his own auditor should give such a report. It is particularly remarkable in that it came barely an hour before the Hurley-Cooper Executive VP, Mercedes Feliz, personally delivered datachip evidence indicating that the heads of the Metascience Group have been conspiring to embezzle about thirteen million nuyen. One individual in particular, a Dr. Hill, has no less than three million nuyen in a hidden account at the UCAS Bank. The evidence suggests that this account was used to funnel embezzled funds into questionable channels that may actually lead to shadowrunners and other criminals.

"Amy Berman collected most of this data," Mercedes Feliz reported, "acting under my direction."

Enoshi rubs at his brow, anticipating the rise of a headache.

His aide comes to announce the arrival of Usami Gek, his senior security operative, and the mage recently dispatched by KFK North America to aid in the investigation: Kajitori Saru. The mage was in New York barely a day when all hell broke loose.

Usami reports, "It appears that the disturbance at the Metascience facility began with an explosion of undetermined origin. Group personnel report that a paranormal creature being used as a test subject has escaped. Numerous persons were injured. Three are dead: Dr. Liron Phalen, Dr. Benjamin Hill, and an aide. Dr. Phalen appears to have succumbed to violence of an arcane nature. Preliminary evidence suggests that Dr. Ben Hill may have killed the aide before taking his own life. The exact sequence of events is still being evaluated by my personnel."

Enoshi struggles to maintain his composure. The loss of Phalen and Hill will no doubt have a detrimental effect on Hurley-Cooper research. The effect of such violent deaths on the firm's reputation, and that of Kono-Furata-Ko International, could be incalculable. He is perhaps facing a crisis of nightmare proportions. He must soon make a report via telecom to the Vice-Chairman of KFK, Torakido Buntaro.

Usami adds, "We have ascertained through surveillance records that Mr. Scott Berman was present at the facility when the explosion occurred."

"Was Amy Berman present?"

Usami nods. "Yes, Enoshi-*sama*. She was present prior to the outbreak of violence, in conference with Dr. Liron Phalen. Surveillance records show that Kurushima Jussai joined this conference, as did Mr. Scott Berman. Neither Ms. Amy Berman nor Mr. Scott Berman remained on site after the explosion. It is not yet known how they left the facility nor where they have gone."

It is mind-boggling. Enoshi struggles to sort it all out. One might suppose that Amy Berman has participated in a deliberate effort to destroy critical Hurley-Cooper assets, such as Doctors Phalen and Hill, and has somehow drawn KFK's own auditor, Kurushima Jussai, into the conspiracy. However, Enoshi is wary of such obvious suppositions. "How did Scott Berman gain access to the Metascience facility?"

"Through arcane means still to be determined," Usami replies. "It is unclear what role Ms. Amy Berman or Mr. Scott Berman may have played in Dr. Liron Phalen's death."

Here, the mage, Kajitori Saru, coughs.

"Have you something to add?" Enoshi asks.

Kajitori says, "Yes."

"Please continue."

"It is my belief that Scott Berman and Liron Phalen engaged in magical conflict. The signs are clear, Enoshi-*sama*. It is also my belief that some third party or entity, perhaps of metaplanar origin, was involved in the conflict."

Enoshi considers that, and says, "Are you suggesting that Scott Berman called on some metaphysical entity with the intention of assassinating Dr. Phalen?"

"I believe that the entity entered the conflict on Phalen's side. I also believe that it was of a malignant nature."

"Malignant?"

"Malevolent."

Enoshi wonders what to make of this. "Was this entity of a type that a mage might ordinarily call on to aid in a magical conflict?"

"It was possibly a form of entity I have never encountered," Kajitori replies. "However, I do not believe that any mage would call on such a malignant entity unless forced to it in some way, or unless the mage was of a similarly malevolent nature."

"Are you suggesting that Dr. Liron Phalen was of a malevolent nature?"

"It is of course possible that the entity had control of Phalen from the start. That he was influenced or possessed."

A most remarkable, wholly unsubstantiated theory. Enoshi will withhold judgment until more facts have been assembled. He directs Usami and Kajitori to continue their search for such facts, and for Amy Berman, who has many things to attempt to explain. Enoshi then goes down the hallway to his bedroom and to the small sitting room adjacent. One of his guards stands watch at the door.

Inside, on the intricately carved furniture provided by the Waldorf Park East Hotel, sits his mistress, Frederique, and a man named Harman Franck-Natali. They are having tea. Franck-Natali is smiling like a man under some form of enchantment.

As Enoshi enters, Frederique excuses herself and glides out of the room. Enoshi marvels that he would consent to letting his mistress become so involved with corporate affairs as to let her speak with this man. He cannot help marveling over the result. Frederique has learned more from Harman Franck-Natali with a smile and a few softly spoken words than Usami's operatives managed to glean with all their sophisticated techniques. Furthermore, Frederique believes she has persuaded Franck-Natali that his abduction and interrogation was at least partly the result of over-zealous security agents, and an event Enoshi sincerely regrets.

"Utterly charming," Franck-Natali says, once Frederique has departed. He sips at his tea. Enoshi sits down opposite, considering how to take up from where they last left off.

They have been discussing the local units of Mitsuhama Computer Technologies. In speaking with Frederique, Franck-Natali has revealed great dissatisfaction with MCT and appears willing, perhaps even eager, to change corporate affiliations. Enoshi wonders whether to accept this as genuine. It is certainly possible that Harman Franck-Natali has accepted none of Frederique's explanations, that he is merely biding his time.

Possibly, there is some very specific objective underlying Franck-Natali's cooperative manner and all that he says—some ulterior motive—just as there is a very definite objective underlying Enoshi's handling of this matter.

Kono-Furata-Ko International plans to continue diversifying in order to meet the challenges of the future. Those plans include the possible acquisition of certain MCT subsidiaries. Enoshi is keenly aware that Harman Franck-Natali may have valuable knowledge about these subsidiaries.

"I believe you indicated," Enoshi says, "that Amy Berman has been pressuring you to join Hurley-Cooper Laboratories."

"Well," Franck-Natali replies, "in recent weeks, we have been turning to discussions concerning the future. Amy knows how I feel about the situation at Mitsuhama. Primarily, she's concerned that I get out. She hasn't mentioned any corp specifically, but I imagine she would be pleased if I decided to approach Hurley-Cooper."

"This would add to her status within the corporation."

"Likely, that's so, but I think Amy would be pleased due to the expectation that I would be happier at Hurley-Cooper, and that I could do a lot for Hurley-Cooper in sales, perhaps even in a marketing venue."

"Do you feel that Amy Berman is a loyal corporate executive?"

"Oh, certainly." Franck-Natali pauses to smile. He does this often. The habit gives Enoshi the impression that the man considers his every word very carefully. "She's unquestionably a loyal executive."

"Please explain."

"Well, you would have to know Amy to really understand."

"I would like very much to know her," Enoshi says, "so that I might better understand her motives. KFK International places a very high value on understanding. I would like to feel that I know Amy Berman in a personal manner. As a friend and colleague."

"Well," Franck-Natali says, smiling. "Where shall I begin?"

86

Inside the small shack fashioned of panels from macroplast crates, Old Man sits facing the fire. Dark Rain Hunter and Pug sit beside him. On the near side of the fire lies Amy, eyes closed, deeply asleep, her body slack.

Getting Amy all the way here to Brooklyn from the Bronx wasn't easy. Just sneaking her off the property of the Metascience building took a few more grams of magical energy than Bandit thought he had to spend, and that was not all he had to do. He's tired, tired enough to collapse, but his ordeal is near its end. Abruptly, he sits, then pulls on his ankles to bend his knees and sit cross-legged.

"The darkness is in her," Old Man says. "It will kill her mind. Eagle and Dog will help her because that is their nature. They are generous, but Raven is greedy. What will you give me to save her?"

Bandit drags the great book from his knapsack, the book with the mystic symbols, rescued from the shattered, smoldering ruins of Phalen's house. Surrendering this book is difficult, for though it is the work of a mage and inexpressibly evil, it contains great power and many secrets. Its value is beyond estimation. It tugs at the Raccoon nature, and Bandit's curiosity. He could probably not give it away if his own sister's life were not at stake. Even if he could never learn the book's secrets, he would like to keep it, hoard it.

"I will give you this."

"I accept it," Old Man says. But it is Dark Rain Hunter who reaches out for the book, and Dark Rain Hunter who slips it into the fire. After a while, Old Man says, "The knowledge in this book should go out of the world. Men are not wise enough to control it."

Bandit nods agreement, and catches himself nodding off, falling asleep. He's tired enough now to agree with almost anything. When this is over, he might just sleep for a month.

"Now we will help your sister," Old Man says. "Pay attention to the song we sing. You might learn something."

Bandit nods.

Abruptly, Pug shakes a rattle. Dark Rain Hunter begins tapping a small drum. Old Man is the first to sing and his softly chanted song drones on for a while, speaking of changes and the world and the ways in which people grow. Dark Rain Hunter sings of nature and the necessity of purifying nature of evil. Pug sings of loyalty and love and the importance of the ties between people and especially people related by blood. The three songs together speak of life and the nature of living and of things that must be done. They tell Bandit that wily Raccoon must sometimes crawl out of the shadows of his favorite pastimes and face the harsher realities visible beneath the all-important light of the sun.

The auras of the three shamans join. The magic gathers slowly, filling the medicine lodge. As it ends, Amy stirs, and sighs.

A darkness flutters across the astral, and vanishes.

Bandit kneels next to Amy and smooths her hair back from her brow. Her eyes open lazily, as if heavy from sleep. The fiery cast is gone. Her eyes are brown now, just brown, like Bandit's own. "Scottie . . . ?" she murmurs. "What happened . . . ? I . . ."

Bandit says, "You're fine now."

"Are you all right?"

Bandit nods. "Everything is."

87

The guide meets her about ten kilometers outside of Boulder on an old logging road halfway up the side of a mountain. He is called Ed Flashing Deer.

Contacts brought him here, very carefully selected contacts. There will be no mistakes this time, and no betrayals. Tikki has made sure that all interested parties understand how great her displeasure will be if anyone causes her trouble again.

"Let's see the eyes," Flashing Deer says.

Tikki slips off her black mirrorshades and glances toward the late afternoon sun. Flashing Deer watches her face. He should see her eyes glint with the light of the late afternoon sun. He was told to look for reflective eyes. He probably assumes that means she's got cybereyes. That suits her purposes.

What happens now is simple. They walk deeper into the mountains and Tikki finds a den for her and the cub. After that? Hard to say. Tikki's got some odd ideas.

Her mother taught her that prey is prey. Two-leg or four makes no difference. Only now she's noticed some differences. That two-leg ork who moaned incessantly about the son killed in Philadelphia; that slag in the white coat who didn't want her to escape, but couldn't quite bring himself to shoot her; and, that magician who neutralized a pair of guards and then told her where to find her cub. All that is making it hard for her to go on believing that all two-legs are the vicious betrayers she's always assumed them to be. The magician especially.

Why did he help her? He gained nothing by it. That's the thing that's really got her thinking. No ordinary animal would have done that, or anything like it. Ordinary animals don't act like that.

Maybe, like the ork, the magician felt something that made him do what he did. Maybe it's all about feelings. Maybe she's got more in common with two-legs than she ever imagined.

It's time Striper retired. She doesn't want to take two-legs as prey any more. She doesn't want to take money for killing them. She doesn't like the thought of what that kind of killing might mean to somebody somewhere, somebody like that ork. She knows what losing her cub meant to her, and now she can almost imagine what it might feel like to lose a cub to some killer in an alley in Philadelphia.

It's not good. Not right.

She'll raise the cub and then forge a new life for herself. New life, new career. Surely, someone with her skills and contacts ought to be able to find something to do. Something interesting. Satisfying. Something that'll suit the hunter inside her, keep instinct content, without forcing her to kill, kill, kill ... Kill others' cubs ...

Abruptly, Ed Flashing Deer crouches down, extending a hand toward her cub. Tikki shifts her weight, preparing to strike, but then stops, noticing the man's wry smile, the innocuous character of his scent.

As the offending hand draws near, the cub snarls and snaps.

"Whoa!" Flashing Deer says, swaying back. He straightens up, smiling like he's amused, checking the hand as if to make sure nothing's missing. "Nice kid," he says. "Got a name?"

Tikki nods, and slips her shades on over her eyes.

The man takes the hint.

ABOUT THE AUTHOR

Nathan Yale Xavier ("Nyx") Smith began his writing career by revising the 23rd Psalm to excoriate Richard Nixon about Watergate, only to be called down to the principal's office, and has been getting into trouble ever since. His early experiences as an altar boy (passing out from the summer heat) perhaps inspired his late-adolescent abhorrence of anything resembling a suit and tie, as well as a lingering aversion to ever becoming a "suit" himself. He has not seen a barber (or other tonsorial artist) in ten years. He has worked as a dishwasher, custodian, landscaper, shipping manager, bookkeeper, and computer operator while making no money for lots of writing. He drives an old car that's very nondescript. He originally thought a cyber-esque world with magic and elves a pretty strange idea, but then Striper came along and asserted it makes perfect sense.

The author strives always to avoid arguing with characters of as menacing a stripe as Striper, and recommends this practice to all those with a hankering toward longevousness.

Nyx Smith continues to live in a basement on Long Island (New York's most notable sandbar) along with a salmagundi of doloris nocturnum, but has traded his Selectrics for a 486/33 that occasionally shows signs of paranatural infestation. He invites readers of SR 11 *Striper Assassin,* SR 13 *Fade To Black,* and this book, SR 16 *Who Hunts The Hunter,* to send him comments, critiques, or complaints about his writing, characters, plots, and so on, in care of the FASA Corporation, 1100 W. Cermak, B305, Chicago, IL, 60608.

▼ 1 ▼
NEVER DEAL
WITH A DRAGON
Secrets of Power Vol. 1
by Robert N. Charrette

Where Man Meets Magic and Machine

The year is 2050. The power of magic and the creatures it brings have returned to the earth, and many of the ancient races have re-emerged. Elves, Orks, Mages and lethal Dragons find a home in a world where technology and human flesh have melded into deadly urban predators. And the multinational mega-corporations hoard the only thing of real value—information.

For Sam Verner, living in the womb of the Renraku conglomerate was easy, until his sister disappeared and the facade of the corporate reality began to disintegrate. Now Sam wants out, but to "extract" himself he has to slide like a whisper through the deadly shadows the corporations cast, through a world where his first wrong move may be his last . . . the world of Shadowrun.

▼ 2 ▼
CHOSE YOUR
ENEMIES CAREFULLY
Secrets of Power Vol. 2
by Robert N. Charrette

When Magic Returns to the Earth

Its power calls Sam Verner. As Sam searches for his sister through the slick and scary streets of 2050, his quest leads him across the ocean to England, where druids rule the streets . . . and the throne. But all is not what it seems, and Sam and his new shadow friends are plunged into a maze of madness on the trail of destruction.

Only when Sam accepts his destiny as a shaman can he embrace the power he needs. But what waits for him in the final confrontation of technology and human flesh is a secret much darker than anything he knew lay waiting in the shadows. . . .

▼ 3 ▼
FIND YOUR
OWN TRUTH
Secrets of Power Vol. 3
by Robert N. Charrette

Find the Magic!

He was only a "beginner" shaman, but Sam Verner had to find a cure to ward off the curse on his sister. Only something of great magic would do the trick. It was this quest that took him to a mystical citadel in Australia, where, with the aid of his shadow-runner friends, he recovered the strange artifact he hoped would prove helpful. But instead of anything that even remotely resembled help, an unexpected and ancient terror was released—a terror that erupted into a shadow war for dominion over an awakened earth. And while the evil kept growing, inexorably drawing him into battle, the curse's power over his sister was also growing, bringing her closer and closer to death. Soon a truly desperate Sam realized that the last and only hope for saving his sister was to find the greatest shaman of the Sixth World, former leader of the Great Ghost Dance—a man who may no longer exist. . . .

▼ 4 ▼
2XS
Secrets of Power Vol. 4
by Nigel Findley

2XS, The Hallucinogenic Chip of Choice

To Excess, that's how they say it on the streets, before it destroys their minds. Dirk Montgomery thinks he knows those streets. He's watched it change with the world, as the power of magic grew and altered the balances of power. He thinks he understands even the deepest shadows and the darkest of hearts. He is wrong.

Now there's something out there beyond his understanding. Something foul and alien. Something that will consume even the most wary soul.

Like Dirk's.

▼ 5 ▼
CHANGELING
by Chris Kubasik

The Magic Is Back

By 2053, the return of magic to the world has filled the streets of Chicago with beings and creatures from mythology. For those in the politically dominant mega-corporations, the underworld, and everywhere in between, it is a time of chaos and wonder, and opportunities ripe for the taking.

For fifteen-year-old Peter Clarris, transformed by his Awakened genes from a human to a troll, the forces of magic are a curse to be combated with science. Torn from the comfortable biotech fast track of his childhood, he becomes an outcast, shunned by friends and strangers alike. Now, living among the outcasts—the underclass of orks and trolls, the criminal societies of gangsters and shadowrunners—he grows up, pursuing the elusive means of controlling his own genes, and ultimately his own destiny. . . .

▼ 6 ▼
NEVER TRUST
AN ELF
by Robert N. Charrette

Who Understands the Ways of
Elves and Dragons?

Some say that the dragons are the most powerful beings on Earth. Certain elves disagree with that belief in the strongest, most violent terms.

An ork of the Seattle ghetto, Kham usually worries about more mundane problems. Day-to-day existence in the now magically active world of 2053 is tough enough. But all that is about to change.

Drawn into a dangerous game of political and magical confrontation, Kham not only learns to never deal with a dragon—he also discovers that trusting an elf may leave you dead. . . .

▼ 7 ▼
INTO THE SHADOWS
by Jordan K. Weisman

Mercs, Magic, and Murder—

In the world of the future, reality has shifted. It is a time where supercorporations are the true rulers, and their corporate wards, power games, and espionage missions all too often rampage out of control. The nation is divided into megaplexes, sprawling urban centers peopled by everything from true humans to elves, dwarves, orks, trolls, werefolk, mages, and the occasional upwardly mobile dragon.

In this world where magic and technology coexist, and where both become far too advanced for comfort, the shadowrunners survive by the quickness of their wits, the sharpness of their fangs and blades, and their skill at riding the computer Matrix. And if the price is right, or the need is great enough, they'll sell their services to any bidder. These are their stories.

▼ 8 ▼
STREETS OF BLOOD
by Carl Sargent

Razors in the Fog

London, 2054. Shadows dance in every fog-bound lane and alley of the historic city—shadows that hide a sadistic murderer, somehow summoned from Victoria's reign to kill once more.

An uncertain alliance of shadowrunners is thrown together by violent death and corporate intrigue. Geraint, noble lord from the Principality of Wales; Adept, politician, bon vivant. Serrin, renegade Elf mage from Seattle, in search of vengeance or forgetfulness. Francesca, high-class decker for hire, haunted by blood-drenched nightmares. Rani, Punjabi Ork street samurai, a true shadow-dweller from the lowest level of British society.

All are drawn into a web of death and deceit; a conspiracy which reaches to the highest powers of the land; an intrigue built upon murder and manipulation.

When death stalks the dark streets of London, no one will be safe from the razor's kiss.

▼ 9 ▼
SHADOWPLAY
by Nigel Findley

Sly is a veteran. She's run more shadows than she cares to remember, and has the physical and emotional scars to prove it. But no matter how violent it became, it had always been business as usual. Until now.

Falcon is a kid. He thinks he hears the call of magic, and the voice of one of the Great Spirits seems to whisper in his ears. He's gone to Seattle, to the urban jungle, to seek his calling.

Thrown together, veteran and novice, Sly and Falcon find themselves embroiled in a deadly confrontation between the world's most powerful corporations. If this confrontation is not stopped, it could turn to all-out warfare, spilling out of the shadows and onto the streets themselves.

▼ 10 ▼
NIGHT'S PAWN
by Tom Dowd

For years Jason Chase was the head of the pack, shadowrunning with the best in the business. When time dulled his flesh and cybernetic edge, he knew it was time to get out, or get dead.

Now his past has come back to haunt him. To protect a young girl from the terrorists who want her dead, Chase must rely on his years of experience, and whatever his body has left to give. And everything he's got, he'll need as he comes face to face with a part of his life he thought he'd left behind, and an enemy left for dead.

STRIPER ASSASSIN
by Nyx Smith

Prey for the Hunter

For the world of humans, she is Striper, the deadly Asian assassin and kick-artist. She has come to the City of Brotherly Love seeking revenge and made it her killing ground. But she is not the only predator stalking the dark underbelly of the Philadelphia metroplex. There are other hunters prowling the night, and some possess a power even greater than hers.

Some may even want her dead.

When the moon rises full and brilliant into the dark pall of the night, the bestial side of her nature battles for dominion, demanding vengeance and death.

Who will survive?

Who dares to hunt the hunter?

▼ 12 ▼
LONE WOLF
by Nigel Findley

Blood and Magic ...

... rage in the streets of Seattle. The shifting of turf by a few blocks costs lives, innocent and guilty, silenced forever and then forgotten in the city's deepest shadows. Lone Star, Seattle's contracted police force, fights a losing battle against Seattle's newest conquerors—the gangs. From his years of undercover work for Lone Star, Rick Larson thinks he knows the score. The gangs rule their territories by guns and spells, force and intimidation, and it's the most capricious of balances that keeps things from exploding into all-out warfare. Inside the Cutter, one of the cities most dangerous gangs, Larson is in a prime position to watch the balance, react to it, and report to his superiors. But when the balance begins to shift unexpectedly, Larson finds himself not only on the wrong side of the fight but on the wrong side of the law as well.

▼ 13 ▼
FADE TO BLACK
by Nyx Smith

Honor, Loyalty, Rep

In 2055, Newark is an overcrowded urban nightmare populated by hordes of SIN-less indigents. Millions live in abject poverty. Violence is rampant. Brutal gangs and vicious criminals control many sections of the city like feudal lords. Amid this harrowing landscape Rico gathers his team: Shank, Thorvin, Piper, and the eccentric shaman known as Bandit. The job is to free a man from a corporate contract that is the moral equivalent of slavery, but that is only the beginning. The runners' diverse skills and talents are swiftly put to the test. Rico's challenge is to keep the team alive as they sort through a maze of corporate intrigue and misdirection, but without discarding honor, for without honor a man is nothing. Honor alone distinguishes a man from the ravaging dogs that fill the streets, and as the runners soon learn, the price of honor is high.

▼ 14 ▼
NOSFERATU
by Carl Sargent and Marc Gasoigne

Nowhere to Hide

Serrin Shamander, rootless mage and part-time shadowrunner, is on the run. First he flees New York, hoping to find refuge in Europe. But somebody is determined to corner him—he doesn't know who or why. On the run with Serrin is a brilliant decker named Michael and a burned-out troll samurai named Tom. Behind them is Kristen, a street kid from Capetown with a list of names . . . or victims, if you will. Now Serrin and his friends are driven by mounting panic. Everywhere they go they feel evil eyes, elven eyes, watching them. Gradually they learn of their enemy's plan to wipe humanity from the face of the earth, and they are desperate to confront him. Their enemy, however, is in no such hurry. Why should he be? Restless, powerful, demonic, hasn't he already been waiting for more than three hundred years . . . ?

▼ 15 ▼
BURNING BRIGHT
by Tom Dowd

Spare No Expense

Missing: Mitch Truman, heir apparent to an entertainment mega-corporation. He may have fled his parents for the sake of love, but if magic is involved the reason could be darker. . . .

Wealthy: Dan Truman, CEO of media giant Truman Technologies, doesn't care how much it costs—he wants his son back. He'll hire the best to find his heir, even if their motives are suspect. . . .

Experienced: Kyle Teller's done this job before. He knows the tricks of the trade, and not only because he's a mage. He think finding the missing boy will be easy. Why shouldn't it be?

But will money and experience be enough to defeat the terrible power growing beneath the city of Chicago?

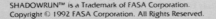